OF NINE SO BOLD

FOREVER AFTER: CRIMSON SNOW
BOOK FOUR

SIERRA ROWAN

MOUNTAIN TREE PRESS

eBook ISBN: 978-1-955991-23-0
Paperback ISBN: 978-1-955991-24-7
Hardcover ISBN: 978-1-955991-25-4

First published: December 2024
Urbana, IL, USA

v.0.2

AUTHOR'S NOTE

If you would like content guidance, please see the author's website at sierrarowan.com.

1

MELISANDRE

Cries of mourning for the dead and the dying rang through Lumilia as the sun rose. Standing by the window of my castle chambers, I smiled. The dull skyline of this pathetic city was no more. Only rubble remained where countless homes and businesses once stood, the debris spilling out into the roadways like party favors left scattered after the celebration had come to an end. Here and there, bodies lay on the cobblestones like so much left-over garbage—corpses of the poor, the destitute, and the rich alike.

Soon, they would start to stink. That was if the monsters roaming the city didn't devour them first.

I chuckled as I watched smoke drift like a gray shroud over the morning sky. Wood burned. Stone crumbled. Humans bled and died.

Nothing was permanent... except me.

"You've made a mistake."

A contemptuous sneer tugged my lips at the sound of

the hissing-clicking voice. I cast a glance over my shoulder. Though before, I would have seen a muscular man with long brown hair and a strong jaw, now I saw only a shell. The truth hid inside the shifter, invisible to anyone besides me or his own kind. A twist of smoke and darkness lurked under his skin, glaring out at the world with metallic spikes for teeth and burning yellow eyes.

One of the Voidborn.

"I don't make mistakes."

My words were met with silence. Those smoke-like creatures hated me, I knew. They resented me for how I'd destroyed Alaric, their insufferable leader who'd crawled inside my head and deluded himself into thinking he could make me his *pet*.

But they feared me too, for that same reason.

Smirking at them briefly, I turned back to the smoke rising over the city. The Voidborn were such cowards. Born of the empty realms between worlds, they couldn't survive the sheer force of reality without hiding like frightened children inside creatures like those behind me —formerly extinct monsters they'd resurrected to serve as vessels. They *hated* reality for that and a thousand more reasons, and so their brilliant solution to that was to consume and destroy it all.

Rather than crush it beneath them and bend it to their will.

And yes, I'd bargained with them once, decades ago. Fate had left me no choice, cursing me to be born as a lowly carbon witch, destined by the hierarchy of the Jeweled Coven to spend my life serving at the feet of those who thought themselves better than me.

So I bent fate to my will as well.

The Voidborn transformed me from a lowly carbon witch into a mistress of magic who surpassed the diamond witches themselves. They'd made me a vampire. And in exchange for giving me the power and might to annihilate the Jeweled Coven, I was meant to sacrifice myself to them... eventually.

As if I would ever keep such a deal.

In the end, *Alaric* was the one who'd made a mistake. After my infuriating stepdaughter failed to fulfill her purpose and die in my place, he'd thought to use me as his shell, to hide him in this reality. He'd thought me his *plaything*. Using my magic, my *body*, he'd tracked the ley lines of power flowing through this world, following them back to each nexus where they met so he could consume them and destroy all that I intended to rule.

But he'd underestimated me. People often did—until I stood over their broken bodies and watched them die.

The smoke hanging over Lumilia suddenly twisted, forming a face. A *laughing* face.

Alaric.

I flinched back with a sharp breath of alarm.

The image disappeared, becoming billowing smoke once more.

A shiver rolled through me. Alaric was gone. *Dead* gone. I'd taken control of the nexus he thought to destroy and I'd used its magic to consume *his* power and essence like he once thought to do to my world. I'd triumphed again, and with that victory, I gained even more strength. I could understand the hiss-click language of the Voidborn. I was even connected to them, just as he had been, allowing me to *feel* them throughout the land.

I was their queen, and nothing of that bastard remained.

"You won't survive this."

I whirled to face the Voidborn hiding within the shifter. A twist of my fingers sent the creature and the man writhing. "I *always* survive."

Quivers of power rushed over me as I pinned him, an obedient surge of magic from the nexus I'd made my own.

Fur sprouted all over the shifter's body as the animal inside him tried to escape. His muscles and skin rippled, unable to complete the shift. "Reality... will... crumble..."

I tightened my magical grip, making his body spasm. "*I* control reality."

"*Your* reality..." A choked howl left the shifter's mouth as the Voidborn attempted to flee and couldn't. "You... *used* Alaric. Made his knowledge... his power... part of you."

"Imagine what I could do to you, then."

The man's head shook. He was merely a puppet of the Voidborn within, and when that creature bared its teeth at me, the shifter did too. "We are... anti-life. We are... beyond mere death. You made a *mistake*... consuming him."

With an irritated sound, I snapped my fingers. The Voidborn's scream joined the shifter's as the man's limbs suddenly contorted beyond the limits of his joints and his organs collapsed.

The body dropped like a sack of bloodied meat to the

floor. Fragmented wisps of the Voidborn's smoke drifted from the corpse, but still the dying creature made the dead man's lips move. "Madness... comes... for you."

The last of the smoke faded.

"Anyone else wish to accuse your queen of impending insanity?" I asked the remaining Voidborn.

The creatures were silent.

"I thought not."

A tentative knock came at the door to my chambers.

"Highness?" Harran's nervous voice carried past the spells covering the thick wood. The gray-haired palace steward still lived—and remained human—if only to deal with the irritating populace who'd survived the arrival of the Voidborn in Lumilia.

I'd kill him eventually. But the man was useful in a way, and such a coward that, for now, it was rather entertaining to watch this defender of Aneiran propriety flounder as I tore his understanding of order and decency apart.

"The, um..." Harran's feet shuffled on the tile. "Your people wish to know if it's safe to, uh... to venture outside now that your... your *guests* seem to have stopped their, um... their..."

I restrained an amused scoff, watching him flail about in the search for a word besides *attack*. "Only if they wish to be eaten. Now, has any word come from my Huntsmen?"

"No, Your Majesty."

My mouth tightened as I turned back to the window. I'd sent my Huntsmen out mere moments after I defeated Alaric, though of course I hadn't let them go alone. Voidborn hid within several of the soldiers in their company.

The creatures were being recalcitrant. They gave me only what information I demanded, nothing more.

I'd learned they'd had some success with their mission. They'd captured one of Gwyneira's Erenlian allies. A young man who could have been mistaken for a human, if one were a fool. But thanks to the soldiers' incompetence and the cowardice of the Voidborn, my irritating stepdaughter remained at large with several other giants and the descendent of an angel in tow.

A hiss-click sound left an orc beside the door. "The Nine chase the boy. The girl leads them."

And then there was *that* nonsense.

With effort, I pushed my irritation down, though my hand still tightened around the hilt of the sword that lay on the windowsill. It was an ugly weapon, with a grotesque face on its hilt and too much bulk to be fitting of a queen.

But it was also the sword Alaric claimed as a souvenir when he'd marched me like a puppet across this land. Thus it was a lovely reminder to the Voidborn that it was by *my* hand he'd died.

I gave the orc a contemptuous glance. "The Nine are a ridiculous fairytale, and my pathetic stepdaughter couldn't lead a *goose*, let alone anything to threaten us. If my Huntsmen don't find her, my trap will snare her, or she'll die when my plans come to fruition. She has no way out, and thus she and her allies are irrelevant. I will prove that to you."

Harran cast a confused look at me and the orcs alike. I ignored him.

The orc's glowing eyes narrowed. "How?"

They would learn not to question me soon.

Reaching for a glass bowl at the center of a nearby table, I lifted out an apple with crimson, unblemished skin. For every single day of the past nineteen years that I'd pretended to be the loving wife of the king and stepmother to Gwyneira, a servant had placed these fruits upon a table in my chambers. They were the symbol of the queen of Aneira, after all. A symbol that went back generations until no one could remember why it had even become such a thing in the first place.

And that, in its way, was the entire point.

"Do you know why the witches believe apples are at the heart of so many stories?" I asked mildly.

The orcs shared a wary glance, saying nothing. Still confused, Harran apparently believed I was speaking to him, and thus the old man's head shook, his wide, watery eyes never leaving me. "N-no, Your Majesty."

My lips curled into a smile, willing to indulge him, even though it was the orcs to whom I truly wished to make my point. "Because they say that, once upon a time, the term *apple* was a generic word used to describe any number of things. Tomatoes. Cucumbers. Even nuts. And thus countless stories were filled with them, because an *apple* could be anything. Yet, over time, languages changed. Those other objects fell away, being labeled with different words instead. But the term itself remained, drawing down until it applied predominantly to this little fruit, the one found in countless realms—both existing and now destroyed."

I pinned the orcs with a pointed glance. Their eyes narrowed again, distrustful of where I might be going with this.

"Fascinating, Your Majesty."

I didn't bother to acknowledge Harran's obsequious response. "But the important part of this—" I chuckled, "—this *story* is that all the incredible energy of meaning and intent didn't disappear when languages changed. That power wasn't reduced simply because it was used to describe fewer fruits or nuts or what-have-you. Quite the opposite. Because the power of story and words can never *actually* be erased. Be rid of one word, life will only find another to describe the thing at hand. Kill one prophet, another only arises. Sometimes years later, yes, but story..." I made an admiring noise. "Story is power. Story finds a way to survive."

A low rumble of displeasure came from the orcs. They didn't like the idea of *anything* surviving.

They were fools.

"Therefore," I continued, "even as the other objects *behind* those stories became known by the words we use now, the word itself *within* those stories didn't change. And thus the power of apples only grew. This little fruit became everything from the food of the gods, bestowing immortality, to a carrier of the knowledge of good and so-called evil. All that power, and all of it focused right here, until the energy became pure. Concentrated. Refined by the pressures of meaning. Honed by surviving the test of time. Almost..." Satisfaction curled my lips. "Like a diamond."

The questions faded from the orcs' expressions, and cold hunger took their place. Here was a magic equal to some of the strongest in this world, but it was a magic that could be consumed, unlike a simple *jewel*.

Thoughtfully, I turned the fruit around in my hand, admiring how its blood-red skin glistened in the morning light. "It hardly matters whether the Nine are real, if they are warriors who believe they'll save the world or if they're the cause of its destruction just as Alaric claimed. The truth is, I killed that girl with an apple once." My smile turned cruel. "This time, I'll do something worse."

2

NIKO

The world swam in and out of focus like a fish darting beneath the surface of a murky lake. A flash of yellowed grass beside a brown swath of dirt. Of blue sky with white puffs and a bright glare. I reached for my magic only for the darkness to take everything away again, and through it all, words reached me in a blur, barely making sense.

"—you long enough. Why the hell did you—"

"—made the best time we could. The others fought back and—"

My confusion grew. Others?

Jumbled memories rose. Roan returning with Gwyneira after the monster he'd hidden inside himself kidnapped her. Ozias revealing he was a monster too. Both of them had been lying to us this entire time, and even after they admitted the truth, nature still whispered to me that something *more* was off about Roan, something he hadn't revealed.

Rage bubbled up in me, the feeling weird and echo-y amid the heavy cobwebs gripping my mind. I'd been furious at them for their lies. Furious that Roan was *still* hiding something too. I'd been *so* furious, in fact, that I stormed off into the forest like an idiot, only to realize too late that it'd been *myself* I was mad at as much as anything.

All this time, I'd known Ozias and Roan were hiding something, even if I hadn't known what. But I never said anything because I trusted they wouldn't endanger us or our treluria, Gwyneira. Moreover, I'd lashed out at *her* in my anger.

And that was the worst part of all.

A groan tried to escape my lips, but I couldn't make a sound. I'd tried to return to her. I'd wanted to tell her how sorry I was for my behavior. But my foolishness had left me vulnerable.

And then the Aneirans had attacked.

"—following you then?"

Someone made a disgusted, negating noise. "We took care of that. They don't stand a chance of catching up now."

I didn't like the sound of that, especially since something about the needling, contemptuous voice who spoke the words seemed familiar, and not in a good way.

More memories swirled past. The Aneirans... they hadn't been like any others I'd ever encountered. Somehow, they'd been able to hide themselves from my magic. Suppress my powers too, all without ever laying a hand on me.

My heart raced. With effort, I tried to force my eyes fully open.

Brown wood lay directly in front of me, smashed against my cheek and side. When I tried to move, something restrained my arms and legs, biting like little teeth on my flesh and holding me in place. My eyes were the only thing I could move without pain, and even that took effort.

Slats of wood were beside me. The upper curve of a wheel too.

A cart. I was tied up and lying in the back of a cart. I could smell the horses now, even if I couldn't feel them with my powers. My magic was still gone like it had been after the Aneirans attacked, my affinity to nature as dead to me as a limb gone entirely numb. But maybe if I—

Beyond the slats, figures swam into view. Humans, judging by their size. Light glinted in sharp flecks that speared my eyes—metal, maybe. Armor?

Soldiers.

Oh no.

Other people were with them too. Ones that might've been wearing leather and... Wait, was that an axe over the shoulder of the blurry figure nearest to me?

Hope flared. Ozias. Yes, I was furious at him for hiding whatever the hell he was. And sure, I had no idea where that left him in terms of being trustworthy. But right now, I'd take that over being the prisoner of Aneirans.

My vision cleared a bit more as the figure turned, revealing a dark-haired man with a cruel twist to his lips and nothing but ice in his brown eyes. The emblem clasped to his chest shone in the sunlight.

Dread sank over me. Not Ozias. A Huntsman of the queen.

Gods, this wasn't good.

"—get those winged bitches and fly him, then." The Huntsman's words pushed past the thick feeling in my ears. "The queen ordered us to deliver him quickly, not waste time slogging along this—"

An irritated sound came from near me, cutting the man off. "Dammit, the stoneskin's awake."

Gods help me, I *knew* that needling voice. Something strange had happened when last I heard it, before all of this. Something...

The memory of eyes flashing brilliant orange raced through my mind, and adrenaline followed. That wasn't really a man at all, but a Voidborn, at least on the inside.

On the wood floor of the cart, I attempted to wriggle away, but I couldn't move fast enough.

Something jabbed my neck.

"Stubborn bastard," the Huntsman chuckled. A screeching cry like an enormous bird came in the distance. "He'll wish he stayed unconscious soon."

I tried to open my mouth to swear at him every bit as vehemently as Clay might have done, but it was too late.

The world swirled and disappeared again.

3
GWYNEIRA

There were several roads to Lumilia, but this had always been the fastest.

Until now.

"Fuck." Clay glared at the shattered bridge ahead of us. Posts of splintered wood stuck up like broken bones from the riverbank, all that remained of the bridge's anchors, and beneath the pink-gold light of dawn, the raging river that the bridge once spanned glinted and flashed, almost as if it wished to taunt us with how fast and dangerous its waters would be to cross.

Raking a hand through his blond hair as if to pull the gold strands out by the roots, Clay threw us all a frustrated look. "They knew we were going to follow, didn't they?"

Gods, I prayed he was wrong. We'd all been soaked by the heavy rain last night, as if even the weather had conspired to slow us down in our pursuit of Niko. Maybe the fact the bridge had collapsed into the river was mere coincidence brought about by time and nature.

Though that didn't explain why Clay, whose power over water was incredible, couldn't help us continue past it.

"What's the problem?" Dex asked as if thinking the same thing. Tightening his legs on his horse, he sent the creature forward to where Clay stood holding the reins of his own mount. The former soldier was the de facto leader of the giants around me, owing to the fact he was always thinking three steps ahead, if not more. To hear the others talk, he was a significant part of why they'd survived the war between their nation of Erenelle and my own country, years ago.

Clay flung his free hand at the river in irritation. "Damn water doesn't want to listen to me."

"Could it be more of those bracelet things?" asked his twin brother, Lars.

"How?" Clay gave him an incredulous look. "What'd they do, lace the river with those—"

"They anchored bodies to the riverbed," Casimir interrupted, certainty in his voice. "Possibly ones with those 'bracelets,' as you call them, attached."

"What?" I turned to the vampire in alarm, and my sudden motion made my horse dance beneath me, sending a dull throb through my middle. My body was healing faster thanks to Clay and Lars both letting me bite their wrists while we rode through the night. But I still ached where a soldier's crossbow bolt had torn through my shadowy vampire form.

The king of Zenirya's expression turned slightly

apologetic for his words, but it was Roan who spoke, his voice quiet and reserved. "There's blood in the water."

Dread sank over me, though my chest still did a hot little twist when Roan's coal-black eyes found me, the concern in them still taking me aback. Up until his demon broke free during the Voidborn attack on the city of Duteliera, he'd done everything in his power to treat me like he couldn't care less about me, if not outright hated me.

But to my shock, that hadn't been the truth. In reality, he'd been trying to protect me. He'd spent years living in fear that everyone around him would die if the demon emerged. After all, that's what happened to his family. So he was convinced if he didn't push me away, I'd die too. Even after he shifted back that first time and discovered his demon had kidnapped me away from the other men, he'd been sure every last one of his friends was dead, murdered by the monster he hid inside.

Finding out the demon hadn't done anything of the sort had nearly sent him to his knees.

But it didn't mean everything was better now. He'd still been hiding the truth from his friends for years. He still didn't trust the creature inside himself. And the demon itself was so strange, so *alien*, in its ways that I still wasn't sure what to make of it.

It was demanding. Unhinged with an almost black-and-white simplicity to its thinking. And willing to unleash a level of violence to get what it wanted that even my vampire side found surprising. The soldiers who'd thought to capture us—all but one of whom were now lying dead in a forest missing their limbs or, in one shocking example, a heart—were clear testament to that.

Roan hadn't said much when he shifted back after that. He'd barely met anyone's eyes, and to their credit, the other men hadn't pressed for more. The secrets between us all had torn everything apart, but figuring that out would have to wait. Right now, we needed to save Niko.

And to get across this damn river.

Bracing myself, I urged my horse closer to the rushing water. The scent of blood began to tinge the air, so faint that if I'd still been a human, there'd be no way I could have detected it.

But my vampire side stirred with hunger.

"He's right," I said tightly.

"Holy shit..." Clay backed away from the water. "What the fuck did they kill?"

Casimir gave a considering look to Roan, as if waiting for the man to speak, and when he didn't, the vampire shook his head. "That, I cannot tell you. The blood is human, though. It's barely detectible, but..." His brow rose and fell. "It seems unlikely they would destroy their fellow soldiers. Perhaps our unwilling friend would know more." He tilted his head back toward the Aneiran soldier we'd captured.

Pinned by Ozias's grip on the ropes binding him, the man blanched. "I-I don't—" A growl from Ozias cut off his sputtering. "These don't come off without the key. We didn't have a key holder with us."

"So they *did* kill their allies after all," Casimir amended.

Sickened looks passed among the others, while Ozias glanced at me. Like Roan, he hid another side to himself. He could shift into a horned wolf creature that made him look like a forest god, and he'd bonded with me as his mate. We shared a magical connection now, one that let us know each other's emotions.

Which meant he could feel the dread inside me, and it mirrored his own.

A strained sense of reassurance followed soon after, though, and I was grateful. Especially since I could feel how he was trying to offer that for my sake.

In truth, he was worried. Deeply. Even if Niko never spoke to him again, he still didn't want anything to happen to the younger man.

I sent him back as much reassurance as I could before returning my eyes to the water.

My stomach churned. My people had committed so many crimes. But killing our own just to block a road?

For the thousandth time since I returned to Aneira, I found myself wondering what in the names of *all* the gods had become of my home country.

"In that case," Byron began, his meticulously careful manner of speaking clearly struggling to cover the scholar's alarm. "How do we go about crossing this?"

I bit my lip. I could think of one way to deal with the bodies down there and clear them from our path, but I didn't like it.

I'd never been comfortable around the dead.

"I can clear them away," I made myself say anyway, because it was that or let my stepmother's forces get farther ahead of us with Niko. "I'll just shift and go down there to move them. It's not like I need to breathe, so it shouldn't take—"

Ruhl made an irritated noise, and then the shadow wolf surged forward, turning into smoke and diving into the river.

"What the..." Clay started.

"I rather think our canine companion is no more enamored of letting the princess handle the bodies than we are." Casimir regarded the water with an annoyance that seemed reserved for the obstacle in our path rather than the wolf currently clearing it away.

But then, I suspected he'd be helping Ruhl if he could.

Which was the problem. Somehow, Casimir could no longer shift like a vampire, changing to a smoky, ephemeral form that could have followed Ruhl beneath the water. I gathered it'd happened as a result of the wounds Roan's demon inflicted when he took me. But it wasn't going away.

"It's working," Ozias said in a low rumble, jerking his chin at the water.

I pulled my attention back to the river, watching Clay as he extended his hands toward the tumbling water again.

The flow started to churn against itself.

"Oz?" Clay called.

My mate tossed the rope holding the soldier to Dex and then awkwardly urged his horse closer to the river. Like most of my giants, he clearly wasn't comfortable on horseback, and he held the reins with a tight grip as he glared at the water.

Or, more likely, the riverbed beneath it.

A shiver went through the ground beneath me, making my mount skitter to the side before I calmed the dark brown gelding as best I could. The horse didn't like me any more than most of my men liked their rides. But in my case, I suspected it was because I was a vampire.

The horse stilled, but I could feel how it trembled a bit even now.

Ahead, the quivering in the ground grew stronger, and then suddenly, the earth began to crest above the water. Before my eyes, a bridge of land rose, arching across the river while leaving an empty space beneath it for the water to pass through.

With a small grunt, Clay lowered his hands carefully. The tumbling, churning water flowed forward again. But Clay was still in command of it, even now. Instead of surging forward like a dam breaking, the water released a little at a time, keeping it from moving at a speed that would be fast enough to do any damage to the bridge.

Air rushed from Clay as he finally let his hands drop completely. "Anyone see the wolf?"

As if summoned—though that was definitely not the case—Ruhl flowed up from the river like a sentient cloud of smoke. Taking wolf form, he shook himself hard, just like a dog trying to remove water from his fur. The look he gave us all seemed to ask why we weren't moving already.

In spite of everything, a smile tugged at my lips. I had no idea what Ruhl really was, where he came from, or anything about his goals at all. He was definitely more than a wolf, that much I knew. Back at Lord Thomas's castle, he'd somehow shown me his memories, though they were made more of emotion than sight or sound. Someone had sent him here—*ordered* him and his fellow wolves to come here, more specifically—and the shadow wolves were looking for something.

But what that was, I couldn't be sure. In the meantime, however, Ruhl had decided to join us, while the rest of his pack were back at Casimir's home in Zenirya, somehow keeping the deranged magic of the Wild Lands from swallowing the castle whole. Given how many times Ruhl had saved our lives, I had no reason to distrust him.

Even if there were always more questions than answers around the wolf.

"Okay, then," Dex said, eyeing Ruhl with a touch of respect and amusement too. "Let's get—"

The sound of pounding hoofbeats made me whirl, and he cut off.

"What is it?" he asked cautiously.

"Horses," Ozias said. Like me and Casimir, his hearing exceeded that of any Erenlian or human.

"Great." Clay drew his sword. "Anyone expecting guests?"

No one answered as half a dozen people crested the rise behind us and continued on at high speed.

Surprise shot through me when I spotted the one in the lead.

Lars seemed equally shocked. "Is that—"

"Lord Thomas's bodyguard, yes," Casimir filled in, suspicion thick in his voice. "But how they followed us here…"

My horse turned skittish beneath me as my vampire side suddenly fought the urge to let my fangs out. My men had chased Roan's demon across the prairie in an entirely different direction than we now traveled. There was no way Valeria and her people should have known to follow us here.

Moreover, during all our hard riding to chase down the ones who'd taken Niko, I'd heard bits and pieces of what'd passed between my men and the Lord of Sinaria. After the Voidborn attacked the city and Roan's demon kidnapped me, my men had had no choice but to reveal to Lord Thomas that they were Erenlian—my people's sworn enemies, owing to the supposed assassination of my mother, the queen, by agents of Erenelle.

Never mind that it'd all been a lie. My stepmother was the one who'd killed Queen Eira. But Aneira still started a war to avenge her.

Yet, instead of imprisoning them as enemies of the crown, Lord Thomas *supported* them.

It was amazing. A relief too, given that the man was an Aneiran war hero, praised for his actions during the war with Erenelle. He'd given my men horses and supplies, sending them on their way.

But he hadn't indicated any plan of diverting his people from their efforts to secure his city. So what were they doing here now?

Dex never took his eyes from the approaching riders. "Circle up," he ordered the others. "Princess, stay behind us."

I frowned, but the other men were already moving between me and the humans coming our way.

"Hold," Valeria called to her companions, lifting a fist.

The humans' horses slowed and came to a stop. Just like in the city of Duteliera, the people with her were obviously not soldiers, for all that they obeyed her commands. From their clothes and appearance, they seemed like farmers. A few were old enough for gray hair to stick out around their rusted helmets, while several others were so young, I doubted they'd ever been a dozen miles from their homes before this.

But every real soldier Lord Thomas possessed, save Valeria, had been sent north to defend the border against the army of monsters that had inexplicably been approaching.

Not a single soldier had returned.

Valeria rode closer on a large chestnut stallion that I suspected had spent part of its life as a warhorse, if the way it moved was any indication. She wore armor that had obviously seen plenty of use in the past, and her brown hair was lashed back in a tight braid, same as the first time we met her. A sword was tucked into her horse's tack and another was sheathed in a scabbard on her back. When she slowed, she gave us no greeting, saying only, "I see you found the princess."

"Why are you here?" Dex called back rather than respond to the obvious.

She skimmed her dark eyes over all of us quickly, pausing only briefly at the bound soldier and then slightly longer at the sight of Roan. Her brow twitched up, but she buried the hint of surprise quickly. "Lord Thomas sent us in case you needed assistance."

Silence followed the words for a heartbeat.

"Well, uh—" Clay chuckled. "We're good, thanks."

Dex's face was carefully blank. "How did you know which direction we would go? What road we'd be on?"

Curiosity flashed over her face, but she merely replied, "We didn't. Not for certain. But if the creature who took the princess worked for the same ones that attacked our city, then it made sense it'd pursue a course to join its brethren. Last we heard, those brethren were in the north, possibly heading for Lumilia." Her brow rose and fell like the conclusion was obvious.

Wary looks passed between my men.

"Yet Lord Thomas no longer required your assistance in dealing with the destruction suffered by Duteliera?" Casimir asked her.

"He does," she allowed. "But he also wanted to make sure the princess didn't die." Her mouth tightened as if our distrust irritated her. "But obviously you've already found her, so the need for our help has passed. Princess, if you're okay, then we'll get back to—"

"What exactly were his orders?" Dex interrupted.

Valeria paused, her eyes narrowing. "To give you any help you may require."

From Dex's expression, I could tell a plan was forming in his mind. I just wasn't sure what it could be.

"Even if that means helping us against other Aneirans?" he persisted.

Oh. Now I could see what he was planning, but it was... risky. Potentially a necessity if we were going to save Niko, yes. But still. After all, my men were Erenlians and Casimir was a vampire from a dead nation. Meanwhile, as far as my people were concerned, I was an assassin fleeing prosecution for the death of my father.

But Valeria and her people were simply citizens of Aneira, and she was a former soldier of it as well. They could go where we could not.

Assuming we could trust them.

Wariness lived in Valeria's gaze. "What are you asking?"

"One of our allies has been taken," I said. "Niko. The one who used vines and roots to hold up walls in your city and keep them from crushing people."

I hoped bringing up what he'd done to help save the innocent in Duteliera would help sway them. From the conflicted expressions that flashed over several faces, I suspected I was right.

"The shorter giant," Valeria said, as if placing him. "The one who didn't want to keep any secrets or tell us lies about who you all were."

Discomfort crossed a few of my men's faces. I hadn't been there for whatever conversation she was describing —chances were, it had happened after Roan's demon took me—but I could guess. It was essentially the same thing as what Niko had said, and why he was so angry at Roan and Ozias.

And me.

"Niko, yes," Dex said. "If Lord Thomas's orders could give us any help we might need, then..."

Valeria's eyes narrowed. "I say again, what *exactly* are you asking?"

"He's been taken by Aneiran soldiers. Queen's orders. Our *guest* here says they're likely headed for the mines, and that they took this road toward Lumilia." Dex nodded back at the soldier wrapped in ropes under Ozias's watchful eye. "We're trying to intercept them before they make it that far, for reasons that I'm sure need no explanation."

The woman was silent for a moment. "Do they know the princess is with you? Will they be watching for her?"

Dex made a neutral sound. "Possibly."

Valeria frowned for a moment. "Then the princess is still in danger, and so our mission isn't done. What do you need us to do?"

4
NIKO

Pain jolted me awake.

I was on something cold. Something hard. My left side throbbed as if I'd slammed down onto it.

This wasn't right. I'd been in a cart and—

Irritated screeches came from above, followed by the sound of wings flapping.

Panic shot through me. I knew that cry. Harpies. Winged creatures who harbored Voidborn inside them. They had bodies like women but claws and beaks like birds, and they'd attacked us in Lord Thomas's city.

But that... that was *days* ago.

My eyes burned when I opened them. A white blur lay before me. After a moment, it resolved into a long stretch of striated marble tile severed by a red carpet like a straight and bloody river. And beyond it...

Horror shuddered in my veins. Towering pillars and walls of white stone stood around me, all of them cast in gray by the thick curtains pulled over every tall window. Only thin streaks of sunlight managed to make it past the dense fabric, and when the harpies slipped by them and disappeared outside, the curtains muffled every trace of sound beyond this room. Marble steps waited at the end of the red carpet, leading up to a throne of glinting gold inlaid with rubies. Two smaller thrones flanked it, each crafted in silver, and the one to the right bore the jewel-encrusted shape of an apple at its peak, placed so that it would rise just above the head of whoever claimed that seat.

But both the smaller thrones were empty. Only the gold one at the center held an occupant. And not just *any* occupant...

Oh hell.

I'd never seen the queen of Aneira. When the others would watch through the magic mirror at our cabin, I would go to tend my plants instead. But I'd heard descriptions of her long and golden hair, her icy blue eyes, and her skin so pale, it was as if death's hand had caressed her like a lover. That she was cruel and heartless was also a given, considering what she'd done to my treluria and my nation.

None of that had prepared me for seeing her in the flesh.

"Do you fear me, boy?" she asked, her quiet voice nevertheless carrying through the silent throne room. The sound was as sultry and sinuous as smoke, and as poisonous too. It brought to mind images of a snake idly twisting through tall grass, knowing it had all the time in the world to devour its cornered prey.

I fought back a shiver as I pushed myself to my feet, struggling past the way my legs wanted to give out beneath me. "Should I?"

She chuckled.

Doing my best to ignore how the sound made my skin crawl, I reached for my own magic again, seeking anything that would help me. When I was captured, the Aneirans had somehow managed to hide themselves from my sense of nature, and their net had suppressed my ability to ask any of the plants or trees around me for help.

But that was then. Now—

A biting, burning sensation on my left wrist made me flinch.

"You wouldn't be trying to *attack* me, would you?"

Ignoring the queen's jibe, I tugged my sleeve back. A thick band of dark metal and brass wrapped my wrist, unfamiliar symbols and odd black stones glinting on its side. It was nearly skin-tight, giving me no way to work my fingers under it or pry it loose, and it had no latch or lock.

What in the world?

"Care to try again and see how much pain you can withstand?" Queen Melisandre asked, almost as if she'd enjoy watching me try.

I reached for my magic anyway.

It felt like my wrist was being chewed by a rabid dog with knives for teeth.

Her laughter was the first thing I heard when the pain finally abated.

"Such fools. Even when you Erenlians look like men,

you never listen." Her brow rose and fell. "But then again, it's not like men do either." She folded her long fingers in front of her. "The manacle suppresses your powers, rendering you incapable of attacking or using them to free yourself. And when you attempt to use them around me, the manacle reacts as you've just experienced. Trust when I say it can get worse. The more you try, the less likely you are to survive your own stupidity."

Gods help me.

Heart pounding, I tried to keep from showing my horror. But my eyes still darted around, seeking out an escape route as well as attempting to locate any *other* nightmarish threats—though the gods knew she was more than enough. My legs shook with residual agony and with the aftereffects of whatever sedative the soldiers had given me, but I still managed to straighten to my full height.

I wasn't nearly as tall as the massive creatures by the doors to my left and right, though.

Stunned, I stared at them for as long as I dared. Her guards weren't Huntsmen. Weren't human or Erenlian either. There were four total—two on each side—and their torsos were like oversized barrels while their limbs were thick as logs. Their skin was green like unripe fruit, and they wore nothing but loincloths of fur, necklaces of bleached bones, and leather straps crisscrossing their chests, the latter of which held more weapons than I cared to think about.

But their eyes were familiar, if only because of the eerie glow they held. Yellow lights. Pink ones. Colors that —even though I knew nothing about whatever these creatures were—I could swear were not natural to their species.

No, Voidborn were inside these creatures, and that alone made me pity these monsters who otherwise looked like they would happily kill me and add my bones to the necklaces hanging around their thick throats.

Queen Melisandre's smile remained in place when my attention returned to her. The more I looked at her, the more I realized the expression was… wrong. All of this was, of course, but her smile was just *flat*, like the soulless smile of a painting that had somehow been brought to a semblance of life.

"Come closer." The command could have come the shadows of a cave, where a predator planned to lure me to my death.

When I didn't move, low hissing sounds came from the monsters on either side of the throne room. Bone rattled and leather creaked as they took a threatening step closer.

Drawing myself up, I walked a few paces forward.

More details became clear, and suddenly my skin went from crawling to staging a full-blown riot, demanding I get away from her *right now.*

With effort, I held my ground, nothing in me foolish enough to believe I'd survive a retreat.

Her eyes weren't merely blue. They were striated by virulent yellow, almost like a strange amalgam of human eyes and those of a creature possessed by the Voidborn. Fangs peeked past her red lips, while her deathly pale skin held the faintest sheen of silver, as if she was becoming one with the same metal as the thrones on either side of her. She gripped the arms of the throne with nails that had clearly worn grooves into the gold, if the scratches below where her fingertips rested were any indication.

But it was the look in her eyes that made every instinct I possessed scream for me to flee, because it was clear she wasn't *only* a predator.

She was insane.

"You allied yourself with my traitorous stepdaughter, did you not?" At my silence, she merely smiled again. "I think I'll send you back to her as a gift."

Unease swirled in my gut. I was no warrior, but I could imagine the horrible implications of those words. How none of them meant I'd be returning to my treluria alive.

Or in one piece.

Deep inside, my heart broke at the prospect of never seeing Gwyneira again. Never caressing her beautiful skin or kissing her soft lips. I'd wished to hold her close and cherish her for the rest of my days, though it had not escaped me that the length of my days and hers would differ greatly.

My beloved was a vampire. From all I'd seen of other vampires over these past several weeks, I'd been able to deduce that her lifespan would be measured in far greater lengths of time than mine. Decades, most likely. Possibly even centuries.

There always would have come a day when we were parted by my death.

I just hadn't anticipated it would come this soon.

Drawing myself up, I held my voice steady and calm

as I said, "Do what you will. But know that I will never betray her, and she will never stop seeking justice for all you've destroyed. Nothing will change that."

"You think I plan to send her your body?" She chuckled. "I *do*..." Her lips curled, her smile becoming more of a cruel smirk. "After a fashion."

She twitched her chin at one of the green monsters by the door.

The creature's body lurched, and then a twist of smoke rose from its chest, writhing like a snake in the air.

A Voidborn.

Hovering in the air, I could feel it watching me. Gods, I could feel it smirking at me too, like a contemptuous predator eyeing unworthy prey.

One that couldn't escape no matter how fast I might try to run.

Behind it, the green-skinned creature stumbled. But unlike the humans I'd seen possessed by a Voidborn, he didn't fall dead to the ground. Instead, he blinked as if disoriented, his eyes no longer glowing orange. Dazed, his gaze stuttered across the room, only to stop when he spotted the other creature next to him.

A strange cry left him, one filled with rage and shock and a desperate sort of agony that was painful to hear. Though I knew nothing about what he was, I could still recognize the horrified cry of a fellow sentient being.

But he didn't go for his weapons. No, with one hand, he grabbed at the bone necklace at his throat, ripping it away and then slamming it to the chest of the man next to him.

Guttural speech came from his lips, rhythmic. Frantic. Pleading and ordering and making the hairs on my arms stand on end.

Magic.

For a moment, the body of the Voidborn-inhabited creature next to him shuddered. Struggle flashed over the other man's face, the yellow light in his eyes flickering.

Oh gods, the first guy was trying to cast a spell to save his friend.

But suddenly, the second creature's shuddering gave way. He lurched, and then the struggle disappeared from his face while the yellow light returned even brighter than before.

I gasped. "Watch ou—"

It was too late. With lightning-quick speed, the Voidborn-inhabited man drew a weapon and stabbed it through the chest of the one trying to save him.

The green-skinned man choked, but desperately, he still attempted to press the bone necklace to the other one's chest. Still tried to grit out a spell.

I started forward. I knew nothing of what they were, but I had still trained with a healer throughout my childhood. I couldn't just stand here and let him die.

Or let the Voidborn win.

Before I made it more than a step, the Voidborn-possessed man yanked his weapon free and swung it around to slash across the dying man's throat.

Green blood splattered the white marble. The man crashed down so hard, I could feel his impact with the glistening tile.

The Voidborn-inhabited creature turned his glowing eyes to me. Lifting the blade, he dragged his tongue along it, licking away the blood. Nearby, the smoky form of the free-floating Voidborn vibrated.

Gods, it was *laughing*.

I wasn't just disgusted, but I was too upset by the pointless, desperate death before me to be scared. If the man who'd just died was any indication, the true owners of these green-skinned creatures' bodies were each still alive in there.

Could they see what just happened? Were they screaming to get out?

"I'm sorry," I said to the one holding the blade, even though I had no idea if he could hear me. "I'm so sorry for your friend."

Still seated on her throne, the queen made a contemptuous noise. "Oh, please. Destroy this soft-hearted simpleton. He bores me."

Like a snake, the smoky Voidborn began gliding through the air, heading straight for me.

My eyes darted around, but I knew what I'd find. There was nowhere to go. No way to escape. The touch of the Voidborn turned everything from trees to bushes to animals into ash.

But... how was that part of her plan?

My heart beat so hard, it felt like it was choking my throat. "If you turn me to ash," I asked, backing up anyway and trying to buy time—for what, I wasn't sure. But that didn't stop me from trying. "Then what are you sending to Gwyneira?"

"You think *that* is what I intend, boy?" The queen's

smile was clear in her voice. "Hardly. I have something much more fun in mind."

Horror and understanding choked me. Oh gods, I was a fool. She meant for the Voidborn to take me over, same as it had with those green-skinned men.

At a hissing sound from the queen, the Voidborn suddenly lunged. Speeding across the remaining distance, it dove straight at my chest.

I stumbled away, but there was no escape.

Fire burned across my chest as the Voidborn struck. Every nerve in my body screamed, begging me to run, to do *anything* if only to flee this horror. Black smoke surged over me, and a screeching noise drowned every other sound like it was determined to claw its way straight through my ears into my brain.

But as fast as the sensations arrived, another rose as well. A crystalline feeling, as if I was suddenly encased in thick quartz. Yet there was no darkness. Instead, the world was made of light that shimmered like a river of rainbows beneath a brilliant sun.

The screeching noise grew louder, like its owner was being stretched and tortured beyond what it could bear.

And then silence swallowed it whole.

The rainbow light and crystalline sensation disappeared. The throne room returned, seeming all the dimmer for the sudden loss of the brilliance that had surrounded me. For a moment, the air sparkled like glittering dust was slowly fading away.

Shivers gripped me. My eyes darted around, seeking the Voidborn. Was it in me? Was this what being possessed by those creatures felt like?

The queen stared. "What *are* you, boy?"

Wait, what?

"You..." Rage suffused her face. "That shouldn't be possible. That—"

She cut off with a look like she was suddenly listening to someone speaking.

Except I couldn't hear anybody. Even the green-skinned men around the room had gone totally silent.

What the hell had just happened?

Her eyes slid back to me, scathing. "You Erenlians think you're so clever. Sneaking *you* away from that dying land. Planting you as the one I captured instead of your friends. Your plans won't work. You won't gather any information for my bitch stepdaughter, and that damned spell of yours *will* fail. And then you'll break, same as all the others. It's only a matter of time."

I was lost. Sneaking me away from where? When? And planting me to be captured? The Aneirans had found me, not the other way around. I'd been stupidly storming through the forest out of anger at my friends, not executing some plot to get myself separated from my treluria.

The queen truly was insane. That was the only explanation.

But then, what had that crystalline feeling been? And where had the Voidborn gone?

"You." The queen turned her furious gaze to the green-skinned men. "Take him away."

From either side of the throne room, the Voidborn-possessed men marched over and snagged my arms. A hissing-clicking noise left one of them, almost like a question.

The queen sneered. "Perfect."

Without another sound, they hauled me between them toward the door.

"You should have let my creature possess you, boy," the queen called behind me. "This death will be so much worse."

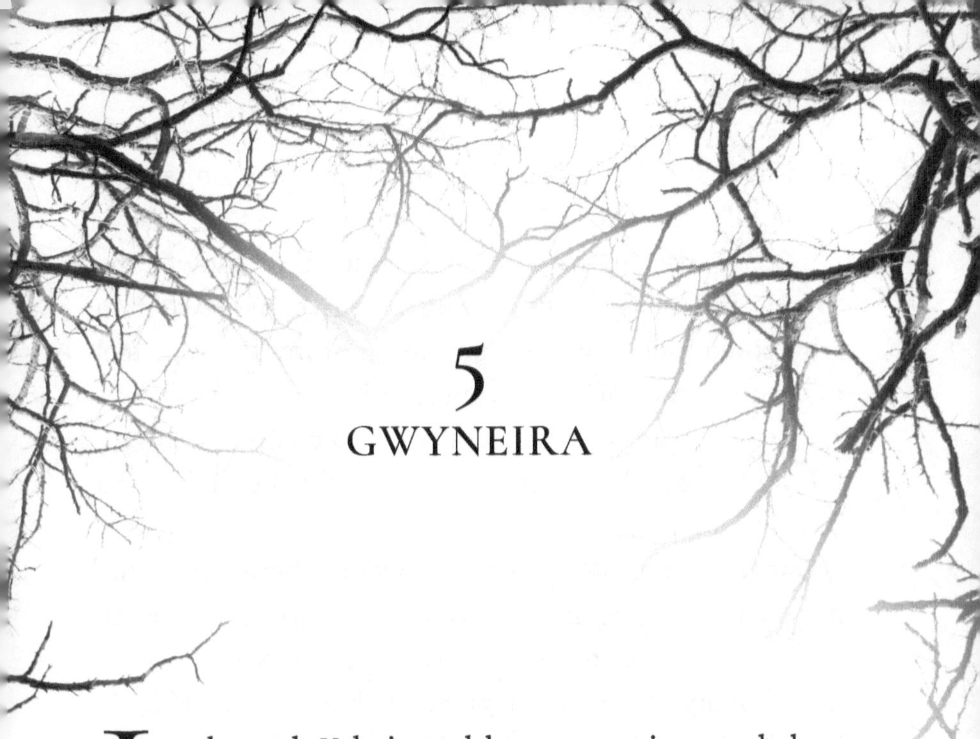

5

GWYNEIRA

In the end, Valeria and her companions ended up stealing a carriage.

Not that I was entirely certain it counted as *stealing* anymore. The village where we found the black wooden carriage had been abandoned—and quickly. Doors stood open to the elements. Belongings lay scattered in the streets, rotting amid the cobblestones and mud. There were no bodies to speak of, nor any signs of what transpired to leave the place so silent and eerie.

But my imagination was only too eager to fill in the blanks.

Seated next to me on the cushioned bench, Casimir reached over and took my hand, giving it a gentle squeeze. "Your people will be avenged, princess," he murmured so quietly that I doubted the bound soldier seated across from me could hear his words. But my vampire senses had no such difficulty, nor did Ozias where he sat next to the prisoner, holding the man's bindings. Support radiated along my mate's connection to me, silently echoing Casimir's reassurances.

Obviously, any training I possessed that allowed me to hide my reactions was failing, at least where two men who could hear the tense pounding of my heart or feel my aching emotions were concerned.

By the time we reached a place to camp that night, I'd started to feel as if my nerves were like the strings of a minstrel's instrument, tightened to the point they were about to snap. Wherever we went, there was only destruction. Never mind that the soldiers transporting Niko *should* have stopped to investigate it. No, they only dragged my sweet, kind giant farther north, bringing him back to the queen with no care for what was happening around them.

And I could do nothing to change that.

Seated by the campfire, I breathed slowly as I watched the flames. I was being self-indulgent, I knew, in letting my emotions get away from me. What would my father think if he saw me sitting here, worrying instead of planning?

That thought didn't help much at all.

I looked away from the flames only to find Valeria sitting on the other side of the blaze. Her eyes were on the night beyond our small campsite, where the orange glow of the fire played against the tall grass.

Sadness lingered in her eyes.

Curious, I rose. My men and the guards from Dute-liera glanced over. The humans and my giants had finished their dinner some time before, and while Lars and a few of the guards were preparing places for us all to sleep, Dex, Roan, and several humans were keeping watch by the edges of the camp.

None moved to intercept me as I circled the flames.

When Valeria spotted me, her expression closed down, but I didn't let that deter me. "Are you okay?" I asked quietly.

The murmurs from the others fell silent for a second before returning, as if the humans wanted to pretend they weren't listening and my men wanted to give us space.

I wasn't fooled. Neither was she, if the way her attention flashed across the others was any indication.

"Of course," she said flatly.

"It's just... you seem sad."

She regarded me for a moment. I doubted it was my imagination that she seemed to be deciding how far to extend her trust.

"My lord is putting himself at risk, sending me here," she explained at last. "I worry for him."

I nodded. "You don't have to stay. Gods know we could use your help, but—"

"I have my orders, princess," she cut in sharply and then caught herself, blanching slightly. "Apologies, Your Highness. Thank you for the suggestion, but with your permission, I respectfully decline."

I smiled at the tight propriety. "It's okay. We're all on edge. And I prefer honesty to decorum, just so you know."

A heartbeat passed, and then she nodded, just once. She never looked at me.

I watched her, debating. I didn't want to make things

worse than they were already, but I also didn't want to treat her like furniture, present to support us but not worth acknowledging beyond that.

If our lives were going to be in her hands, I wanted to know I could trust her. And regardless, everyone deserved better than to be treated that way.

Gently, I continued. "You're close to Lord Thomas."

I heard her breath catch ever so slightly.

"He is a good leader," she said, her voice carefully neutral. "All our people are fond of him."

I made a noise of acknowledgment. She didn't move, her eyes on the middle distance between us as if she wouldn't quite let herself look at me to see what I thought of her words.

Because gods knew, the lords in Lumilia would have *plenty* of opinions about what I suspected existed between the two of them. Not one of those opinions would be kind. A soldier and likely a commoner by birth in any sort of *formal* relationship with a man of Lord Thomas's stature would reflect badly on him in their eyes. And an informal relationship wouldn't be much better. It would change his reputation, at a minimum, and likely hers as well.

If she loved him, she wouldn't want his position to suffer. If he loved her, he wouldn't want her viewed as an opportunist sleeping her way to authority.

Secrecy was their best defense.

"I swear you'll find no judgment from me if it's more than that," I told her in a quiet voice. "For him or for you. I only mean to say that I will do all I can to make sure your orders are fulfilled and you can return to him soon."

Now her gaze flicked up to me, assessing and cautious. Her head bowed just a tiny bit.

Moments ticked past.

"If I may, princess?" she murmured.

I nodded for her to go on.

"You are not what I expected." Her eyes skimmed over the others. "None of you. What you are to one another is... intriguing."

I tensed at the realization she knew about me and my men. She was dancing around it, yes, but when she looked back at me, there was no question of her true meaning.

She gave me a small smile. "You will find no judgment from me either," she continued, her voice low. "Love is a gift. I know that well. But I have to ask, how did you come to—" She seemed to search for words. "To see the world as you do?"

"What do you mean?"

Her mouth tightened briefly. "I meant no offense. I—"

"And I took none."

She hesitated. "I only meant... *some* people in your position would seek to uphold what came before them. To regain power and then hold on to it by reassuring everyone nothing under them would change. But you..." Her eyes darted around the camp. "You're changing everything. And from all I can tell, you're not doing it out of some grand gesture, but out of love and belief that it's right, and that is..." Her tiny smile from a moment ago returned. "Not what I would have expected."

I blinked, taken aback. "I suppose..." I thought about

it, and then an amused sound escaped me at the truth. "When it comes to things like—" I nodded at her rather than state the nature of either of our relationships out loud where others might hear. "It's because I read stories I wasn't supposed to, growing up. Stories of true love and other pleasures that were tucked in the back of the castle library, and that would never have been considered 'proper' for a young lady of my station to read. Books were the start of everything, I guess. And then, later—" I smiled at Clay when he sat down on the other side of the fire, and he grinned back. "I met people who showed me the world was more complex and nuanced than I'd been led to believe. More beautiful too."

Valeria was quiet for a moment. "The day Lord Thomas showed me his libraries, I thought I'd died and found the afterlife."

I glanced at her in surprise.

She shrugged. "My mother taught me to read. She was a tutor in one of the border cities before I lost her to the war."

Sympathy made my heart ache for her. "I'm so sorry."

Silent, she nodded.

"When this is over," I continued, "perhaps you'd like to see the libraries in Lumilia too?"

She appeared startled. "It would be a great honor, princess. Thank you."

I smiled, and she returned the expression, suddenly looking younger and much less like a hardened soldier. More like a woman being offered something she adored.

Maybe even like someone I could eventually call a friend.

Silence settled between us again, companionable where before it'd felt tense. I didn't make a sound to break it. I'd never had many friends at the castle. There'd been a handful of children of various lords and ladies when I was younger, but most had gone to live elsewhere by the time I was a teen. Beyond them, the person who had come closest to being my friend was Fironia, my maid—and even I could see how sad *that* was.

Never mind how her proximity to me had gotten her killed, thanks to my stepmother.

Guilt dulled the edge of my mood. Valeria and the rest would be in danger, too, if they stayed with me.

And that thought only made me feel worse.

With another smile to Valeria—one that, this time, hid how strained I felt inside—I rose and walked away from the fire, heading for the far end of the camp. I didn't want to give in to sadness, but it was hard when Niko was still missing and the gods only knew what was waiting for us closer to Lumilia—to say nothing of the destruction we'd seen already.

"You okay?"

I flinched. In the shadows, Roan leaned against the side of the carriage. His dark eyes were on me, and between his black hair and pale skin, he looked like a ghost in the night.

At my alarm, he shrugged away from the black lacquered wood, straightening. "Sorry. Didn't mean to startle you."

I shook my head. "It's fine."

"You're distracted." It wasn't a question, but it also didn't carry the note of angry accusation his words had always possessed before his secret came out.

I shrugged. "I'm worried."

His brow furrowed briefly, and then he reached out, gesturing for me to come closer.

Not moving, I glanced back at the camp. It wouldn't do for the humans to see me acting "too familiar" with any of the giants. Not when—Valeria aside—they might change their minds about supporting us if they thought I was behaving scandalously with any of these men.

To say nothing of the truth about all of us.

But none of the guards were looking this way, and though Dex's and the twins' eyes flicked toward me every few seconds, they made no motion to draw attention to what I was doing.

I stepped into the shadow cast by the carriage. Roan took my hand, pulling me closer, and a breath left me, some of my tension easing away at his touch.

Silence hung between us, broken only by the soft sounds of the camp and the whickering of horses. Roan's hand stayed on mine, even as his eyes remained focused on the prairie. Tension made his jaw muscles twitch, but there was a sadness around his eyes that gave me pause.

"Are *you* okay?" I asked softly.

A long moment passed before he gave a small nod.

I didn't believe that. "What's wrong?"

He glanced at me askance. "I was looking to comfort *you*, princess, not the other way around."

Stubborn man. "So comfort can only go in one direction?"

He looked away.

I sighed. He was still him. Determined to the point of bordering on bull-headed. Silent more often than not. The fact we'd learned about his demon's existence hadn't changed that.

"This is my fault."

I looked back at him, confused. "What?"

His eyes remained on the prairie. "If I'd told the truth from the start, Niko would still be here."

Discomfort swirled in my gut. "But would *you* be?"

"That's not the point."

"It matters, though. If you'd told the others the truth years ago and left after that, there's a very good chance we'd all be dead right now."

He frowned.

"That dragon would have killed us," I continued. "Or who knows what else might have. Plus—" I squeezed his hand. "—you and I wouldn't have met. And that would have been a tragedy, as far as I'm concerned."

He put his free hand over mine, a small smile lifting the corners of his lips.

"What-ifs don't fix the past," I told him. "They just make the present hurt more."

Sighing, he nodded.

Seconds ticked by in silence.

I bit my lip, wondering if I should press the question that had been lingering at the back of my mind since Niko was taken.

"About the forest..." I began.

He tensed but said nothing.

"Are you angry at me for asking you to let the demon out?"

At that, he looked over at me, obviously baffled. "What? I'm not angry at you."

A relieved breath left me.

"I'm—" He cast a quick glance back toward the camp and then lowered his voice as if trying to make sure no one overheard. "I'm concerned I might have frightened you away from being with me."

Now it was my turn to be confused. "Why?"

"I saw what the demon did to those soldiers. Just flashes, but... enough."

"Oh."

His brow rose and fell like that was a sufficient response.

Which was hardly the case. "It was shocking, yes. But I'm not afraid of you—or it."

"It ripped out a man's heart right in front of you."

"Yes, but..." I wasn't sure how to explain why that didn't scare me without sounding like a lunatic. "The demon also saved us. *Again*. It's violent, true. But only to protect us." I hesitated. "I get the impression it just isn't familiar with being *part* of anything or cooperating with others."

He was silent for a moment. "Probably not."

I bit my lip briefly. "What would you think of trying to change that?"

His gaze slid to me like I'd just suggested dabbling in suicidal madness could be a fun pastime.

But something else was there too. Some*one* else, slowly heating his dark eyes with curiosity and desire.

A shudder passed through him, and the heat faded.

I sighed, disappointed in spite of myself as he looked away. There couldn't be anything more between the demon and me, not while it insisted on having me only to itself, to hell with what I or my men wanted.

And that didn't bring into it how *Roan* felt.

But that didn't mean we couldn't at least get along. Hopefully, anyway.

Taking a breath, Roan seemed to draw himself out of his thoughts. "I'm not sure how to help Casimir, though. The demon... It's definitely not cooperating about helping him." He scoffed slightly, as if the words were an understatement.

Worry settled like a leaden ball in my stomach.

"But," he finished more resolutely, "if there's anything I can do, I will."

"Thank you."

He nodded.

Behind us, the sounds of the camp had settled down while the others got ready to rest. Roan cast a glance back at it all and then leaned over, kissing the top of my head lightly. "Go get some sleep, love," he whispered. "Tomorrow will be here soon."

6

NIKO

The green-skinned creatures dragged me as far as the castle exit, and then the Huntsmen took over.

At least, I assumed the people holding me were still the Huntsmen. Something had jabbed my neck not long after the green-skinned creatures handed me off to the others. Whatever concoction they gave me sent my consciousness spiraling back into darkness just as it had in the forest where I was taken. A thick hood covered my head now, the fabric so dense it was hard to breathe. I couldn't see or hear much either. A muffled voice here. A shadowy blur there. A few minutes ago, I'd woken to the feeling of wood beneath my bound hands again, along with a rumble like perhaps I was in another cart. But it stopped soon afterward, so I couldn't be sure.

Or tell how long I'd been unconscious.

My stomach gnawed at itself, but that paled in comparison to the dread currently eating me alive.

The hands gripping my bound arms pulled me to a stop, making my suffocated world swim. Whatever they'd given me still had its hooks sunk into my gut, and if not for the fact I had nothing left inside me, I probably would have thrown up somewhere between where I woke up and wherever I was now.

Fingers tugged at the lashes around the bottom of the hood. Marginally fresher air rushed in, and I gasped, only to wince at the glare of torches when the thick fabric was yanked away.

"—just kill it and be done already."

I blinked, frantically trying to make my eyes focus and find the source of that growling voice. I stood in some kind of tunnel of roughhewn stone with torches burning inside notches along the walls. The smoke was doing its best to escape through holes in the ceiling, but there weren't enough of them and a haze still clung to the air, making my lungs burn. In the distance were the familiar sounds of pickaxes striking stone.

Oh gods. I knew this. A mine. They'd brought me to a mine. One of those that served as a prison for the Erenlians captured in the war.

Swallowing hard, I told myself not to panic. Dex and the others knew about the mines. They would likely suspect the queen had sent me there. And any mines they *weren't* aware of, Gwyneira would likely know about.

Well, maybe. Except her father had kept her sheltered from so much about the war. About so many things, really. The locations of the mines were probably no different.

Oh, I was in trouble.

Closing my eyes tightly, I tried to slow my breathing, even as the smoky air scorched my throat. Gods help me, an Aneiran must have created this ridiculous system for letting the smoke escape. My people had mined our mountains and foothills for centuries. No Erenlian would make the mistake of thinking those tiny holes were sufficient.

"You said you needed a way to get through the collapsed sections in the west tunnel. Soldiers refused and the giants were too big. Well, here you go."

Renewed shock snapped my eyes back open. I knew that sniping voice.

I twisted, looking over my shoulder.

My stomach dropped. The skinny man from the forest was here. The one whose eyes had glowed orange right after he shot me with the dart that let the Aneirans knock me out.

No trace of that eerie light shone in his eyes now, but the contempt for me on his face was the same. He looked like the scum beneath his shoe ranked higher in his opinion than me.

But then, from his glare, scum might outrank the disgruntled soldier next to me as well.

"He won't last a week," the soldier spat, irritation on his ruddy face. "What good's that?"

"Good enough to serve the queen's purpose, that's what," the skinny guy replied. "So get on with it."

Without another word, he stalked away through the tunnel like every rock, torch, and speck of dirt offended him.

"Fine."

I turned back to see the soldier—no, the *prison guard*—jerk his chin at two more men standing several yards off. "Get 'im going, then. Fucking lazy bastard."

The men strode toward me and grabbed my arms, hauling me with them as they started down the tunnel. I scrambled to keep my feet under me, if only to avoid the ache of being dragged somewhere yet again. But it was difficult to do that and keep searching for any indication of where they'd taken me.

Because there was *nothing*. Every wall was the same. Every exit from the tunnel bore nothing but thick wooden logs to hold it in place—ones carved with strange symbols, same as the damned manacle still wrapped around my wrist, suppressing my magic. There *were* markings to identify the tunnels themselves, but they said nothing about where the overall mine was located.

I exhaled, trying to stay calm. Okay, fine. So what if I didn't know where I was? That wouldn't matter. It *wouldn't*. There was a mine near Lumilia, and my friends definitely knew about it. Dex and the others had spent years practically making the question of how to break our people out of that one into a daily thought exercise. And given that I'd been in the castle before they brought me here, it stood to reason that this was the Lumilia mine.

Except... the Huntsmen had knocked me out. And I had no idea how long I'd been unconscious.

I pushed that worry down hard. My friends knew

about other mines too. They'd still find me and get me out.

And besides, that assumed *I* didn't find a way to escape first.

A resolute breath entered my lungs, and I damn well ignored the smoke that came with it. Everything would be all right.

The guards came to a stop. Bars reared in front of my face before a clank of metal followed and the barrier swung out of the way.

Roughly, the soldiers tossed me forward. I crashed to the ground and tumbled, coming to a stop with my head spinning so hard, I gagged and only barely managed to keep from losing whatever remained in my stomach.

Metal clanged as the gate closed. Footsteps followed, the soldiers chuckling as they walked away.

I lay there for a heartbeat, breathing shallowly and attempting to get my bearings. I ached all over, but I didn't feel any injuries. No wetness from blood or wounds. Nothing broken. More symbols were engraved on the bars ahead of me, and beyond them was only another tunnel wall and nothing else I could see.

"So they're throwing their own in here now too, huh?" someone muttered nearby.

I tensed. Oh... no.

Moving carefully because of my dizziness and apprehension alike, I rolled over to face the room.

A few torches burned where they'd been shoved into crevices in the rough stone wall, creating patches of light amid the dense shadows of the massive cave. The ceiling hung in darkness far above my head, with the firelight only barely tracing the edges of the stalactites hovering there like spears ready to fall.

And everywhere ahead of me, there were giants.

Dozens, maybe *hundreds* of giants, the myriad shades of their skin so coated in dust that they blended with the drab rags of their clothes and the rough rock walls around them. Small fires burned in dented metal bins at the heart of a few of the groups, providing some measure of warmth. But plenty remained along the walls, huddled beneath the torches or clustered together in the shadows.

To a person, their eyes were fastened on me, the supposed *human* in their midst.

"I'm not Aneiran," I said, inching backward carefully. "I swear I don't want any trouble."

A scoffing sound came from one of the groups to my right. "Like we give a shit what you want."

I tensed as a massive guy rose to his feet from beside one of the largest fires near the wall. His head looked like a rough block of stone, all blunt and square like the universe had given up before he was fully formed. His dirt-colored hair was lashed back tightly against his scalp and gleamed with grease in the firelight, and his skin was pale gray like granite and just as rough. He had a twist to his lips that spoke of cruelty and said he enjoyed it, while his eyes scraped over me with contemptuous anticipation, as if I was a bug he looked forward to crushing.

Certainty settled like a lump of stone in my gut. Clay and Lars used to tell me about guys like this one. Back when the two of them were children and their family had cast them onto the streets in the capital city, they'd avoided giants like him for the sake of self-preservation. The guy was a bully, through and through, and the way the people around him pulled away when he stalked toward me only reinforced the impression.

Several other guys got up behind him, and it didn't take much to mark them as the bully's henchmen. They weren't quite as large, nor quite as intimidating, even if they would still tower over me. The contempt on their faces looked like echoes of his, as if they would as easily mirror their boss's laughter as his rage. They existed to follow his lead, to react how he did because they wanted to belong.

But the sadism in their eyes said they loved every minute of it.

"I say we start with his arms," the head bully commented. "Rip them off and listen to him scream."

His buddies grinned. "Great plan, Norbert," one of them chimed in.

Norbert? This behemoth's name was *Norbert*?

Like it mattered. His name wouldn't stop him from killing me.

My fingers pressed into the rock, straining for any trace of nature to help me, even underground. Pain like pinprick needles stabbed into my wrist from the manacle clamped there, while my powers were just as absent as they'd been when I was dragged before the queen.

My heart raced. Dex had always insisted on training us to fight. My friends and I had spent years up in the mountains, drilling everything from individual combat to how to wage battle as a team.

But I had no illusions that would help me survive now. If anything, I'd be lucky to leave a bruise on any of these guys before they tore my head off.

"Yeah, you tell 'im," another henchman said with a grin. "Watch him bleed out."

Norbert the Bully ignored the agreement like he expected it. Holding up a hand, he didn't even glance over at his henchmen when they came to a stop like trained dogs.

His cruel grin widened. "But first, let's give him a little payback for how his human buddies have treated us." He snapped his fingers and then pointed at me.

The henchmen started forward again. I scooted backward across the rocky floor, my legs too shaky to allow me to stand in my hurry to put distance between them and myself.

"But what if this is exactly what the Aneirans want?" came a voice from somewhere to my left.

Norbert made an irritated noise. His henchmen stopped moving, as if they were suddenly torn on what their leader wanted them to do.

Rustling followed. Near where the voice originated, people moved out of the way.

An old man walked from the shadows. His face was weathered and wrinkled. There were creases in his dark gray, stone-like skin like what one often saw in the deepest parts of a cave, when water had dripped for so long that it made the rocks look like they possessed countless ripples. His gnarled hair looked like dried gray moss, tangled and grown out past his shoulders, while his equally gray beard was long and unkempt. His dark robes were so old and threadbare, it took me a moment to recognize the symbols stitched into the hem in faded gold.

The Order of Berinlian. Byron drew those for me once in a melancholy moment on a holy day for the scholars—not that anyone but he had been left to celebrate it. For a long time, he'd thought the entire Order had been destroyed, and even all these years later we'd only ever met one other monk still living after the fall of Erenelle. Dathan, my friend's mentor, had survived because of a magical gateway that carried him all the way to the remnants of the Jeweled Coven hiding in the mountains of the Wild Lands.

But while Dathan had helped us and Byron had been my friend for years, I wasn't so naïve as to imagine that meant *all* monks of the Order could be trusted.

I hoped he was a better option than dismemberment by Norbert the Bully, though.

"Fuck off, Ignatius," Norbert growled.

The older giant ignored the insult. "Why would the Aneirans throw this human in here except to have us kill him on their behalf? If we play into their hands, what will they do? Punish us for the murder? Use it as an excuse to send more of us into the unstable western tunnels to be crushed?"

My eyes darted across the other giants, praying they thought this was a good argument for keeping me alive and un-dismembered. But while looks of discomfort passed among some, others just stared at me like they weren't sure they cared about Aneiran retribution anymore. Still others just *watched* me, their stone-like faces so unreadable, they could have been statues.

I shivered as one rose from beside the fire where Norbert had been. He was even bigger than Norbert. Even more built like a mountain that gave up halfway to becoming a man. His hair was the color of sand, tangled and gnarled like the rest, and his eyes were like ice chips that might stab me through.

The scholar, Ignatius, took the silence as an opportunity to keep speaking. "The Aneirans seek *any* opportunity to break our spirit. You know this. And yet they hand us this human like a boon?" The old man shook his head with a chiding expression. "It cannot be that simple."

"The old man's got a point," commented the sandy-haired giant mildly.

I swallowed hard, faint hope rising that maybe *someone* around that fire didn't want me dead after all.

Norbert made a rude noise. "Oh, fuck off, Brock," he spat at the sandy-haired man. "Who cares if it's what those bastards want? I say we take advantage of every opening we get and kill as many as we can!"

Scattered rumbles of agreement rose. Brock's brow rose and fell like the insult mattered even less than whether I died. Sneering, Norbert gestured sharply and sent his henchmen toward me again.

I struggled to make my legs wake up and support me. If I was going to die, I'd do it on my feet like Dex would have wanted.

And I'd damn well make my treluria proud.

"Hold."

As tense as the moment had been, it had nothing on

the way the air changed around me now. Everyone in the cavern paused. Even Norbert pulled up short, though his teeth flashed in an angry grimace like an attack dog jerked to a stop by a leash.

People turned. Others drew back, clearing a path to the fire where Norbert and Brock had been sitting. Across the faces of Norbert's henchmen, I saw flashes of fear, while Brock stood motionless with an expression so flat and unreadable, he might as well have been part of the wall.

Oh, this couldn't be good.

By the largest fire in the room, a giant sat with his back leaning casually against the cave wall. His arms were crossed like he was lounging in a tavern, not trapped in a cage with hundreds of other Erenlians. While his clothes were faded, they didn't appear as worn or haggard as the people's around him, and the richness of the fabric was more than clear. He had a long, dark beard tied with a thong of tooled leather and brass, keeping it under control rather than wild like so many of the others around me, and his dark hair was lashed back as well. His skin was the color of pale marble, and there was a fullness to his face that was lacking in everyone else's—his cheeks were less gaunt, his eyes less sunken. He ate well, I suspected, compared to everyone else here. He was older than Norbert or Brock, but younger than Ignatius. Even the few wrinkles around his eyes seemed like they were afraid of being noticed.

My mind raced, reevaluating the power dynamics quickly. Norbert wasn't in charge here, no matter how he acted. Neither was Ignatius nor Brock.

This man ruled them all.

Frustration flashed over Norbert's face, but it never came close to insubordination. When he glanced back, everything in his bearing made clear he was waiting on the other man's command before opening his mouth again.

"Let the human live," the man said. "For now. He may have information that proves useful. Ignatius, check him over. Make sure he's not diseased."

Small gasps and shuffling sounds rose, and anyone near me pulled back in fear I might be carrying some contagion.

Ignatius bowed his head, the subservient motion impeccable and yet somehow artificial at the same time, like the textbook definition of how to execute a bow rather than a natural action. The scholar came toward me.

I didn't move, save for how my eyes darted between the monk and the other giants. The scholar didn't seem to *want* to obey the man by the fire. But Ignatius wasn't challenging him either.

Who was that guy? He obviously had power, and his rich clothes fit him well, so he probably hadn't taken them from someone else. Maybe he was someone who'd been powerful in Erenlian society. A royal, even. Except Dathan said they were all dead.

Maybe he'd been wrong.

I scooted back again as Ignatius came closer. I'd never really understood how Erenlian society functioned, beyond what I read in books and what the healer who raised me had described. Some of the royals had been kind, Marnira had said. Power didn't *always* corrupt —and I only had to look at Gwyneira to know that was true. But some royals could be petty and foolish, caring more for their position than their people.

I'd never understood why *those* ones were able to remain in power when it was clear they weren't there to help others.

In a rustle of fabric, Ignatius sank down. "What's your name, son?" The old man's voice was low enough that the other giants likely wouldn't hear—especially since they'd all retreated from me in case I might be infected with a plague.

I weighed whether to answer truthfully, but there likely wasn't anything to be gained by lying. "Niko."

Ignatius nodded. "Why are you in here with us, Niko?"

That question, on the other hand, was definitely dangerous. "I, um..."

Gods, what did I say? Generally speaking, Erenlians didn't take kindly to people who looked like me or my friends. *Dwarves*, they called us. They'd done everything from treat us with mild contempt to make our lives a living hell. Dex had been cast out as a child, and he'd survived by hiding among the humans until they tried to kill him. Clay and Lars had spent their childhoods as punching bags for their high-society parents before being thrown out onto the streets because their parents' friends began looking down on the whole family for having children who were "flawed." Byron never said much about the Order, but I'd gotten the impression even he had struggled to find acceptance.

Thus, it was anyone's guess what Ignatius would think if he found out I was a human rather than a "dwarf."

At my anxious silence, Ignatius's mouth thinned. "If the Aneirans tossed a human in here, they likely don't want you to survive. Strategically, you've got better odds with us on your side than going alone."

That was a good point... except for the part where I wasn't human at all.

But then, while I couldn't be sure Ignatius would be my ally, he also didn't want me dead. That was something. Yet if my silence made him suspicious I truly was a spy, he might not intervene to stop the bullies a second time.

"I'm Erenlian," I whispered. "A... a dwarf from the Forest of Azurine. The soldiers captured me in southern Aneira, and they brought me here." I grimaced. "Wherever here is. But I can't reach my magic to do anything about it."

Ignatius went still for a long moment. "You realize that means there's no way to verify your story," he said finally. "Even dwarves are generally bigger than you."

I swallowed dryly. I knew I was smaller than the others. Barely larger than a human male.

Gods, I'd never wished I was as large as Ozias or Dex more than I did at this moment.

"You're from the Order of Berinlian, right?" I nodded toward his robes. "Did you know a scholar named Byron? Or one called Dathan?"

Ignatius was quiet again. I got the feeling he always

thought before he spoke. Normally, I was the same. But right now, the silence made my heart race.

"Describe them." His voice gave nothing away. "Something that you would only know if you'd met them while they were alive."

Every thought abandoned me. I scrubbed a hand over my face, trying to make myself calm down enough to coherently describe the friend I'd known for years.

Ignatius straightened. "They bound you."

I hesitated, lowering my hand. "What?"

"Your wrist." He twitched his chin at the manacle peeking past my sleeve.

"Um, yeah, I guess?" I glanced around at the other giants nervously, keeping my voice low. "What is this thing? Is there a way to take it off?"

His mouth tightened. "No. It binds our magic. Keeps us from being able to fight back. The Aneirans wear them too, but they serve a different purpose for the soldiers. The shift leaders among the soldiers can lessen the suppressive power if they choose, though. Just enough for us to access our abilities if they decide it's needed for the mining, though that usually only happens when a tunnel is about to collapse. And it's never enough power for us to harm them or escape."

I shifted uncomfortably on the stone.

Ignatius's eyes narrowed. "There may be truth to what you claim, but I would still hear an answer to my request."

It'd hardly sounded like a *request*. More like a condition of whether he would believe I wasn't a human spy. Nevertheless, I racked my mind, seeking something that would satisfy him. "Byron took his oaths on his nineteenth birthday. He said it's all he ever wanted, to become a scholar, and he's never wavered on holding true to that, not for a single moment since. Dathan was his mentor. When Byron took his vows, Dathan gave him the gift of a simple leather satchel that he could tuck under his robes so he could carry even more books, because Dathan said a scholar could never have too many." I hesitated. "Byron always regretted that he couldn't bring it with him when he fled the Aneiran assault on the temple where he lived."

Again, Ignatius was quiet.

I glanced around, hoping none of the other giants were thinking of ways to take out their frustrations on the dwarf in their midst. That'd been a favorite pastime of Clay and Lars' family, I recalled them saying.

Kick the dwarf. Watch him fly. Wonder how long it'll take him to die.

Gods, the singsong words they recounted from their family's sadistic games still gave me shivers.

"I taught Dathan many years ago when he was an initiate," Ignatius said at last. "That sounds like him. I recall he later took on a trainee dwarf as well. He was quite proud of the young man." The giant drew a breath as if centering himself. "Where are they?"

"I... I'm not sure at the moment. The Aneirans grabbed me in a forest when I was on my own. But I've been in hiding with Byron for years, and we found Dathan recently too."

Ignatius's eyes brightened a bit at that, so I pressed

onward. "He's been in the mountains of the Wild Lands this whole time with about twenty other giants."

Hesitation flickered over his face, and then he sighed. "So few."

I winced at the tightly restrained pain in his tone. "But *alive*."

Ignatius nodded thoughtfully but offered me nothing more.

Movement caught my eye. Norbert was settling back by the largest fire. When he spotted me looking at him, he grinned, the sadistic expression like the promise of pain to come.

Suppressing a shudder, I turned back to Ignatius. "Who are they?" I asked, my eyes sliding to the side briefly to indicate Norbert and his friends.

The old scholar's mouth tightened, and his voice dropped lower, making me strain to hear him. "They are what happens when desperate people are trapped for years with no hope of power but what they can claim over their fellow prisoners. Norbert, Brock, and their companions were young when Erenelle fell. This is very nearly all they've ever known. They're now the closest thing we have to the top of a social order in this place."

"And the man they all answer to?"

Again, he was quiet, and I worked hard to hold on to whatever shreds of calm I still possessed. I'd never thought of myself as impatient. I'd always believed other people had their reasons for the time they took.

But apparently I had a limit to my patience, and it was this.

"Duke Deter Ensid," Ignatius said at last. "Norbert's father and Brock's uncle."

Oh gods, they were all related?

Every thought of finding an ally over there instantly died.

"Once the duke was eighth in line to the throne," Ignatius continued, "but after the deaths of the king and his family, he's the only royal we know of who is still alive. That makes his word law." Ignatius's lips compressed briefly. "And makes him king."

Oh, this was bad. I didn't even know the man, and I could still tell this was very, *very* bad.

To say nothing of how the duke looked at me like a fisherman would regard a worm he was debating whether to put on a hook.

I drew a breath, trying to stay calm and focused like Byron would. Or think analytically like Dex would. One problem at a time, as the former soldier would say. Solve the most pressing issue first, then worry about the rest. "How do these bind our magic?" I asked, nodding at the manacle.

Ignatius tugged up the edge of the threadbare sleeve of his robe. Like me, he wore a band around his wrist. The metal was so tight, his skin was pinched around it, and the sight made me wince in sympathy. "Harmonic energies with the bands on the soldiers' arms, I suspect. From what I've been able to tell over the years, there are traces of witch magic in these, but strange."

My stomach churned. "Did the queen make them?"

A sharp look came into his gaze. "Possibly."

Great. More bad things.

Focus, I chastised myself. *What would Dex do?*

"So." I cleared my throat. "What happens now? When they dragged me in, the soldiers said something about the western tunnels?"

Ignatius became even more still than he'd been before, like a statue of wisdom suddenly turning fully to stone. "They wish to send you there? Those tunnels are a death sentence."

Fear tried to bubble up higher inside me, choking my throat. I made myself breathe through it.

But Ignatius's expression didn't help. "I'm sorry, young man. They clearly don't mean you to stay alive for long."

The certainty in his voice was chilling, and my natural hopefulness struggled hard against it. My treluria was out there, waiting for me. I couldn't lose her now. I'd just found her after longing for her my entire life.

Gods help me, I didn't want to die before getting a chance at a life with her.

"My friends will save us," I told the scholar as confidently as I could manage. "They're some of the strongest people in the world, and they won't leave me behind. They'll figure out I've been taken to the mines, and they'll make sure we all escape."

Ignatius was silent, but in a weird way. Like he knew what he needed to say but also knew it was going to hurt.

My heart started to pound harder. "What?"

"Where do you believe we are, young man?"

"I, um..."

Oh gods, oh gods.

I drew another breath, determinedly fighting my rising tide of panic. "I'm not sure. I was in Lumilia, but even if we're not in the mines near that city, I know my friends will..."

I trailed off at his pitying expression. Why was he looking at me like that?

But Ignatius only sighed like I'd confirmed something. "If your friends go to look at any of the *known* mines, they won't find you. These are the mines of Eliantra. As far as the outside world is aware, they don't exist."

My mouth opened, but I couldn't make a sound.

"Most everyone here was brought to this place over the years from other mines for one reason or another. This is where they take the prisoners they want to make disappear. The ones they don't intend to *ever* set free, no matter what political changes might happen in Aneira. This entire mining complex is hidden, the ground laced with so much magic and spell-bound metal, not even a diamond witch of the Jeweled Coven would know it was here, much less anyone else. So no matter how strong or loyal they are, your friends will never find us." He shook his head. "I'm sorry, son, but this is where you are going to die."

7
ROAN

I hadn't lied to Gwyneira when I said I would try to help Casimir, and "not lying"—for anyone keeping score—wasn't exactly my strong suit.

I just couldn't think of what to do to help him.

Or anyone.

The demon rolled beneath my skin, making the horses whinny with anxiety. The poor animals were miserable with me in the driver's seat of the black carriage—and I didn't blame them. I suspected they were wondering why this terrifying giant was here and Niko was not, and when they might get the nicer, kinder giant back again.

If only I had an answer for that.

I scanned the prairie, my eyes aching. I wasn't the only one looking out of them, assessing our safety and seeking any clue to where the ones who'd taken Niko had gone. Even though the demon had relinquished control of my body when we left the forest, the damned creature hadn't gone back to sleep in the slightest.

My head ached with the pressure of us both in it.

"You need to switch?" Clay asked.

I tensed, only to belatedly realize he wasn't talking about my situation with the demon. "No, I'm fine."

The horses suddenly tried to start trotting. Wincing, I pulled them back under control. We were pretending to be servants and guards protecting a minor noble on their way to the capital. It was imperative we seemed naturally comfortable around the beasts and not like a collection of giants who'd barely been within a hundred feet of the things in their lives.

Seconds ticked past. Atop his own horse, Clay didn't attempt to ride onward.

His presence gnawed at me. When I shifted back as we set off after Niko, the others hadn't spoken much, and although I appreciated what Gwyneira had said, I also knew why they maintained their silence.

This *was* my fault. Niko would be here if not for me.

"I'm sorry," I said, keeping my voice low so the humans riding ahead of us wouldn't hear. True, they seemed intent upon remaining near Valeria. Since none of them were soldiers, they often appeared less like any sort of military unit and more like baby chicks staying near their mother hen in the hope she'd tell them what to do.

That didn't mean they weren't dangerous.

Clay glanced over at me. "For what?"

"This. All of it."

He gave me a confused look. "This isn't your fault, man."

Oh for the gods' sakes, did he think me a fool? I knew that wasn't true.

At my disbelieving expression, Clay scoffed and motioned to his brother. Lars rode closer, followed by Dex and Byron.

Which was just lovely. Maybe they could *all* act like I was an idiot, and then this could get even more fucked up.

I struggled to bury my frustration. Regardless of what they did, I knew damn well that I owed them all an apology and a promise this wouldn't happen again, even if that meant leaving once Niko was safe.

Might as well get it over with.

Clay beat me to it. "Roan here thinks this shit is his fault."

Well, I supposed that saved me any preamble. "I know I caused all this trouble to—"

"This is the Aneirans," Byron cut in like it was obvious and he couldn't understand how I'd missed that. "*They* took Niko."

"Yes, but—"

Clay made a rude noise. "What, like you helped them?"

"No, but he was in the forest because I—"

"None of us went after him when he stormed off," Byron pointed out. "Would you prefer we blame ourselves for that?"

"Of course not."

"Then you're being illogical, my friend."

My mouth opened and then closed, words failing me. "I... I'm not being illogical. I know this happened because I—"

Dex cut in. "Things went wrong because we didn't talk to each other, Roan. That's it. We didn't trust each other."

And gods, if *that* didn't cut like a knife.

I winced, ashamed.

"But we don't fix that by focusing on the past," he continued. "We fix that by taking different steps in the future. Right?"

The others nodded, and I swallowed hard, doing the same.

"Well, okay, then," Clay announced. "You hiding any more secret monsters inside you?"

I shook my head.

Lars gave me a smile, the expression filled with all the familiar optimism that I'd never understood how he possessed. "Apology accepted, then."

"I..." Oh, fuck, I was getting choked up. I swallowed again and pushed the words out as evenly as I could. "Thank you."

Clay shrugged. "We're family."

My chest ached at the words, the sensation sharp and painful and yet warm. There was no way in *hell* I could trust my voice if I tried to speak again.

Family...

It's all I wanted. All I thought I'd lose if the truth came to light.

And here they were offering it to me anyway.

Settling for a grunt of agreement, I nodded tightly.

We didn't speak much again as the hours slid onward, but the silence wasn't anything like before. Or, really, it was like *long* before, when the seven of us lived at the cabin and everything had been simpler.

Except this time, I wasn't lying to them.

That made it sort of amazing.

By nightfall, the terrain had started to change, becoming rougher, with stony hillsides shoving past the rolling prairie grass. Trees clustered beside a winding river, alternating between shielding the water from view and letting it peek out at us like a glistening ribbon in the darkness. The moon shone down from the black sky, but the lack of a single cloud let any residual trace of the day's warmth escape, leaving a bitter chill on the wintry air. As we passed a bend in the river where a collection of trees had fallen, providing a clearing and wood for a fire besides, Dex finally motioned for us to make camp.

When I pulled the carriage to a stop, Gwyneira followed Casimir out immediately.

"I heard everything they said," she told me in a soft voice the moment I climbed down from the driver's seat.

I hesitated, but her grin made her thoughts more than clear.

"Told you it could be okay," she murmured, arching an eyebrow at me.

Gods, I wanted to tie her up, kiss her silly, and then spank her for that teasing look in her eyes. I'd never tried such a thing—hell, I thought I'd die a virgin just to stop the demon from killing any bed partners. But now that I could keep that side of me contained, there were all kinds of things I wanted to try. Tying her down and turning that beautiful ass of hers pink was only the start.

I suspected she'd enjoy it too.

"Brat," I murmured back.

Her eyes widened in surprise.

I grinned.

"She is that," Casimir chimed in from the rear of the carriage where he was retrieving our bags.

Old resentment flared like a bad habit. Exhaling slowly, I squashed it down. I'd meant what I told Gwyneira in the forest, back before everything went wrong and Niko was stolen. I'd hated the vampire for kidnapping her, no matter how desperate he was at the time or how he handled himself since. I would have sooner forgiven the world for exploding than extend an inch of grace to him for taking my treluria away.

But I was starting to suspect the way I'd viewed the vampire ever since had more to do with *me* than with him or his choices.

Gods, I'd taken my pain out on so many people.

Time to start fixing that.

Squeezing Gwyneira's arm briefly, I walked over to the vampire. "Casimir. A word?"

His brow rose, but he nodded. Letting Dex take over on the bags, he followed me away from the carriage to the edge of the camp. "Yes?"

Fuck, how to do this? "I... I'm sorry for what the demon did to you."

Inside my head, the demon grumbled and eyed the vampire distrustfully, waiting for a fellow predator to take advantage of this potential display of weakness.

Casimir straightened slightly, and it took effort to hold myself still rather than make any threatening movements. The vampire was a decent amount shorter than me—and trapped in human form besides—but that hardly meant he was incapable of doing damage.

"I am sorry as well," he replied. "Stealing the princess away as I did when we all first met... You and your demon showed admirable restraint in the face of that offense."

I blinked. Wait, did he just—

Casimir chuckled like he could see my shock. "I had quite a bit of time to think while we chased your demon across the countryside."

I was speechless.

"Perhaps you and I are not that dissimilar," he continued.

The demon twisted inside my skin, not liking that.

But, in a way, I could see the vampire's point. "Maybe so."

He nodded. "Truce, then? I would much rather have you as an ally than an enemy."

The demon grumbled something contemptuous about the vampire needing that because we were stronger.

"And," Casimir continued, "I'm sure Gwyneira would prefer that as well."

The demon stilled. It hadn't thought about that part.

"I agree." I cleared my throat, trying to keep the demon from fucking this up. "And I wanted to say, if there's a way I can help with what the demon did to you..."

Casimir chuckled, very little humor in the sound. "Yes, that is rather frustrating."

I fought back a wince.

"Would you happen to know how to reverse whatever it did?"

The wince won. "No."

"I see."

I cursed internally, while the demon just gloated and muttered something about not wanting to help vampire-angel things anyway.

Which wasn't fucking useful. We weren't going to win anyone's trust this way, not long term. It'd always be there, the fact we'd done something to Casimir to damage his vampire powers.

The fact that, by extension, we could do it to Gwyneira too.

The demon froze. It *definitely* hadn't considered that, and though it didn't say a word, I could still interpret with crystalline clarity what it was thinking now.

Oh shit, oh shit, oh shit...

"But I'm willing to help if I can," I said to Casimir. "Maybe if we ask Byron, then between all of us..." I glared at the demon internally, but the creature didn't argue. It was too busy panicking about how its mate had yet another reason to push it away.

I took a breath, silently ordering the demon to calm the fuck down. "Perhaps we could fix this."

"I would appreciate that," Casimir replied.

I nodded tightly and glanced around, searching for the scholar.

My eyes found Gwyneira first, and I faltered at the smile she was giving me.

Gods, it warmed me like she'd filled my chest with the sun.

Still grinning, she turned toward where the others were getting their bedding ready for the night. "Byron?"

At the sound of her voice, he paused in straightening his blanket. I didn't have to be a scholar to read the tension that shot through him, nor to interpret the carefully controlled expression on his face when he turned. I'd likely looked the same as him for weeks—albeit while also behaving like more of an asshole than Byron would ever be. I had *no* illusions about that part.

But it was clear the man was trying to keep her from affecting him. And fuck if it wasn't *also* clear he was failing miserably.

I suppressed a wry sound. No matter what we did, it never mattered in the end. All of us could sooner resist gravity than fight our pull to Gwyneira.

Byron rose to his feet. When the princess nodded toward us, he walked over with a hint of relief that was probably owed to the fact she hadn't wanted him to come closer to her.

But I didn't comment on it. I wasn't *that* much of an asshole. "We'd like your help."

"With what?"

"Whatever the demon did to him." I nodded at Casimir.

Byron's head tilted back, considering. "I see." An odd sort of consternation crossed his face.

My heart sank. If the demon had permanently fucked up Casimir's powers...

The creature surged beneath my skin. It wouldn't allow that. Not if that meant Gwyneira had another reason to reject it.

Gritting my teeth, I fought to keep the monster contained, cursing internally. Acting rashly would scare everyone, Gwyneira included. And *that* would be stupid as hell.

The demon growled at me, but it also stopped thrashing around for control of my body.

"Fixing this could be difficult," Byron said, apparently oblivious to my silent argument with the monster in my mind. "But I may have an idea."

A breath of relief left me.

"It is complex, though," he warned. "And risky. And..."

That same strange, frustrated look flashed over his face again like he was cursing something.

"What?" I asked.

He exhaled sharply. "And we won't be able to do it without the princess's help."

8

MELISANDRE

I drummed my fingers on the arm of my throne and then scowled, stilling the ridiculous display of tension. The throne room was an abyss, not a candle or torch lighting the cavernous space. Humans would even think it silent, considering neither I nor the orcs keeping watch over the doors made a single sound.

They would be wrong.

The Voidborn rattled in my head like a thousand chattering birds. Gone were their soft, sibilant whispers. Their insidiously quiet clicks and hisses. What happened with that boy several hours ago should have been impossible. They knew that like they knew all the realms should fall.

As did I.

I closed my eyes, but the darkness only made their protests louder. They railed at the fact that irritating young man had dared to avoid being possessed. They ranted about the destruction of one of their own and the mere existence of *anything* that could resist their will.

But that was where they were wrong. It was *my* will he'd resisted. *My* power he'd opposed. I ruled them now, and for that boy—that *giant*—to have stopped what I planned...

My fingernails dug into the scrolled armrests of the throne, making the gold plating bend and chip. The throne was weak, just like the former king. A monstrosity of gold overlaying its common wooden core. It had been the seat of the ruler for generations, and once I secured my hold on this world and banished any memory of Gwyneira's family from the minds of the populace, I would have it replaced with something that did not reek of human frailty.

A throne of magic, perhaps. Of darkness and despair. Something to remind anyone who set foot in this place that only one being would ever sit upon the throne of Aneira again.

Me.

It was a pleasant enough thought, but the seething Voidborn and their irritating cries overwhelmed it almost instantly, distracting me once more.

"Shut. *Up.*"

My hissed command carried into the dark throne room. In the shadows, the orcs straightened, their glowing eyes twitching to me.

"I will solve this," I snarled at them. "Whatever that boy did, he will not slow us down."

A second slunk past as if unwilling to be noticed, and then the damned Voidborn quieted their protests.

Finally.

I steepled my fingers, thinking. The giants were devious. Everyone knew this. Yes, I'd set them up as scapegoats for my assassination of Queen Eira, but they were still capable of all manner of schemes.

The war had proven that in spades, after all. For years, the Erenlians had tried countless tricks to keep me out of their country, and their scholars had worked day and night to hold my magic back. But it was when the war ended that the true extent of their desperate refusal to bend became clear.

In the last days of the war, a magical barrier rose around Erenelle. An unschooled human might have thought it identical to the Warden Wall I'd crafted around Aneira, and in *some* ways, maybe that was true. Just as my wall burned alive any giant who dared attempt to cross, the Erenlian Wall killed anyone who touched its surface.

Even the Erenlian prisoners I'd ordered the soldiers to drive against it.

Even the soldiers themselves.

Old irritation rose again at the memory. I would have sent hundreds at that barrier. Thousands, even, if that was what it took to defeat the thing that dared to stand in my path. But after the first dozen or so deaths, I'd been forced to stop testing. The king had gotten squeamish. He didn't like ordering his soldiers to die against a wall that never changed, and he believed the Erenlian prisoners were better used in the mines, rather than dying "pointlessly."

Fool. It was his fault that damned wall still stood around Erenelle, sealing away whatever remained inside and taunting me with its refusal to fall.

But until now, I'd never seen that magic around one of the giants themselves, and *that*...

My fingertips pressed against one another harder.

That shouldn't have been possible.

A sliver of light pierced the darkened throne room. "Y-your Majesty?"

Harran peered around the doorway, his aging body silhouetted by the chandeliers burning in the hall. At the sight of my orcs standing on either side of the door, he audibly gulped, but propriety demanded he step farther inside now that he knew I was likely here. His watery eyes squinted in the darkness as he walked toward the throne, and his veiny hands wrung themselves like he would strangle his own fingers from fear. "If... If I may, Your Majesty...?"

I contemplated draining him just to be rid of him, but I would only need to find someone else to fill his place. After all, I needed to keep *some* of the city's inhabitants around to feed myself and my servants. I couldn't be bothered to speak to the human cattle at any given moment, and my vampires and orcs couldn't either—the former because they couldn't go out in daylight to enforce my commands, and the latter because they could barely speak at all.

Thus the annoying steward lived another day.

"What?" I replied.

"Your subjects are restless once again. Your *allies*

have… Well, they seem to be *eating* the dead. Several of the living they captured too. Your subjects wish to know if this will continue, and if not, when your allies might be leaving?"

The Voidborn hissed in my mind, wondering the latter as well.

Fools. All of them. Daring to question me…

But sitting here gained me nothing.

"Very well." I rose to my feet. "I shall answer their concerns."

Swiftly, I took up the sword from where it rested against the smaller throne at my side. This ridiculous nation had set that silver seat aside for the queen, just as the one opposite it was meant for the first-born heir of whatever *male* ruler they had at the time. Had I followed their rules, I would have been expected to sit as regent to their precious Gwyneira, leaving the golden throne empty until the day she married some fool who would take her father's place.

And that idiot child would have gone along with it. She was complacent. Dull. Pathologically trusting, to the point of never questioning any of the countless lies I fed her over the years. In truth, I doubted Gwyneira could even hold an original thought in her head, much less recognize one if someone presented it to her. She would have no sooner rebelled against giving up power to her husband as her people expected than she'd have grown wings and flown to the moon.

But then, all of Aneira was like that. Countless sheep merrily trotting along paths that said *this was right, this was wrong*. Not one would step beyond the lines some long-dead king had put in place for reasons no one living still knew.

Little did they know how *vulnerable* that made them.

They'd spent years being taught to fear anything outside their precious lines. Anything that wasn't like them or that didn't fit into the world as they'd been taught to see it. But fear was a beautiful, vicious tool. Twisted just right, it could be aimed by the person who controlled that fear at any target they wished.

I should know. Years before, I'd manipulated their king into starting a war that *should* have delivered to me the magic of Erenelle. But now—oh, *now*—I would turn this nation into a wheel of blood and death that would roll over the world and bring it *all* under my control.

I had no intention of leaving Aneira.

Not when everything I needed was here.

Harran stumbled out of my way as I strode from my throne room and down the hall toward the castle courtyard.

Dozens of orcs and harpies and other monstrous creatures were waiting outside.

The crowd of beasts parted, clearing my path to the gnarled and aging apple tree that stood inside a large circle of stone and dirt at the center of the courtyard. None of the Voidborn-possessed monsters had come near it, which was just as well. No matter how long other apple trees lived, this particular one was so old, I had never found someone who could tell me its true age. But these creatures would likely kill it.

In all honesty, given what I'd told the Voidborn about apples—along with the fact a few of the dark

crimson winter fruits still clung to the tree's branches—
it was somewhat surprising the creatures hadn't decided
to try gnawing on it already.

The Voidborn had a tendency, I'd realized, to be
incredibly literal.

Ignoring the way their glowing eyes tracked me, I
walked up to the tree. Beneath my feet, I swore the roots
shivered, while the leaves quivered in fear when I rested
my fingertips on the mottled flesh of a single apple
within my reach.

I smiled. Like the damned castle, this tree was right
to fear me. Everything should. Between my magic and
the power I'd taken in when I killed Alaric—

A shiver crawled over my skin between my shoulder
blades.

Alarmed, I spun, scanning the crowd.

The orcs and harpies and all manner of creatures
remained as they had been, their glowing eyes trained on
me and the tree alike. Harran was long gone, off to
attend to some insufferably domestic task or other.

What had that been? Some traitor lurking in my
midst? Any of these creatures would happily kill me
given the chance. But that was hardly a threat.

I'd destroyed Alaric. I'd destroy them too.

A chill crept over my skin again, like cold and
inhuman fingers tracing down my spine. The slow and
steady rhythm of my heart began to speed up.

No. No, that bastard was *gone*. What I'd done to him
was more than death. It was *annihilation*.

My muscles twitched, as if a bug had landed on my
arm and instinct made me flinch to dislodge it. Whirling

back to face the tree, I glanced down surreptitiously, but my body was of course the same. No insect was upon me. Nothing in this world would *dare* touch me.

On the sword in my grip, the gruesome face carved into the hilt writhed.

A short breath of alarm stuttered into my lungs.

I stilled the reaction quickly, not moving. Between one eye blink and the next, the face was still again, as if it had never moved at all.

I ground my teeth. Obviously, this was a trick of the light. Admittedly, there wasn't much, given that it was night and the moon and stars were shrouded by clouds. But torches still burned by the gate and in the castle. Any one of them could have made the face appear to move in the darkness.

Enough of this foolishness.

Resolutely, I returned my attention to the apple tree. Passing beneath its branches, I lifted my free hand and rested my fingertips on the cold, rough bark of the trunk.

Even though any *other* tree should have been forced by its nature to remain motionless, I swore *this* tree still tried to recoil from my touch.

I smiled and sent my power rushing into it, down through it, racing along the corridors and avenues of its being into its roots.

Riding the flow of its energy into the earth.

My smile grew. I'd been right.

This gnarled old tree was so much more than merely a tree. Its roots stretched deep into the earth. Its apples grew even in the depths of winter. And that was because over these many years of growing directly above a powerful nexus, *story* had been at work, twisting and changing the tree's nature, both with the power of apples and through its identity as the symbol of the Aneiran queen.

But Alaric hadn't foreseen this. He'd thought the best way to control the nexus—to control everything—was to go deep into the earth. To descend through the castle and draw as close to the nexus *physically* as possible in order to strike.

Such linear, literal strategists, all of them.

This was true power.

I closed my eyes, letting my consciousness descend with my magic into the earth. In my mind, the glow of the nexus appeared, a swirling mass of bright light and deep shadow that grew larger the closer I came. Broken ley lines were scattered around it, irrelevant. They bled their light out into the earth like torn veins, their connection to the nexus severed when Alaric had attacked. Those that remained were striated with my darkness.

And that darkness writhed as if recognizing me.

Carefully, delicately, I began to weave my spell, sending my will into the shadow and infusing it with the power of story and belief. Pulses of dark energy surged out from the nexus, pumping like blood from a poisoned heart into the remaining ley lines that traced their sinuous paths out from Lumilia and into the rest of the land.

In the distance, I felt the mountains tremble. Felt the trees and rivers shiver with fear.

And I laughed.

The Voidborn saw only straight lines to their targets. I saw a web that gave a thousand routes to victory. A forest that would carpet the world in my might, crushing my enemies no matter where they might hide.

And it all would start with a simple apple.

9
GWYNEIRA

Seated beside the fire, I froze when I overheard Byron's words. "Wait, what?" I turned, struggling to keep my voice down. The humans were tending to the horses beside the river, but they might still overhear if I spoke too loudly.

The scholar didn't look at me when I pushed to my feet and hurried over to where he stood with Casimir and Roan.

"How am *I* the linchpin for whether this works?" I demanded in an urgent whisper.

Byron frowned, still not meeting my eyes. "Because it is a modification of a spell for mirroring like to like. Casimir's vampire powers are damaged. Yours are not. Thus if I draw on the demon's magic to identify the traces of its power, I should be able to isolate what parts of Casimir's abilities are harmed, match them to yours which are unharmed, and then use that model to..." He bobbed his head. "Fix them." A flicker of hesitation crossed his face. "Maybe."

"*Maybe?*" I repeated. "Just how dangerous is this spell?"

"It is... somewhat risky."

My mouth moved at the careful statement. Or, given Byron's tone, *understatement*.

"If there's any backlash," Roan said. "Aim it at me. I should be able to take it." Darkness ghosted through his eyes when he finished speaking, as if his demon seconded the words. "All right?"

Byron hesitated.

"What?" I asked.

He let out a breath, short and resolute. "Nothing. That'll be fine. But we should get on with it then, yes?" He looked to me expectantly.

I faltered. Just because they were in agreement hardly meant *I* was.

Except what choice was there? Casimir would be in danger if there was a fight when we found the soldiers who took Niko. Hell, we'd all be in danger without his help too.

"Can I help?" Lars spoke up from behind us. When we looked at him in alarm, he shrugged. "It sounds a bit like the spells I use for food."

"It is a *bit* more complex than that," Byron countered.

Lars shrugged. "I'll be another buffer then. Like Roan."

I stared at him, and when he glanced at me, my heart melted a little bit. I'd swear he knew I was worried.

And he was trying to help.

"Me too," Clay chimed in. "Just in case."

Dammit. I wanted to thank them and I wanted to yell at them for risking themselves.

"Ozias and I will keep watch," Dex said.

Ruhl made a yipping sound, almost as if telling us he would stay for the same reason.

Dex eyed him briefly and then gave a small nod. "Your help would be appreciated."

Clearly I wasn't the only one who'd decided the wolf understood us all just fine.

With a solemn look at us, Dex continued, "You all get this fixed."

I turned away, biting back a curse of frustration. "We should stay away from the humans," I muttered.

"Agreed." Casimir scanned our surroundings and then nodded toward the woods beyond the horses. "Perhaps beyond that forest we will have enough distance to shield our magic from view?"

Byron made a noise of agreement. With Clay and Lars following and Ruhl flowing along beside us, we crossed the camp, gaining curious looks from the humans when we passed.

"Is everything all right, princess?" Valeria called.

"Fine. Just... getting some air."

She definitely looked like she didn't believe that response. But thank the gods, she also didn't ask for more.

No one spoke as we wove through the forest, the rise and fall of the terrain slowly swallowing any glimmer of firelight or whisper of sound from the camp, even to my ears.

"Okay, what now?" I asked when we reached the far edge of the trees and had put so much distance between us and the camp that I suspected even Ozias wouldn't be able to hear if anything went wrong.

The thought wasn't comforting. But the brush of his reassurance across my mind let me know that, even if he couldn't hear us, he was with me.

"Now," Byron replied shortly. "You both stay still." At the others' expressions, he winced, adding, "Please."

I didn't dare move a muscle.

Frowning, Byron lifted his hands, looking between me and Casimir like he was weighing something I couldn't see.

Seconds ticked past.

Nothing happened.

"Whenever you are ready, scholar." Casimir's tone was polite, but questions lived inside it.

Closing his eyes, Byron scowled, muttering something under his breath in a language I couldn't identify.

It definitely sounded like swearing, though.

"Byron," I started warily. "Are you sure this is a—"

Exhaling sharply, he opened his eyes and snapped something else I couldn't understand.

Magic rushed from his extended hands like a crystalline cloud. It swept past me, past Casimir and Roan, and broke like a crashing wave beyond Clay and Lars, leaving us all surrounded. Starlight danced in the air, drifting like dust in the misty magic that was slowly becoming still.

In the heart of a world of fog and starlight, we all stood.

"What the—" Clay started.

"Quiet." Byron's fingers began moving like he was plucking invisible strings. Here and there, the starlight dust twitched, shifting position. "No one... move..."

I didn't even breathe.

Gradually, the flecks of light began to move together. They coiled around Roan and ghosted past me to flow in a spiral around Casimir. Over and over, specks of light wound around Roan and I, serpentine, only to spiral into oblivion around Casimir without ever touching my skin.

My eyes slid to the side, seeking Byron. This magic was *way* beyond anything I could imagine. I had no idea if it was working.

The small beads of sweat on his brow weren't encouraging.

"Roan." He spoke the other man's name between clenched teeth. "This..." He swore again as the flecks of starlight stilled, hovering motionless in the fog surrounding us all. "We need the demon."

Already pale, Roan's face lost the last of its color. "The—"

"Now."

Roan's mouth moved, no words coming out. He looked at me, his worry obvious.

I didn't dare nod, but I willed every bit of reassurance into my eyes that I could. The demon had helped us before. If it was ever going to learn to *work* with us, not just fight with us, we had to give it a chance.

And pray to the gods we weren't making a mistake.

Roan shuddered, worry still lingering in his gaze. But

after a moment, reluctant agreement took its place. "Okay."

With an expression like he was swearing inside, he closed his eyes.

Cracks lit by fire ripped through the area around his eyes, his temples. His skin turned the color of dark ash, like the fire inside him was charring it all. His body warped, growing, transforming. Enormous wings erupted from his back, tipped by curved bone as sharp as knives, and a thick, sinuous tail hung down from the base of his spine. The bone structure of his skull became sharp and pronounced, savage with its severity and only barely like his Erenlian face. Thick black horns rose from his head and vicious claws extended from his fingers, all of them gleaming in the starlight. Two long fangs glinted past his black lips, but he didn't grin like every time I'd seen him before.

I braced myself.

The demon's eyes were fire with a dark star at their center. They were trained on me, but devoid of their arrogance.

Somehow, it felt like the demon was bracing himself too.

"I..." He spoke like he was choosing his words carefully. "...will help."

A tiny breath escaped me before I could stop it. "Thank you."

In his fiery gaze, a painfully desperate sort of hope flared. He squelched it quickly, though, sliding his burning eyes to Byron. "Begin. Now."

The scholar didn't respond, but the flecks of starlight began moving again.

Standing rigid, the demon's blazing eyes twitched from side to side, distrustfully tracking the glints of light. But as the seconds ticked into a minute and then another, he returned his attention to Byron, consternation on his face. "You are restraining yourself. Why?"

Byron flinched and then caught himself. "Quiet."

"You are keeping your power from touching Gwyneira. You will not be able to feel the nuances necessary to complete the spell."

At the edge of the fog, Clay made a choked sound of incredulity. "Is the big guy telling you how to do magic, Byron?"

The demon's gaze snapped to Clay, heated by his temper as much as fire. "I am telling him how to *help*." His pointed glare faltered, and his attention darted back to me. Worry flickered across his face like he feared I'd be mad at him before it vanished once more behind a stone-like expression.

I stared, stunned. This was the creature who'd ripped out a man's heart for being rude to me. And now he was concerned about taking an irritated tone?

Lars cleared his throat. "Maybe demon guy has a point?"

"*Quiet.*" Byron bit off the word.

Apprehensive looks passed between the twins. Even Casimir seemed like he was becoming concerned.

Byron scowled.

The coiling specks of starlight suddenly drew in, flowing across my skin before twisting onward to

Casimir. The fog grew thicker, obscuring our forms, turning us into ghostly shapes in the mist.

But the starlight never stopped. At first, they were threads, separate and easily traced. But then there were more. And more. So many I lost count.

And gods they felt... good.

I trembled, fighting to keep myself from moving as the sparkling energy drew in farther, sinking into me even as it sank into Casimir. I couldn't see the light beneath my skin, but that hardly mattered. I could feel it spiraling through me, tracing something, mapping every inch of it in a way so intimate, it was a good thing I didn't need to breathe.

But damn, I wanted to moan, and so did the vampire inside me.

The spiraling light coiled tighter, wrapping something so deep within, it nearly made my legs go weak. My core clenched. My breasts ached. This power was like the intimate touch of a lover, caressing my innermost parts until it was all I could do to stay standing.

But Byron wasn't even looking my way. His bearing rigid, he stared at the space between Casimir and me like neither one of us actually existed.

This couldn't be him. Admittedly, yes, the feeling hadn't started until the demon insisted Byron let his power actually touch me. But surely the scholar would be exhibiting *some* kind of reaction to this if it was his doing?

Nobody could be *that* controlled.

A tightly choked growl came from Casimir. Across from me, I could just make him out in the mist.

His eyes were absolutely riveted on me. To my right, the demon's were too, his gaze like twin balls of flame in the fog. Both the vampire and the demon were quivering like they were on the verge of lunging at me, consequences to the spell be damned.

This had to be caused by one of them. Which one, I had no idea, because both of them looked ready to fuck me until I screamed.

And dammit, I didn't mind that idea a *bit* right now.

The spiraling magic inside me coiled tighter, a strange sense of resonance coming from it, like it was vibrating in harmony with something else around me.

But that only made my body ache worse. Everything in me strained to be touched by whatever this was, because it needed me as badly as I needed it.

The resonance grew stronger, and I barely restrained a whimper. I was going to melt if I couldn't find relief soon. I knew I had to stay still. Stay quiet because this magic was dangerous. But my legs were on the verge of giving out beneath me. My nipples felt like raw nerves attached straight to my throbbing clit. My hands shook with the urge to reach between my legs, if only to find relief. My pussy was clenching, empty and desperate, and the way this magic kept touching me was just—

The magic pulsed sharply, striking everything within me in one mind-blowing surge of energy. The fog disappeared. The dust and starlight too.

All my restraint went with it.

But I wasn't the only one.

Casimir was on me in an instant. My back hit the ground and his leg shoved between my thighs, crushing against my clit. I cried out, my back arching to rub my breasts against his chest.

"Say yes, my beautiful fucktoy," he gasped. "I beg you."

I clutched at his clothes, desperate to rip them off. "Yes. Oh gods, yes. Please fuck me. *Please, I—*"

He shredded my coat and blouse with both hands. His fangs flashed for an instant before they sank into my breast.

I lost the world, screaming as I came. Pleasure rocketed through me, scattering my thoughts to a constellation of bliss. But my body kept moving like it was possessed, instinctively grinding against him in a wordless plea for more. Gods, *more.*

His hands ripped away my pants even as he kept feeding from me. I caught a glimpse of Clay and Lars, their clothes gone and their cocks hard as stone. Byron was nowhere to be seen, but beyond the twins, the demon stood, naked and huge and gods, *so* hard.

Fear skittered at the edge of my awareness, reminding me I should worry. I should... should *think* because the demon... Dammit, he...

I cried out, my thoughts scattering into a senseless blur as Casimir's fingers slipped into me and his thumb massaged my clit. My hips jolted up, thrusting against his hand with reckless abandon.

But I needed more than this. Desperate, wordless, pleading sounds tore from me. Noises I barely even recognized. My eyes locked on the twins and the demon, my entire body clamoring that they needed to be inside me *now.* I couldn't think past it. Couldn't comprehend *anything* but the fact I had more holes aching to be filled.

Casimir's tongue lashed my breast and nipple, sealing his bite. My mouth moved, struggling for words.

"Please," I begged, praying they'd understand. "Please, I need—"

Clay and Lars moved as one. When Casimir drew back, they took my hands and pulled me away from the ground. I was on my feet for only a moment, though, before Lars yanked me closer. Crushing his lips to mine, he sank back to the earth, pulling me down to straddle him. In only a moment, he had me lined up where he wanted me, his strong hands moving me into position.

With a long, slow stroke, he drove his cock into me, his length thick and hard and stretching me just right. I moaned wantonly at the pleasure and pain of him entering my body, every piece of me coming alive. I pushed my breasts forward as his hand slid up my torso. More moans escaped me when he gripped my breast, pinching and rolling my nipple between his fingers.

Gasping cries ripped from my throat. "More," I begged. "More. I need..."

Casimir was there immediately, taking my hips. Reaching between us, he got his fingers wet with my slick and then smeared that across his cock.

I whimpered, angling my hips for him, wordlessly pleading once again.

"We will fill you, little fucktoy," he growled in my ear. "Never fear. You will have all the cum you crave inside you soon."

Nodding frantically, I rocked back against him as he

pressed his cock to my rear entrance. The thick ring of muscle resisted for a moment, only for a jolt of dizzying pleasure to shoot through my veins as he penetrated me. He began thrusting in slow, strong rhythm, moving at the same time as Lars. Both of them stretched me so much, it made my womb clench and spasm.

Clay crouched in front of me. He rested one hand on my head, his other gripping his cock, and his eyes held the same kind of desperation I knew had to be in my own.

"Yes," I gasped. "Oh, gods, yes, fuck my mouth. Fuck my—"

His fingers curled, making a fist of my hair. Guiding me to his cock, he thrust between my waiting lips.

I moaned, all my other senses vanishing as my body wholly submitted to being taken in this way. I was a mindless creature of need. Of fucking. I knew nothing beyond the fact I craved them inside my body.

And gods help me, I'd never felt so pent up, so frantically overwhelmed by my need for release in my *life*. It was like I'd never come before. Like I'd die if I didn't get relief right now. Like I—

Gray skin flashed at the corner of my gaze. The demon was beside us. His body quivered with tension. His fiery gaze was riveted on me.

But it wasn't anger on his face. It was desire. With one hand, he stroked his enormous cock, pumping himself in time to my other men's thrusts.

Below me, Lars's grip shifted, supporting my weight, and I couldn't resist the implicit invitation. Instinct was in control of me now. In control of us all. I was nothing but my dazed and insatiable need for release, and it drove me to reach out, straining to touch the demon no matter how much I knew he wanted me only for himself.

But then, he was letting the others fuck me too, wasn't he?

At my motion, the demon groaned, half-falling to his knees at my side. My hand took his cock, his girth so massive, I couldn't wrap my fingers all the way around.

That didn't stop me. As I licked and sucked Clay, I slid my hand along the demon too. His hips jerked instinctively, thrusting while his clawed fingers scraped lightly up and down on my spine.

It was so possessive. So dangerous, too, given how wickedly sharp I knew those claws to be. The sensation sent hot quivers of vulnerability twisting through my body, stoking my pleasure higher.

Gods, how had I ever thought I wasn't his as well? It was so clear right now. I was his. Theirs. And they were mine. And we... oh gods, we...

Hot and demanding pressure coiled between my legs, growing quickly.

We... we needed to be closer... we...

The pressure built higher, taking over my core. My breasts. My mouth and lips where Clay was fighting not to jerk deeper than I could take him. My thoughts drown in the buzz building up inside my head.

But I had to... gods, I had to take them all even... even *deeper.* Not into my body, but into my...

The pressure broke like it was struck by lightning. My orgasm ripped through me, obliterating my thoughts, my senses. I was weightless in a world of blinding light and kaleidoscopic color. I was nothing but a mindless being floating on tingling waves of pleasure that had finally, finally found me.

Slowly, awareness of my body returned, all of it awash with soft, fuzzy release. My men still held me. Lars's hips jerked as the last of his cum pumped into my clenching pussy. Casimir gripped me, his cock twitching with his own release. My throat convulsed, instinctively swallowing, but it wasn't just Clay's cum I tasted in my mouth.

I tensed, realizing my fangs had sunk into his cock after he came.

Clay's fingers tightened on my hair. "Fuck, baby, don't stop," he urged, his voice shaking. "This is the hottest thing I—" He groaned, clearly fighting to stay still in my mouth. "I've ever..."

I took one more gulp and then retracted my fangs as his cock began to soften. Licking him carefully, I sealed the wounds.

He shuddered, sagging back onto his heels. "Holy *shit*, that was incredible," he whispered to himself, his eyes dazed.

As Casimir and Lars eased from within me, a satisfied grunt came from nearby. I glanced over to find the demon still at my side. Hot, thick ropes of his cum coated my arm and back, all of it glowing faintly with orange flecks like embers, as if it was burning from the inside. With one massive hand, he reached out, smearing the sticky release over my back, my sides, my breasts and ass, like he was intent upon it covering every inch of my skin.

"Think the big guy is claiming you, baby," Clay continued, still sounding sex-dazed. "That's fucking hot too."

Staring at the demon, I nodded, my body tingling. Even after the intensity of my orgasm, a tiny coil of heat still gathered in my core at the feeling of his release marking me. Of how it sparked with magic as it absorbed into my skin.

But if I could have it *in* me...

The thought seemed to take control. Instantly, I sank back into a sitting position, and my legs fell open in offering.

The demon grinned, his eyes tracing a line from my breasts to my wet core. "Mine."

I hesitated, tensing. Did that mean he wasn't going to continue sharing?

He seemed to see my apprehension. His eyes narrowed, flicking to the others. I held my breath, bracing for what he'd do or say.

Pushing to his feet, he stalked toward me. My body responded instantly, like instinct was still driving my muscles instead of my brain. Leaning back onto my elbows, I arched my back, pushing my breasts toward him while my legs spread wider. Wet, hot need pooled between my legs, making me ready to accept his cock. I didn't even know if he'd fit, but I ached for him to try.

But my mind was torn, faltering between how he'd just shared me and how he might not want to do so after this.

Bracing himself with one hand on the dirt, he

lowered himself over me, his sinuous tail flicking the air behind him.

Need quaked through me as my gaze tracked it. "Put... put that in me too. Put..."

His clawed finger took my chin, tilting my head up toward him so my eyes had to meet his. The dark star at the heart of his fiery gaze transfixed me. My hips raised for him immediately, offering myself to be fucked. My pussy quivered when he gave a low, rumbling purr.

"Take me," I gasped. "Please. Now."

"Mine," he murmured again, nodding. "Mate you. Breed you. Feed you blood until you swell up with little ones."

"Whoa..." Clay murmured somewhere nearby.

"Is that even possible?" Lars whispered.

A hint of a snarl left the demon, as if he didn't like the question.

Worry flickered in my mind, stronger this time, trying to remind me that I needed to get a few more things straight with the demon before I let him drive himself into me. But my body didn't care. It rocked toward him, dripping with arousal, utterly lost in its mindless readiness for him to do everything he said and more.

A tiny muscle spasm twitched his face, seeming involuntary.

My worry returned, this time for him. "Are you—"

The twitch returned.

My body still clamored to let him fuck me, all rational thought be damned, but my apprehension was getting strong enough now that I could overcome that.

Carefully, I eased up from my elbows, watching him. "Demon?"

"Mine," he growled, but it didn't sound like he was talking to me anymore. "Mine *wants* me now. Wants me to—"

He cut off with an infuriated sound.

"Princess..." Casimir reached down for me, never taking his eyes off the demon. "I think *perhaps* you should—"

The demon snarled viciously, baring his fangs at the vampire.

Alarm shattered the hold lust had on my muscles. Scooting back fast on the dirt, I shoved to my feet and put myself between Casimir and the demon. "Don't you dare!"

The demon froze. His eyes darted from me to the vampire and back, horror and confusion spreading across his face. "I... Vampire was..."

"You just got done helping. Would you seriously hurt him again?"

A strangled sound escaped the demon, like he was panicked and furious and frightened, all at the same time. His face twitched once more and the fire in his gaze dimmed, something in his eyes changing in a way that took me a heartbeat to identify.

"Is Roan trying to come back?" I asked. "Does he—"

A shudder rolled through me, like cold fingers had suddenly brushed over my naked skin.

I shook my head, trying to dispel the strange feeling and focus. "Does Roan—"

The cold sensation grew stronger. On some unnameable impulse, my eyes went to the east, searching, but I only saw the bushes, fallen branches, and trees.

My skin crawled. Trees... something about trees...

Leaves and bark and roots and it hurt... I hurt...

I flinched back from the bizarre thought. But like the filament threads of a spider web, it clung to me, echoing with fear and pain.

My mouth tasted apples. The juice filled my throat. But the flavor swiftly turned to mush and vinegar, twisting my insides with nausea and making me want to gag.

"Princess?" Worry threaded through Lars's tone. "Are you okay? You look queasy."

I swallowed hard, trying to keep my stomach down. "Something's wrong," I whispered, terrified of speaking too loudly, though I couldn't explain why. "Something about the trees, but I don't—"

Icy cold sent a violent shiver coursing through my body, if the temperature in the forest had suddenly dropped so dramatically, everything should have frozen in an instant.

"Do you feel that?" I breathed.

At their silence, I twitched my eyes toward them, no matter how much it scared me to take my attention from the forest for too long.

Climbing to his feet, Clay didn't take his eyes from me as he motioned briefly, conjuring clothes over us all. "Feel what, princess?"

But even wool and leather didn't dispel the chill ghosting across my skin.

The cold felt like it had already gotten inside me.

Wordlessly, the demon raked his fiery gaze across the woods, every trace of Roan gone now from his eyes. A low growl left him, like a predator who knew a threat was near.

I couldn't be scared of the sound. Not when *I* felt like we were all prey who'd suddenly found themselves in a trap.

Casimir's brow twitched down. "Something *is* odd, but..." His head shook slowly, and his attention slid to the trees.

I followed his gaze. "Can you tell what it—"

A twisting, stabbing sensation ripped into my gut before I could finish the sentence. My knees hit the ground with a thud, the sharp pain of the impact nothing compared to the shredding agony tearing through me.

"Gwyneira!" Casimir's hands grabbed my arms, stopping me from falling all the way to the earth. "Speak to me. What is—"

A scream tore from my throat as the pain grew stronger. His mouth was moving, but I couldn't hear him anymore. His terrified expression broke my heart, but only until agony stole my sight. Blinding red and black and white lights swallowed my vision, like my entire being was losing its ability to function in the face of this torture.

But I wouldn't have known what to tell him anyway.

Darkness swelled, devouring the flashing lights, the searing agony. But this pitch-black hell wasn't empty.

I swore I heard it laughing.

10
DEMON

I reached my mate's side with a speed that would have rivaled that damn vampire, scooping her away from him and nestling her in my arms. But her screams didn't stop. Her body began to seize and spasm, her vampire strength giving her convulsions such force that they nearly threw her from my grasp.

"What the fuck is this?" Clay cried. "What's wrong with her?"

Lars stared with horror, wordless.

I, too, was beyond my ability to speak.

But words would not be needed to kill that which harmed my mate.

Holding her close, I raked eyes over the forest. *Something* was out there. I could not smell it. Could not hear it.

But it was here *somewhere*.

"Cas, help her," Clay begged. "Please!"

The vampire extended his hands toward my mate. I started to snarl.

Don't you fucking dare, the broken one snapped.

I snarled at him instead.

"This..." The vampire's eyes went from my mate to the forest and back. "It's fighting me. I cannot protect her and locate the source at the same..." He swore, dropping his hands. "Perhaps Byron can—"

I did not wait for more. Beating my wings hard, I took to the air. The scholar had abandoned the clearing some time ago, the moment it became apparent what was about to occur with my mate. Whether he realized that it was his own suppressed desires that had been the catalyst for the intensity of my mate's need and the other men's reactions, I could not tell. Perhaps that was why he had resisted allowing his magic to touch her in the first place, never mind that such opposition was foolish. His spell never would have worked that way.

Yeah, and what about your *part in it, huh?* the broken one snapped, contempt thick in his voice.

I swatted at him in my mind. He wanted to place blame? He, who thought himself capable of taking control of my body and stopping me from claiming my mate when she lay before me, ready and willing?

Willing? the broken one's voice was a roar of rage, his fury burning as hot as my flames. *She was under the influence of magic, you primitive son of a bitch! You saw her face, and I* damn *well know you smelled her confusion. Her body wasn't fully under her control, which meant no, that didn't count as fucking* willing! *But could you bother to care about that? No, you were still going to rut her like a damn* animal!

I growled, but his words still stung. She... yes, fine, had possessed a hint of confusion in her scent. And her eyes flickered with worry. But perhaps that was for *him* and how he'd tried to take control rather than let us lay together.

Except... what if it hadn't? What if I had been mistaken yet again?

Shame began to gnaw at my belly.

The broken one continued, his voice scathing. *The minute she's safe, you're done, you hear me? We're done. We can't be trusted near her. Not if you can't respect her like she deserves.*

That drew another snarl from me. Like hell he'd keep me from my mate.

In my arms, she twisted again, agony on her face.

Dammit, fly faster, you—

I shoved him down hard. I'd had enough of him. Of all of this. I knew what needed to happen. The scholar had likely fled to the camp after leaving the clearing. That was miles from here, but I was fast. I would reach it in moments.

And there, the scholar would cast spells to stop her pain while I hunted down the source of her suffering, because whatever harmed my mate *would* die. Bloody. In pieces.

And then I would kill it again for good measure.

The black blur of the vampire shot through the forest below. Some distance back, the twins ran, leaping logs and tearing through branches, moving fast even if their top speed was no match for my own.

In my arms, the princess's struggles slowed, but one

glance told me it was not because her invisible assailant had fled in fear. Her skin held the bloodless pallor of death. Her breaths were as weak as a dying breeze.

This was killing her.

I roared, rage and fear pounding through me. No, she would *not* die. I would hunt down and kill the threat to her first, and then everyone would be grateful. They would understand they did not need to protect her from me. That they did not need to pull her away, encouraging her to retreat to supposed safety when I was inches from filling her sweet pussy with my cum. My mate would forgive my mistakes in the clearing, the broken one would leave me be, and then everything would be all right.

Deep inside, the broken one glared at me, believing none of that.

To hell with him. This was his fault as much as anything. How, I was uncertain, but surely he also shared blame for—

A gray and brown blur raced through the forest, coming this way, with a cloud of black smoke on its heels. The creature was larger than my mate's men, with horns on its head and the body of a wolf, but running on two legs.

The beast-man and that shadow mutt.

At the sight of me, the beast let out a howl. Bloodthirsty threat was in the sound. Promises of torturous retribution from which the escape of death would be a mercy.

He thought *I* did this?

He was a fool.

Another convulsion rolled through my mate. In the forest below, the beast stumbled, crashing into the undergrowth like his legs had gone out from beneath him. The smoke-wolf swirled around him, shoving him back upright. But still the beast's howl turned anguished, a cry of horror for my mate's pain.

But I would save her. I would fix this. He would be grateful because I would—

My enemy raced over the horizon.

A snarl tore from me, my fangs bared. In a wave of black ink, the twisted magic coursed through the ground like poison racing along the earth's veins.

And it was coming for us.

For *her*.

The camp came into sight below. The fragile humans were on their feet, staring around, and a shout went up when they spotted me. My roar must have reached even their small and dull ears. But near the side of the clearing closest to where the beast-man had run into the forest, the one called Dex stood, his sword drawn. The scholar was nearby, his bag of magical tricks gripped tightly in one hand and his weapon clutched in the other, as if he hadn't been able to decide whether magic or metal was needed.

Swiftly, I dove to the earth. All around the camp, the horses went mad, rearing and making their annoying, shrill noises of fear. I did not care for those creatures. They became twitchy when the broken one went near them.

But now the horses' fear was not for me.

They knew something was coming too.

At the sight of Gwyneira, Byron immediately dropped his sword and raced toward me. "What happened? Where is everyone else?"

The vampire flew into the clearing. Coalescing into solid form without ever slowing his pace, the vampire ran toward us.

"Do you feel that, scholar?" he called. "The threat on the horizon?"

Byron looked around quickly, confusion on his face. "Feel…" His face went slack with horror. "Oh gods."

Dex wasted no time with questions. "Demon, get the princess to the carriage. Byron, Casimir, do whatever it takes to help her. General! We've got to move!"

A dark-haired woman nodded once at his words and then began shouting orders at the humans. I liked that one. She was efficient, and she made my treluria happy in some way I couldn't quite define.

Like a friend, you idiot, the broken one snapped from deep inside. *The word is* friend.

Damn him! How was it he was *still* here, even after I shoved him away? And on top of that, now the vampire and scholar were coming toward me as if to take my mate from my arms. That would *not* happen. I was the demon. *I* could protect her better than those two ever could—and certainly better than some foolish box of wood on wheels.

And if whatever the fuck that is tries to attack her physically? the broken one argued furiously. *The carriage could take the blows instead of her.*

I growled. How dare he delay me, then?

I strode for the carriage.

The ground began to rumble before I made it three steps. I dug my feet into the dirt, fighting to stay upright while humans shouted and my mate writhed, short and sharp noises of agony escaping her.

I would kill this. I would burn it to ash for the pain it caused.

And then I would hunt down the gods and burn them too for allowing her a moment of suffering.

The beast-man rushed into the clearing, that irritating shadow dog beside him. Humans began panicking yet again at the sight of them, but the beast-man shifted quickly. Rage on his face, he strode toward me. The ground became steadier the closer he came, as if he was stabilizing it even in his fury.

"What did you—" he started.

"The demon did not cause this," the vampire interrupted.

He *defended* me?

I did not trust that.

The beast-man looked barely mollified. "Then what the hell is happening to—" Cutting off, he whirled quickly, staring to the east.

In the distance, my superior vision caught how the ground began to crack. Fissures ran through the rocks and soil like tree roots were ripping through the earth.

Casimir's senses were adequate enough to allow the vampire to spot the damage a moment after I did. A curse in another language slipped from him before he spun to me, shouting, "Forget the carriage! Fly!"

How dare the vampire give me orders like a—

Fucking fly, you idiot! the broken one shouted so

loudly in my mind that my wings beat the air like his fury had propelled their motion.

How had he—

FLY!

I snarled as my wings spasmed again. To hell with them both. I would fly, but only because it was what I would have chosen to do anyway.

Beating my wings hard, I took to the air again, cradling my mate in my arms. On the far end of the clearing, the twins raced into view, breathing hard and smudged with dirt from their desperate attempt to catch up to me.

But even though I lifted my mate away from the earth, she continued writhing as if attempting to escape her pain.

Furious, I turned my eyes to the east again. Whoever cast this magic to torment her would beg me for death by the time I was through.

The fissures were fools, though. They underestimated my power, continuing to race closer like deranged arrows seeking their target, darting left and right across the terrain with every passing second.

But they weren't like those the broken one had seen before, when the foul Voidborn tried to enter this reality to unleash their destruction. This time, gnarled vines shot up from the darkness within the cracks, twisting and thickening with unnatural speed until they became trunks and branches.

Trees, but not like those in the rest of the forest. These reached for the sky as if they were diseased hands, their branches clawing like the fingers of the damned.

Sickly leaves sprouted from their mottled bark, each encrusted with virulent pustules that steamed in the cold air.

The vampire-angel muttered another curse when he spotted the diseased trees as well. "All of you!" His arm sliced the air as he gestured. "Run!"

The humans looked around in confusion, as if uncertain whether to obey Casimir's orders. But the giants had no such trouble. Immediately, they ran for the horses. But while Dex hauled his panicking animal around and swung up onto its back like he was accustomed to handling a horse on the verge of bolting, the others struggled.

I growled in frustration. The men were not familiar with how to control those infernal, braying creatures. Neither was I, but that would not have slowed me. The horses would have obeyed me or died.

That's not fucking helpful, the broken one pointed out testily. *But the horses* will *run from us if we come close or use any fire, so stay away.*

He was *infuriating.* Surely he could see that the men needed to move? The cracks were coming closer. And while I wouldn't have cared previously, these men were less annoying than most.

Besides, my princess would be upset if the giants and the vampire died.

One by one, most of the giants managed to clamber onto the beasts, until only Clay remained struggling.

"Here!" On a massive horse built like it was intended for war, the dark-haired woman charged toward Clay.

Valeria, the broken one snapped. *Her name is Valeria, dammit. I know these names.*

What was that supposed to mean?

The one called Valeria reached a hand down to Clay and then shifted her position on the horse so that he could scramble onto the large creature. "You heard the Zeniryan king!" she shouted to the humans. "Move!"

The humans and giants took off, while the vampire and that infuriating shadow mutt did the same. Beating my wings, I held my princess close and cast another glance at our approaching enemy. The fissures were moving faster now, slicing the earth like lightning bolts.

But as the fleeing horses ran, the cracks split off. As if guided by a powerful hand, the jagged lines moved to cut off any escape.

In my arms, the princess gasped, her body spasming like those tears were actual lightning striking her.

The fissures encircled the humans and giants. The horses reared and whinnied, sending several riders toppling to the ground. Trees shot up from the cracks, growing at high speed.

Their branches wove together, forming a net between me and the people below.

A furious roar tore from my throat, echoed by the beast-man as he stared up through the branches at the princess in my arms. But he needn't have worried. I would burn these impudent trees. I would scorch them from the earth itself for daring to—

The branches began to change.

Against my chest, the princess whimpered as if too weak to even cry out anymore.

Like bulging, jaundiced eyes glaring up at us, round growths swelled to life between the rot-encrusted leaves. As yellow as a pus-filled wound, they grew until they were the size of a human man's fist.

And then their surface changed. Darkening to bloody red, they glistened brighter than the forest around them and steamed in the cold night air like they were heated from the inside.

Oh, gods, the broken one breathed in my mind.

What? I demanded silently, before snarling at myself for how ridiculous it was to respond at all. I didn't need his input.

He answered anyway. *Apples. Like in the forest where the queen killed her.*

His memories rose, playing out like a nightmare. The snowy slopes of a mountain range. A desperate attempt to escape the queen's pursuit. A forest like death, where decaying red spheres clung to leafless gray trees, rotting before our eyes and plunking to the earth like globs of filth.

But in those brief moments when she'd been beyond our sight, the princess had taken one of them. Eaten one of them.

And died.

Rage coursed through me, hotter than the fire that lived inside my veins. The world would burn before I let anything take her away. And if Death itself thought to visit her again, I would prove that even *that* could not survive *me.*

"Swords at the ready!" Valeria called to the humans. "Jakob, Erlek, take the lead and—"

She cut off as suddenly, a crooning sound rose. It twisted around us, seeming to come from everywhere. Soft and gentle and soothing, it used no words as it promised that now, oh yes now, everything was fine. Peaceful. Safe.

I flinched, confused. How could that be true? Moreover, my ears swore I was not actually hearing a thing. No, this strange melody spoke to me like the broken one. Like it was in my mind. Yet it was not him.

Maybe that was fine too…

Air spilled from my wings, dropping me closer to the branches before I could stop myself. But I didn't need to worry about that, the crooning sound whispered. All threats were gone now. It was safe to come down among the trees. Nothing would hurt me.

Beneath the interwoven branches, several humans slipped from their horses, moving like they were in a dream. In fits and starts, Ozias tried to shift back into his beast, but he failed, his body seeming to resist obeying his command. Appearing dazed, he shook his head hard as if attempting to dispel a persistent bug buzzing around his ears.

Like a man with numbed limbs, Byron fumbled for his bag. "Don't…" He grunted, struggling with something. "Don't lis— Gods…"

Nearby, Casimir dropped to his knees, gasping in air. His shadow dog paced around him, the creature's infuriating snarling discordant amid the crooning, making the beast even more irritating than normal.

No, the broken one gasped as if he was struggling too. *Listen to Ruhl. Focus on him.*

Why would I pay attention to that annoying mutt?

Because this is a lie. The broken one's voice was a distant whisper now, nearly drowned beneath the lullaby. Air spilled from my wings again, dropping us down until we were only a few feet above the trees. *It's a—*

His whisper turned to wordless choking, as if even he couldn't keep speaking over this sound.

But why should I care? Everything was fine now.

More air spilled from my wings. My claws were only inches from the trees, and it would only take a small flex of my muscles to grasp one of the glistening apples perched high in the branches.

And they would taste wonderful. I knew that, even without the crooning noise murmuring such promises. I would be fine if I landed on these silly little trees. I could relax now. I didn't need to fight or protect the girl in my arms anymore. I could just let her go.

I jerked my foot away from the tree branch. Wait, this... this *noise* would dare to tell me not to protect my mate?

I scoffed. That was a mistake.

My lips pulled back from my fangs and a low growl rumbled through my chest. The broken one was right. This was a lie. Nothing on this *earth* could tell me that I should not defend my treluria. Especially not when she was curled silently in my arms, her eyes squeezed shut with pain while tears slipped down her bloodlessly pale cheeks.

Heat built in my chest. This forest deserved to die.

"Hold..." Valeria's voice carried up to me past the net

of branches. She rocked on her saddle like even her own body was fighting her order to remain still. "Hold positions. Stay where you—"

I snorted. I would not. This crooning sound deserved death for what it was doing.

Wait, the broken one gasped. *Think, dammit.*

Of what? I would burn this forest and everything in it would...

Oh.

Then everyone here would burn too.

I shook my head hard, fighting the vestiges of the crooning. There had to be a solution. I was the demon. I would find a way.

"*Hold,* dammit." Valeria's voice was strained. "Look for... for a way out of..."

But the humans weren't listening to their commander, and they were only making things worse. Stumbling away from their horses, they staggered toward the very trees I intended to burn as if they were being pulled by tethers.

"Stay... stay put!" Dex barked, his tight grip on the reins blanching his light-brown knuckles to the color of bone. "Dammit, Byron, can you—"

"It's everywhere." The redheaded giant grunted and shook his head in pain. "I can't—"

"Jakob!" Valeria shouted.

A brown-haired human stretched up for the nearest of the putrescent apples dangling from a tree. With an enraptured expression, he plucked the fruit.

"Don't," Valeria gasped, her voice weakening. "That's an order—"

The man sank his teeth into the apple's red flesh, while all around him, other humans plucked fruits to do the same.

Bliss took up residence on their faces.

"You'll want this, General." Jakob approached her, extending the bitten apple.

Valeria shuddered, but her hand rose as if it wasn't under her control.

The man smiled. "Take a bite. Do it. You—"

Clay grabbed the reins from her, yanking the horse into a retreat before Valeria could grasp the fruit. "Get that fucking thing away from us," he rasped.

"But you don't understand," Jakob protested kindly, undeterred. "You'll want this. You—"

A shudder suddenly coursed through his entire body. For a moment, he froze, overcome by a stillness so profound it was like he'd become a painting of a man.

But then his smile grew, stretching to the limits of his muscles and skin. A giddy chuckle escaped him, the sound utterly deranged. His gaze slid upward, finding me.

Finding my princess.

Darkness swirled through his eyes like ink in milk. When he spoke, it wasn't his voice but a woman's. "I see you, Gwyneira."

Like a wild animal, Jakob sprang into the nearest tree and scrambled upward. His eyes never left my treluria. His mouth never stopped grinning madly.

I beat my wings, lifting higher in the air.

Or trying to.

Suddenly, it was as if I was fighting my way through

sludge. Like the crooning sound that even now still twisted on the air was dulling my reactions.

But not his—nor those below him.

The humans who'd bitten apples spun, their mouths pulled wide in rictus-like snarls. They lunged at the giants and the other humans.

We... we need to help... the broken one's voice was muted like he was fighting to speak through suffocating cotton.

I fought to beat my wings harder, but I could barely move. Below me, horses went down, knocked over by assailants who were ruthlessly determined to grab their riders. Dex tumbled away, rolling as he hit the dirt and barely managing to draw his sword when he rose. Nearby, Casimir and the shadow mutt shifted to smoke and tried to rush through the group, fighting desperately to drive the feral humans back.

But not everyone could stop them. Humans fell and their movements were too slow, too unskilled to beat the rush of their attackers.

They aren't warriors, the broken one gasped. *They're farmers and villagers. We have to help—*

From the topmost branches of the diseased tree, Jakob lunged upward and grabbed my ankle. Hauling on me with impossible strength, he began to drag me down.

Fury surged through me, hot enough to start burning back the thick numbness coating my limbs. Kicking hard, I dislodged his grip and beat my wings faster, lifting beyond his reach.

"Mine," I snarled down at him.

"Dead," he snarled back, inky darkness swirling in his eyes.

And then his body spasmed like something was trying to crawl up his throat. Strange words choked out of him. Horrible, twisted sounds that slithered around like invisible oil on the air.

"No..." Gwyneira's whispered plea startled me. My shocked gaze darted from the possessed man to my beloved.

She never opened her eyes. The pallor of her skin was becoming deathly white.

But her body began to jerk like she was being prodded by knives.

"Stop him!" Byron shouted below. "That's the language of the witches! He's—"

I didn't need more. Spinning tightly, I swung as fast as I could through the sludge-like air.

My claws took the man's throat—and his head besides. Blood splattered the trees as his corpse toppled through the branches on its way to the ground.

Gwyneira whimpered. Her shaking ceased.

But still she did not wake.

Below, the other possessed humans didn't pause. Shrieking like savage beasts, they shoved fistfuls of the apples into the mouths of their pinned prey. The humans forced to consume the corrupt fruits began to lurch and shake. Their eyes rolled back in their heads.

They lunged to their feet and charged at the giants.

I wrapped my arms tighter around my treluria, torn. I couldn't help the ones below. Not with my flames, anyway. The attackers were too close to my beloved's allies. I would only burn everyone.

And to go down there would only risk her.

"Demon!" Lars shouted. "Use your fire!"

I balked. Was he insane?

The blond madman shoved a human attacker away and fumbled desperately to hold back another with his sword. "Do it now!"

He... he can control flames, the broken one stammered. *But surely he doesn't think he could actually—*

Ozias roared as three humans flung themselves at him in an attempt to pin him to the ground. Across the small clearing, Clay toppled from Valeria's horse as the beast reared wildly, surrounded by attacking humans.

Indecision ripped me apart. Not to try would break my treluria's heart.

To be responsible for their deaths would too.

"Now, dammit!" Lars yelled. He flung a hand upward, his magic heating the air.

The flame within me answered. Fire rushed through my veins, surging to life like a trapped blaze that had suddenly found air.

Put her down, put her down, put her down! the broken one cried in my mind. *You'll burn her, you crazy son of a—*

No, I wouldn't.

Tucking my beloved safely to my chest, I let my blaze roar out, breathing fire down upon the forest as if it was the dragon I'd defeated days ago. That scaly beast was still out there, wounded but not dead, and different now that the Voidborn had abandoned its body. If the dragon returned to threaten us, I would burn it again. But it wasn't my concern now.

This corrupt forest hurt my mate.

Time for it to die.

My fire slammed down upon the trees like a hammer. Tearing through the branches, it consumed everything in its path. But before the blaze could reach the people below, the flames split like they were the waters of a river and they'd collided with a boulder.

Because Lars's magic was there to control them.

At his motion, they raced off to either side, splitting again and again, turning into dozens of burning streams. Twisting in the air with his magic, the blaze arced around the humans, the giants, even the vampire and his dog, only to lash the trees again.

I grinned.

Because in the face of that onslaught, the forest *screamed*.

Branches thrashed. Trees split. Apples whipped through the air as if shot from a sling, splattering the earth and horses and humans alike.

"Get down!" Dex shouted.

Valeria and the few remaining non-possessed humans hit the dirt. The giants did the same, even Lars ducking as low as he could while sending my fire at the trees. Shifting back to his human-like shape, the vampire pressed himself to the earth while his annoying dog covered him like a protective cloud of smoke.

But all the while, the dog's glowing green eyes stayed trained on me, an intense sort of *knowing* in his gaze.

Why is he watching us like that? the broken one asked, watching the mongrel.

Like I cared.

Ignoring them both, I kept my flames going as the irritating-but-useful blond giant sent fire across every fissure and tree root. Nothing would remain after this. Nothing would threaten my mate again.

Except suddenly, the possessed humans stood up.

And charged.

Dex was on his feet immediately, his sword cutting a man down when he flung himself at Lars. Ozias's axe took another, sending the attacker flying backward into the burning trees.

An inarticulate cry of anguish and fury left Lars. But before I could order him to get on with it, he did what was required anyway.

Fire struck the possessed humans. One by one, the humans fell, howling, never to threaten my treluria or those she cared about again.

Good.

I smiled as the forest burned. Its disgusting branches became ash and charcoal, crumbling into the flame-blasted dirt. Its twisted trunks cracked and fell into the fissures, where nothing tried to emerge again. At the center of my blaze, Lars remained standing, his arms outstretched, diverting threads of fire after any leaf, twig, or glob of decaying apple that dared to fling itself his way.

And soon, charred landscape and the blackened bones of the dead were all that remained.

Carefully holding my treluria close, I descended, the

beating of my wings sending swirls of smoke and ash spiraling in the air. Around me, the giants and remaining humans climbed to their feet, staring in shock.

And horror.

"They killed them!" a young man among the humans cried. "They killed all of them! They didn't even try to—"

Valeria caught him across the chest as he tried to lunge at Lars.

I growled. That twin may irritate me, but he had still been useful. Yet this pathetic boy complained when we just saved his life?

"They didn't have a choice, Nerak." Valeria held him fast when he fought to push past her again. "There was nothing to be done."

The boy's face screwed up, and he made a choked sound that was on the verge of becoming a sob. "They didn't even *try*..."

At Valeria's nod, a gray-haired man among the human survivors took the boy. The older man's dark eyes tracked us while he led the boy away, his intent gaze not leaving us even as sobs began to escape the younger one's lips.

I did not care for the way that gray-haired man was watching us. Reproach lived in that gaze, and only the fact the old fool was not worth my energy kept me from growling.

But would he have preferred we let him die?

Lars took the judgment more to heart, however. Closing his eyes with an expression of regret, the blond man turned away. He said nothing as Clay put a hand to his shoulder.

He's never liked killing, the broken one murmured, sympathy radiating from him.

The emotion was strange and foreign to me, as was the entire concept that upset them. What did it matter if he *liked* killing or not? Protecting Gwyneira was the point, and killing our enemies had accomplished that.

If they hadn't wanted to die, they shouldn't have threatened my mate.

Dismissing the blond man's bizarre reaction, I turned my attention to my princess. In my arms, she was motionless, her chest still, her heart not beating.

A shudder crept through me. Death had not taken her. I would not allow it.

"Demon." Dex's voice was carefully controlled. "Is she…"

"Tell me she's not dead," Clay demanded tightly.

Shivers crept through my muscles. "No, she is not dead."

Clay nodded, though worried looks still passed among the others.

I did not care. My words would be true—because if they were otherwise, I would hunt her down in the after-life, bring her back, and *make* them be true anyway.

"Here." Ozias strode closer, extending his arm. A quick swipe of his blade across his wrist left blood welling in its wake.

She did not stir when it dripped onto her lips, nor when I carefully opened her mouth and let it fall onto her tongue.

Fear gripped Lars's voice when he spoke. "A-are you sure she's not—"

"No." Ozias glared at him briefly before turning his attention back to Gwyneira. "I would know if she was gone."

His fist clenched, urging more blood to flow from his wound. "Drink, little mate. Wake up."

I bit back a snarl. She was *my* mate.

His too, the broken one pointed out.

Shut up, I snapped back, not caring how ridiculous it was to respond.

Dex, the twins, and Byron came closer, their eyes trained on her. Nearby, Casimir stood with Ruhl at his side. The vampire's eyes were closed, his brow furrowed as if he strained after something. A moment later, he cursed under his breath, opening his eyes once more.

"Nothing." A desperate note clung to his voice. "I cannot hear even the faintest breath or heartbeat from her."

Fear grew on the faces of the giants.

"What do we do?" Clay asked.

I racked my mind for an answer. I was the demon, after all. I would know.

I could not think of any solution.

"Lower her down," Byron said. "Gently."

I tensed. Yes, I traveled all this way for him to use his magic to help her. But releasing her from my arms was asking for something else entirely.

You need to listen to him, the broken one urged.

"Please," Byron continued, almost as if answering the broken one's pleading. "If there's any way to bring her back from wherever her spirit has gone, it will mean unraveling what just happened here. That may take time, and it will be substantially harder if your power overshadows hers. You need to put her down so I can try."

A wary noise left the vampire. "Are you planning to delve into the power that threatened this place? My friend, that could kill you."

The scholar didn't even blink. "It's killing *her*. I'll die before I let it do that."

Rage snarled through me. I would not allow that either.

Except... there was nothing here to attack. Nothing to kill now that the forest was gone.

Fuck, I didn't know what to do.

Grim resolve came from the broken one. Confidence too. If anyone besides us could save her from this horrible magic, it would be Byron. And while the broken one did not want this man to lose his life, he understood the willingness to sacrifice for her. He would do the same.

As would I.

"Very well." I lowered my beloved, laying her carefully on the ground. "Do it."

11

MELISANDRE

Veins of magic flowed up through the nexus and into the royal tree, feeding pure unadulterated *power* into me. Though I stood where I'd been, my hand on its trunk at the heart of the castle courtyard, my mind was not so limited by mere physicality.

I could feel everything. See everything. Throughout Aneira, smaller nexuses fell to my will one after the other while my trees, my apples, tracked the ley lines coursing through the ground, twisting and warping the landscape, the people, the *world*.

In Aneira...

In Cioloren...

In Gentresqua...

National borders meant nothing. Neither did their silly magical defenses. None could stand against me.

Except one.

My teeth ground as the shimmering force of

Erenelle's border wall resisted my onslaught. Even now, that infuriating country wouldn't break. Every spell I'd turned against it all these years said that no one was even still *alive* within its borders, the entire nation reduced to a wasteland populated only by ghosts.

Their wall sheltered *nothing*. Yet still it wouldn't fall.

Seething, I pressed my hand harder to the trunk of the apple tree and turned my attention away from that dead nation. When the entire world bent to my will, I would deal with Erenelle. Or perhaps I would leave it as a graveyard, a testimony to the fact the only outcome of resisting me would be subjugation or death.

And until that day...

I smiled as, one by one, humans anywhere near the ley lines succumbed to my spell, becoming my pawns. My *subjects* in the truest sense. For years, they'd bent their knee to me or others in fealty. In respect, feigned or real. But whether that honor had once been truth or lie no longer mattered.

Now their entire *beings* would bend, and I would be the only one they served. All because they took one little bite of an—

I paused as a tiny speck of light glinted in the dark night of my power.

Gwyneira was here.

Amusement rippled through my expansive awareness. Like a snow-white gnat flying at the edge of my vision, her presence flitted about, as lost and helpless as a feather in a storm.

The child could no more control magic than she could learn to breathe underwater. So some fragment of the magic in Lumilia's ley lines must have drawn her here, pulling her hapless awareness away from her body and out into the maelstrom of my power.

It would be her destruction.

"The so-called *Nine*," I scoffed. "And how easy it is to simply snuff you out."

My magic drew down upon her location. Already, some of the humans with her had made themselves my subjects. It was nothing to shove the melting remnants of one of their feeble minds out of the way of my will, erasing all that was left of the commoner called Jakob and replacing that with *me*.

Sight, blurry and wild, became clear to me, revealing the scene. My trees. My apples. Humans, giants, and a vampire were surrounded by them all. Some strange slip of smoke darted around as if it was alive and possessed its own mind.

But up above the head of my pawn...

Disgust filled me. That child was so helpless, she was being *carried*. But the creature holding her was... odd.

Wait. Was that a *demon*? How had she come across *that*?

I chuckled to myself. Several decades ago, there'd been rumor one might have slipped into this world, but the stories had never been substantiated and the Jeweled Coven eventually dismissed it all as the fantasy of villagers who'd had one too many drinks. Prior to that, demonkind hadn't been seen in centuries. Not outside of fading illustrations on crumbling manuscripts.

But, oh, to make *that* creature my subject...

I focused more power upon the lulling song of my

spell. The monster's face twisted with resistance, but the struggle was fruitless. I could already see I was winning. Demon or not, he would bend to my will.

And as for the pathetic girl in his arms…

My subject's lips curled when mine did. "I see you, Gwyneira," I said.

At my command, the man leapt.

The demon's wings beat harder as he fought to rise in the air. My pawn grabbed the creature's ankle and began dragging him back to earth anyway.

Anticipation shivered through me. I could feel this demon's power. It was like staring into the heart of a volcano.

Forget bending him to my will. I would consume this power. Drain it. Make it part of my essence the way I'd done with—

Me.

I flinched. What the—

Rage twisted the demon's face. With more force than he should still have been capable of summoning, he kicked my subject's grip away.

"Mine," the vicious beast snarled.

Cursing to myself, I refocused on claiming my victory. The demon could actually talk, and he dared use his words to resist me.

When I killed Gwyneira, perhaps I would make him watch.

"Dead," I promised him.

I smiled as I made my pawn speak my spell out into the air. Meanwhile, I could feel the Voidborn still hiding out inside one of the other humans. That insidious spy of mine was biding its time, pretending quite convincingly to be horrified by what was occurring.

Once my magic was done destroying this pathetic excuse for the supposed *Nine*, the Voidborn would make sure any of the humans left were bent to my will.

What an overblown fairytale this prophecy had been.

"No..." Gwyneira's little presence in the infinite dark whispered the plea at the same time as her dying body did. Crystalline glints of light drifted around her, like specks of dust glittering in moonlight.

Her presence melted away, lost to the darkness completely.

Contempt filled me. That was it, then. She'd thought to challenge me, and in the end, she was no more permanent than a snowflake on the breeze.

What a pathetic little—

Pet.

I tensed at the sibilant whisper. That... that wasn't possible.

My awareness jolted as the connection to my pawn disappeared in a splash of blood and pain. But my link to the others held, and through the eyes of my other subjects, I saw my pawn's head fly while his body tumbled from the branches, the two parts ripped asunder by the demon's claws.

The rough whisper of a chuckle rasped like grit-filled smoke across my skin.

No. Alaric was gone. Dead. I'd consumed his power and—

Taken it.

Bound it.

Used it.

Made it you.

No!

Outrage flooded me—because I would be *damned* if I allowed space inside myself for fear. Hatred was my power. My strength. The thing others feared and scorned. The thing that I embraced.

My hatred had burned that bastard once. It would stop whatever game Gwyneira's allies were playing to make me think I heard him now.

Like poisonous water, my fury rushed out into my subjects. In only a heartbeat, they leapt at anyone around them who had yet to bend to my will. More and more, my power spread through the humans, while Gwyneira's allies shouted and fought and scrambled to stay alive.

But I would destroy them. They *dared* to stand against me, to try to manipulate me, and for that I would—

Fire slammed down upon my forest.

I stumbled backward from the apple tree in the castle courtyard, my awareness reeling between Lumilia and the forest where Gwyneira's allies should have died. This was more than ordinary flame.

It was the nature of fire itself, and it wanted to devour me.

I screamed.

My connection to my subjects near Gwyneira fragmented like a broken mirror, showing pieces of the scene but nothing whole. Still, my pawns served me, trying to tear down her allies, fighting to reach her and destroy that girl who didn't deserve anyone's loyalty.

But the fire was everywhere.

The connection to my subjects in the forest vanished as the fire consumed them completely. My power withdrew from the trees as the trunks and branches and roots all died, leaving only ashes in the fissures I'd torn through the soil. Throughout the land, the rest of my subjects paused, their eyes turning in the direction of that distant, dying forest as if they too were appalled by what Gwyneira's monstrous allies had done.

Shivers racked me while the pain of the forest's burning faded away.

A hiss-click came from one of the Voidborn. A question of what had just happened.

Without looking at him, I flung my hand out. Bones snapped. Organs squished. The slip of shadow tried to flee, only to evaporate as I pinned him in the light of the rising sun.

Silence followed the thud of the dead body hitting the ground.

A shudder rolled through me. "Harran."

The silence remained.

"Harran!"

Another several seconds ticked past, and then hurried footsteps rushed across the cobblestone courtyard. "Yes, Your Majesty?"

"Where were you?"

"C-cleaning the library. It's really rather dusty since most of the staff no longer—"

"Quiet. Find me a mirror."

"A mirror?"

My head twitched toward him in irritation, though my eyes didn't leave the west.

"Yes, Majesty. Right away." His footsteps fled the courtyard.

My jaw clenched and my fangs bared. Behind me, no Voidborn made a single sound. No human nor creature did either.

And there wasn't a damned *trace* of Alaric's voice to be heard.

Because of course there wasn't.

I straightened in the light of the rising sun, its radiance unable to burn me as it danced across the gold and silver glints in my skin. I'd defeated that eel-faced bastard. I'd consumed the blood of Gwyneira's angel and defeated the light of the sun as well.

And when this was done, I would stand upon the grave that held all her men.

"If you survive the dark, Gwyneira," I whispered, "know this. Demons die. And so will you."

12

GWYNEIRA

"Hello?"

Nothing.

"Roan? Ozias? Is anyone there?"

Silence.

In the dark, I twisted and turned, lost in a place where there was no trace of up or down. I couldn't feel my body. See my own hands before my face. There was just... me.

And the darkness.

"Please! Can anyone hear me?" My terrified voice barely pierced the emptiness. "Casimir? Byron? Any—"

Low laughter rolled through the night, cruel and familiar. "I see you, Gwyneira."

Oh gods.

Panic gripped me, and before I could think to question, I was already fleeing into the dark. I couldn't let her catch me. Not if I wanted to survive.

But... where was the way out?

The darkness grew thicker. Colder. Emptier in a way that felt like nothing of substance or form could survive. I'd made a mistake coming here.

White as snow...

I slowed at the faint traces of a woman's voice drifting through the darkness.

Red as blood...

I twisted and turned, searching. I... I *knew* that voice. I'd heard it on the edge of a dream.

Dark as ebony...

"Hello?" I called, but the emptiness swallowed my cry.

Yet a ghost of sensation brushed me, like a hand against my cheek. *Hold on, my precious one. They're coming.*

Far in the distance, a thread of glittering power flickered to life in glistening white and gold, shining like dust made from the stars and the sun. It wound its way back and forth through the night, searching, battling the darkness to find me.

I knew that light.

"Byron! Casimir!" I strained toward it. "I'm here! I'm—"

The dark was too great. The gold light fell back, unable to continue. But still the silver-white glitter of stars continued on, struggling with all its might.

Byron. But he was fading.

"No, please!" With everything I had, I summoned up my own magic. Whatever I could find in this empty, awful place where light was an abomination and my stepmother's darkness still reigned.

He was going. Draining away.

My power touched his.

A shock jolted through me, and I could feel the same reverberate through him. Like threads of light, our energy wove together, blending and twisting into each other until it was impossible to tell where one ended and the other began.

Until they became the rope that could pull me from this horrible night.

But it wasn't just our power that joined. Images suddenly hit me, as if I'd plunged into strange, frigid water that engulfed me in sight and sound.

Marble floors glittered beneath me, and all around, carved columns rose up to a distant domed ceiling that shone with sunlight and inlaid jewels. Robed figures stood in a circle, surrounding me, each of them several feet taller than I was and broader besides. The smell of incense hung heavy on the air. I was cold beneath my velvet robes. Nervous too, but resolute. This was all I'd ever wanted, and excitement fluttered like trapped birds in my chest at the fact this day had finally come.

Not all the Order had thought I should be admitted into their ranks. I wasn't like them, and many had openly questioned whether someone like me could handle the burden of this calling.

But every single day, I swore to myself that I would prove them wrong. I would be worthy of this. I would never falter.

Not now, not ever.

The robed figure ahead of me stepped forward. "Do you swear your life to the Order of Berinlian, forsaking all others for the pursuit of higher knowledge? Do you swear to have no

other love but that of learning, abstaining from all attach-
ments and keeping your mind, body, and soul dedicated solely
to the holy communion of magical wisdom?"

I held my face still, reflecting the solemnity of the occasion
no matter how much I wanted to grin with pride. "I do."

I gasped, the rush of images vanishing into light as I opened my eyes and saw blue sky above me again.

And Byron.

I stared at him. That... that was him. His past. I could feel it as viscerally as if I'd stood there myself.

His fear. His pride. His desperate need to prove everyone wrong. To be every inch the scholar so many swore he couldn't be.

And he had. Gods, did he know how truly he had? He was amazing, and I ached for how much I hoped he knew that.

Just as much as I ached for how I knew now why he and I would never be together.

13
BYRON

The princess opened her eyes, and I took my first real breath in what felt like days.

No, not *felt*. It *had* been days, at least if my spotty and exhausted memory served.

With a thud, I flopped onto my back on the blanket under me. My friends had set it up three—no, four?—days ago when we reached this hillside, miles from where the cursed apple trees had attacked, and it had become clear continuing our travels was not going to be an option.

Saving Gwyneira took precedence. I couldn't even compensate for something as simple as the rocking of a carriage when all my focus, all my magic and energy and *soul*, were needed to rescue our princess from the darkness that wanted to steal her away.

Again.

A pained whimper left the princess, but my friends were there, gathering around her as if each was trying to be the one to help her if needed. Meanwhile, the humans hung back with looks that ranged from curious to wary.

Valeria's orders still held sway, however. While she'd sent a few human survivors on horseback to warn Lord Thomas about the poisonous apple trees that had ripped through the earth, she'd commanded the rest to stand guard. Or, more specifically, for the humans to protect us while "that giant did whatever the hell he's doing."

Blunt words or not, I appreciated the sentiment. From the way Valeria's eyes frequently went to the horizon, she was worried for her lord. I suspected it was more than worry, and likely love that made her send those riders to warn him. But still she stayed, following his command to guard the princess and making sure those under her charge did the same.

At the moment, I was more grateful than ever for it. I ached all over and doubted I could form words right now, to say nothing of helping with an attack. Wrung out like a sodden rag, my skills had been reduced to lying here, holding this blanket on the earth.

But the exhaustion was worth it, if only because Gwyneira was still with us.

I stared up at the night sky, a distant part of my mind listing the constellations and using them to calculate the approximate date. I didn't particularly care about the result, but I could no more turn off my brain than I could fly to the stars themselves.

Gods, how many times had we almost lost her? I'd say I had lost count, but the truth was I only *wished* I had. Because every time was one too many, and each weighed on me like a boulder crushing my soul.

And this time might have been the worst of all. No, it hadn't been like when we found her dead in the forest, or when the vampire king took her and we had no idea where she'd gone.

But what it had taken to save her this time, what happened in those days of endless toil to bring her back to life...

A horrible, warm-cold shiver rolled through me, radiating from my middle. The others didn't know, and I wouldn't tell them. Not unless Gwyneira—

"Here. Drink."

Casimir's voice came from somewhere to my right, startling me from my thoughts. When I rolled my head to the side, I found him holding a small cup.

"It's only water," he said to my questioning look, a wry glint in his eyes. As I struggled to rise, he was there to assist me in sitting up, his vampire strength more than compensating for our difference in size.

A breath escaped me after the water was gone. "Thank you."

He nodded, but his attention was only partially on me. Clay and Lars were helping Gwyneira to her feet, while Dex and Ozias were at the ready to catch her if anything should go wrong.

"I'm fine," I assured him. "Go help Gwyneira."

Gratitude flashed over his face, but still he paused before leaving. "Well done, my friend."

Would he say that if he knew what this *truly* took?

Thankfully, he didn't seem to need a response. Nodding once more to me, he joined the others.

For a moment, I debated staying put, but the

gnawing anxiety in my gut was growing stronger by the second.

After all, the princess might glance my way and then, maybe, *questions* would come.

Biting back a groan, I pushed to my feet and walked away as steadily as I could.

I probably looked like a staggering drunkard.

Scowling at myself, I kept going. I knew I should be ashamed of fleeing like this, but I couldn't help that. Humans stared as I retreated, and it wasn't until I reached the far side of the carriage that they seemed to decide Gwyneira should have more of their focus than me.

Thank the gods.

I leaned against the black lacquered wall of the carriage, closing my eyes. My body was waking up slowly to the fact I hadn't eaten in days, and my limbs were steadily becoming shakier for their awareness of that lack. On my own, the amount of power I'd just expended would probably have killed me, though even now I couldn't find it in myself to care.

There hadn't been a choice. No one else could help. Not the demon or any of my friends. Casimir had tried, as his power was the closest to mine in a way, but even he couldn't stay long in that endless night. It drained him, dragging at his soul and sanity. If not for Ruhl somehow anchoring him here, I feared we would have lost him to the darkness too.

And that had left me as Gwyneira's only hope. The only one out of us all whose magic was enough like hers to even stand a chance of bringing her back. My friends' magical gifts held affinities to elements of the natural world. Wood and water and the like. But my affinity was to energy itself. And though, yes, on some level, even solid matter was *energy,* I couldn't manipulate fire or wood or water the way they could.

But I *could* reach through the cosmos itself to find our treluria.

Shivers cascaded over my skin at the memory. Bright and crystalline energy, shining like a star in the eternal night. To the others, she'd been lost, and even Casimir's gifts from the angels couldn't find her light.

But she called to me.

She *always* called to me, even in the darkest night, even in the empty realms themselves—or as near to them as anyone could survive. She was there.

I would cross them all to save her.

Footsteps came from the camp, pulling my eyes open again. Biting back a groan, I pushed away from the carriage, trying to stay upright on legs that felt as weak as grass blades. But thankfully, the footsteps moved away a moment later, and in relief, I sagged back against the black lacquered wall again.

I knew I'd need to face the others sooner or later, if only to find something to eat. But more than food, my body craved something I could never, ever give it. Something that surpassed even the intensity of my power touching her body when I cast the spell to protect her from the sunlight.

Something I never should have known in the first place, and *that* was the entire problem.

She ran through the palace, laughing, as her pigtails

bounced against her back and her pet marmoset squeaked with alarm. The little brown creature with its white tufted ears was a gift from a trading vessel that had landed to the south last month. A pet for the princess, they'd said. She had adored it from the first moment she cradled it in her arms.

Servants jumped out of the way as she ran, some of the higher-ranking ones calling admonishments to be careful, but she ignored them all. The walls rang and echoed strangely with her laughter, the twists and turns of the castle bending the sound in a way that seemed wrong, but she never noticed. Even when the stones shifted beneath her feet to keep her from falling, it never struck her as odd.

It never would.

But the marmoset would only be a part of her life for a few months before it would disappear one day, never to be seen again. Her stepmother would claim it ran away and that the princess had been irresponsible with its care, and though in her memory, the princess believed her, there was no way the words could have been true. She'd treasured that creature, same as she treasured her friendships that would inexplicably always come to sudden ends and the letters she'd write to those friends that would never be returned.

She had been so trusting, never knowing she was putting her faith in a creature who was systematically isolating her and who would only ever see her as a pawn and as prey.

Time passed and the memories changed. She grew older, turning from a small child into a young woman. Seated with her legs curled up beneath her skirts, she nestled in a padded leather chair in the back corner of a library so beautiful, it should have made the gods weep. A stack of dusty tomes on Aneiran history sat on the polished wooden table *beside her, assignments from her tutors. Another enormous book was in her lap, held up as if she was reading it intently.*

But a second, smaller book rested secretly on its pages. One made of thin paper and held together by little more than string, as if it was scarcely worth binding. One she'd just found tucked away in a back corner of the library, hidden like contraband, its original owner unknown.

And that book... was magic.

Not magic like witches and giants wielded. Not the kind that, at the time of this memory, she still feared. No, this was the magic of possibilities. Of windows opening in her mind, revealing a life she could scarcely imagine living. A life where pleasure mattered. Where love mattered. Where women were more than mere ornaments to adorn the arms of men, bearing them children and managing their homes as if that could only ever be the extent of their dreams.

This book was the beginning, and there would be others. "Silly" romance stories she would find secreted away in the far corners of dusty shelves. Together, they would open her eyes to dreams and desires and beautiful possibilities she had never imagined. They'd form the cracks in the walls of Aneiran propriety and culture that would one day lead a princess to challenge her entire nation, all to save the lives of giants she'd only ever been taught to fear.

Together, these books would change the world.

A breath rushed from me, and I swiped a hand across my face, dashing away the prickling in my eyes. Gods, did she know how magnificent she was? Had anyone told her? This breathtaking woman who sought out books the ways others sought light and food and air? Who'd studied everything her tutors gave her and more, yet never let that be the end of what she learned?

I'd never felt awe for the *gods* the way I felt awe for her.

Sheltered in a life where she had every reason to conform to how she'd been taught to think, she'd still chosen a different way. Despite her tutors' best efforts, she'd held strong to her secret conviction that there was more to reading than merely memorizing facts or her forebears' ways of thinking. She'd clung to the belief there was beauty and love and creativity and worlds upon worlds to discover.

All within the pages of books.

It was so like, and yet unlike, my own road. I'd adored books and learning, stories and myth, ever since I was a small child in the massive halls of the Order. But for me, being part of the world of books meant making certain choices.

Ones that were the opposite of hers.

A sharp breath entered my lungs as thunder rumbled on the horizon, promising a storm to come. I shouldn't have been able to see those things. I almost wished I hadn't.

Except... it hurt to think that. No, it wasn't right that I knew this about her. But now that I did, it was all so... dammit, so *beautiful* that I never wanted to let it go.

And so shameful that it burned like a hot coal in my hand.

Because while following her passion for knowledge and reading had led her to change the world, for me it meant turning my back on the very things she'd discovered in those precious books.

Love. Passion. Everything my treluria and I should have been able to share.

"Byron?"

I froze, curse words from every language I knew blurring through my head in an instant.

Gwyneira stepped around the side of the carriage.

Carefully concealing any trace of my reaction, I shifted my weight to face her. "Yes?"

My voice was still rough from days without much food or water, and cold besides, but she didn't care. She walked closer.

I remembered several curse words I'd left out.

"Are you okay?" she asked.

My internal swearing went silent. *That* was her question? Everything she'd gone through, the fact she could have died, and she asked about me?

Gods, how did one *begin* to deserve her?

Fighting down the tangle of anguish, need, and awe that was choking me, I kept my voice tightly controlled as I replied, "I'm fine."

From the corner of my eye, I saw her nod. For a moment, she was silent, and then she asked. "What was that?"

With effort, I kept my face still. "What was what?"

She was silent.

Shame began eating at my gut like acidic rot. Damn me, I was feigning ignorance to save myself when I should have been acting with more honor. I hadn't *intended* what happened, no, but I still needed to own up to it rather than acting like a coward and leaving her to—

"What you did," she said.

Gods, it felt as if we were sword fighting, each testing the other with careful strikes, seeing where our opponent's weak points lay.

I didn't want to be her opponent.

But I didn't want her to hate me for what had happened either.

And I was starting to fear I really *was* a coward.

"I reached out to you with my magic," I said, not looking at her. "Is that what you mean?"

She made a noise of agreement.

And left the answer up to me.

Strike, defend. Strike, defend.

I'd never been good at sword fighting.

"I'm sorry." My heart began pounding. "I swear, I would never intentionally—"

"Did you see my memories?"

I froze. Her words felt like a peace offering extended over a possible trap. If I said yes, would she lash out in rage for the violation?

Closing my eyes, I cursed myself silently. I didn't need to be a scholar to know that was a foolish question. Gwyneira wouldn't. She'd put distance between us, yes. My friends would take care of beating me senseless.

And I'd deserve every blow.

Bracing myself, I made myself look up. "I'm sorry. Truly. I never meant to—"

"I saw yours too."

The sorrow in her eyes brought all my self-protective babbling to a halt.

Oh, gods, I was an *idiot.*

"Princess..." Every horrible moment of the war raced through my mind, each one made all the *more* horrible because I might have inadvertently inflicted them on *her.* "What did you see?"

A heartbeat passed. "The Order."

Oh, gods, no. They'd died so horrifically, I still had nightmares even after all these years. "I'm so sorry, I never would have wished you to—"

"I get it now."

I faltered, my words falling silent so hers could be the ones to emerge. In the distance, thunder came again, closer now.

"I understand why you retreat when the others are with me," she said. "Why the two of us can't be like that, even if you once called me your treluria. I saw the day you swore your oaths to the Order. I felt how much it meant to you. How important that is, even now." A sweet smile crossed her face, but because I knew her, I could still see the trace of sadness in her eyes. "Byron, it was beautiful."

Quivers spread through me. If this was a sword fight, she'd just cut me to the core. "*B-beautiful?*"

She nodded, a trace of amusement in her eyes like somehow my reaction was endearing.

But then it faded. "I'm so sorry for what happened to them."

My heart tripped over itself in panic. "Did you see that? The—"

She was already shaking her head. "Just the day you swore your oaths."

Relief crushed a breath from my chest.

Her smile returned, kind and soft. She was looking at me like I was something mysterious and incredible, but even that couldn't fully mask her sadness.

And I couldn't reach out to her. I couldn't make her pain better or bask in the wonder of seeing that respect in her eyes. And she'd seen my past, so she knew *why* I couldn't.

Somehow that fact didn't help at all. It *should* have. A week ago, I likely would have been relieved. Ecstatic even that the woman I couldn't get out of my mind now understood and accepted that I could never be with her the way the others could. A week ago, I would have seen that as an unequivocally *good* thing.

It didn't feel good now.

"Did you see anything about me?" Her brow rose, curious.

"I... I, um..."

"It's okay to say so."

The kindness on her face was heartbreakingly genuine. I hesitated all the same, choosing my words carefully. "I saw a marmoset."

Her smile returned, but once again, it held pain.

It goaded me onward. "It wasn't your fault, princess. The fact he disappeared. Your stepmother lied to you. I saw how much you cared for that creature. You never would have let him slip away if... if she hadn't taken him from you."

I knew I couldn't prove that last. But I also knew without a shred of doubt that my words were true.

Her gaze dropped to the yellowed grass beneath us. Seconds ticked by before she said softly, "She did, didn't she?"

"I'm sorry." My fingers curled as I fought the urge to reach out to her.

She nodded in acknowledgement. "Did you see anything else?"

At my silence, she glanced up again.

"The library." The words felt like they were being dragged from me by sheer virtue of the fact I couldn't bring myself to lie. "The day you found the first of those small romance novels you love."

Her brow rose. "Oh. I, um... Oh, dear." Her cheeks flushed pink and she chuckled, retreating a step in embarrassment. "Should I apologize? I—"

"Not at all!" My hands caught hers before I realized what I'd done. Blanching, I released her quickly.

Gods, her skin was as soft as rose petals against the roughness of my own.

Clearing my throat, I shoved that discovery to the depths of my incessantly observant brain. "I... I didn't mind."

For a moment, she was still as only a vampire could be still. At last, she gave a tiny nod. "Okay."

The silence stretched.

"Did, um..." In spite of myself, I motioned for her to sit on the step below the carriage door. She had to be tired, after all.

And gods help me, I didn't want her to go. Not yet. "Did you ever find out who left them there?"

She hesitated and then sank down. "No." A rueful smile tugged at the corners of her lips. "I never asked, either. I was too scared someone would take them away if anyone realized they were there."

"Perhaps when you claim the throne again, you can get more. Create a whole section so you never run out of stories and don't have to hide what you love."

And if she did, gods help me, there wouldn't be a corner in this world that could hide a book she desired. I'd find each and every one. I swore that by Berinlian himself. I'd fill shelf after shelf until she needed whole buildings to house them all.

Just to see her smile.

She glanced up. "I'd like that."

I couldn't breathe. That beautiful joy in her eyes stopped my heart and lit up my soul. Words pressed at me, leaving my entire being teetering on the edge of blurting out something I shouldn't—*couldn't*—ever say.

"There you are!" Clay leaned around the rear of the carriage.

I flinched back, a sharp breath shooting into my lungs. On the carriage step, Gwyneira straightened, blinking hard and turning away from me.

Clay gave us both a curious look. "You two okay?"

Did wanting to punch him count?

Shuddering, I drew myself up with effort. I shouldn't punch him. I should thank him for saving me from making a fool of myself. "Fine."

He gave me an odd look. "Okay, well, the humans

want to get moving, and with this storm coming in, we probably should listen and head out soon."

I nodded tightly. "I understand."

He didn't go.

The urge to punch him was starting to win.

"We'll be there in a moment," Gwyneira told him.

That same odd look lingered for a heartbeat. "Okay." Flashing her a grin, he disappeared back around the corner of the carriage.

Scattered raindrops plopped on my head as if to prove Clay's point.

Sighing, Gwyneira rose to her feet. Turning to me, she rested her hand gently on my arm, where it looked so delicate and small. "Thank you," she said softly. "For saving me and... and for everything."

My mouth moved, searching for an answer and finding only the truth. "Always."

She smiled.

Even through my coat, I swore I could feel the loss of her warmth when she lowered her hand and walked away.

14
GWYNEIRA

My mind was rattling every bit as hard as the rain pounding on the carriage roof.

Sitting on the slightly clammy seat of the carriage, I chewed my lip and stared past the sliver of an opening in the curtain-covered window. Lightning speared across the dark gray sky every few minutes, while thunder rumbled soon after, adding to the constant noise that left the carriage feeling like the interior of a drum. Dampness clung to everything from my clothes to my skin, and each blast of wind sent the carriage rocking on its wheels.

I felt terrible for my men riding outside, and for their horses too. But although the terrain was becoming hillier and we were leaving the prairie behind, there'd been nowhere to find shelter from this storm for hours.

And no resolution to the confusion tumbling inside me either.

Ozias's hand came to rest on my knee, and I flinched, so lost in thought I hadn't even felt him move.

"You're going to rip that." He nodded toward my lap.

I glanced down at the hem of my coat and the button I'd been absently picking at without realizing it. Releasing it, I folded my hands in my lap, but the urge to fidget returned immediately.

He put his arm around my shoulders. "Breathe, little mate."

A shuddering breath entered my lungs, but my eyes darted to the side. Seated across from us, Casimir was watching out the opposite window, while Ruhl was curled like a pillow made of black smoke nearby. Even though the storm drowned many of the noises from outside, I could tell Casimir's vampire hearing still picked up Ozias's endearment for me.

But beyond the way his lips curled a bit, my vampire didn't react, never turning away from the other window. Ruhl remained as he had been, his smoke tumbling slowly as he rested. And the emotions I could feel from Ozias via our connection weren't disturbed by the idea Casimir or the shadow wolf might overhear.

He was willing to risk being himself around the others, just a bit, and that fact was wonderful.

I wished I could focus on it more.

Ozias's arm tightened around me. "We'll find Niko."

I nodded, trying to believe that. But it was only the tip of the mountain of problems before us, and that mountain had only grown.

Apparently, I'd been unconscious for *days*. Days in which Niko could have died. Days in which my stepmother could have done any number of horrible things, none of which I knew how to prepare for. At any moment, the road we traveled could be washed out by this monstrous storm, delaying us even longer.

And then there was whatever Byron had done to save me. What I'd seen from him. What he saw from me.

How it made me feel.

I hadn't told the others about what had happened between us yet. Originally, I'd wanted to talk to him at camp about it, but then we were all packing up because of the storm coming in and there wasn't time. Not without saying something in front of the humans, anyway.

As understanding as Valeria had been about everything so far, I couldn't be sure the others wouldn't panic at the idea the Aneiran princess was somehow sharing memories with an Erenlian monk.

But beyond all of that, there was me. Even all these hours after waking from unconsciousness, I felt *odd* somehow. Tingly, like the sensation of a limb waking up after being asleep, but in my veins and mind.

What if something went wrong in that strange darkness? What if I wasn't *right* anymore?

"Your heart is pounding quite hard, princess." Casimir turned from the window. "And I suspect your mate can feel whatever fear is gripping you right now. Would you care to tell us what has you so scared? Is it Niko or something else?"

I cast Ozias an apologetic look, but he only raised an eyebrow at me, his scarred face calm and curious. Comfort radiated through our connection.

Biting my lip, I tried to think how to respond without making them think there was cause to worry. "I-I just wonder, in the days I was unconscious, if something—"

Shouts came from outside. The carriage suddenly lurched hard to the right, sending me toppling into Ozias.

And then tumbling farther as the carriage itself rolled onto its side.

I crashed into Ozias, trying to shift to avoid hurting him, but everything was moving too quickly. My head slammed into the wooden wall, pain blinding me for a moment. When I tried to move, my hands landed in mud, all of it squelching through the window as the carriage steadily sank into the muck.

More shouting penetrated the ringing in my ears. The clang of swords came from outside.

"Go!" Casimir ordered Ruhl.

The shadow wolf rushed upward, pouring out of the window that was now above our heads. Screams followed.

"Are you okay?" my vampire continued to me.

I tried to nod, but it only made my head spin. "Yes." Carefully, I glanced at Ozias. My mate lay at an awkward angle, his shoulder crushed against the interior corner. Pain radiated through our connection.

But he was already struggling to rise. "Stay down," he snarled at me.

Not waiting to see if I would listen, he straightened carefully. His nose twitched, and then a low growl left him.

Moving fast, he lunged up through the window. A

shout followed, but it cut off quickly as he snapped the neck of the man who'd been climbing to reach us.

A small object tumbled from the man's hand, clattering through the carriage.

Only to burst into flame a moment later.

Fire rushed over the upholstery like it couldn't devour it fast enough. Only the mud saved the sodden curtains beneath me from joining it.

"Shift!" Casimir snapped at me.

I didn't need the order. Swiftly, I abandoned human form, rushing upward as fast as I could and grabbing Ozias as I passed.

He was huge. Heavy.

Thank the gods for vampire strength.

But outside was chaos, and my strange senses in this form took it all in at once. Enormous men attacked from every side. They moved like a unit, wielding their weapons with lethal precision. Their uniforms were terrifyingly familiar.

Huntsmen. My *stepmother's* Huntsmen.

Leather armor covered them, with crimson sashes across their chests pinned by emblems of Aneiran silver apples. Leather masks made each of their faces the same, and they bore more weapons than any other soldier could hope to carry. From axes to swords to bows, they were masters of them all.

A Huntsman had spared my life once, leaving me in the mountains rather than cutting out my heart and returning it to my stepmother like she'd ordered.

None of these seemed inclined to spare anyone.

Bodies lay on the road. The humans who'd been with

us, and of their number, the survivors were barely holding their ground. Valeria was shouting to her people, trying to keep them together, but the Huntsmen were too strong. Steadily, they broke through the humans' lines of defense, separating my allies' numbers into smaller groups where they would be more easily picked off. Dex and Byron were likewise trapped, fending off attacks from all sides. Nearby, Lars and Clay were backed up against the carriage, and Clay cursed vehemently as smoke began pouring from the window behind me.

Surging forward, Casimir charged at the Huntsmen attacking Dex and Byron, Ruhl at his side. The Huntsmen screamed as the vampire and shadow wolf tore into them. In my grip, Ozias snarled something unintelligible. I could feel him urging me to let him go.

But panic held me fast. Everyone was here, fighting and attempting not to die.

Except Roan.

Oh gods, I couldn't find Roan anywhere. The demon either.

On the air, a trace of his blood caught me, drawing me like a beacon. I dropped over the side of the carriage.

He was there. On the ground in human form, half pinned beneath the carriage and the driver's seat.

Rage and horror flooded me. He wasn't moving. Blood coated his face from a savage gash on his temple.

My vampire senses pierced my terror. I could hear the slow thud of his heartbeat. The shallow breaths in his lungs. Both were faint, but it didn't matter. He was alive.

Oh, thank the gods.

I dove for him, releasing Ozias as I went. My mate was already shifting form before his feet hit the ground. In only a moment, a massive beast stood where he had been.

The Huntsmen charging at us balked. Behind the leather face masks, their eyes went wide.

Relief flashed over my giants' faces. "Want to gut some fuckers, Oz?" Clay called.

Throwing his wolf-shaped head back, Ozias howled. Lunging forward, he snagged the nearest Huntsman. The man's blood splattered the mud a heartbeat later.

I kept moving, surging toward an attacker trying to circle the carriage to where Roan lay. The Huntsman screamed, falling to the ground as I surrounded him in shadow form and then tore into him.

"Damn," Clay commented, sounding impressed but taken aback.

I dropped down to Roan's side and shifted. "Roan? Roan, please wake up. We're under attack."

A yelp behind me sent my attention whipping around. At the heart of a group of Huntsmen there stood one who wasn't like the rest. Bigger. Covered in dirt with scuffs on his leather armor and tears on the red sash, like neither had been repaired or even removed in ages. He held his hand aloft, and in his grasp, Ruhl twisted, thrashing with fangs and claws, fighting to break free.

In the form of shadow and smoke, Casimir sped toward them, only to be knocked aside by the Huntsman's free hand.

My eyes went wide with horror. How had he—

With a sharp gesture, the Huntsman flung Ruhl away. The shadow wolf crashed into the boulders beside the road and then tumbled limply to the ground.

Ignoring him entirely, the Huntsman started toward us.

"Roan, please!" I cried.

He didn't stir.

Fear choked me. If the wound to Roan's head was bad enough, or if some other part of him that I couldn't see was injured...

Squeezing my eyes shut, I reached inside myself for my magic. I'd helped Ozias once. I could help Roan too.

A shiver of ice rushed through me, coursing down to where my hands gripped Roan. It was like a frigid breeze on my skin, but it was more *real* than before. Not stronger exactly.

But something was different.

Roan drew a sharp breath, his eyes flying wide. Beneath my palms, he suddenly shifted. His body grew. His clothing shredded away. Enormous wings spread from his back, one of them arching over me like a protective shield.

Something struck the wing an instant later. I whirled, gasping. The horrible Huntsman hadn't reached us yet, but another had just swung his sword at me. The blade was now lodged in a thick bone of the demon's wing, wedged there like the man had struck stone.

The Huntsman cursed. Swiftly, he went for his knife.

A fanged snarl left the demon. His eerie black eyes found me. "Mine." He turned to the man. "You tried to hurt *mine.*"

And then he was moving. His massive, clawed hands grasped the Huntsman. The man's screams lasted only a moment, and then pieces of him flew in every direction, smashing into the rocks with sickening, squelching sounds. A blast of wind buffeted me as the demon took to the air, naked and clearly furious.

Shouts rose from the other Huntsmen. They grabbed for their bows.

The strange one who'd hurt Ruhl and Casimir merely stopped. His head cocked to one side as he regarded Roan's demon rising into the air.

Fear gripped me. Could he hurt the demon too?

"Twin Lars!" the demon shouted.

Ducking under the swing of another Huntsman's sword, Lars called back, "What?"

The demon's lips pulled back in a grin. "Time to play with fire."

Flames erupted from him and poured down like he'd unleashed a river that'd been blocked by a dam.

My breath caught. But before the fire could reach anyone, it separated. Flames twisted through the battle like living ropes. Wrapping around the Huntsmen, the blaze poured over their bodies, consuming them and leaving the humans and my men unscathed.

I looked from the demon to Lars. Eyes intent with focus, the blond giant held his hands outstretched. His fingers moved like a weaver, all while the demon kept the flow of fire coming, his fangs bared in a wide grin.

Despite everything, a chuckle escaped me. The demon really could work with us. Be a part of our group, at least in this way. Yes, I'd seen him helping the others in the forest after Niko was taken, but this... this was amazing.

With every passing second, the battle slowed. The Huntsmen fell, fewer and fewer of them left alive to strike out at our allies. At last, none moved again.

Breathing hard, Lars lowered his hands.

"You okay there, brother?" Clay called.

Lars nodded, a wary hint of exhilaration in his eyes. "That's just... damn. Hell of a rush, every time." He let out a breath, regrouping. "Is everyone okay?"

As the others nodded, I scanned the road. Casimir was with Ruhl. The shadow wolf was back on his feet, shaking his fur like a dog trying to dispel an irritant.

Relief threaded through me, growing stronger when Casimir caught my eye with a reassuring smile and nod, as if to tell me they both were okay.

Thank the gods.

While some of the surviving humans checked on their comrades, the rest were headed in our direction. My relief grew to see Valeria with them. She kept an eye to the demon overhead, balking a bit when he dropped back to the earth and growled.

A bit of my exhilaration dimmed. He was still feral, the demon.

Maybe we could work on that.

"Clay," I called. "Would you please...?" I twitched my head toward the demon who, as always, was totally naked after shifting.

The blond man nodded. With a few quick gestures, he conjured clothing. "Remind me to ask Roan about a non-nudist solution for you, buddy."

A displeased growl left the demon, but at a glance from me, he quelled the sound quickly, discomfort flashing across his face. His fiery gaze dropped away like he didn't want to meet my eyes.

Which was strange, because this was a creature who hadn't cared one bit about being naked or growling at others before. Yet now he looked… ashamed.

But only when he looked at me.

I didn't have time to ask what prompted that reaction. Ozias strode toward us, shifting back from the form of his beast as he moved. "One still lives." He jerked his chin at the burned bodies of the Huntsmen.

My stomach sank with the heavy certainty of which one that would be.

The demon snarled with irritation. "Magic one," he snarled over his shoulder as he stalked toward the survivor. "You. Byron. Come here now."

Glancing warily at the others, Byron trailed him. I hurried after them both.

"Princess," Dex started.

I cast him a worried look, but I didn't stop. I couldn't.

I needed to know what the hell this man was.

The stench of burned flesh surrounded me as I trailed Byron to where the demon waited, and I pressed my sleeve to my mouth and nose, trying to smother it. Even if I technically didn't need to breathe, I still didn't want any of this to work its way into my lungs.

Burned like the others, the strange Huntsman lay on the ground. But *unlike* the rest, he was still trying to rise, even though his body was a wreck. Groaning, he attempted to lift his sword.

"Surrender," Dex commanded him, coming up beside me. "Now."

The Huntsman's head shook. "I... cannot..."

His words were rough, as if his throat could barely make sounds past the damage to his body. But there was also a weary note of defeat to his gravelly voice. A sorrow that confused me. He sounded as if he would give anything to stop, yet still he moved.

I stepped closer, peering down at him.

Recognition teased at the edge of my memory. Something about him was familiar. His eyes, maybe. Or the harsh lines of his face, burned though it was.

The truth hit me. "I... I know him. He's the Huntsman the queen ordered to take me into the mountains and cut out my heart. But he didn't. He spared me and let me escape." A breath rushed from me, wonder and horror so tightly entangled in my chest, I couldn't separate them. "He's the reason I survived to meet you all."

My men froze.

"He swore it wasn't mercy, leaving me in the mountains like that. He said it'd be better to let him kill me so I wouldn't suffer the cold. But when I begged to live... he disobeyed her command and let me run anyway."

On the ground, the Huntsman struggled to rise, even though his body was so burned, movement had to be excruciating. His sword slipped away from the slick flesh of his melted fingers, but still he reached for it over and over again.

I couldn't understand why he kept trying. "Stop. Please. We're not going to hurt you."

"Can't..." Agony filled his eyes, even as he continued straining to grab the sword. "Can't..."

Slow horror spread through me as a terrible possibility presented itself. My stepmother had a way about her. A trick I hadn't seen until the night she framed me for the murder of my father.

She'd whispered in my maid's ear and made Fironia say things she otherwise never would have. She'd turned that sweet girl into her puppet.

But this was so much worse.

"Um, *why* can't you stop?" Lars asked warily, as if he had the same suspicion I did.

"Queen's... command..."

"Fuck," Clay whispered.

The demon harrumphed. With one clawed foot, he pinned the Huntsman's arm.

Agony deepened on the Huntsman's face at the weight of the demon on his burns. But sorrow was there too. Grief so deep, it surpassed even his pain.

And still his shoulder lurched like he was trying to move.

I stared at him. "She did this to you?"

His head twitched in a nod. "Bound me... as punishment. The oath to serve the queen... became this. I let you live, so now I... I can't..." A raspy, rattling sound left him, like a breath from lungs so damaged, they shouldn't still be able to draw air. "I can't die."

My mouth moved in horror, at a loss for words.

"Tied me to her service." He groaned, his shoulder lurching in an attempt to break the demon's hold. "Never to stop, not even for death."

"That is dark and terrible magic." Appearing stunned, Byron lowered his hands where he'd extended them toward the Huntsman. "Even for her."

"Princess." The Huntsman rocked harder, struggling to rise though nothing on his face said he wanted to. "Her power... binds me. My words. Can't... can't speak for long. This creature's fire loosened the spell... but it's coming back. I feel it."

"What do you need?" I asked him. "What can we do?"

"Kill me."

Oh gods.

"I beg you." His voice turned desperate as his body rocked again, fighting to stand. "Please. Kill me. Let me die."

I wanted to cry. To scream in horror that she would do this to someone whose only crime had been to spare me.

And now the only thanks I could give him for that would be death.

With effort, I made myself nod. "Okay. We—" I glanced at my men, seeing gut-wrenched looks all around.

But Byron's eyes were narrowed, his eyes running over the Huntsman like he was seeing more than merely the burned wreckage of a man.

"We will," I continued to the Huntsman. "Somehow, we will."

Several of my giants nodded, but Dex didn't move. "Before we do that, tell us why you and the others were here?"

The Huntsman's chest rattled again. His body struggled harder. "Please."

"We will help you," Dex said with a firm glance to me as if to reassure me of his words too. "But there's nothing for miles around, yet you and the others attacked us."

A shudder rolled through the Huntsman. "Trap. Queen knew... you'd come this way."

"Why?"

"The boy."

My stomach turned to lead. "Niko?"

The Huntsman nodded. "Said... you'd think he went... to the mines... at Lumilia."

Cold dread sank over me.

"That we'd *think* he went there?" Clay repeated.

A sickened look crossed Lars's face. "But he didn't."

"No."

Clay made an incredulous noise. "Where the hell is he, then?"

Another shudder racked the Huntsman. "Please. Her power... coming back. Please."

My heart raced. "Where is he?"

The Huntsman groaned, agony in the sound. But something else was too. A savagery like a predator discovering it was in a trap.

"Where?" I pressed. "Please!"

He snarled, his head turning back and forth. His body began to thrash so hard, he appeared to be close to dislodging the demon's foot.

The demon scowled, pressing down harder.

"Please," I begged.

He only snarled again.

Anguish crushed down on me. If Niko wasn't at the mines of Lumilia like we'd thought, he could be anywhere.

And I didn't know where to begin.

Thrashing on the ground, the Huntsman tried to tear at the demon's leg, though his burned fingers could do no damage, only leaving bloody trails that made the demon's lips curl in disgust.

"Dammit," Dex cursed under his breath, resignation in the sound.

My heart ached. I wanted to ask more. To wait and see if somehow he responded. But it was a childish wish. My stepmother's curse had him well in its grip, tormenting him with rage and unending pain.

We couldn't force him to stay like this any longer.

I lifted my hand to extend what magic I could toward the man.

"Don't." Byron caught my arm, alarm on his face. He shook his head. "Whatever she did to him, it could harm you too."

The Huntsman roared in rage, shoving at the demon's leg.

"If that guy could hurt Ruhl and Cas here," Clay said with a nod to the vampire, "I'm guessing our demon friend won't hold him forever either."

The demon sneered. "He will not escape me."

Snarling, the Huntsman shoved him so hard, his weight rocked a bit. Incredulity widened the demon's eyes.

"Weapons," Ozias suggested shortly. "The ore in our blades. We take his head."

Unease rose at the thought, but Byron only made a considering noise. "It once severed the power she used to attack the princess, yes. But if it doesn't work, it could be worse than this—for him and for us."

I could hear the implication, and nausea swirled in my stomach at the possibility his body and head would continue this grotesque "life" even if they were separated.

"That's *definitely* our last resort," Dex agreed, sounding sickened too.

"Allow me to try a few of the Order's unbinding spells first," Byron said. "And if they go wrong, then…" He gestured permissively, leaving the rest unsaid.

"But it could hurt you too," I protested.

He glanced back at me. "This man made meeting you possible. Without his actions…" He shook his head resolutely. "If this is the only thanks we can give him, then let it be done quickly." A grim look crossed his face as he turned back to the Huntsman. "I would not leave him bound to an oath that never should have been used against him like this."

His words caught me, making my heart twist with regret. Bound to an oath, he said.

He'd know. No, the Huntsman's situation wasn't the same as Byron's. I knew that.

But I could see the similarities all the same.

Dex took my arm, pulling me back with him to give Byron and the Huntsman space. The demon didn't move, harrumphing as if indignant at the very thought. But even his face became more solemn as he looked down at the burned man.

"If this does not work, magic one," the demon promised Byron, "I will burn him until not even ash remains."

I shivered, not wanting to imagine the pain the Huntsman would suffer before *that* end.

But Byron just nodded. With a last look at us all, he extended his hands toward the Huntsman.

15
CASIMIR

Apprehension gripped me as the scholar reached out toward the Huntsman. The man had become something beyond cursed. Something touched by magic so foul, it could affect even creatures of smoke and shadow like Ruhl and myself.

Yet, if memory of my history books served, in Aneiran society his regiment's original duty had been ceremonial at best. Their job was merely to protect the queen's "innocence" by enabling her to participate in royal hunts, all without her ever needing to do such a supposedly masculine thing as hunting. Barely more than muscular surrogates, Huntsmen were never taken to war or valued for more than their skill in tracking game.

From the look of it, under the current queen that had changed. The Huntsmen were now tasked with doing her dirty work—including executing a princess accused of the queen's own crimes.

Except this one had disobeyed. He'd spared Gwyneira.

And for that mercy, he'd paid dearly.

Snarling, the cursed Huntsman rocked again, still pinned by the demon's foot yet trying to break free. That he was even still capable of moving at all was horrifying, given the extent of his injuries.

The witch who had destroyed my nation was a monster, yes, but even she hadn't cursed a fatally wounded man to never die.

At least... not like this.

Pushing aside the irony of my own situation—seemingly immortal, never dying because of a vampire witch's bite—I frowned. The gods had brought mercy to me, and that mercy's name was Gwyneira.

In our own way, perhaps we could be a mercy for this man too.

Drawing a steadying breath, Byron began chanting in a low, barely audible voice. In only a moment, I felt the stirrings of his magic in the air.

Curiosity drew me a step closer to his work. His power was intriguing. Unquestionably Erenlian, yes, but closely aligned to the princess's gifts as well. I'd felt the resonance of their abilities when I was aiding him in bringing her consciousness back from wherever that horrific spell had cast her. Indeed, I'd barely left his side during all those dreadful days when she lay unconscious, her body unable to be moved for fear of sending her once again into a seizure. So I'd had ample opportunity to study them both.

His determination and power throughout that

terrible time had only increased my respect for him. If anyone could help this creature, I suspected it would be the scholar.

Continuing to whisper under his breath, Byron twisted his magic around the Huntsman, seeking an opening in the dark spellwork that gripped the burned man. In my mind's eye, I tracked his progress. My years of training with monks in my home country had made my perception a matter of more than mere sight. The power wrapped around the Huntsman was like a scaly black ribbon, covering him from head to toe, impenetrable.

Or… almost.

Byron spotted the opening in the spell at the same moment I did. In my mind, I could see his gifts dive into the weak point like a needle made of light. The Huntsman lurched, and then his struggles against the demon pinning him to the ground ceased for a moment.

Satisfaction coiled inside me. Progress, then.

Never ceasing the spells he whispered under his breath, Byron watched the man intently. His eyes darted back and forth like he was reading a wealth of history from the ribbons of spellwork. What had been done, perhaps. What the man had suffered.

A low, rumbling growl started deep within the Huntsman's chest.

Horror hit me. That wasn't a growl.

That was *laughter*.

"Got… you."

A woman's voice emerged from the Huntsman's burned throat, her tone filled with contempt and glee.

"The queen," Byron gasped. He stumbled as suddenly the thread of his power jerked deeper into the Huntsman, as if someone held the other end of a rope and was using it to drag him forward.

Gwyneira started toward him. "Byron?" Dex caught her before she could come closer. "What's happening?"

Digging in his heels, the scholar fought to keep from being pulled toward the Huntsman. "Can't... Trap."

He lurched forward another step. Lars grabbed him as if to hold him back.

But the pull on his magic only grew stronger, making both men fight to keep their feet.

And then the princess cried out. Stumbling, only Ozias's grip on her kept her from crashing to her knees.

"What the fuck is this?" Clay demanded.

My eyes flew between them all, my sight and my magical perception alike racing to track what was happening.

And my blood went cold.

In my mind's eye, the light of the princess's magic glowed bright. When we first met, her power had been so deeply under wraps, I hadn't even perceived it, and had she not worn her diamond pendant marking her as a witch, I may never have even known. But with all she'd suffered and survived, her power had only grown, until now it was as brilliant as winter frost in sunlight, shimmering and radiant but with a ghost of a dark shadow twisting through its core.

But that wasn't what froze me.

A radiant beam of her power stretched out, and it

wasn't alone. Another light was with it, bright like a star and recognizable too.

The scholar. Their two gifts met like a bridge, merging together so intricately, I would swear they were as close as any two people could be in this life or any other. I wouldn't know where to begin in separating them, if I even could.

But that was the problem.

The trap inside the Huntsman was pulling on Byron's gifts, trying to drain his power. But because of this beautiful, breathtaking connection between them, it would soon grab hold of the princess too. Even if it didn't, to drain one of them would be to drain the other.

And kill them both.

Instinct born of years of training propelled my power to reach out quickly. I couldn't fully see the shape of the trap within the Huntsman. But I could see the black ribbons on its surface that were trying to consume Byron's power and absorb it into that horrible spell.

The hell it would.

I strode forward, distantly noting Lars stumble when I pushed him aside so that I could grab Byron's shoulder.

I would apologize for my rudeness later. Right now, there wasn't a moment to waste.

My magic flowed through the scholar, burning with the light of my ancestors' angelic gifts, bright and gold like the sun. But the spell fought back, snapping and snarling like a fanged snake, determined to inject its poison into my abilities as well.

Rage and fire suddenly surged toward me from one side, nearly startling me into ceding ground to the poisonous spell. Dark and deadly like a flow of lava from beneath the earth, it barreled toward my power. This wasn't the spell.

It was the demon.

The antithesis of my own abilities.

Opening my eyes, I gasped out, "Demon, what are you—"

The demon snarled, his fangs bared. He stood on the other side of Byron, one massive hand gripping the scholar's opposite shoulder. On the ground, his tail still held the Huntsman down, while the vicious claw at the end of one wing pierced the cursed man's shoulder, pinning him to the dirt.

"Focus, angel," the demon snapped.

Holy gods.

I balked at taking orders from the creature, but it also had a point. Even now, the trap was gaining ground.

Closing my eyes, I scanned the battle before me. I'd just regained my abilities as a vampire, and part of my gifts was tied up in the fight I now faced. Coming close to the demon's power could weaken me once again, doing untold damage to me *and* the others. But if I did nothing—

A cool sensation swelled in my mind, coming from behind me. Frost and crystalline light, as radiant as a winter goddess but laced with shadow.

Gwyneira.

Her power flowed around me. The pain of the demon's gifts abated as if a soothing balm now separated us, allowing us to act without harming each other.

How in the gods' names was she doing this?

"Hurry," the princess gasped.

Details were irrelevant.

I would *never* fail her.

My magic raced across the surface of the spell, seeking a way to dislodge its grip. Nearby, the demon growled, the sound hungry and savage like a predator intent on destroying its prey. "Mine. Don't touch *mine.*"

The threat reverberated through his magic. His power followed, tearing into the curse like his magic had claws.

The trap shuddered.

I took the opening.

Using my magic like a knife, I sliced at the spell, carving away piece after piece that tried to reach the princess and Byron. Over and over, the curse tried to fight me, but the demon's power was there every time, shielding my flanks, burning it before it could strike at my back.

Time lost all meaning. My awareness of the others around me slowly faded away. There was only the curse, only the battle. Only the princess who was somehow aiding me even as this horrific magic tried to consume her and the scholar whole.

Again.

I could feel my fangs pressing into my chin, as long as they'd ever been. My heart had long ago stopped beating. No matter what I did, Gwyneira was always in danger. Always on a knife's edge, a hair's breadth from tipping into darkness. It was enough to drive one mad.

I'd relish the moment we removed the queen from this world and protected Gwyneira once and for all.

The trap faltered. Its grip on the Huntsman lay in tatters, the black ribbons of its presence nothing but fragments now. I didn't relent, striking at each one, slicing at them while the demon's magic burned every fragment left in my wake, until the last hung like a threadbare strip of aging fabric before my mind's eye.

The queen's cold, contemptuous snarl filtered through my mind. "You still won't win."

With a shriek, the last ribbon of the spell flew apart and evaporated like smoke dissipating in sunlight.

Leaving nothing behind.

I shuddered, withdrawing my power carefully, and opened my eyes. The princess stood nearby. Byron too, and both were alive. Across from me, the demon glared at the Huntsman like he was daring the spell to return.

A rattling gasp left the cursed man. Pain was etched deep on his burned face. The agony of the dying.

But gratitude mingled with the anguish in his eyes.

An ache throbbed through me, one that had nothing to do with the spell or the queen.

I knew that look only too well. The look of the dying, grateful to be released from their pain. I'd seen it on so many faces in my own country when I ended their suffering because it was the only thing I could do.

"Thank you," the Huntsman whispered to the princess.

Gwyneira nodded. "Please. Where can we find our friend?"

His body shuddered again, his gaze moving away from her to turn toward something in a distance that only he could perceive. "Eliantra. There are mines hidden by magic in the hills south of the village, ten miles west of here." A ragged breath made his chest shake. "Look for a dead tree. And then a pond. The entrance... is there."

His eyes started to lose focus. "Forgive me, princess. I shouldn't have left you to die."

Gwyneira shook her head. "You left me to *live*, Huntsman. There's nothing to forgive."

Despite his pain, a smile drifted across his burned and ravaged face. "You will be a good queen."

A rattling breath escaped his chest.

And then he went still.

I looked over at Gwyneira as the last of his heartbeats came to an end. Tears shone in her eyes, and my soul ached for her.

I knew this pain too.

Pushing to her feet, she turned away. "We should go." Without another word, she walked away from everyone.

Her men glanced at one another, some unspoken communication passing between them. But I didn't bother attempting to follow it.

Not when I suspected what she was telling herself right now.

With a brief nod to Ozias and Dex, I followed her. "Princess."

"I'll just be a moment."

"I'd rather you weren't."

She stopped, but still she didn't look toward me. "What?"

My mouth tightened as I came up beside her. "If I may?" I gestured to the rocks beside the road.

Confusion furrowed her brow, and frustration was there too, but she followed me all the same. Once the rocks were between us and the others, leaving only her mate and possibly the demon able to hear our words, I continued. "Might I ask what you are thinking now, princess?"

She looked away, not meeting my eyes. "We have more important things to worry about right now. Niko needs us to—"

"Princess."

She fell silent. "It doesn't matter."

My eyes narrowed. On many occasions, her stubbornness was arousing. But this was not one of them. Now, it only served to hurt her, and therefore I couldn't let it continue. "Then allow me to guess. You blame yourself."

"No, I—" She shook her head but didn't continue.

Indeed.

"Do you know how many of my people I killed?" I asked her.

That drew her attention, making her look up at me in alarm.

"Hundreds. Possibly more. I stopped counting after a time because I couldn't stand the pain of that knowledge any longer. But that's how many of my friends and servants and citizens were turned or left to suffer by the witch. I tried all I could to save them, but even with all my magic and training, I couldn't change a thing. Those who'd been turned were monsters, and their victims..." I shuddered even now at the memory of their cries. "They were clinging to life. Bleeding out on the city streets or left to die in macabre displays made by the vampires for sport—all with the blood of the turned smeared on their lips so that they would only rise again. In the end, granting them true death was the only mercy I could bestow."

I reached out, taking her hand. "You feel that you did the wrong thing, letting him die. That perhaps you could have found something, *done* something, that would have changed his end. But waiting only would have prolonged his suffering, and the outcome would likely have been the same. So let me say, from one ruler to another... I understand. I've felt that too. But this *was* mercy, princess. Not murder. I saw that magic. I felt the viciousness of that spell. I know for a *fact* there was nothing else you could have done."

Her eyes closed. Gently, I pulled her closer, wrapping my arms around her and comforting her in the agony I knew so well.

Moments slid past, and then she drew back, looking up at me. "You're not breathing."

"I'll be fine."

She was already pulling her hair aside to expose her beautiful neck.

I stilled her hand and shook my head. "I will not feed from you, princess. Not when you need all your strength to recover from all the ordeals you only recently survived."

Her intent to argue was clear on her face, and I placed a finger to her lips. "I will feed after we rescue Niko. Trust that I have ample experience withstanding a little bit of hunger after thirty years on my own."

She hesitated, but after a moment, she nodded. "I'll hold you to that promise."

My lip twitched. Gods, it was so easy to love her.

Footsteps came on the gravel beyond the rock shielding where we stood. From the sound, I suspected it was Ozias. Given how quietly he could move, he likely only made noise to give me some warning he was there.

It was a thoughtful gesture, one I could respect and appreciate.

"Little mate?" he murmured when he stepped around the large boulder.

With a smile to me, Gwyneira went to him. He drew her into his arms, his much larger body wrapping hers in a hug that couldn't have been more gentle and careful than if she'd been made of glass.

She was so precious to us all.

"We need to go," she said as if responding to some unspoken reminder. "I know."

He nodded, saying nothing. Arms still around her, his eyes rose to me.

His head bowed in a solemn gesture of thanks. I nodded once in acknowledgement.

Keeping her close, Ozias turned and started back toward the others. I trailed after them, noting the new pile of earth and stone beside the road and that the Huntsman's body was now gone.

Buried by Ozias's gifts, I suspected, and thus placed out of view so that Gwyneira would no longer be confronted with what her stepmother had done.

As ever, I found myself grateful she had these men.

Some of them in new ways now.

I studied Byron as the others prepared to head out. Did he know his power had become so inextricably intertwined with Gwyneira's? Did she? Their magic was like two trees that had grown together so closely, there was no way to separate them any longer.

A cold feeling swelled in my gut. That was the problem, though, wasn't it? They really *couldn't* be separated.

Not without killing one or both of them.

Byron started to turn as if feeling the pressure of my attention, and with vampiric speed, I looked away. It was just as well my heartbeat was still from hunger. It wouldn't have helped anything for Gwyneira to hear it pound.

Because my beloved was a vampire. A precious, beautiful, intoxicating vampire unlike anyone I'd ever known. But that also meant she was immortal, or damn near as close to it as anything even vaguely living could be.

But Byron wasn't. None of her giants were, not as far as I could tell. Before, that had been a source of far-off anguish I knew she'd feel some day. But now...

My cold horror only grew. I respected these men. Cared for them even. I would never willingly harm them.

But now everything had changed. And if anything happened to Byron in all the battles ahead of us, if a stray arrow or knife ended his life...

Gwyneira looked back at me, a question in her eyes like she'd seen something on my face that gave her pause. Drawing on every scrap of royal training I possessed, I buried my horror swiftly and offered back a smile.

It changed nothing. Her curious expression remained.

Desperate, I turned away. Gods help me, there was no choice. I had to wait for my moment and act with the same horrible determination I'd possessed when my nation fell and death was the only available version of mercy. I'd be as careful as I could be, of course. But I still had to find a way to break this bond between them, even if doing so might kill Byron.

Because if I didn't, then the only woman I would ever love might die.

16

MELISANDRE

My hand slammed down on the magic mirror, shattering it.

Damn that angel. That demon.

And *especially* damn Gwyneira.

She'd escaped the dark. She'd escaped my spell *again*. And now she'd destroyed the Huntsmen I'd sent to stop her—including *that* Huntsman, broken toy though he had been.

How the hell did that brat *still* manage to survive?

I wrapped my hand around the sword that lay on the table beside me. The grotesque emblem upon its hilt hadn't warped or twisted recently—because of course it had not. That had been merely my imagination.

And to every hell with the Voidborn who swore I was going mad.

My hand tightened. I could be rid of the thing. But it would be infinitely more satisfying to keep it just long enough to ram the ugly blade straight through that annoying girl's ribs.

"The Nine have changed course," one of the Voidborn hissed and clicked at me.

"Forget the damned *Nine!*" I flung a hand out, crushing the Voidborn-possessed shifter who had dared to speak.

The creature howled and died. The other Voidborn recoiled, a rumble of discontent passing through them.

Ignoring them, I looked back down at the sword. Damn those imbecilic Voidborn and their obsession with a fairytale. I knew Gwyneira had changed course. The Voidborn among her people still whispered of where they were going, so I hardly needed the information repeated to me now.

And besides, didn't they understand it scarcely mattered *what* Gwyneira and her band of misfit creatures were, much less where they went? I had plans within plans, and no matter how many obstacles that child survived, in the end she would still die.

My lips curled into a cold grin.

It took a moment for my reflection to smile back.

I tensed. That... that had been my imagination. A glitch of my attention caused by too long enduring the presence of fools. I needed rest. Perhaps to feed on another commoner—or a lord, since their blood was all the sweeter from their diet of fine foods. That was all.

Drawing myself back up, I turned my focus resolutely to the map on my table.

The bowl of apples burst into flame.

I gasped, recoiling. Swiftly, I spun, searching for the

witch or sorcerer responsible. "Don't just stand there, you fools!" I snapped at the Voidborn, pointing at the bowl. "Put out the fire!"

"Fire?" one of them hissed.

Red apples glistened in the glass bowl, untouched by any trace of flames.

I stared, my chest heaving. "There... they..."

Dark, mocking laughter echoed in the distance. *Familiar* laughter.

I bit back a snarl, my eyes raking the room. This was a trick. Some ploy of the Voidborn to destabilize me. But it wouldn't work. No matter what they tried, I knew Alaric was dead.

The laughter grew louder.

Dammit, Alaric. Was. *Dead.*

Something moved at the corner of my eye. I whirled, fangs bared.

On the far end of the room, the gilded frame of my mirror hung. The glass lay shattered on the floor beneath it, same as it had for days now.

I didn't know who had destroyed it. Perhaps a servant or maybe the Voidborn themselves after I left to capture Gwyneira in the mountains, back before that brat of a girl drove me into the empty realms. I scarcely cared, since the Voidborn no longer used it to speak to me.

But now, glints of light caught my eye on the thick rug beneath the mirror's frame.

Growling low, I stalked closer. I'd forbidden anyone into my chambers, with the exception of the Voidborn and that idiot steward, Harran—and while the former wouldn't dream of cleaning this room, the latter was too terrified to even try. Thus, shards of glass no bigger than my palm lay scattered about, reflecting the stone ceiling pointlessly.

Except now... they didn't.

In every shard, the ceiling's reflection drowned beneath swirling fog as the glass grew dark and murky.

Just like it had when the Voidborn used it to communicate with me.

A face began to emerge from the fog. Alaric's hissing voice surrounded me. "You made a mistake, pet."

Snarling, I recoiled from the glass. "I know you're doing this," I spat at the Voidborn-possessed monsters behind me. "How dare you continue to play games with me?"

Their faces were inscrutable. Cursing them, I spun back, raising my hand to smash the glass shards.

The glass reflected only the stone ceiling again.

My heart pounded. This *was* a trick. All of it. The Voidborn resented me, and so they thought to play with my mind.

The sword quivered in my hand. When I looked down, the blade's surface was dark and swirled with fog.

What in the—

A timid knock came at the door. "Your Majesty?"

I shrieked, flinging my hand at the thick wood. My chamber door exploded into kindling.

Surrounded by shattered wood, Harran blinked in shock. Only the idiotic gods knew how the destruction hadn't turned him into a pin cushion.

"What?" I demanded.

"Th-the lords are here, my queen."

I scowled. Of course they chose *now* to arrive. Never mind that I'd ordered them here. They chose to present themselves together like a collection of rabbits pretending to be wolves, thinking their numbers would serve as intimidation.

They'd learn differently soon.

My eyes twitched toward the shards of the mirror. Nothing stirred in the reflection. And on the blade, no trace of fog or darkness remained.

This was the Voidborn's trickery.

But they wouldn't win.

"I will see the so-called lords now," I snapped at him over my shoulder. "But be certain my instructions are followed to the letter by the kitchen staff."

"Yes, Your Majesty." Harran bolted for the servants' stairway as fast as his old legs could carry him.

"You should be embracing my power."

I froze at the sound of Alaric's voice again. My eyes darted around, landing at last on the blade.

The grotesque face on the hilt curved its gaping mouth into a devilish grin.

Rage surged within me. "Get out," I snapped at the Voidborn. "Now!"

The creatures paused, glancing at one another questioningly rather than obeying.

A twist of my fingers had them screaming as they died.

"Or should I say," Alaric commented as their cries faded, "embracing *more* of it."

I looked down at the sword again. "What is this? Did you hide in the blade?"

Alaric chuckled. Between one eye blink and the next, the face on the hilt snapped back to its ordinary appearance.

But the mirror shards were gray again.

"Do you remember, pet?" he mused. "How our power twisted and formed you into this? Why do you hide from it now?"

"I hide from *nothing*," I snarled.

His chuckle made me stalk back toward the mirror. In the shards, the gray fog gave way to his face. He didn't look the same as when I killed him. No, he looked like when I first met him after escaping the empty realms. His skin was once again made of silver scales. His face was blunt like an eel's, with only slits for his nostrils.

"Once upon a time, you were unafraid of us."

"I am *not* afraid!"

He grinned, his mouth full of metallic fangs. "Prove it. Remember how you reached across the miles without ever leaving this room. Remember how you bent the world based on your will alone."

My teeth ground. "I still do."

"Really? A few apples. A few trees." He scoffed. "You've barely scratched the surface of what you *could* do."

An angry sound escaped me. Damn these Voidborn for trying to toy with me. How they'd continued their ruse when none of them even remained in this room, I wasn't certain. But I would cease bothering with it immediately, and I sure as all *hell* wouldn't let them succeed in thwarting me.

Alaric's inhuman face turned taunting. "Or admit you are going mad, not from power but from fear."

My fingers curled into a fist. I shouldn't respond to him. This was merely a trick.

"I *know* you're afraid, pet."

To hell with it. "I fear nothing."

He merely regarded me in mocking silence.

My fists shook. They thought me afraid and weak, these Voidborn fools who taunted me with false visions? They thought my power was a joke?

I'd show them.

Whipping around, I strode from the room and stalked through the corridors, silently summoning more of the Voidborn bastards to join me in the main dining hall. My servants had made quick work of the preparations, arraying a feast on the long table that served as the center point of the room. Chandeliers hung overhead, resplendent with candles and crystals, while gold-lined plates filled the long spread beneath them, awaiting the delicacies that would emerge from the kitchen when I gave the order.

The Voidborn mocked, but they understood nothing. Victory was mine.

And only one food would be served tonight.

"Queen Melisandre of Aneira," announced the servant at the door when I entered, and to his credit, the man's voice only shook a little.

Around the table, the lords looked over at me. Several

tried to stand up out of respect, only to be tsked and tugged down by their glaring counterparts.

Arrogant fools. As if their displeasure could possibly matter.

"You think to host a party as your city lies in ruins, *queen*?" called a lord near the head of the table. His thinning, gray strands were slicked over the top of his balding head, each one desperately trying to portray itself as being still among all its brethren, rather than a lonely, useless pretender to a crown of hair. Like all the other lords here, he wore robes that likely cost more than a peasant family would see in its lifetime, trimmed by luxurious furs and threads of gold. Though I knew he hadn't *earned* his title—it was an inheritance, same as many others here, and privately the king had confessed the man irritated him to no end—he was still the lord of a powerful province in the Aneiran economy. His position at the table would have been one of honor in the late king's court.

I scarcely cared enough to bother remembering his name.

"I think to do as I wish, Lord Antieron," I replied, pacing past the long line of foolish men on my way to the chair at the head of the table. "And I wish to speak to those who believe themselves in charge of this nation. Are you suggesting there is someone more important to whom I should speak?"

The man scowled, giving a harrumph of displeasure. But he could hardly argue, since doing so would simply make him look like even more of a fool.

I suppressed a smile. "Very well then." Turning, I seated myself at the head of the table, eliciting several more disgruntled looks from the lords. By their view, I should have left this seat empty, awaiting whatever next male would take the late king's position.

Aneira would never have another ruler besides me. Neither would this world.

A spiral of darkness drew my eye to the empty metal goblet before me. Alaric's grinning face swirled into view on its side. "But you only scratch the surface, pet. Remember how it *could* be."

Snapping my eyes back to the lords, I tossed a napkin over the goblet, smothering him. "Gentlemen," I said calmly. "I am certain it has escaped none of your notice that our nation was recently under attack."

"*Was?*" Lord Antieron looked at his fellow lords incredulously. "You sit here surrounded by these *things,* looking halfway on the path to being one of them, and you dare to claim the attack has ceased?"

Around the room, the orcs and other Voidborn-possessed creatures shifted position slightly, hissing-clicks passing between them, and though I knew the lords did not understand a thing, several of the men still glanced around warily.

I smiled. "These *things,* as you call them, answer to me now. I took command of them from the one who dared to torch our fair city, and now they do as I wish." At my glance, the Voidborn stepped forward.

Alaric's voice was muffled. "But how much more could they do?"

My smile unfazed, I shoved the goblet off the edge of the table, ignoring it as it clattered to the floor. "So yes, Lord Antieron, I say the attack has ceased. I willed it so. And as for your insinuation that my appearance is somehow not becoming of a fair queen, well..."

My fangs slid past my lips.

Lord Antieron recoiled while around the room, several lords gasped, and others shoved to their feet. They raced for the door only to find it locked and bolted from the outside.

From the goblet on the floor, Alaric's muffled laughter rose.

In spite of myself, my lip twitched. Illusion or not, that dead Voidborn bastard had a point. It *was* amusing to watch the vermin run.

"You trap us here?" one of the lords demanded, a note of panic beneath his polished tone.

"Deceiver," Lord Antieron spat.

I made a dismissive sound and then gestured to the Voidborn-possessed creatures beside a small door to my right. One of them pushed past the opening, returning a few moments later leading several servants who carried silver trays.

Each platter held a mound of glistening red apples.

The effect on the room was immediate. Even the lords trying to escape past the locked doors suddenly paused, their gazes fixing upon the glistening fruits.

In silence, the servants placed the platters on the table and then left the room.

"What... what is this?" Lord Antieron asked, his

attention also transfixed by the fruits. His face twitched as if he was at war with himself while his fingers wrapped around the ends of the arms of his chair, digging into the plush velvet.

"My answer to your impolite questions." I glanced at the lords. "Eat, gentlemen. Far be it from me to stop you."

Several of them snatched the apples, shoving the fruits into their mouths. Others hesitated, struggling to resist the lure.

Alaric's voice was tiny, coming from a sliver of reflection on a fork at my side. "This is barely the beginning of what you *could* do, pet."

But this was so satisfying.

I smiled as I watched the annoying noble wage a war with himself. Lord Antieron's hand shook as he reached for an apple, but then his other hand grasped his wrist as if he was fighting to keep from taking the fruit. "Y-you... you trick us. *Monster.* You manipulated us into—"

His eyes flicked to the others as, around the room, the lords started to choke. Alarm spread over the lord's face.

I lifted one of the apples and placed it in his outstretched hand. Relief and horror battled in his expression. In spite of himself, he drew the fruit toward his mouth.

"Oh, on the contrary, Lord Antieron," I said while he bit down. Ecstasy filled his eyes as the apple took effect, transforming him into my pawn. "I'm no monster, and I'm hardly a manipulator."

Alaric scoffed from the cutlery.

Ignoring him, I didn't take my eyes from the lord. "I simply make the world work the way it *should* work. No fear. No compromise. Better than any monster, witch, or mere human could dream. In reality, I think you'll find —" I leaned back in my chair, watching the pretentious bastard fall to the ground. "—I'm the fairest of them all."

17
NIKO

I refused to die here.

Gripping the pickaxe tightly, I swung it at the rocky wall and repeated the mantra to myself silently. I didn't know how many times the sun had risen and fallen since I'd been dragged down to this place. The surface world might as well have not existed, and the guards seemed to maintain erratic schedules all their own.

They liked to keep us disoriented, Ignatius said. To rob us of even the most basic level of stability, so that we could never relax, never rest or gain any semblance of calm. Instead, we were always on edge, waiting for them to return.

At every turn, they found new ways to be cruel.

I suspected it had been days, though. Maybe a week or more since I arrived. So far, the humans hadn't taken me to the western tunnels, though the gods only knew what they were waiting for. The threat of being sent into that death trap hung over my head like a sword suspended on a fraying string, and at any moment it could snap and end my life.

But I was determined not to think about that. No, I would focus on the problem in front of me like Byron would. I'd keep my eyes open and wait for the first slip from the human guards, just like Dex would. I'd draw on the strength that all my friends had shown me throughout all the years we'd spent running and hiding and surviving the war, and then... then I'd escape.

Because I *refused* to die here.

I needed to see my treluria again.

My swing faltered as fear tried to bubble up, bringing panic on its heels.

"Keep going, scum!" a guard shouted.

My hands quivered, the fear turning into rage that had no outlet. Adjusting my grip on the pickaxe, I choked down a breath of stale, musty air and swung at the wall harder. I'd already ruled out using the tool to attack the guards. They were smart and stayed at the far end of the tunnel while they watched us. I'd never make it within a dozen feet of them before they activated the manacle wrapped around my wrist.

I'd seen what *that* did three shifts ago when they thought Norbert wasn't moving fast enough. The guy was a jerk, but his screams had been the stuff of nightmares. And with what I knew of medicine and the mortal body, I had no illusions that someone my size would survive the kind of pain meant to keep giants in line. More likely it would just stop my heart.

But I *fucking* refused to die here.

By the time the guards called an end to the day, my back and arms had given up trying to tell me they were in pain. Mining with my friends had kept me in shape, but it hadn't prepared me for this level of torture. Yes, the seven of us had used tools in our work. Our magic wasn't inexhaustible and it was smart to keep some in reserve at all times. Using it all up to draw ore from the ground might have meant we were screwed in case of a cave-in.

But this was something else entirely.

The Aneirans *wanted* to work us to death.

At long last, I shuffled back to the massive cavern with the rest of the giants, too tired to even seethe at the guards watching us. Because it was what Dex would do, I made myself look back and watch the humans when they locked the gate again, taking note of where they put the key and what they did with the manacles on their own wrists to secure the magic in the bars. When they turned to leave, the guy in charge waved his arm at the wall on the opposite side of the tunnel, the same as a guard would do every day.

I couldn't see any reason for the motion, but Ignatius told me the Erenlians suspected there was some kind of spell there that enabled the Aneirans to watch us from a location somewhere else in the mines. A security station of some kind. If they wanted, the Aneirans could even make their voices carry all the way down here from else-where, though they rarely used that spell and no one had been able to figure out its source.

More ways to make sure we never made it out of here.

Sinking down against the rock wall—it was best to keep the stone at my back so no one could come up on me from behind, I'd learned—I leaned my head against the rocks and struggled to repeat my mantra to myself, fighting to believe the words. It didn't matter what the Aneirans did. How long it took. I wouldn't die here. I would make it back to my treluria.

For her, I had to survive. To die would be to leave her with one less person to protect her, and I would never fail her like that.

A commotion rose as the guards returned with a single bucket of food. Tossing the contents through the bars, they laughed as the giants scrambled after the rolls of bread that tumbled across the stone floor.

I didn't move, praying someone would miss a crumb or, gods help me, an entire roll in the chaos. I'd learned on the first day that chasing the food was a great way to get stepped on. As it was, I'd narrowly avoided that fate a dozen times that day, just trying to get something to eat.

Hungry people were desperate.

But I also hadn't eaten in nearly two shifts.

"Here, boy." Ignatius sat down next to me with a sigh and tore the roll in his hands in half. There was mold on the bread, but he barely seemed to notice beyond giving me the part with fewer of the tiny invaders.

I hesitated. My stomach felt like a gaping void made of hunger, but the scholar was one of the oldest people in here and he needed every bit of sustenance he could get. "You don't have to do that."

"Eat."

I frowned, but I took the bread. "Thank you."

He just grunted and began to eat, clearly too exhausted to respond.

My eyes closed in relief the moment I gulped down a bite.

"Pace yourself, son."

Breathing heavily, I tried to slow down and do as he said.

"You're holding up well," Ignatius commented after a moment. "I admit, I didn't expect you would make it this far."

I wasn't sure how to respond—or what that meant for how long I'd really been here. "Um, well, my friends and I mined in the mountains beyond Lumil—"

A shriek interrupted me, and my attention snapped around to the opposite side of the cavern.

One of Norbert's henchmen had a young female giant by the throat, while a skinny little girl cried at her side. His buddies laughed at the sight, and one of them shoved the child, sending her sprawling to the stone floor. Nearby, Brock glanced up, and tension flashed across his face—the most emotion I'd ever seen the big sandy-haired giant express. His eyes darted from the woman to someone else in the crowd, and his jaw clenched at whatever he saw.

Meanwhile, Norbert only smirked and rose to his feet. "Nadine, Nadine," he chided. "Getting above your station now, aren't you? Now why would that be?"

He looked in the same direction as Brock had, but still, I couldn't tell why.

"She wasn't trying to take more," the woman pled. "I swear."

Norbert made a tutting sound. "You calling us liars? The king's own guard who act on his behalf?" He chuckled. "You know the rules. Disrespecting the king is punishable by death. You weren't doing that, now were you?"

The woman clamped her mouth shut, her eyes wide with fear.

"Guess not." Norbert smirked. "Brock, would you care to remind Nadine here what the price is for giving brats more than a quarter ration?"

Brock glanced again at the crowd. His jaw tightened, but after a heartbeat, the reaction vanished. Leaning back, he took a bite of his own roll and shrugged his brow as if to say he couldn't be expected to speak with his mouth full.

The bully's henchmen snickered. "Brock wants some of her ass too."

Rage surged hot in my veins.

Ignatius caught my arm, stopping me when I started to shove to my feet. At my incredulous look, he only made a cautioning noise, shaking his head.

"Yeah, that bitch of his is all dried up," Norbert agreed. "We'll let him have the leftovers, how about that?"

His buddy's sound of agreement made my rage burn hotter.

Yanking her closer, the henchman sneered. "Who says anything'll be left over?" He took up a tangled strand of her hair with his free hand and sniffed it.

She whimpered.

Aghast, I looked around the cavern. None of the

other giants were moving to intervene. Most were turning away like they were pretending they didn't notice what was going on. Brock hadn't looked up again, and even Ignatius only grimaced regretfully, as if the old giant couldn't do a damn thing and he knew it.

Seated by a fire, Duke Ensid merely glanced at his son and his henchmen before calmly starting in on a second bread roll.

This was madness. How could they just—

"Now..." Norbert took the woman's chin, forcing her face toward his. "You want the brat to eat or don't you?"

My blood boiled. "Stop!"

The bastard paused, but only to turn an incredulous look on me. "You got something to say, human?"

My heart raced. I was outmatched and definitely outsized, and there was no way in hell I wouldn't get crushed in a fight between me and the enormous giant. They still didn't know I was Erenlian—Ignatius insisted on keeping my identity as a dwarf a secret—but even that wouldn't have changed my odds.

Basically, this was suicide, and a guarantee that I would never see my treluria again.

But I couldn't just sit here and do *nothing*.

I tugged my arm free of Ignatius's grasp. "Let her go."

"What, you want a piece of her too?" Norbert chuckled. "Her cunt might be a bit big for a tiny human cock like yours."

My fingers curled into fists. "She's a *person*, not an object. You shouldn't treat her like this."

The giant's brow rose. He glanced around at his buddies as if silently asking them if they heard me too.

When they scoffed, his grin returned. "You hearing this, Brock?"

Brock looked up from his meal, regarding Norbert for a heartbeat before turning a flat, cold expression on me. "Humans don't get a say in how things are run down here."

"Any *decent* being should have a say against this," I countered.

Norbert snarled. "Wait, are you *insulting* us, pipsqueak? Didn't you hear what I told my friend Nadine?" Thrusting the woman away from him, he ignored how she stumbled as he stalked across the cavern. "I represent the king, and disrespecting the king—" he grinned cruelly, "—is punishable by death."

Behind me, Ignatius muttered something in a language I didn't know. But the tone definitely said, "Oh shit."

Norbert's massive hand took my arm, pulling me up to my tiptoes.

"They *want* us to kill him, Norbert," Ignatius cautioned.

"Shut up, old man." Norbert hauled me closer. "You think you know how to keep order in this place?"

A hand caught his arm. I looked past him to Brock.

"Your father says give it a second," he said flatly. "Humans are coming."

"Yeah, well, how about we let them see us crush their little spy, eh?" His grip tightened, grinding my muscles against bone. "Show 'em they don't have the strength to survive like we do."

Brock scowled. He didn't let go of Norbert, but he didn't say anything else either.

Trembling, I drew myself up as best I could. "This isn't strength. A good leader takes care of the people under them. They make sure the youngest and weakest have what they need so that the *souls* of their people survive, not just their bodies." Rage shivered through my voice. "And they don't *rape* innocent women."

Norbert scoffed. "Oh, please. The bitch is asking for it."

Brock's jaw muscles jumped.

"I think you can be better than this," I urged, keeping my attention on the sandy-haired giant instead of the one currently on his way to crushing my arm. "*More* than this."

His ice-chip eyes returned to me.

Norbert just laughed. "What the fuck do you know?" Turning, he hauled me around and then flung me forward. Pain shot through my arm from the motion, and then my shoulder joined the chorus when I tumbled across the cavern floor.

His henchmen stalked past him, grinning viciously.

"Pipsqueak here wants to lecture us on leadership," Norbert called to his father. "I say we show him how *real* leaders deal with insubordination, eh?"

Still standing where he was, Brock didn't move to follow the others.

"Yeah," one of the henchmen chimed in. "I want to see how quick we can tear a human apart when they don't have their little tools to protect them!"

I scrambled to my feet and backed up, trying to keep

Norbert and his buddies in view. "Please," I said. "This isn't who Erenlians are. This is what the Aneirans want you to become."

Ignatius shook his head, pain and regret on his face. Nearby, Brock just looked on, his dead expression unreadable.

The bullies circled me.

"This is how they want to break you," I pressed. "By making you hurt anyone weaker than you, when you should be helping each other survive and stay strong."

"Well, then," Duke Ensid offered calmly, like he had all the time in the world. Even now, he hadn't moved from where he sat on the other side of the cavern. "I see the humans think they can tell us who we are now."

Hate twisted Norbert's face. "The hell they can." He grabbed for me.

Ducking fast, I darted between him and his buddy. Whirling, the giants started after me, driving me to retreat until the gate bars bumped into my back.

The metal burned. I gasped at the bite of magic, stumbling forward a step just to escape the pain.

Norbert stopped, the hatred on his face flickering toward confusion. "What the fuck is your problem, pipsqueak? The bars don't hurt humans."

Oh crap.

I swallowed hard. "I... I'm not—"

"Enough." Duke Ensid rose to his feet.

Appearing confused and wary again, Norbert half-turned, his attention going between me and the duke. Behind him, his buddies hesitated as if they weren't sure what to do now.

Duke Ensid scanned the room imperiously, drawing all focus to himself. His shrewd gaze seemed to be reading everyone, and when he glanced at me, there was a gleam in his eyes like he'd finally found a use for the worm on his hook.

"The arrogance of humans knows no bounds, does it, my friends?" His voice was reserved and quiet, like a leader delivering painful news. A unique bend of the stone walls where he stood amplified the sound, making his words carry through the cavern.

Rumbles of agreement followed from the crowd, and the duke nodded as if in shared understanding. "It shouldn't shock us, not after all we've suffered. Yet it still does, no? For a people to be so depraved? So violent? Humans lock us up. They take our magic. They use us until our bodies break and kill any who get in their way. And now—*now*!" He shook his head as if dumbfounded. "They think they can tell us what *strength* means?"

He made a contemptuous noise, somehow communicating derision and yet also pride. "But humans don't know us. Our history. Our legacy that will endure no matter how they try to break us down. They don't know that *true* strength isn't something they can understand. It isn't something *they* could ever possess, because strength doesn't come from humans. True strength belongs to Erenlians!"

Around the cavern, cries of agreement rose.

The duke gestured toward me as if re-introducing me to the crowd. "Yet here they are, sending in one of their own. They wrap him in spells to make it *appear* like their magic hurts him. They pretend he's defenseless and trapped in here with us, when we all know they would come to his aid at the first *real* moment of need." He sneered. "They think we're such fools that we'll trust him. That we'll let him in on the plans that will one day set us free."

I glanced at Ignatius, confused. Wait, what was he talking about?

The scholar's eyes never left Duke Ensid, and his wary expression provided no answers.

With a rude noise, the duke continued, "How dare this fool think he—small and pathetic as he is—could tell us who *true* Erenlians are? What the power of a *true* Erenlian is?" The look he leveled at me was so scathing, it could have carved my flesh from my bones.

But it was his icy words that made a cold spike of fear shoot through my veins.

The duke knew I was a dwarf. He hadn't said it outright, not yet. But "true" Erenlian was code enough for me to read between those gaping lines.

He gave me a cruel smile. "We are more than this weak creature dreams. We are capable of more than the Aneirans know." He turned back to the room, lifting a fist in the air. "And we are greater than any cage!"

Cries of support came from around the cavern. Proud rage took up residence on so many faces.

But not all. Even as some giants called for my head on a pike, others tried to sink back into the stone like maybe they could hide. And I wasn't so much of a fool to think the duke didn't notice the difference and know exactly how these people were responding to his words. The reaction was the *point*. To keep the biggest and strongest united in rage and hate behind him, while the others knew to stay in line.

Or else.

Turning back to me, Duke Ensid's smirk didn't reach his eyes. No, those were as cold as a grave. "I say it's time to remind the humans why Erenlians make them so afraid."

At his motion, Norbert grabbed my arm.

"My lord," Ignatius called. "This is what they want us to—"

"Enough, scholar," the duke retorted without taking his attention from me. "We've given the humans our blood and sweat. We don't need to give them our mercy too."

I yanked at Norbert's grasp, but there was no way to escape it. "I'm not human!"

Norbert scoffed. "Bullshit."

Panic rose. I had one chance. One, and it was risky beyond measure. "I'm not, I swear! I'm a dwarf. I was found as an infant in the Forest of Azurine, and I survived the war with six other dwarves. My magic is bound just like yours, but I swear I'm—"

Norbert grabbed my other arm, jerking me forward. "Please. I've known dwarves, *human*. They're bigger than you."

I stared at him. When had he—

"How many pieces?" he continued to Duke Ensid.

The duke smiled. "One for every year we've been trapped here."

My heart was racing so fast, I couldn't breathe. Instinctively, I reached for my magic, but nothing was there. "You're killing your own kind if you kill me! Erenlians are better than this! Erenlians are more than bullies who prey on—"

The blaring sound of the next workday's alarm cut me off. Footsteps carried down the tunnel.

Norbert snarled while his buddies stared at me, incredulous. "Guess Dad was right," he spat. "Huh, *human?*"

I didn't know what to say. There couldn't be truth to what the duke claimed. The Aneirans had thrown me in here to die, same as all the rest. They wouldn't show up to save me now.

But maybe the gods were looking out for me, making coincidence work in my favor.

That meager hope died when I saw the faces of the giants in the cavern. This wasn't a favor from the gods. This was confirmation in the eyes of every prisoner here that I was human and deserved everything the duke claimed and more.

And from the cruel smirk on the duke's face, he knew it.

The guards came into view. "Get up, you lazy brutes," the one in the lead called. "You've had all night to rest. Time to get back to work."

I faltered, thrown by the blatant lie as much as their presence. And I knew protest was probably useless. My options were work or dismemberment, and none of the Erenlians would believe I was on their side regardless. But the exhaustion on the faces of the giants around me drove the words from my lips anyway. "You just threw us in here minutes ago. You can't expect us to go back to work this soon."

The lead guard scoffed and tapped the metal ring on his wrist.

Pain shot through me so fast and hard, I didn't even have time to scream. My vision blacked out, and I couldn't feel anything except the agony roaring through every single inch and ounce of my being.

"See, runt?" The guard's words swam out of the darkness. "Your stoneskin pals here know better than to call us liars. We say you've had a night's rest, then that's what you've had."

Trembling all over, I opened my eyes. I was on the cavern floor, my heart tumbling over itself just to stay beating. My breath caught in my throat, making me cough like maybe I had been screaming without knowing it. My face burned and felt tacky with blood from where it'd hit the stone floor when I fell.

Every giant around me was staring, confused distrust on their faces.

"Maybe the pipsqueak isn't human after all?" one of the henchmen offered.

Norbert punched him in the gut without a word.

Shaking hard, I pushed away from the ground on arms that felt as limp as the branches of a willow tree.

The guard smirked at me. "These brutes thought you were human?" He snorted with disgust. "You should be so fucking lucky."

Anger swirled in my gut for his bigotry and the duke's alike. "You have no idea how lucky I am," I gritted out.

I was a man who'd found his treluria. Who would be damned if he didn't see her again.

And who was *nothing* like any of these bastards mocking me simply for how I'd been born.

If that wasn't luck, nothing was.

The guard scoffed. "That so? Well, that *luck* of yours means we've got a special assignment for you today. You and these brutes alike." He raised his voice so the cavern could hear. "We got approval from the warden to start clearing out the collapsed western tunnels." His stained teeth showed when he grinned. "And the runt is going to lead the way."

18

GWYNEIRA

Every second we crept along the road left me on edge. Casimir had taken to the air a short while ago and spotted soldiers hiding in the forest several miles beyond where the poor Huntsman finally died. But that had been ten minutes ago. They may have moved.

To say nothing about all the other threats that might be out here.

"We still good?" Clay whispered to those up ahead.

Clearly I wasn't the only one worried.

In the lead with Casimir and Byron, Dex nodded back wordlessly. Valeria and her soldiers waited behind them, hands on the hilts of their sheathed swords, ready to draw them at a moment's notice. We'd left the horses behind several miles ago, just in case the animals made a noise at the wrong moment, and a few of her people had stayed to keep watch over the mounts.

But of the humans, there were so many fewer than

before. It pained me. My stepmother's Huntsmen and her spell in the forest had cost us *so* many allies.

At my side, Ozias reached over, putting a hand to my arm in silent comfort. I exhaled slowly, appreciating the gesture, especially since I could feel his apprehension through our connection no matter how he tried to suppress it.

My stepmother had not only done damage. She'd also created wristbands that could block Erenlian magic. And what else might she have done? She wasn't the only vampire in the world, obviously. Had she made something that would thwart Casimir's and my senses too? Or what about weapons against creatures like Ozias or Roan?

My heart racing, I exhaled slowly, ordering myself for the thousandth time to stay calm. Stay focused. Worry wasn't helping anything, and I needed to concentrate if I was going to keep myself and my allies alive.

Up ahead, Dex suddenly came to a halt with a brief warning gesture.

I slowed, craning my neck to see what caused him to stop.

A dead tree stood to one side of the road, its trunk split and blackened by a long-ago lightning strike. Casimir had paused before it, and he was eying the charred wood like it might bite.

"Are you seeing this?" he asked Byron.

While the scholar bent closer, Clay called in a low voice, "What's wrong?"

Casimir's brow furrowed with concern. "There's something here, tucked within the tree." He made no move to come closer to the trunk. "It wasn't visible from the air."

With another brief look at Byron, he murmured something I could only barely hear, even with my heightened senses. "Huntsman knew... warned us... might alert..."

I swallowed hard, guessing the rest. Whatever was there, the Huntsman had tried to tell us about a dead tree.

Maybe he'd wanted to warn us.

At Casimir's words, Byron made a considering sound. Crouching down, he reached for something within his bag. I caught a glimpse of a tiny nugget of ore in a sliver of moonlight before he tossed it into the gap in the split tree trunk.

A strange sensation like prickly feathers ghosted over my skin and then faded, leaving the sensation of something *less* in the air, even if I hadn't noticed anything before.

"Excellent," Casimir said. "It is likely neutralized."

"*Likely*?" Clay repeated.

Byron gave the blond man a tired look. "A warning spell was tied to a token tucked within the fallen tree. It was probably designed to alert those in the mines if someone was approaching. It shouldn't trigger now when we pass."

Dex nodded. "We move quickly, then. Just in case."

As the others started forward, Clay shook his head, mumbling something about people hardly being reassuring.

Nervously, I trailed after them, straining my senses for any sign of someone on the path ahead. The forest gave no hint of that, though. Only the occasional rustle from the undergrowth broke the silence. I'd flinched at first, worried, but each sound proved time and again to merely be a small animal racing from our path, their brown fur darting swiftly beneath bushes or around trees. Bats swooped by overhead, squeaking intermittently, and nothing about the path seemed to say a mine lay at the other end with the giants my father and stepmother had imprisoned.

But then, maybe that was the way of things. Nature continued on while people inflicted horrors on one another, and even though it seemed like all the world should mark the nightmare of what we'd done, somehow... it didn't. The sun still rose. The trees still grew. You wanted it to stop, somehow. To recoil in horror because what was happening was so wrong, and yet nature carried on.

Because it was bigger than you. Older. It would be here after all the horrors were gone.

Was it my imagination that the forest still felt hushed, though? That the air was sharper, clearer, like cut crystal through which everything held a strange sort of focus? That even though the bats squeaked and the little creatures scurried, somehow I could *feel* the pain of all those trapped in the mines as if it was carried on the air?

Or would this seem like any other forest if I didn't know what was waiting at the end of this path? Or if I still believed the stories I'd grown up hearing, that all these prisoners were my nation's enemies? That they deserved this horror somehow?

Would I still feel this pain if I'd chosen to see the world the way my father had?

Ozias came up beside me and placed a hand on my shoulder. I glanced up at him, torn between relief and guilt for where my thoughts were going—and what might have been.

"Breathe, little mate," he murmured to me, so low only Casimir could have heard. "Breathe."

I nodded, trying to do as he said.

In the lead with Casimir and Byron at his side, Dex held up a hand and then glanced back at Ozias, nodding briefly for the bearded man to join them.

No way was I staying behind.

Dex's mouth tightened a bit at the sight of me, but he only said, "Noises up ahead," when we reached them.

Casimir pointed down the path and then to the left. "I hear at least two voices. Six heartbeats. They're not moving much."

"Soldiers," Valeria murmured, coming up behind us.

The others nodded.

"Can you feel anything about the mines?" Dex asked Ozias. "Anything at all?"

My mate closed his eyes, and it only took a moment before I could feel the frustration coming from him.

"Nothing. Their little charms make the earth lie."

"So what's the play?" Clay prompted, coming closer. "Go in swords swinging or…?"

Dex cast a concerned look at the narrow track, but it

was Casimir who spoke first. "Ruhl and I could remove them."

"And if they raise the alarm first?" Roan countered.

"I can help," I said before Casimir could respond.

A chorus of whispered protests rose, and frustration surged in me. Yes, fine, I wasn't a fighter like them. But I was hardly helpless.

And every second we waited meant Niko spent more time with people who might kill him.

"Let me rephrase that," I whisper-shouted over their protests. "I'm going. I can shift like Casimir, and three against six is better than two."

"No," Dex replied immediately. "If they catch you, there's no telling what they'll do. You—"

"They won't," I said.

From his expression, he clearly wasn't willing to gamble my safety on that. Neither were the others.

"Are you prepared to hurt your own people, princess?" Casimir asked quietly.

I looked away, my stomach churning. "We need to help Niko."

"And if your stepmother has more traps and spells waiting?" Lars pointed out. "Ones that could hurt vampires too?"

I didn't know how to respond to that. I knew it was a risk. For the gods' sakes, I'd just been worrying about the same thing. But what was I supposed to do? Stay hiding back here while they raced in, risking their lives, when I was one of the few who could get close enough to disarm the soldiers before they hurt anyone?

To hell with that.

I shifted and took off into the forest, leaving the men scrambling in my wake.

"Shouldn't have mentioned the damn queen," I heard Clay hiss at his brother.

Beyond the next rise, a small valley came into sight, clustered with trees and holding a pond at its heart. Moonlight reflected from the water's still surface, and nothing moved on the rocky banks. The shadows in the forest were deep, and even with my visual abilities in this form, it took me a moment to pick out the telltale shape of a man hiding in the undergrowth.

A dull gleam came from the darkened metal of his breastplate, marking him as a soldier. His sword was sheathed at his side, and his expression was bored as he idly scanned the pond and the surrounding hillsides.

I raced at him, sticking close to the tree line to hide among the shadows.

He didn't even turn.

Slamming into him, I knocked him down and muffled his mouth before he could shout. He thrashed in my grip, struggling to reach his weapon, but my strength as a vampire was more than his as a man.

My vampire side pounded through me, urging me to bite him, end this, stop him from hurting anyone ever again. I held on tight as I fought it, but that side's instincts were louder in this form. Stronger.

His motions slowed. He stilled and went limp. I released him carefully, relieved I could still hear the thud of his heartbeat in his chest.

One down.

I turned, making myself focus past the drumming of

hunger from my vampire side. I'd need to feed again soon.

But not from humans. Never from humans. Not if I wanted to stay sane.

The vampire side of me didn't like that.

Snarling at it silently, I lunged at another soldier walking into view. He'd been strolling along, likely following a route he'd walked hundreds of times, and he gave no sign of having heard his fellow soldier's struggles. Just before I reached him, his eyes fell on the man I'd knocked unconscious, and he opened his mouth to yell.

I drove him backward into the bushes, muffling his cries. He was even easier to subdue than the previous one—as if, now that I'd figured out how to do this, my vampire side enjoyed tearing the soldiers down a little *too* much.

A smoky form rushed past me when I drew back from the soldier, and Ruhl's green eyes gleamed as he became his wolf form in the darkness. His tongue lolled between long fangs, and I'd swear he was grinning at me.

I glanced around, searching for Casimir. Somewhere to my left, a faint grunt came from beyond the bushes and then fell silent.

Worried, I started toward it, only for Casimir to emerge and shift into his human form. "Are you all right?" he whispered.

"Yes. You?"

"Quite." He smiled, his fangs showing. "Though I suspect Dex and your mate may wish to express some *opinions* later about your insistence on being the one on the front line."

Casimir's eyes held a gleam of amused anticipation as he spoke, and my core twisted hotly at the implication.

His expression turned more businesslike as he scanned the forest. "The rest are down. We need to get moving." Notching his head to the side, he motioned for me to follow and then shifted back into smoke and shadow. I flew after him as he wove through the underbrush, coming to a stop and shifting back to human form a few moments later in the shelter of a large tree.

A fissure showed in the surface of the hillside ahead, as tall as three men standing atop one another and wide enough that a cart could drive through. The faintest traces of firelight gleamed inside, barely an orange blush in the depths of the entrance. In the distance, I could just make out a whisper of voices from farther within, though I couldn't hear what they were saying.

But it was enough. That had to be the entrance to the mines.

I glanced at Casimir. With a grim look on his face, he regarded the fissure for a moment. "Do you feel that?" he murmured.

I gave the valley a wary look. "Feel what?"

He frowned. "Nothing. No mines. No people. Just... nothing." Expression unchanged, he nodded briefly to the side. Silently, I followed him as he shifted and raced back to where we'd left the others.

Casimir had not been wrong. My giants were *not* happy when I returned to human form in front of them.

"The soldiers are gone," I told them, trying to stave off whatever they were about to say. "And we found the way into the mines."

They hardly looked pacified by the news.

"You *cannot* risk yourself like that," Dex said, his voice hard. "If not because of what it would do to us, then because of what it will mean for your country if you're caught. Your stepmother will make an example of you—and that's just the beginning."

Discomfort twisted in me at his words. He wasn't wrong.

But I couldn't stay behind. "I'm not going to hide while you all do the fighting for me."

"And if you get killed?" Ozias asked, and my discomfort grew to feel his horror at his own words, no matter how neutral his voice sounded.

"There is another issue," Casimir said carefully into the awkward silence. "I have reason to believe our arrival may have been anticipated."

"What?" Lars turned to him, alarmed.

"How so?" Byron asked.

"There are spells within the ground," he said. "There have to be. They're strange. Possibly inverted upon themselves somehow. But not only could I detect no trace of the mines, I could not even detect the guards within the entrance itself."

"So it's a trap," Clay translated flatly. "Great."

"Or it's meant to be so well hidden," Byron said, "no one could find it unless they knew where to look."

Unsettled silence fell over our group.

"We have to save Niko," Roan said quietly. "We can't leave him down there."

Dex frowned, his eyes turning to me.

"I'm not staying put," I told him immediately.

His frown deepened, but he only turned to the others and said, "When we get in there, no one say Gwyneira's name or title, understood? The guards or the Erenlians might recognize her anyway, but let's not give anyone help in figuring out who she is—just in case."

Murmured agreement came from all the men around me.

Dex gave me a pointed look. "Stay *behind* us."

I scowled, wanting to protest, but I knew it wouldn't help anything. Roan was right. We needed to go save Niko, not argue about where I would be standing in the battle that lay before us. "I'll do my best."

Dex's expression turned exasperated, and he took my arms, physically moving me back. I couldn't stop myself from giving a startled and thoroughly undignified squeak of offense, but he didn't stop until we reached the rear of the group.

One of his hands released my shoulder only to take my chin, tilting my face up toward his. "Your safety matters more than anything to us, do you understand? More than life, more than death, and I *promise* you, Niko would say it matters more than him. Each of us would die to protect you, so don't go forcing us to do that by being a brat about this."

My eyes went wide with indignation. "I am not being a—"

His thumb landed on my lips, stifling my words.

"Enough." His face tightened. "Please." When I didn't protest, his eyes narrowed, a tad distrusting and a tad playful. "And remind me to repay you later for all this worry you're causing us, princess." The pad of his thumb tugged briefly at my bottom lip.

My indignation drowned as my insides turned molten. Gods, first Casimir and now him.

I managed a nod.

Dex's lip twitched. "Good girl." His hand released my chin. "*Stay.*"

Without waiting to see if I obeyed, he turned and strode back to the front of the group, drawing his sword as he went. "Move out."

I stared after him, my body and mind reeling from what just happened. When I blinked and finally pulled my gaze away, it only landed on the others.

Clay winked at me, grinning like he could guess what had just transpired, while Ozias growled so low with desire, it was more of a sensation prickling across my skin than a sound. Meanwhile, Casimir gave me a wicked smile, undoubtedly having heard every word.

My mate and my dominant vampire were clearly looking forward to helping my equally dominant giant "repay" me, just as Dex promised.

Taking a breath, I turned away, only for my eyes to catch on Roan. He looked stricken. Pained, almost. But before I could ask what in the world was wrong, he buried the expression and spun to follow Dex.

That was... odd.

Promising myself I'd ask him later, I set the worry aside and ordered myself to focus. I would never ignore

Roan's pain, but we all needed every bit of attention and readiness for what was about to happen.

And I wasn't a dog, so like hell was I *staying* anywhere. I wouldn't let these men die to protect me. I didn't care what I had to do.

They could repay me all they wanted later—*after* they survived.

"All right, friends," Clay chuckled darkly as he drew his sword and started toward the mines. "Here goes nothing."

19
NIKO

Every curse word I'd learned from Clay rattled in my head as I followed the guard toward the western tunnel, so many giants in chains trailing after me. Fear quivered through my gut, and my heart thudded so hard, it choked my throat. With every step, I tried to make myself think like Dex. To observe the resources at my disposal and come up with a masterful plan like he would.

Except there were no resources, and so I had no plan.

Gods, I didn't want to die down here.

The collapsed section of the tunnel came into view around the turn ahead, and my heart sank. Boulders filled the opening ahead from top to bottom, and in the light of the torches the guards held, the shadows between the rocks danced. I swore they looked like the taunting maws of hungry beasts, as if each little opening between the rocks was just waiting to devour me.

Which, basically, was true.

I swallowed hard, ordering myself to think like Dex. Like Ozias. Like anyone who might've known what the hell to do right now. But while I didn't have Ozias's skills with the earth—and what gifts I *did* have were suppressed anyway—I'd still done enough mining to know a death trap when I saw one.

It wasn't just the rocks blocking the tunnel that were the problem. If you knew what to look for, it became obvious that the surrounding earth itself was clearly unstable, run through with traces of water and weaker strata of stone that would crumble the moment they were disturbed. And while someone like Ozias could have held it all steady long enough for people to get through, even he would have needed a significant amount of power, effort, and time to remold the earth around the tunnel into something that wouldn't collapse again the moment he let it go.

Assuming it was even possible.

"Get in there, runt," the guard ordered, coming to a stop forty feet from the pile of rubble and stone blocking the rest of the tunnel. "Start clearing that shit out."

I shook my head. "I can't just—"

He tapped the bracelet on his wrist.

Every nerve in my arm screamed like my skin was on fire.

Shuddering racked me as the pain faded, and I blinked hard, somehow now lying on the ground. Chuckling, the guard looked down at me, a contemptuous curl to his mouth. "You were saying?"

I stared up at him, speechless for a moment. "The ceiling will come down if I—"

Pain shrieked through my arm again, climbing farther, all the way to my shoulders like it had acid-tipped claws.

"Let me explain something to you, runt." The guard's voice surfaced past the ringing in my ears as the agony faded again. "There's a seam of gold down there. These lazy brutes located it before a bunch of them decided to be stupid enough to let the tunnel collapse on their heads. So now you're going to get it for us, or I'm going to watch you shit yourself while I burn up your arm with my little toy." He held up his wrist, and the bracelet glinted in the dim torchlight. "And then I'll do the same to every stoneskin here. Understand?"

My whole body was shaking. My eyes crept over to the other giants. Norbert was there. Brock and Ignatius too, along with so many more whose faces I recognized but whose names I'd never learned. Contrary to what it seemed when the guards arrived, they hadn't ordered all the giants to come back to work so soon. No, they'd left about fifty in the cavern, mostly the women and children, as well as the duke and a few of his henchmen.

It wasn't mercy. It was power. The Erenlians knew this was suicide, but each group would stay calm for the sake of protecting the other—at least where everyone besides the duke and his fellow "every Erenlian for themselves" types were concerned.

Even Norbert appeared on edge right now. He was a bully, but he didn't want to suffer or die any more than anyone else did.

I couldn't let the guards torture them. And I couldn't

get back to my treluria if I got my brain and body fried by the guard.

But going forward was certain death too.

"What's it going to be, runt?" The guard rested his hand near his bracelet in implicit threat.

I shuddered again. "Okay." Bracing myself, I climbed to my feet. On my ankle, a shackle clanked where it chained me to all the others. "I'll get to work, like you said."

The guard snorted derisively, like he expected the answer.

I tensed as he tapped the bracelet again, but this time, no pain followed. Instead, a tingling sensation spread through me, like a dull, muted version of when a limb would go numb and then begin waking, but across the entirety of my body. I blinked fast, my mind reeling at the sudden awareness—dim and muffled though it was—of the tiny threads of mold and fungus growing through the stone around me.

My magic was back. Just a bit, but back.

Breathless, I darted a glance at the soldier. They let us access a tiny amount of our magic every time we mined. Never enough to hurt them, not with how far away the guards stayed from us at all times in the tunnels.

But this man was standing so much nearer than any of the guards had come in the entire time I'd been here.

The guy just smirked like he could see what I was thinking. "Any idea you get in that rocky head of yours about taking this from me and getting those stoneskin abilities of yours back, trust we've already thought of it.

So get your ass moving, runt, or we'll see how the *little* stoneskins like paying for your laziness." He tapped the bracelet meaningfully. "Or maybe I'll just send them down here in your place. They're tiny. Maybe they'll fit between the stones better than you. After all, we like having them to remind you brutes to stay in line, but it's not as if we need *all* of them for that."

My gut clenched. Kids? He'd hurt the kids in that cavern?

I'd kill him first.

The thought came out of nowhere, but it was as hard as stone and burned like lava in my veins. I wasn't a killer. Never had been. I knew death happened in nature, but the wanton killing that humans and Erenlians and others engaged in was anathema to me.

But this? This was rage. Protective, defensive *rage* built of the gods only knew how many days in this place, where this sick bastard and all his buddies threatened to harm *children* if I didn't crawl into a death trap, simply because our lives didn't mean as much to them as the potential for *fucking gold*.

Still smirking, he shoved my shoulder to get me moving.

That was his next mistake.

Side-stepping his hand, I grabbed his wrist and spun. For once, the fact I was only slightly taller than an average human worked in my favor, giving me the angle I needed. I slammed an elbow backward into his midsection but I didn't let his arm drop. No, that I pinned above me and shoved upward with my shoulder, dislocating the joint.

Dex always insisted we needed to know how to fight. He'd made us train constantly over the years, all to make sure we could protect ourselves if necessary.

Gods willing, I'd get the chance to thank him someday.

The guard screamed, but my attention was on the other Aneirans in the hall. They reached for the bracelets on their wrists like they all were racing to be the first to burn my nerves to crisps.

"Stop or I kill him!" I barked.

The other guards froze, their eyes going from me to the man I'd pinned and back. I got the feeling this guy was in charge somehow, and like the duke's henchmen, when the guy in charge wasn't giving them orders, they weren't sure what to do.

"Unchain them." I jerked my chin toward the giants, never taking my gaze from the Aneirans.

"This won't work," gasped the man I held. "You won't—"

I yanked his arm upward higher, and he choked on a scream. Keeping my attention on the others, I suppressed a wince at the sickening feeling of tendons and ligaments stretching beyond what was natural.

Violence wasn't my way. But there wasn't a choice.

"Unchain them," I repeated. "Now."

"Don't you fucking dare," snapped the guard I held, his voice breathless with pain.

None of the other humans moved. Some even eased their hands away from their bracelets, a strange look on their faces, like they weren't as worried about stopping us anymore.

Which made no sense.

My eyes darted around the tunnel, but I couldn't see anyone else coming. Couldn't hear any shouts or running footsteps.

This didn't make sense.

I was also burning time.

Exhaling sharply, I thought hard, letting the endless days of forcing myself to study the guards even when exhaustion made me want to weep play back in my mind.

Right.

Gripping his arm tightly, I reached over with my free hand and pressed my fingertips to the bracelet in the pattern I'd seen the humans use.

Nothing happened.

The guard I held let out a rasping chuckle. "They don't work for stoneskins, runt."

I must have gotten the pattern wrong. I pressed my fingers to the metal again. And again. And again.

Nothing.

Desperation drove a furious cry from my lips. Gods, no. I had to get out of here. Find my treluria. Save these people before the Aneirans sent kids down here in my place.

"Let me go," the man continued, "and we'll make your death quick."

My hand clenched down on his arm, and he grunted in pain. "Then *you* release us," I said, tossing a quick look at the other guards. None had moved to put their hands anywhere near their own bracelets, waiting to see what their leader would do. "You fucking reach over and push the sequence to—"

Pain screamed through my nerves like my entire body had been dropped into the heart of a volcano. I lost the tunnel, the world, in a blinding wave of agony that abated only long enough for me to hear the other giants screaming.

What... what *happened*? I'd been *watching* them, dammit. How had the Aneirans...

The guard's voice came near my ear. "Backup security system, asshole. We've got eyes on you everywhere." He chuckled. "You're all going to die for this."

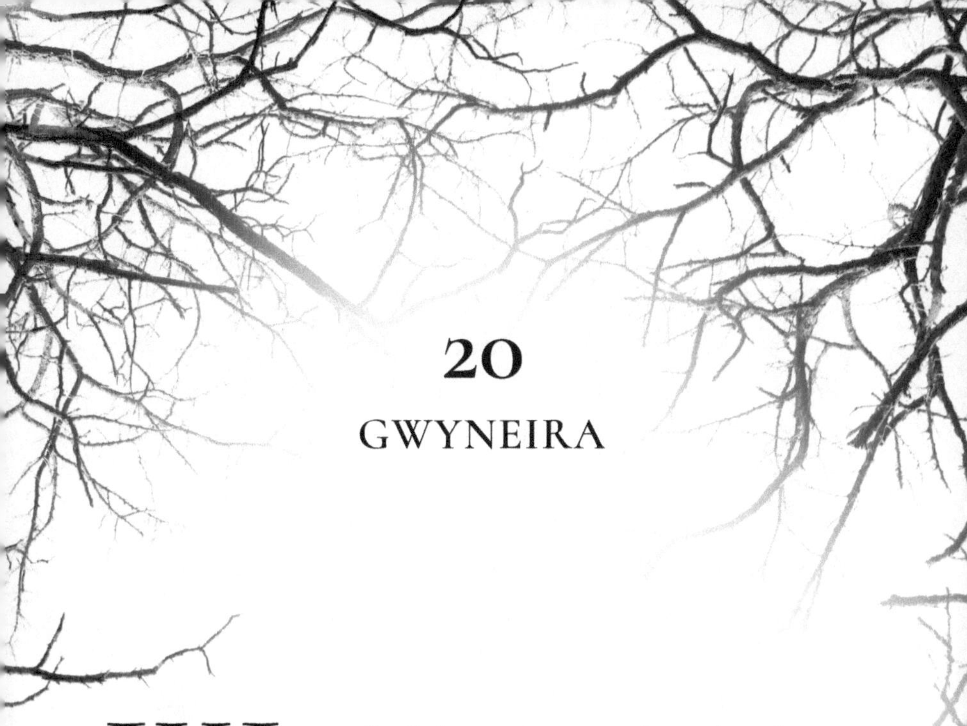

20

GWYNEIRA

We reached the entrance to the mines just as a new contingent of soldiers was coming to check on the ones Casimir and I had already subdued.

They didn't get the chance to raise an alarm either.

"Ozias, Casimir, take the lead with me," Dex ordered, scanning the tunnel ahead of us. At our backs, the moonlit night was still beyond the fissure leading to the mines, all the guards tied up and gagged in the bushes out there. "Valeria, can your people strip these soldiers and take their uniforms? Cover the front and make it look like everything is fine, in case anyone comes this way?"

The woman nodded once firmly.

"Good. And princess—"

"I'm coming with you."

Dex scowled.

"She'll just sneak after us anyway, man," Clay said with a shrug.

Huffing out a breath, Dex nodded. "Fine. Stay behind us." He cast a quick glance at the others. "Let's go."

I started after them, but Valeria caught my arm before I made it more than a few steps. "Be careful, princess," she whispered. "Your men aren't wrong. We need you to survive."

I swallowed hard, hating the sudden twist of apprehension in my gut. While we were all together, I could protect her and the other humans too. If we split up…

"Take care," I made myself say instead of voicing any of my fears.

She nodded once in return before turning resolutely to her people. "Nerak, gather the armor. Merias, get the weapons."

The humans nodded, though the young one she'd called Nerak still watched us as he walked away. Seeming barely older than me, he had the sun-darkened skin of a farmer and the look of someone who'd seen more than any farmer ever should. He'd also seemed displeased with us since I woke, though the others wouldn't say why, only that he'd lost someone in the battle that occurred before I woke.

"All right," Dex's voice pulled my attention back around. Determination in every line of his body, he addressed the giants and Casimir. "Guard the princess. Find Niko. Kill anyone who tries to stop you from doing either. Got it?"

My men nodded, but I resisted the urge to scowl. I

was on board with the latter of those two things, but I wasn't in favor of any plan that meant I was expected *not* to use my abilities to protect my men.

Casimir gave me a pointed look, the heated promise of retribution if I disobeyed Dex in his eyes. Nearby, Ozias echoed that with a dark, hot surge of insistence along our connection.

Gods save me from these men and their annoyingly sexy protective instincts. "Dammit, focus on Niko. Do not worry about me."

"Then don't give us reason to worry," Ozias growled.

Oh for the love of—

Ruhl shifted back to his wolf form at my side. The sardonic look in his glowing green eyes didn't help anything.

"Shut up," I muttered to him.

I could swear amusement joined the shadow wolf's expression now.

Before I could protest this nonsense—I was a vampire, for pity's sake; I could take care of myself—Dex nodded at the others and said, "Go."

They raced deeper into the tunnels, and I followed immediately. The stone around us was roughhewn and jagged, liable to tear at us if we came too close, but the tunnel itself was so huge, there was little chance we'd come anywhere near it.

Giants, on the other hand...

My stomach twisted with a sickened feeling. Beyond the tight fissure of an entrance that would force a group of giants to pass single file—the easier to control them and cut them down if they tried to flee—the tunnel itself was wide enough for a line of giants to stand while human guards could come and go easily around them. The ceiling was tall, yes, but only to a human like me. For the Erenlians' massive forms, it would still force them to hunch over for every step.

I knew it wasn't thoughtlessness. No, even in the tiniest of ways, my people had found methods of being cruel—all while believing they were justified for doing so.

The floor sank downward at a steep angle, and up ahead, the tunnel split into a three-pronged fork that made my heart sink too. The leftmost was narrow, barely wide or tall enough for humans to get through, but the others were wider, like the tunnel in which we now stood. Yet there were no signs on the wall. No indications of which of those two larger tunnels led to the prisoners here.

Panic started a steady drumbeat in the back of my mind. I hadn't expected this, but then, I'd never been in a mine before. All I knew was that it was a tunnel into the ground. But this place was more massive than I expected, and Niko could be anywhere. If the guards received any warning we were coming, there were countless ways they could hurt him before we even knew where he might be found.

Before the fork in the tunnel, Casimir pulled up sharply, casting a quick glance at Dex. Jerking his head to the left, he held up seven fingers.

Oh gods...

Dex nodded. Glancing back at us, he motioned for us to stay put and keep quiet.

With Clay and Casimir, he darted into the smaller, leftmost fork in the tunnel. Crashing sounds followed, and shouts too, but all fell silent in rapid succession, leaving only the faint sound of someone gasping in fear.

"Clear," Clay called.

I rushed after the others around the turn.

A splintered door of metal and wood lay in pieces ahead, before an open doorway with a remarkably ordinary room inside. The walls were plastered and painted white, though blood now dripped from a few. Wooden tables lined the walls on either side, and chairs had been set before them, at least until the latter were shattered moments ago. One table had an icebox for food beneath it and a stack of plates off to one side—remarkably unbroken—while another had an array that stopped me in my tracks.

Mirrors. *Magic* mirrors, if the images playing across their reflective surfaces were any indication.

I swallowed hard, stepping around the fallen bodies of soldiers as I came into the room. Most had been cut down in the midst of trying to attack, while one sat in the chair ahead of the magic mirrors.

He was still breathing. The rest were clearly dead.

My stomach churned, but I ordered myself to stay steady. The soldier in the chair was younger, with wide dark eyes and an ashen cast of terror to his light-brown skin. I could see him shaking from the doorway, his whole body frozen while Dex held a blade to his throat.

"Where are the prisoners?" Casimir asked the young man.

A resolute expression coming onto his frightened face, the soldier clamped his lips shut.

I looked at the magic mirrors, scanning them fast. Most showed empty tunnels. Some showed human guards leaning against the walls, chatting and oblivious to what we were doing here.

One showed a wall of bars, behind which was a cavern full of giants.

A shallow breath left me. In the firelight and shadows of the cavern, I couldn't see all the way to the back to find Niko in there. He wasn't up front, though, and the ones I could see just looked tired, terrified, or like they were hanging onto their resolve to survive by their fingernails.

Gods...

My eyes caught on another mirror. More giants, this time in a tunnel. They were on the ground, writhing in pain with human guards around them.

And at the corner of the image in the mirror was Niko, a guard standing over where he lay on the ground. Pain etched my giant's face. Pure agony, while the guard just grinned.

Inside me, the vampire snarled.

"Where is that?" Dex demanded of the soldier, pointing at the magic mirror showing Niko.

When the young man didn't answer, Dex's blade bit his neck, sending a trickle of blood running down his throat. "Tell us *now*."

Casimir growled, and at the sight of that blood, the

urge to do the same rumbled through me. I was hungry. So damn hungry and that...

I shuddered hard, my fangs aching.

"Answer or we give you to my friend here," Clay said to the soldier, nodding toward Casimir. "Trust me, it won't go well for you."

Worry filtered past my hunger at the threat. Human blood would be like poison for us. Unlike giant blood, it would strip away our ability to still *be* us, turning us into ravenous beasts like every other vampire. Clay knew that, so chances were that his threat was only to make the guard give us answers.

But I still glanced at Casimir, worried.

His eyes flicked over to meet mine when the guard turned toward the mirror. The feral look in his gaze took on a different edge, less insane and much more teasing. He winked at me.

My shudders took on a decidedly heated quality, but I wasn't completely reassured, mostly because I couldn't see him breathing.

Not all of this was an act. Like me, he needed to feed and this was testing his self-control.

The guard cast another glance at him, and quickly, the vicious look in Casimir's eyes returned. He bared his fangs at the young man.

"Clock's ticking, my guy," Clay pressed.

"The cell's in the mid-northern quadrant. That's the western tunnels, subsection D." A shuddering hint of stubbornness came into the guard's eyes. "But you won't reach them in time. The shackles are designed to kill them if we see any sign of resistance. Even if I turn them off, those stoneskins are already dead."

The vampire in me didn't pause to question, and my human side couldn't stop it from reacting, no matter what my men had said.

I shifted and took off.

21
NIKO

Everything was pain. I couldn't even hear the other giants screaming anymore.

I couldn't hear myself screaming either.

And then the agony disappeared.

Gasping, my throat aching and raw, I blinked at the stony ceiling. Shouting still rang from the tunnel walls, and the laughter of the guards too. Every nerve in my body still thrummed with the aftereffects of that excruciating torture.

But the pain was just *gone*.

I struggled to push myself away from the ground, twisting to see what the hell was going on.

The giants were still writhing in agony. The guards still stood above them. But behind me...

Horror hit me like a wall.

Gwyneira was on the ground against the fallen boulders blocking the rest of the tunnel. She was curled up as if in pain, and wisps of smoke flickered around her body like she was struggling to resume human form. A metal bracelet lay near her, fallen against the rocks. But the guard stood over her, sword drawn.

"I said what the fuck *are* you?" he shouted. "Answer me, you freakish bitch!"

My eyes flashed from the bracelet on his arm to the one on the ground to my wrist.

Which was bare.

Awareness of my powers flooded me. They weren't as strong as normal. The earth above me still felt like a thick, wet blanket trying to smother my gifts.

But my rage and terror for my treluria *more* than compensated for that.

Magic surged in me, stretching out and calling to the debris. The humans had killed so many giants down here. Over and over again, they'd sent my people into that death trap chasing their fucking gold. And when that hadn't worked, when the earth only claimed more, it hadn't stopped them. So what if dozens upon dozens of giants were dead, their flesh and bones crushed and their bodies left to rot? There were always *kids* to condemn to death too.

But rot was part of nature too.

And that was the humans' mistake.

At my magical call, every tiny bit of mold and decay between those rocks surged out, growing and expanding and building on top of each other until they became like vines.

"You little..." The guard started to swing his sword at Gwyneira.

A makeshift vine snagged his wrist.

He faltered, starting to turn. "What the—"

The vines weren't done. Crawling across his wrist, his arm, his torso, they wrapped him until they covered him from head to toe.

"Life from death, you bastard," I whispered.

His horrified eyes stared at me between the vines. Behind the gag of nature choking him, he tried to shout an order for his people to strike me down.

I shuddered. It would be so easy to send the vines inside him. Mold and decay were nature's way of consuming the remains of the living, after all. They could devour him just as easily.

And then he would never be able to hurt the innocent again.

"Niko..." Gwyneira's voice came as if from a distance, but the sound still pulled me back from the brink. My eyes snapped over to her, my chest rising and falling fast in rapid breaths.

"It's okay," she said. "We're okay."

My shuddering grew stronger.

She crawled over to me and pressed a hand to my cheek. "We're *okay*."

I stared at her, shaking like a leaf with only one thought making a damned bit of sense in my mind. "I'm sorry. I'm so, *so* sorry. I was horrible to you in the forest. I never should have snapped at you or left you or—"

Her lips found mine, cutting off my fumbling words. Ecstasy and relief flooded me, stealing anything else I would have said. I could only stare at her in shock when she pulled back again.

She smiled. "I forgive you."

My eyes stung and my breaths turned ragged. A new kind of pain radiated through me, like something was cracking inside my chest and it hurt.

Hurt...

I spun, cursing myself. The other giants were still in trouble, and I—

But they weren't, because my vines hadn't stopped. They'd coursed across the ground to wrap every guard in the hallway, pinning the humans to the walls like flies caught in a web. Beyond them, Casimir stood with Ruhl at his side, smoke still vanishing into the vampire's form like he'd just gotten here, while nearby, the other giants were climbing to their feet, gaping at the guards, the vines, me and Gwyneira alike.

Snarling with rage, Norbert started toward one of the humans, pulling his foot back as if to kick the man into paste on the stone wall.

"Norbert, stop!" I called, my voice rough from all the screaming.

He threw me a dirty look. "Fuck off, pipsqueak." He swung.

The vines caught him, yanking him off balance and sending him crashing onto his ass.

Norbert snarled, trying to scramble upright again, but the vines wouldn't let go. He tried to lunge for me, falling short when a vine tugged him backward.

I trembled. Everything hurt so much, like I was made of paper and glass and both were on the verge of crumbling. I hadn't eaten more than a few scraps of moldy bread in ages, hadn't slept much in that long either. I couldn't keep this up forever.

It was a miracle I'd done this at all.

Gwyneira pushed to her feet. "Niko just saved you, and this is how you thank him?"

Footsteps thudded in the tunnel. My heart climbed my throat, choking me, only to tumble down on itself when Dex and the others raced into view.

Things had been such a mess when last I saw them. But here they were anyway, rescuing me.

Gods, how did I respond to that? *Thank you* would make me seem like an entitled ass who thought he deserved the risk they must have taken to find me.

I retreated a step as my friends skidded to a stop in front of our princess.

"Dammit!" Clay cried, glaring at Gwyneira. "You were supposed to stay behind us!"

Wait, why was he yelling at her? He shouldn't treat her that—

"Niko was in trouble," Gwyneira snapped back. "Another minute and he might've died."

Clay floundered, raking a hand through his hair and then freezing when he seemed to register the other giants. At his side, Lars was watching the larger Erenlians too, his whole body tense. At the edge of our group, Byron had become like a statue, his eyes locked on Ignatius. I couldn't even tell if the scholar was breathing.

"Okay, well..." Dex's voice pulled my attention back to him. He cast the princess a grim glance and then gave a more relieved look to me. "You good?"

I nodded. "Yeah, I—" Reality caught up to me. "Well, no. We're not the only ones down here. The Aneirans have prisoners. Kids. But—"

"Kids?" Dex repeated, while nearby, Casimir's head snapped around to lock a deadly expression on me. At the vampire's side, Ruhl snarled, making a few giants recoil.

Ozias's voice was a growl. "Where?"

"Back that way." I pointed. "But they've got these bindings on us, suppressing our magic." I gestured to the bracelet on the ground. "We can't remove them, but she did, so first we need to—"

"Wait, she—" Clay gave Gwyneira a quizzical look. "How'd you do that?"

When she hesitated, Ozias spoke up again. "Painfully." He glared at her.

Anger surged like a hot rush of fire in my chest. He was still treating her like that? And Clay hadn't been any better. What the hell was wrong with my friends that they would speak to our treluria like—

The worried, apologetic look she gave him brought my indignation to a halt. "Sorry," she murmured back to him. "Are you okay?"

Now I was lost.

"It *hurt* you," Ozias growled, something desperate and possessive in the sound.

I blinked while she put a hand to his arm as if to comfort him. It hurt her so she comforted him like *he'd* been the one in pain? How did that make sense?

"Might I suggest we get moving before we continue this conversation?" Casimir commented from the back of the group. The vampire gave an uncomfortable glance to the tunnel, as if he could hear more than we could. "Our friend in the security station deactivated the pain-inducing spell within these little metal nightmares before we rendered him unconscious, but I doubt that is the extent of the threats in this place."

Oh.

I swallowed hard, finding my voice again. "The soldiers have a device. It can lessen the suppressing power of the bracelets. But giants can't use it. It doesn't respond to us. But if the prin—"

Gwyneira's hand clamped over my mouth. She shook her head, making an "uh-uh" sound.

Confused, I glanced at the others.

Dex's eyes pointedly went to the princess and then he shook his head.

Understanding dawned on me. Oh gods, I was an idiot. We were in a tunnel full of Erenlians who would crush the Aneiran princess given half the chance, and soldiers who would absolutely deliver her to the queen if they could.

Of course we were keeping Gwyneira's name and title a secret.

I nodded at Dex, letting him know I got it, and then continued as calmly as I could. "But if my *friend* here could undo it, that might help."

Apprehension twinged in me after I said that, and my eyes went to Norbert. Brock too. Letting either of them have their powers back was dicey.

In Norbert's case, it might be suicide.

"Okay," Dex said, though his tone was measured. "Then we need to—"

Nearby, Ozias grunted, holding up a hand. He turned, regarding the tunnel beyond the giants.

"Ozias…" Gwyneira started, a strange note in her voice. "What… what is that?"

A low, displeased rumble left him. "Something is changing. The earth…" He trailed off, his head slowly cocking to one side as if he was trying to read something from the stone around us. "The earth is wrong."

Byron jerked his attention away from Ignatius. "Wrong?" He scanned the walls. "Oh."

"What?" Clay demanded.

"It's the metal and spellwork that hides this place," Byron said. "The force that suppressed our powers on the surface doesn't extend this far down into the earth, but there is still *something* woven into the stones above us."

"Indeed," Casimir agreed pointedly. "And as I was saying, I *highly* suggest we begin moving toward the—"

The ground rumbled. Cracks spread through the stone overhead.

"Oh, fuck," Clay swore. "Run!"

I scrambled up, grabbing the princess and pulling her with me. Around us, the giants stumbled and tripped over one another, the shackles on their legs keeping them from fleeing.

Dex swung his sword, slamming it down on the lock holding Ignatius's ankle. Nearby, Clay and Lars did the same, while Byron extended his hands, chanting something under his breath.

The locks clattered to the floor. The giants took off running, my friends on their heels.

"Pipsqueak, you bastard!" Terror filled Norbert's voice past the rage. "You let me go or I swear I'll—"

A flick of my hand sent the vines around Norbert crumbling. He surged to his feet, his hands balled into fists.

Gravel and dust began falling from overhead. A tremendous groan went through the earth.

Norbert looked at the cracking ceiling and then ran for it instead.

I paused, glancing back. The soldiers were still pinned by the vines, writhing in their restraints as rocks began raining down around them.

They'd killed so many...

"Niko!" Several yards farther down the tunnel, Gwyneira motioned frantically for me to keep moving.

These men chose to make themselves my enemies. They'd killed so many innocents. Even threatened *children*.

But I couldn't be like them.

The vines disintegrated at my gesture. The guards stumbled away from the breaking walls.

"Go!" I shouted.

The humans took off, scrambling across the shaking rocks to escape the tunnel. At the rear of their group, the guard who'd tried to kill me frantically ran after them.

But the ceiling couldn't hold any longer.

Rocks gave way. Boulders crashed down. The last thing I saw was his horrified face, and then the earth took its own revenge.

Gwyneira grabbed my arm and pulled me with her, the tunnel collapsing in our wake.

22

GWYNEIRA

If we made it out of here, I'd never go underground again. Forget mines. Forget caves.

This was enough for a lifetime of nightmares.

"Oz!" Clay shouted. "Can't you do something to—" He cut off, ducking out of the way of a falling boulder.

Ozias didn't answer, and I couldn't either. But Ozias *was* helping. Our connection vibrated like a bowstring with the magical effort he was expending to keep the earth from crushing us all.

It was him versus countless tons of rock above us. Even he couldn't beat gravity forever.

I pulled on Niko, urging him to run faster. Where were Valeria and her humans? They were supposed to be watching the surface, guarding against anyone trying to attack from there.

"Dammit, I thought we took out the security station!" Lars shouted like he'd had the same thought.

One of the guards scoffed. "We have backup stations

and eyes *everywhere*. You traitors will never get away with—"

Norbert backhanded the man, sending him flying into the wall. The impact destabilized the already crumbling stones, sending them cascading down and crushing the man before he could get to his feet.

Holy gods.

Norbert just grinned and kept running.

A cold feeling undercut my panic. After how he'd treated Niko, there was no doubt in my mind Norbert was trouble. Or maybe *would* be trouble once we got out of here.

If we did.

We rounded a corner, racing toward the junction. Four other tunnels led off from there, including one to the mineshaft and the lift that would get us out. But all around the support beams holding up the exit, symbols glowed on the dark wood.

Dread gripped me. Those hadn't been glowing when I came down here...

In the lead, several giants faltered at the sight, but they were helpless against the stampede of others fleeing behind them. Shoved forward, they fell past the glowing support beams.

No screams rose. Nothing about the beams changed.

Okay...

I braced myself, racing after the others past the beams.

The symbols grew brighter.

A tingling thud passed through the air.

The tunnel behind me came crashing down, boulders

and gravel roaring to the ground. A cloud of dust rolled out into the junction, turning the air into a brown fog.

But the destruction didn't continue onward.

I covered my mouth with my sleeve. Around this intersection of tunnels, I could see other symbols glowing through the fog.

More support beams, this time for the other tunnels —two of which were clogged with crumbled stones as well.

"So, uh…" Clay began. Through the fog, I saw him cast a worried look at Ozias. "I take it those glowing things are keeping the collapse at bay, yeah?"

Ozias grunted, eyeing the beams distrustfully.

"Great." Clay nodded mostly to himself. "But since they didn't work so well on the tunnels themselves, how about we keep moving?"

"We still have to help the prisoners," Niko said.

Clay frowned, his eyes going to Norbert like he was debating that.

The massive giant never even looked our way. Grabbing two of the guards before they could make a run for it, he sneered as they struggled in his grip. "This way, worms." He hauled the men toward an open tunnel, several other giants doing the same behind him. The rest brought up the rear, with a few of them glancing over their shoulders as if questioning whether we would follow.

"Seems like they've got it under control," Clay said. "We should just go."

"They're starving and weak," Niko replied, lowering

his voice like he didn't want anyone else to hear. "If we leave them, they may not all make it out of here."

Clay's jaw worked around. Beside him, Lars seemed torn, while Byron avoided everyone's eyes entirely.

What was wrong with them?

Roan started walking toward the tunnel, not waiting for anyone else to agree. "We'll be fast," he said over his shoulder. "We can't leave kids."

Clay sighed. "Okay, fine. Good point."

"Keep an eye to the walls," Dex ordered as he strode after Roan.

Dread returned, making my heart sink.

We have backup stations, the guard had said. *And we have eyes everywhere.*

If those backups were the reason for the tunnel collapse...

I hurried after Dex. "Do you think they can see us somehow?"

"Byron?" he asked shortly.

The scholar flinched. "Wha— Right. Yes." Clearing his throat, Byron scanned the walls. "The magic mirrors at the guard station must be connected to a sight spell, but..." His brow furrowed. "I'm having trouble tracking it."

"Thing is," Lars offered from the back of our group, "the exit is open, right? So maybe we should go make sure it stays that way while the giants get themselves out."

Niko gave him an incredulous look. "We can't leave them. Kids, remember?"

Lars winced. "Yeah, but who knows when there might be another—"

Rumbling suddenly carried through the floor.

"You just *had* to jinx it!" Clay protested to his brother.

Crashing sounds came from the mineshaft.

"Run!" Dex shouted.

There was only one way to go. We raced down the tunnel after the Erenlians and the guards. Dust filled the air behind us, and the roar of falling stones was so loud, I couldn't hear what the others were shouting.

And if the guards brought the entire mine down on top of us...

My body vibrated with the need to shift and move faster. I was already in danger of outdistancing my men with my vampiric speed. But if I got ahead of them and then something happened...

Gods, panic made me want to scream.

We rounded a turn and the other giants came into view. A long row of bars lined one side of the tunnel, the thick metal poles driven into the floor and ceiling far above. The giants we'd helped were standing beside them. Norbert had a guard in his grip as he snarled something at the man that I couldn't make out over the collapsing roar.

Behind the bars, countless giants stood.

I gasped, throwing a glance back at my men as the rumbling slowed behind us. The ceiling overhead remained intact. Maybe we had the support beams around the tunnel entrance to thank for that.

For the time being, anyway.

"Are these all the other prisoners?" Dex asked Niko behind me.

Before he could answer, Norbert snarled at Dex, "Shut it, human." Turning his attention back to the guard, he pressed the man harder against the bars. "Open the lock or I break your neck like the last guy's."

Confused, I looked around. The crumpled form of a guard lay beyond Norbert's feet.

My stomach sank. No, those Aneirans weren't good people. But Norbert looked like he wasn't going to stop with just the guards.

And we all looked human too.

"It won't matter." The guard was trembling so hard, his voice shook. "They've taken the shaft down. We're trapped here until the queen comes."

My blood went cold. "What?"

Norbert ignored me, smashing the man harder against the bars. "Open the damn gate."

"Answer me," I insisted, my tension rising. "The queen is coming here?"

Norbert's hand clenched on the guard so tightly, the man's neck broke with a crunch. Tossing him aside, the giant turned to me. "Shut it, bitch. No one needs to hear from some human whore—"

In smoke form, Casimir slammed into him, whipped around his torso, and then flung Norbert to the ground. Reforming swiftly, he pinned the massive giant with one foot, his vampire strength holding the Erenlian down. "Speak to her like that again and I shall introduce you to the taste of your own liver, is that clear?"

Norbert roared with fury. The other giants backed away from Casimir, eyes wide.

Except one. Standing on the far side of the bars, a single giant didn't move a muscle. Older than some, he had his beard tied by a leather thong, one of the few adornments anybody here possessed. Likewise, his clothes were in better condition than the other prisoners', and he seemed better fed. His eyes narrowed at Casimir pinning Norbert to the stone floor, but there was no fear in his expression, only calculation.

He reminded me of some of my father's lords. The unscrupulous, power-hungry ones.

"*Fuck*," Clay whispered under his breath. "He's here too?"

I threw a glance over my shoulder. Both he and Lars had their eyes locked on that giant. The sickened, angry looks on their faces were like nothing I'd ever seen from them.

Casimir ignored them. "What lies down that tunnel?" he asked the guards, gesturing to the curving tunnel that continued past the barred prison cell.

The guards scowled at Casimir. "You think we didn't plan for this, freak?" one snarled. "You think the *queen* didn't plan for you all to come save this pathetic—"

Ozias reached out, grabbing the man and hoisting him into the air. At his side, Ruhl flowed forward and reformed before the other guards, his teeth bared.

"No insults," Ozias growled at the human in his grip. "Just answers."

The man trembled. A stink rose as moisture soaked through the front of his pants.

"Lovely answer," Casimir commented. "Anyone else care to be more helpful?"

Shaking, the guards remained silent.

I frowned. I could order the guards to speak. Maybe they'd even listen. But it would mean revealing everything.

Dex muttered a curse like he'd come to the same conclusion. "Byron, do what you can to open that gate. We'll get the giants and then just get the hell out of—"

Running footsteps came from the tunnel ahead.

Clay swore vehemently and grabbed for his sword. Around him, the others did the same.

Soldiers rounded the turn. They aimed their cross-bows straight at us.

And they didn't hesitate.

Crossbow bolts shot through the air.

23

DEX

As strategies went, this shit was everything I would have expected from Aneirans.

I dove for the princess as the crossbow bolts tore through the air. Colliding with her, I twisted to keep from crushing her even as we both fell to the ground.

Behind where she had been standing, a giant screamed.

I threw a glance back, but I barely needed the confirmation. I already knew what I'd see.

Aneira was so fond of horrific weaponry.

The prisoner's stone-like skin began to crack. Pitch-black rot crawled out from the fissures, spreading across his skin. He clawed at the damage while more screams rose—other giants, other rotting wounds.

My stomach clenched, old memories fighting to rise. At the start of the war, the Aneirans had been outmatched by the Erenlians' sheer power and innate skill with magic. But they'd found ways to compensate for that.

Brutally.

One of the guards pressed his wristband to the bars. The gate to the massive prison cavern opened.

Giants rushed the gate, but the Aneirans were ready. Crossbow bolts shot out. Screams followed.

"Get in there, scum!" the first guard shouted at us over the sound of giants dying. "Now, you traitors, or we kill everyone!"

I snarled a curse, keeping Gwyneira behind me. Scenarios raced through my mind at high speed. So far, none of my friends had been hit by those damned bolts, but that was only because the guards were aiming higher, intent on eliminating the more physically threatening Erenlians first.

It wouldn't last. Meanwhile, the tunnel behind us was blocked. The prison cell beside us was a death sentence.

Which left straight ahead, through those bastards.

"Roan!" I shouted.

Flattened to the ground, my friend's gaze snapped to me.

"We need the demon."

For a heartbeat, his face was grim. I knew that somber expression of his so well.

And then he muttered a curse and nodded.

His eyes went black. His lips pulled back in a vicious snarl. Skin and muscles rippling, his body shifted, wings sprouting from his back and his hands growing savage claws.

Crying out in shock, the guards stumbled back and scrambled to aim their crossbows at him.

Ruhl slammed into the nearest guard, while Casimir turned to smoke and slashed past another.

In my grasp, the princess shifted into her vampire form.

"Dammit!" I snapped. "Don't—"

She was already attacking the guards.

Gods, that woman. If we survived this, the things I'd do as repayment...

I exhaled sharply. Now was *not* the time for sexual fantasies.

Ordering myself to focus, I scanned the battle, but it was obvious there was little need to worry about anyone's strategy. Gwyneira, Casimir, and the shadow wolf knocked the Aneirans down in rapid succession, the three of them moving like they'd been fighting together forever. They raced away again as the demon strode forward like he already knew exactly how he wanted to destroy the guards.

Gwyneira shifted back beside me. I took her arm, pulling her to my side and giving her a stern glare that she met with an unrepentant look.

She'd be the death of me, my stubborn little treluria.

Folding his hands behind his back like a school master with an errant pupil, the demon bent over the leader of the Aneirans. His tail sliced back and forth like a cat about to pounce. "Pathetic." He grinned. "And squishy."

His claws moved like lightning, driving into the man's chest.

I winced. I'd seen a lot of bloodshed, yes. I wasn't squeamish.

It was still strange to watch the creature my friend had become unleash such violence. Roan had always been anxious about anyone getting hurt. He'd worried constantly about everything from knives being left in the kitchen to a fire burning unattended—though given how I now knew his family had burned to death, I supposed that last bit made sense. But in his own way, he'd been something of a pacifist.

Perhaps that'd only been because he was afraid of the hell he—or the monster inside him—could wreak.

Because the demon clearly enjoyed the violence.

"Now," the demon continued to the other guards, still grinning. "How fast can you run?"

The humans began scrambling to their feet, clearly taking him up on the offer to run for their lives.

He growled with satisfaction. The air began to heat up around him.

Oh hell.

"Get back!" I barked at the Erenlians. "Stay away from—"

The ground began rumbling again. Even the demon paused, glancing around. "Beast," he said to Ozias. "Is this your doing?"

A groan went through the earth. Cracks spread through the ceiling even faster than they had in the other tunnel.

"Are these fuckers insane?" Clay cried, backing up.

Retreating as well, Lars scoffed. "I'm guessing the answer to that is 'yes.'"

"Now what, Dex?" Niko called.

I looked around fast, searching for a new way out of here—never mind that the Aneirans clearly intended to collapse this entire place on top of our heads, piece by piece.

Fuck, there was nothing. No escape except—

In a cascade, the tunnel ahead started to fall like an upside-down wave rushing at us.

"Demon!" Gwyneira cried.

I grabbed the princess and ran for the only option I could see.

The cage.

Rocks rained down behind us. Guards cried out, unable to reach the gate before the collapse took them. The giants tumbled through the opening on the heels of my friends, but a few couldn't move fast enough.

The giants at the rear screamed as the rocks buried them. I could only watch in horror, barely breathing for fear the collapse would take us too.

Symbols flared on the bars, same as they had on the support beams in the mine tunnels. The rumbling stopped.

Shuddering, I stared at the wall of stones that now filled the tunnel beyond the metal bars. Gods *damn* these Aneiran sadists. They'd built the whole mine as a series of endless boxes, any one of which they could send crumbling down.

But now, there were no tunnels left.

In my arms, Gwyneira trembled, her breaths coming quick and shallow. "Is there another way out of here?" she whispered.

I couldn't bring myself to respond, not when I had a sinking suspicion of what the answer would be.

Gods, where were the humans we'd left on the surface?

Even as I had the thought, I knew the likely answer. Dead. I may not have trusted Valeria and her Aneiran farmers much, but I doubted they would have betrayed us *this* badly.

They must have fallen to the forces trying to kill us, so help probably wasn't coming from that direction.

Holding Gwyneira close, I scanned the cavern, assessing whatever options remained. My friends were alive. Most of the giants had made it into the cage. The Aneiran guards were gone, crushed by the collapse.

Nothing in me could be sad about the last part, considering they'd wanted to kill us.

"What the *fuck?*" Clay snarled as he climbed to his feet. Swiping dust from his clothes, he glared around the cavern.

"Ozias," I called, "are you picking up on any other exits?"

My friend shoved upright. His lips peeled back over his teeth like he was barely restraining a growl. "No."

Dammit, this made no sense. Why trap us where they couldn't reach us?

Unless this was their endgame. A final measure that, if they could not contain a rebellion or escape attempt, meant they could send the earth itself to entomb their prisoners.

After all, every giant here was bound away from their magic, and the ground at surface level was laced with a layer of silver and spells so thick, even witches couldn't penetrate it. Down here, the suppressive effect was reduced, at least—likely because the Aneirans still wanted to force the Erenlians to use their power when the guards chose. But the magic still served as an impenetrable barricade. Even if the giants *had* overthrown the guards, they couldn't dig through it. The ground was unstable as fuck. Shovels and pickaxes would likely cause a cave-in, if another spell didn't just crush them before they could try.

Gods, it was sadistic and ingenious as fuck.

And if we didn't come up with an escape plan, it'd also get us killed.

Grim resolve settled over me. Us, perhaps. But not Gwyneira. If all else failed, we would dig as close to the surface as we could and then she, Casimir, and Ruhl could shift. The ground was poisoned by magic, and gods knew it'd probably hurt the three of them like hell. But I trusted that the vampire king and his wolf would do everything in their power to protect her while they passed through the tiny cracks in the rock and soil to reach the surface.

After all, Casimir was just as obsessed with Gwyneira as the rest of us. I had plenty of evidence of that. Hell, ever since Byron's magic brought her back after our run-in with those corrupted apple trees, the vampire had been watching her with an almost feral level of concern whenever she wasn't looking.

Even if the rest of us were gone, he would defend her no matter what.

I let out a slow breath, grateful to have a plan, even if

it was a final one. No, it wasn't exactly the end I'd imagined for myself. I'd figured I would die in battle, or perhaps as an old man.

But if it was the last thing I did in this life, I would make sure Gwyneira survived.

"Ozias." I turned back to my friend. "How close to the surface could you get us?"

His eyes narrowed as he studied the cavern ceiling overhead. "Not close enough to break through."

"But close enough for vampires to pass through?"

He met my gaze. Over the years, he'd often kept his own counsel, rarely speaking more than a few words at a time. But I'd never been foolish enough to mistake that for a lack of intelligence.

My friend knew exactly what I was thinking.

Unfortunately, my treluria did too. "No," Gwyneira protested immediately. "I'm not leaving you all down here to—"

"Only for a short time," I cut in, knowing it wouldn't be anything of the sort. "Then we—"

Niko put a hand to my arm, stopping me. He placed a finger to his lips with a wary look. Drawing closer, he whispered, "Ignatius said the guards have ways to hear us down here."

These *fucking* Aneiran—

A crackling sound came from the wall, but not like stone breaking. More like miniature lightning fizzling along the stone. "Attention, prisoners."

"And they have a way to speak to us too," Niko murmured with a dark look at the walls. "They don't use it much so no one has a chance to figure out where the spells are placed, but they're always watching in case—"

"Your disobedience brought this punishment upon you." The voice boomed out from the stone, echoing around the cavern in a dizzying fashion. "You have one chance to avoid being left to die."

This couldn't be good.

"Do you see the humans in your cell?" the guard continued. "They and their beasts are vicious killers and traitors to the crown. The queen promises if you kill them, we will free you. But be warned." I could hear the smile in the guard's voice. "The woman is the most dangerous of all. Be sure to destroy her at any cost."

My friends drew in, circling Gwyneira immediately. Around the cavern, the giants rose, staring at us.

Fuck.

24

MELISANDRE

Hiss-clicks carried through the company of Voidborn, whispering over the miles, telling me what I already knew.

The Nine had been neutralized.

Just as I'd promised they would.

Smiling to myself, I didn't look away from my study of the map on the table before me. It wasn't just territories and national boundaries I saw. No, my mind overlaid the ley lines atop it all, while I played out the strategy of where to take next.

The provinces were mine. True, a few still held out. Lord Thomas and his annoying Duteliera remained obstinate. For some unknown reason, he kept his people behind the city walls and burned any tree that I sent up through the ground, almost like he'd gotten warning of the threat they would present to his precious free will.

"That silly *lord* could be in league with your stepdaughter."

I ignored Alaric's voice coming from the shards of glass on the carpet.

"She probably sent word to him somehow," the irritating bastard pointed out.

"Silence," I spat, not taking my eyes from the map.

"You could find out so easily, though."

I tsked at him. "It hardly matters."

A concerned sound came from the shards. "You're slipping, pet."

"Lord Thomas and his peasants cannot hide forever," I snapped. "They'll starve behind their city walls or they will bend to my will. Either way, I win."

"And the girl?" Alaric teased. "Is this truly all you plan for her?"

Incredulity made me recoil, but I refused to grant him with my full attention. "*All* I plan?"

His silence spoke volumes, most of them mocking.

Growling under my breath, I pressed my fingertips to the tiny, unmarked space on the map that hid the mines of Eliantra. The Voidborn bastard was a fool. That sentimental child had fallen squarely into my trap, lured by emotion and idiotic loyalty that rendered her absurdly predictable. And there she would stay, caged beneath earth laced by magic and silver until she finally starved.

My lips curled with anticipation. Before starvation took her, she'd suffer. Hunger would hound her—and all those infuriating giants as well. One by one, those brutes would fall, the weakest collapsing first and leaving the rest with a choice.

Eat the bodies of your own... or die.

But Gwyneira's punishment would be far worse

because while she could outlast the pathetic mortals around her, she was still a creature I'd made. And that creature would need to feed.

Oh, she'd try to resist. She'd hem and haw, fretting like a ridiculous, emotional child. But every passing day would chip away at her pretentious morals. Before she even realized how it happened, she'd start making compromises, weighing the worth of this life over that one. Until slowly but surely, she'd decide it was okay to just take *one... little... sip*.

Her hunger wouldn't give her a choice.

Of course that wouldn't be the end of it. Eventually starvation meant she would feast on those men she treasured, the ones who stood with her against me, mocking my plans and thinking to condemn *me* to the darkness rather than her.

Maybe they'd even beg her to do it, whether out of their disgusting *love* for her or to put themselves out of their misery.

It wouldn't change the ending.

"When this is done," I told Alaric, "that sentimental child will be nothing but an emaciated ghost surrounded by the dead. All alone in the dark beneath the earth, going mad among the bloodless corpses..." I chuckled. "She'll *wish* I'd been so kind as to leave her to the empty realms."

Alaric made a considering noise. "But didn't you have a *reason* for wanting to feed her to the empty realms in your place?"

In spite of myself, I looked away from the map, and

my eyes found the shards of glass. Within each one, a tiny image of Alaric's eel-like face swirled. "What?"

"A proxy, yes? A sacrifice to spare you the... less pleasant aspects of our bargain, while preserving the better parts for yourself." His brow rose as if waiting for me put the pieces of his puzzle together.

I *had* planned that, it was true. "But what does that matter? I have all the power I could need, and *you* are nothing but a distracting illusion cast by Voidborn fools —ones I will happily kill once I uncover their identities."

He hummed in surprise. "*All* the power? Is there such a thing, pet? It seems rather unlike you to think so."

What was he getting at?

His fangs flashed as he grinned. "Are you *sure* you're still sane?"

Of course I was.

Irritated, I turned away. Simply because I was satisfied with my own progress—I was on my way to ruling the world, after all—he had no reason to question my sanity.

Moreover, why was I even engaging in this debate? Alaric was dead. These images were all some illusion. If anything, I should be hunting down the Voidborn who were toying with me in this way.

Admittedly, none of the Voidborn were in the room with me now. But perhaps they'd left a spell token. I hadn't found anything on my previous searches, it was true. Yet it could be covered in charms and spells to make it invisible. And if there *was* some object bound with magic to make me see—

"What if there was *more* power to be had?" Alaric commented. "Would you truly turn your back on that?"

My eyes twitched over to the glass shards.

The dozens of images of his face all smiled. "You know what to do, pet."

How dare he still call me *pet* when I'd burned him into non-existence? For that matter, how dare he taunt me like that, insinuating that I was turning my back on power?

And why was I even entertaining the fiction of this conversation? Alaric was *dead*. He couldn't—

Hiss-clicking carried through my connection to the Voidborn throughout the castle.

My attention snapped to the door a moment before it opened. An orc stood there, taller than the doorway and very nearly wider than it too. He nodded his head to the left, the creature inside him making his eyes gleam with anticipation.

I drew myself up and strode away from the shattered mirror. To hell with that demented illusion.

But what *had* he meant, "you know what to do"?

Shuddering, I silently ordered myself to ignore that too.

My throne room would have seemed silent to a human when I entered it, but I could hear the fluttering pulses of three prisoners currently on their knees between the Voidborn-possessed harpies. They wore the armor of my guards at the mine of Eliantra, but I was not fooled.

The Voidborn-possessed human standing calmly beside them had informed me of their plans long before

Gwyneira and her pathetic allies had tried to take my mine by surprise.

It had only been a matter of leaving enough soldiers standing guard for them to buy into the ruse, and that foolish girl was mine.

I glanced at the Voidborn-possessed human as I took my seat upon the throne. He appeared perhaps twenty, maybe younger, with sun-darkened, calloused skin from a life of work outside. His eyes were currently dark brown, but I could still see the Voidborn within him radiating its displeasure at being confined by such a *limited* host.

Harpies, orcs, and others at least had claws or fangs or strength. They inspired fear and dread before they killed their enemies.

To the Voidborn, humans were incredibly... *boring*.

Smirking mildly at its displeasure, I turned my attention to the prisoners. Two of them appeared to be nothing more than farmers, their clothes beneath their patchwork Aneiran armor threadbare and stained by mud. Breathless shock still clung to their faces, most likely a byproduct of having been flown here by the harpies.

Humans were so silly about flight, craving it and yet being terrified when it occurred.

But it was the third who made me smile. Unlike the others, she wore her stolen armor with a familiarity that spoke to a military history. With her head unbowed and her jaw set, the dark-haired woman made the fact she was on her knees seem a choice rather than a byproduct of force, and while her eyes tracked me, they showed only determination to die with honor rather than the slightest intent of giving me anything I might want.

Anticipation shivered through me. This one would be fun to break.

"I don't suppose I need to tell you why you've been brought here," I said to the trio. "One does not commit treason by accident, after all. So I'll dispense with the formalities and offer you a choice." I glanced to the side briefly as a Voidborn-possessed orc carried in a tray of apples. "Submit to me now by simply feasting upon the food I've provided you... or die."

The two humans on either side of the woman trembled, their eyes flicking from the apples to the doors to me as if seeking another way out.

They knew what these were, then. That made this even more entertaining.

"Remember the forest," the woman murmured to her people through gritted teeth.

The farmers tensed, swallowing down their nervousness but not moving to take any of the fruit I offered them.

"The gods will damn you as a traitor for this, Nerak," the woman continued to the Voidborn-possessed human standing nearby. "Whatever they offered you to betray us, it will be nothing compared to the punishment you'll find in the realms of hell."

The Voidborn-possessed human smiled, his eyes lighting up with an orange-red glow. "*Nerak* has been dead for days, bitch. And soon, you will be too."

A small shudder went through the woman, her only

reaction to the Voidborn glaring at her from the body of the young farmer.

"Enough." I jerked my chin slightly at the Voidborn. "Find a new host."

With a final smirk, the creature erupted from the boy's body. In a twist of serpentine smoke, it sped from the room, seeking something more interesting in the darkened halls.

"What... what was..." one of the human prisoners gasped, staring after it.

"Quiet," the woman ordered tightly.

The human clamped his mouth shut, visibly trembling.

I smiled. "What is your name, woman?"

She drew herself up higher, the fact she was on her knees with her hands bound at her back be damned. "General Valeria d'Elisan, loyal soldier of the true queen of Aneira—and that *isn't* you."

Alaric's chuckle carried from a sliver of reflection on the tray of apples, though none of the humans or orcs showed any sign of hearing it.

Ignoring him, I lifted an eyebrow at the impetuous woman. "My, such fire. And such unrepentant remorse for your crimes. Tell me—" I turned to the other two humans. "Do you concur with this assessment? That I am *not*, in fact, the true queen?"

They glanced at each other and at their commander. One moved his mouth like he couldn't decide upon words, while the other just whimpered with fear.

I sighed.

In an instant, I shifted form and swept down from

the throne, slashing through the air. The farmers dropped like toppling logs, gasping and thrashing in their restraints, unable to reach the bloodied remains of their throats.

Splattered by their blood, Valeria didn't move, but her accelerating heartbeat betrayed her shock and horror. Likewise, her breathing turned short and quick, though her jaw remained set with determination.

"Oh, pet," Alaric whispered. "You can do better than *that* to break her."

He had no idea.

Shifting back to my human-like form before the woman, I smiled. "They were not nearly as entertaining as I believe you will prove to be."

"Kill me and be done with it," she spat back. "I will never betray my queen or my kingdom."

I chuckled. "Oh, General," My fangs descended. "Yes, you will."

25
CLAY

Even when they'd been starved, beaten, and brutalized, giants could still be idiots—and *total* assholes.

"If any of you fuckers *think* of touching her," I snarled, my sword clenched in both fists, "we'll show you just how *vicious* we can be."

The closest of the giants scoffed, while a few others glanced at their companions like they couldn't believe I thought I could be a threat.

Ozias growled, the sound only barely Erenlian.

That brought the crowd up short.

"What the fuck is he?" one of the giants snapped, fear in his voice.

I grinned, but I couldn't really enjoy the brief stalemate. Not when this whole situation was a great big cosmic joke.

My eyes darted to Brock. It wasn't enough that he was here, oh no. There was also Duke Deter fucking

Ensid and his bloodthirsty son, *Norbert,* along with fuck only knew who else.

If I ever met the gods, I'd punch them straight in their holy faces for this bullshit.

"We're your allies," Gwyneira spoke up. "That's what matters. We want to—"

"I say we kill the humans and take our chances," Norbert called over her. "End this and just—"

Casimir stepped from the group, and Norbert cut off, his eyes widening as they locked on the vampire who'd knocked him down in the tunnel.

But then, he'd always been a fucking coward.

"If you want to make it out of this situation alive," Casimir said, "you won't do as they say. Or do you *honestly* believe the same people who murdered their own with such ease will keep their word and let the people they've treated like animals go free?"

Worry flashed over a few faces. So clearly, they'd thought of the obvious already. They just didn't want to admit it.

Hope being such a seductive bitch and all.

"Regardless of what the Aneirans do," Duke Deter the Asshole said, "there is no reason to keep these *creatures* alive."

His eyes raked past me and my brother, and to anyone else, I'd bet it looked like he was just scanning us all equally.

I didn't believe that for a second. Good ol' Deter knew us, same as we knew him. Meanwhile Norbert was acting like he didn't recognize us at all, and Brock was looking anywhere but our direction.

Fucking cowards, the lot of them.

At Deter's words, several giants started forward. I shifted position, my hands tightening on my sword, and the urge to drive the blade into Deter's face made my muscles quiver.

"Only a fool kills that which may provide his only hope of survival," Casimir replied evenly as Ruhl flowed around his feet like a swirling cloud of impending death. "And as for my point…"

He spread his hands out to either side, and a weird sensation rolled through the air. Bright, but invisible. I'd almost call it shiny, if shiny had a texture. Like if light glinting from a gold surface had a *feeling* to it.

I couldn't see anything of what he was doing, but then again, I didn't really care. The vampire was on our side. Whatever the hell he was up to, it'd be intended to protect Gwyneira, and therefore I was fine with it.

The giants were confused as hell, though. The ones coming toward Casimir stopped, their big stone brows furrowing like creases in rock.

It'd be funny if our treluria wasn't in danger.

"What's he doing?" asked the one at the forefront of the group, a giant who looked about in his late twenties with his hair hacked short and uneven so it stuck out around his head.

Byron spoke up from behind me. "He's showing you what happens if you listen to those Aneirans."

The short-haired giant looked between the vampire and the scholar. "But he isn't changing any—"

"Oh, but I did." Casimir lowered his hands, regarding the massive giants like he couldn't care less that they were twice his size. Everything about the vampire radiated that same royal confidence that had made us hate the guy when we first met him.

Now I just grinned, enjoying the show.

"That was a glamour spell," he continued. "Very old. Very rare. Quite difficult to perform, really, but I believe you'll find it worth my effort in"—his lips curved into an icy smile—"five... four... *perhaps* three..."

The crackling on the walls returned. "Your quick compliance with the queen's command has been noted. You are now granted your freedom... to enter the next life. Kill each other or starve, it makes no difference to us." The guard's voice was sadistic when he finished. "Erenlian scum."

All hell broke loose. Shouts rang throughout the cavern. People started crying, running for nowhere, and banging at the manacles on their wrists like that might work to break the things.

I rolled my eyes. Nobody could panic like a giant.

At a nod from Dex, we retreated with the princess between us, our swords at the ready to stab any fuckers who might come close to stepping on us.

Maybe the Erenlians hadn't *really* believed the Aneiran guards before, but they sure as hell had lost any trace of hope now.

"That is enough!" The air shook as the duke's voice boomed from the walls.

Wincing against the noise, I didn't bother hiding my glare. Obnoxious bastard. He always did know how to gain the attention of a room.

"Creature," Deter continued imperiously to Casimir,

like he hadn't just implied everybody should kill the vampire. "I order you to use your power in the service of Erenelle and enable us to leave this place."

My brow shot so high it made my damn face hurt.

Casimir only chuckled. "You *order* me?"

Deter glanced at Brock, twitching his chin toward the depths of the cavern, and all he said was, "Go."

Brock hesitated, eyeing the duke and the vampire and then the crowd like he was weighing something. But like the good little lapdog he was, the lackey did as he was told, striding off through the crowd.

Ignoring him, Deter walked toward us, drawing himself up as if to emphasize just *how* much bigger he was than the vampire.

He always did love that move.

"I do. I am King Deter Ensid of Erenelle."

I choked at the title.

Next to me, my brother blurted out, "*Excuse me?*"

Deter's eyes raked over us, and he didn't bother trying to hide his disgust. "Silence."

A strangled noise left me. "Not happening. How the hell are you *king*?"

I could feel my friends' eyes on us. Gwyneira's too.

"Do you know this man?" Dex asked.

Deter spoke over him, turning back to Casimir. "You will use your magic to undo these bindings now."

One brow rising like Deter was some bratty child who'd interrupted him, Casimir regarded the guy cooly before turning to me and my brother like the old bastard barely existed. "I take it this man only *claims* the crown, not that he actually possesses it?"

I scoffed, and Lars responded coldly, "He's a duke."

"The dwarves will be silent," Deter snapped.

Casimir continued ignoring him. "And how do you know this duke?"

Deter's jaw clenched with obvious rage at being so completely disregarded.

"He's our uncle," my brother said.

I heard Gwyneira's breath catch, while my friends stared at us or Deter. A low growl left Ozias, making several nearby giants recoil.

Roan spoke up, a hint of the demon's rumble in his voice. "Oh, *is* he now?" His dark eyes slid to Deter, his monster's promises of bloody retribution in his gaze.

I knew I liked that demon.

"But... wait." Niko looked between us and the direction Brock had gone. "That means Norbert's your cousin and... Are you related to Brock too?"

"He's our brother," Lars replied.

Niko's mouth dropped open with surprise.

"Creature," Deter snapped at Casimir, "you will assist us or face the consequences of defying the ki—"

"And *you* will cease referring to me as *creature* this instant. I am Casimir zel Elric ver Altreya, king of Zenirya, and you will speak to me and my associates with respect, or I will rid Erenelle of the one who makes a pretense of claiming its crown."

His fangs on clear display, he leveled an expression on Deter so regal, I would've thought the cave was his throne room. Not waiting for a response, the vampire turned back to us. "May I assume this is not a pleasant reunion?"

I sneered. "Oh, Uncle Deter tried to kill us quite a lot when we were kids. It was his favorite fucking hobby."

"And he was instrumental in convincing our parents that kicking us out onto the streets to die was the best way to remove the 'shame' of our existence," Lars added.

Casimir's brow arched. "Indeed?" His gaze returned to the duke with a predatory gleam, while behind me, Gwyneira gave a small, barely suppressed growl.

I stopped myself from looking back, if only to keep from drawing attention to her. While Casimir could reveal his royal identity and use it to our advantage, Gwyneira's would make all hell break loose.

My restraint didn't help. Deter's gaze ran over her, and the contempt in his eyes made it a gods-damned miracle someone didn't gut him on the spot. "Very well," he snapped like he was barely conceding the point. "But what of this... *woman* the Aneirans wished dead?" he demanded. "I see she possesses teeth like yours. I take it she's Zeniryan as well?"

"Yes."

Casimir didn't elaborate, and after a moment, Deter sniffed and visibly dismissed Gwyneira from his mind. But then, he'd always been a sexist prick and an idiot on top of being a sadist. Rather than spare a moment to consider whether this beautiful woman actually posed a threat, he immediately concluded she wasn't worthy of attention.

Which was good, really, given the situation.

I still wanted to break his teeth for looking at her that way.

Drawing himself up, the old asshole skimmed his

eyes back and forth across Casimir, Ruhl, and the group of us "dwarves" with a look I recognized. The one that said he'd momentarily lost his sense of control over the situation, so now he was redoing his calculations of whom to disregard and whom to manipulate.

Intimidation hadn't paid off. Brute force definitely wouldn't, not if he knew shit about vampires. And since assholes like him really only had three weapons at their disposal and he'd already used contempt and rage, that left...

"If you truly are a king," Deter said, his tone suddenly even and reasonable, "then I propose a treaty between our nations. Zenirya would do well to receive aid from the giants of Erenelle."

Oh, for fuck's sake. His version of charm always had needed work.

Casimir appeared amused. "Even if I believe you possess the authority to form treaties on behalf of Erenelle, the Kingdom of Zenirya has extended its protection to the people you see with me. They are honorary Zeniryan citizens, all of them—including the ones who have just reported your attempts at murdering them. I would never consider such a treaty without my citizens receiving a formal statement of apology and an iron-clad promise that they would never again be subject to any violence—or attempted violence— against them."

For a heartbeat, Deter's face tightened like he'd bitten into a damn lemon, and I choked back a laugh.

"We're Zeniryan now?" Niko hissed to me.

"Oh," I whispered back. "I'll be a three-headed

golden goose if it lets me see that look on that asshole's face again."

Byron spoke up from my right. "And we would need the terms of this treaty spelled out in exacting detail before Zenirya would agree to anything, regardless."

Contempt crept back into Deter's eyes when he regarded Byron. "Who is this?"

"My royal advisor," Casimir replied like it should be obvious. "You will treat him with the same respect you afford me if you wish these discussions to continue."

Fuck, I was loving this. Maybe the vampire king would give us all titles to shove down good ol' Uncle Deter's throat.

The duke regarded Casimir and Byron in silence for a moment, but clearly he couldn't figure out a way around this. If anyone could get those manacles off the giants, it'd be the vampire and the scholar. Even Deter seemed to recognize that, especially since he had no other choice.

"Very well, advisor. Your Highness." That sucking-on-a-lemon tension still lurked under his controlled tone. "We require your magic."

"And why is that?" Casimir replied.

"Because we have another route out of here."

26

GWYNEIRA

My vampire side and I were in wholehearted agreement that something needed to be done about that man who called himself King of Erenelle.

We only differed *slightly* on what.

"And what exactly would this method of escape be?" Casimir replied to the man's claim of a way out.

Deter smiled. "Ignatius."

Nearby, I heard Byron's breath catch.

I couldn't risk turning around, not without drawing attention. I didn't recognize the name from the memory Byron had inadvertently shared with me. But from that reaction, I had to assume he knew the man.

The elderly giant who approached didn't have the sneering look of the duke's henchmen, though. Like many of the giants who didn't seem to be in the duke's inner circle, he appeared tense—and on the verge of starvation. Mining had done just as much damage as age, leaving his wrinkled skin with an ashen, desiccated look, like dust and grime had become a part of him.

"Yes?" he replied.

The duke's eyes narrowed, and I suspected I knew why. No honorific accompanied the short response. His tone was utterly neutral, not offensive but not obsequious in the slightest.

No matter what the duke called himself, clearly some of the Erenlians weren't as comfortable with appointing him as their king as he would have liked.

But the duke also didn't force the issue, which was intriguing. Whoever the older giant was, Deter seemed to need him enough to allow the transgression to pass. "Can you use their power?"

Ignatius nodded. "Potentially."

"Good."

Deter started to turn away as if that settled the matter.

"I would note," Casimir spoke up, "you have yet to answer my question. And we have agreed to nothing."

The duke turned back with a cruel and poisonous smile, and my vampire side surged again. I already distrusted the man, considering he reminded me of some of the lords from my father's court, the ones more interested in power than in helping their people.

But learning that he'd hurt Clay and Lars when they were children...

My vampire side made my lip spasm with the urge to pull back from my fangs. That part of me whispered about swift justice that would be well deserved.

It was difficult to disagree.

The duke never even looked my way. "It would be easier to show you than to explain. If you and your *Zeniryan* citizens will come this way?" There was so much condescension in the word, it made my blood boil. With an ingratiating smile, he gestured toward the far end of the cavern.

Thanks to years of training, I managed to get my reactions under control while Dex and the rest of my men shared a wary look. In the space of minutes, this man had gone from threatening to kill us all to suddenly wanting our assistance and expecting us to wander deeper into the cavern on his word alone.

I didn't trust it for a second.

But on the other hand, we were trapped. Or as good as trapped, considering I refused to abandon them down here.

Dex glanced at me, and whatever he saw in my eyes, it only made him sigh. With a twitch of his chin, he motioned the others to go on ahead. "The previous plan is still on the table," he murmured to me. I opened my mouth to argue, but he continued before I could. "You're getting out of here. That's not up for debate."

Irritation rose in me, but then I noticed the look in his eyes. There was an edge to his gaze I hadn't seen before. A determined sort of desperation that gave me pause.

He looked like he *needed* this. Needed to hang onto the idea that, no matter what happened, I would escape. My men were surrounded by people who, even if they hadn't *personally* tried it, were from the nation that had attempted to kill them when they were younger. Moreover, some of them would almost certainly try to kill me now.

He had to believe I would survive. Otherwise, he'd never be able to focus on getting us out of here.

I exhaled, my breath shallow from how drained I was, and nodded.

Relief flickered through his eyes, and it made me want to reach out to him. But we were still surrounded by potential enemies, and so I settled for a tiny smile that hopefully conveyed my support. Together, we trailed the other giants deeper into the cavern.

The duke strode ahead, his head lifted like he really was a king.

But I refused to call him that. Not unless his people proved they actually wanted him to rule. But wherever the duke went, a space cleared around him like the other prisoners were frightened of coming too close.

My teeth ground. People shouldn't be afraid of rulers. Not like this. Rulers should earn their people's trust and respect because they made choices for the good of the nation and its citizens.

Admittedly, not every ruler succeeded at that. I highly doubted my stepmother had much interest in anything besides instilling fear. But from all I could see, this man thought the position of king was meant to serve *him*, not that leadership was about serving anyone else.

I knew he wasn't the original Erenlian king, the one the country had possessed when my people started the war. King Archerias was dead, as far as I knew. So how the hell this man had gotten the position, I didn't know.

But I could already tell it wasn't going to be easy convincing him to work with me in restoring peaceful relations between our countries, if I succeeded in reclaiming my throne.

If anything, I suspected he'd just want to restart the war.

And if I failed, if my stepmother kept the throne...

I shuddered at the thought. Between Deter and Melisandre, I suspected they'd each burn the world down just so the other couldn't have it.

Picking up on my worry, Ozias cast a sharp look at me, concern in his eyes.

Suppressing the urge to grimace, I tried to send him reassurance instead. "I'm fine. Just... thinking."

His eyes slid to the duke, and he gave a low grunt of understanding.

At the back of the cavern, Brock and several others were crouched around a collection of rocks, doing something that I couldn't see.

For a heartbeat, I studied the sandy-haired giant. Clay and Lars had never said a word about having a brother. But given that he seemed to be in league with Duke Deter and that bully Norbert, I supposed I could imagine why.

"What's that?" Clay asked, eyeing Brock and the others cautiously.

"Is it the way out of here?" Niko asked, directing the question at Ignatius rather than the duke.

But it was the duke who spoke first, ignoring Niko and Clay entirely as he turned to Casimir. "Our people have planned their escape for decades, Your Highness. I think you'll find yourself grateful for the charity of Erenelle when we let you leave with us."

I kept my face still, but inside, I was incredulous. He needed our help, yet he presented it as a gift to *us*?

This man truly would have fit right in among the worst of my father's lords.

Casimir regarded him neutrally. "And where is this escape route that you cannot access without our assistance?"

I suppressed a smile. His nation may have been destroyed, his people gone, but Casimir was still an excellent politician.

And *worlds* better than this bastard at being a good king.

The duke's eyes narrowed ever so slightly. He hadn't missed the implied insult in the vampire's response, but he couldn't say anything about it. Not considering the fact he needed us.

For some reason.

My eyes slid back to the pile of rocks. There was something strange about them, though I couldn't see anything to explain that impression. They just seemed... wrong, somehow. Like they were shells more than stones. Like they wouldn't actually be there if I reached out to touch them.

A chill crept over me the longer I stared at them. I wanted to retreat, but to do so would only draw attention to myself.

"It is a gateway spell," Ignatius said, walking toward Brock and the others, motioning them aside.

Byron gave a startled cough like he'd just choked on his own tongue. "A *gateway*?"

When Ignatius glanced at him, the scholar blanched. He looked away like he suddenly realized he'd drawn the man's notice and wanted to disappear.

"That is *complex* magic," Casimir added, clearly incredulous, "and it requires a great deal of power. How did you accomplish crafting such a thing with your abilities suppressed?"

It was a good question. One that made me suspicious and worried, all at the same time.

The duke's expression turned mildly condescending. "Through the strength of Erenlians."

Behind him, Norbert and several others grinned. But from the expressions on Casimir, Byron, and Niko's faces, I suspected that couldn't really be the answer.

"Our people's magic is suppressed, yes," Ignatius said as if trying to ameliorate the mounting tension. "But the Aneirans still require the use of it, and as such, they can reduce the controlling force of these manacles." He held up the band on his wrist. "Some months into our incarceration, we realized that after they finished forcing us to use our magic and returned the manacles to their standard suppressive settings, a small trace of our powers would linger for a short while. And if we returned here quickly enough, I could—"

"I ordered the scholar to harness this magic and direct it for the good of Erenelle," the duke interrupted.

Oh for pity's sake. Any fool could see that Ignatius was the power behind this, not the duke. For goodness sakes, I'd even wager that Ignatius was the one who came up with the plan in the first place. But the duke still wanted to claim credit.

Gods, that was weak.

A real ruler celebrated the skills of their people. They were proud of their subjects' accomplishments and honored them for what they added to the kingdom.

Overall, Ignatius's face remained neutral at the duke's words, but I thought I saw a hint of tension around his eyes as he said, "My ability to manipulate the magic has been limited to the narrow span of time following our return to this place after mining. But over the years, I've built the beginnings of a gateway spell. It passes through the earth for several miles, beyond the reach of the suppressing spells above us, and then onward to the border of Erenelle. The opposite end rests as close to the Erenlian Wall as possible, roughly seven miles from the temple of Syloria where I served decades ago as a young initiate. In another few years, we likely would have—"

"No need to confuse these Zeniryans with your details, scholar," the duke interrupted.

"We are not confused, I assure you," Casimir said mildly.

The duke sniffed. "We have an escape route. That is what you need to know. To utilize it, we only require the removal of these pathetic Aneiran devices and the application of whatever magic your citizens might possess. As the Aneirans are now dead, whatever key master may have existed among their number is not available to us. Thus, it falls to Zenirya to liberate us. And as a sign of gratitude for their service to the crown, I will grant the *honorary* Zeniryans and their king—" I could hear the sneer in his voice. "—the right to escape with us through our Erenlian gateway."

"Gateways belong to no one," Byron said quietly. "And the beings within them do not take kindly to anyone who believes otherwise."

The duke leveled a look on him that bordered upon contemptuous before turning back to Casimir as if Byron hadn't spoken. "We would have the answer of the Zeniryan king and his entourage now."

Casimir's eyebrow arched. "And I would confer with my advisors."

"The *king* can't just make a decision by himself?" Norbert sneered.

Clay made an angry noise, and I bit back one of my own. People were starving while he and his father clearly weren't, and yet he still had the audacity to think *Casimir* was the weak ruler?

"A good king listens to his people," Casimir replied calmly. "He takes their needs into account and makes decisions that benefit more than just himself."

He never looked at the duke while he spoke, and his tone was neutral with no trace of threat.

But the message was more than clear.

Anger flashed through Duke Ensid's eyes.

Calmly, Casimir turned back to me and my other men. "With me, my advisors." He walked past us, head held high.

"So we're Zeniryan," Dex said without preamble when we reached a space away from the other giants.

Casimir bobbed his head in tacit apology. "Forgive me, my friend. It seemed the best way to protect you all."

"Oh, I'm good with it," Clay replied. "I'm going to need a title, though. Preferably several."

The vampire chuckled. "Consider it done." His humor faded as murmurs came from the duke and his loyal followers. I couldn't make out all the words—they must know something of vampires, since they kept their voices *that* low—and they were speaking Erenlian, regardless. But from the few words I could pick out, it sounded like they were planning how to force us to help.

"Thoughts?" Casimir continued in a more serious tone.

Grim looks passed over the others' faces while I bit my lip nervously. "If we let them out..." I started.

Byron frowned. "With those wristbands in place, there's every chance they would never make it through the gateway, regardless. The deadening power of those devices would likely infuriate the gateway demons."

"Hold on," Clay said. "*Gateway demons*? What the fuck are gateway demons?" He glanced at Roan. "No offense."

Worry hovering in his eyes, Roan didn't respond.

"They are the beings who live within the energy of the gateways," Casimir explained. "Or so many scholars suspect," he added with a nod to Byron.

"They're not like the Voidborn, right?" Niko asked with a worried glance at me.

Anxiety tangled in my gut. We all knew what the Voidborn could do to vampires, and it wasn't good.

My nervousness lessened only slightly when Casimir

shook his head. "Little is known about those creatures, but based on every book I've read... no."

"But is it safe for the princess?" Roan pressed. "Or... any of us?" A slightly nauseated look flickered through his eyes.

"Are you feeling something from that?" I asked him with a nod toward where the strange stones waited near the duke and his bullies.

Roan made a grunt that could mean anything. "I'm fine."

That wasn't what I'd asked.

"We should leave," Ozias stated flatly. "Or get her out, if nothing else." He jerked his head toward me.

"And what?" Niko countered. "We can't just abandon these people here."

Clay and Lars looked like they definitely were considering that option, and Byron just looked like someone had died. Meanwhile, I could feel the distrust seething beneath Ozias's reserved exterior. Nearby, Roan was watching the giants with a mixture of worry and threat, like the demon wanted to come back and deal with them while the man dreaded what would happen if things turned into a real fight.

Dex sighed. "We won't abandon them." Clay straightened a bit like he wanted to protest, but Dex spoke before he could. "Do you want to live the rest of your life knowing you left children to die? That you're no better than the humans who imprisoned them and their parents?"

Clay looked away, scowling. Lars put a hand to his arm in support.

I could only imagine how they felt, given what the duke had done to them. Norbert and Brock too, most likely. I'd never heard the details—not many anyway—but what I *had* heard was bad enough.

Not to mention, how would I feel if it was my stepmother down here?

Discomfort gnawed at me as I tried to push the thought aside. My stepmother was actively trying to kill us.

And the duke wouldn't do the same when he got his abilities back?

Gods, there was no winning here.

I let out a slow breath. No, there was only what Dex had said. The choice of what kind of people we wanted to be. "Niko is right. We can't leave them. But can we power the gateway ourselves?"

"I will try," Casimir said before Byron could respond.

Byron looked a bit pasty, but he nodded. "I can help you—"

"No," Casimir interrupted swiftly. "I will do it. You should remain separate from the spell, just in case anything goes wrong and the others need protecting."

"But the magic is Erenlian," Byron pointed out. "If anything, *I* should try and *you* should stay to protect the—"

"I will not negotiate this, my friend."

The others and I exchanged wary looks. "What's wrong, Casimir?" I asked.

He hesitated and then lowered his voice. "I do not wish to risk you."

I was confused. "But—"

"Please." Insistent urgency threaded through his tone. "Do not argue with me. Not where others may hear."

I bit my lip. Dammit, I hated it, but he had a point.

A small, grateful smile crossed his face. "Allow me to protect you. *All* of you. My tutors were Erenlian. I have experience with their kind of magic *and* with complex spellwork. Please trust me when I say it..." His eyes didn't quite flick to Byron. "It would simply be better if we did things this way."

"Okay, but—" Clay shifted his weight uncomfortably. "—are you sure you can trust this Ignatius guy?"

At that, Casimir glanced at Byron again, questioning. The scholar was silent.

"Byron?" I pressed.

He didn't quite look at me, a strange sort of reluctance flashing over his face.

Clay made an incredulous sound. "Out with it, man."

"It's only that..." Byron frowned. "Ignatius despises dwarves. He was one of the most outspoken opponents of allowing me to join the Order. He believes we aren't capable of strength or integrity." His eyes twitched in my direction without ever meeting my own. "Or of keeping our vows."

My mouth opened but words failed me. Oh... oh gods.

Everything I'd seen in Byron's memories played back. Of course Ignatius hadn't been there when he took his vows. Why would he be, when Byron joining the Order was an affront to everything he believed?

And now our lives depended on this man.

"But..." Niko sounded surprised. "He's been helping me. And he knows what I am. He hasn't treated me that way at all."

Byron didn't appear reassured.

"Maybe he's changed?" I offered.

Niko nodded like that must be the answer.

"Whatever he may think now," Dex said, "we need a way out of here, and they need our help to do it. Casimir, you think you can tell if he tries anything with the spell?"

The vampire nodded.

"Good. Ozias, if anything goes wrong, you get—"

"No," I interrupted firmly. "I'm not leaving you down here."

Dex turned a frustrated look on me. I glared right back.

"Okay, uh, well," Lars began. "I don't think the big folks back there are going to wait much longer, so maybe we should just get on with it?"

Dex nodded. "We break the manacles off Ignatius and any others we need for the gateway spell, and we take that route out of here." His jaw tightened briefly. "No matter what that duke tries to say."

27
BYRON

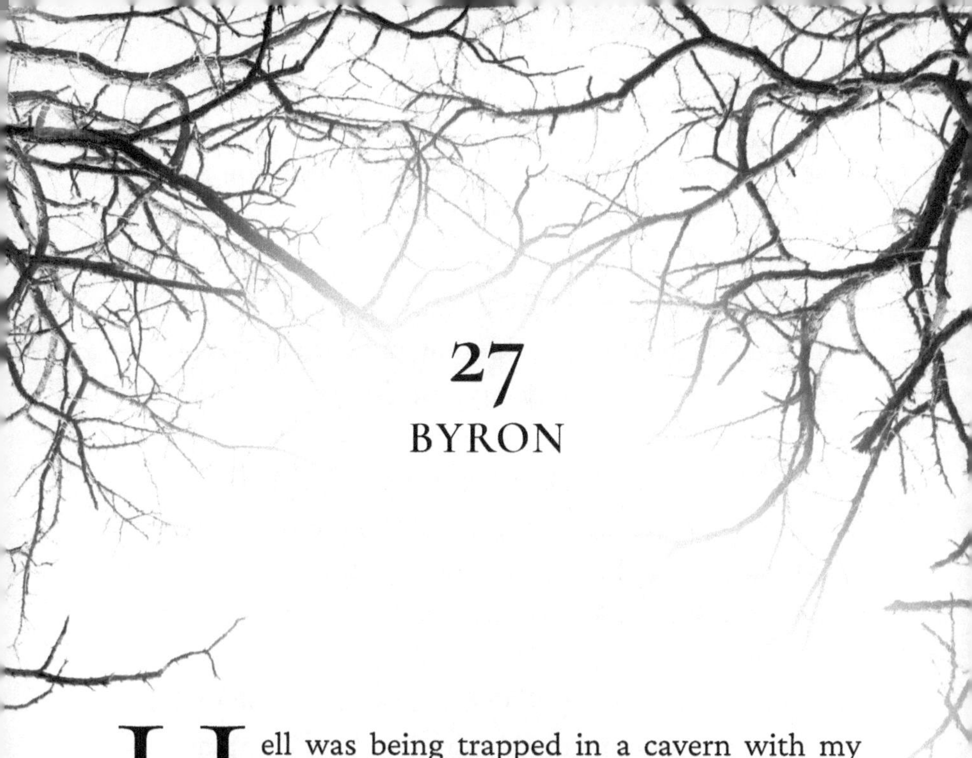

Hell was being trapped in a cavern with my treluria and the man who swore I'd never be able to keep my vows.

Hell was our lives depending upon a spell so complex, it would require all our skill just to manage it, and yet Casimir inexplicably did not want my help.

Hell was here and now.

Following my friends across the room, I scrubbed a hand over my hair and then cursed myself for the obvious sign of distress. Every giant here was looking for a reason to look down upon us. I couldn't be the reason they found one.

The boy is too weak. Mark my words, if you let him into this illustrious body, he will shame us all.

My stomach twisted on itself. Ignatius had never made a secret of his opinions about me. And because he hadn't, the lower ranks of scholars felt they had free rein to vent upon me all their scorn.

Idiot. You failed another test? Those spells are easy for real *giants. Why do you even try?*

My hands curled into fists, my nails digging into palms roughened by years of mining and survival after the Order fell. I'd been different back then. Softer, my body untested by anything but hours of study and meditation.

But I'd never broken. Not when fellow initiates bespelled my clothes to freeze me at night or my work to erase itself. Not when I found dead animals in my bed or mold covering food I'd prepared less than an hour before.

Not when so many of the instructors turned a blind eye to it all or told me a *real* giant wouldn't complain.

Dathan had been one of the few to see through it, and the only one to take me under his wing. But even if his actions made those torments stop, it had done nothing for people like Ignatius, who treated me like dirt under his shoes if he acknowledged me at all.

Let a dwarf take the title of scholar? Next you'll say a mouse could become king of Erenelle!

Gods, he'd always spoken like I couldn't hear his words. Like I was furniture rather than a living being.

No matter what Niko believed, I knew Ignatius would never respect a dwarf.

I avoided the scholar's eyes while we walked up to the group of giants, but that only meant I saw the disgust in the duke's gaze instead. "Have the Zeniryans made their decision?" Duke Ensid asked.

My skin crawled at the scorn beneath his polite veneer.

"We would have the assistance of your scholar," Casimir said with a nod to Ignatius.

The duke paused for a moment. "I see. In that case, my people will, of course, accompany him. To aid him in representing the interests of Erenelle."

Casimir smiled. "We would be honored by their presence."

If smiles were swords, both these men would be drawing blood.

Ignatius motioned to the stones where I could feel the gateway's magic. "This way."

With my friends, I started in the direction he'd indicated. At the duke's nod, several of his henchmen did the same.

But Norbert clearly wasn't willing to wait. Before we made it more than a few yards, he shoved past the other giants, glaring. "No, enough with this fucking around. Are you going to get these things off us or not?"

Coming to a stop with the others, I started to frown at the obnoxious giant. But then I caught sight of Ignatius turning toward me. A bolt of anxiety shot through my veins like lightning. Quickly, I buried the nascent expression.

Such displays weren't the training of the Order. A scholar was somber. Still. They allowed the world to pass before them, observed and catalogued.

Nothing more.

"We have every intention of assisting you," Casimir replied calmly to the giant.

Norbert stuck his wrist out in silent demand that the vampire get on with it.

Casimir smiled but didn't move. The expression was neutral. Utterly unfazed. It could be read any number of different ways, none of which included the vampire king bowing to what anyone else commanded.

Gods, I envied him that control.

"But before we get to that," the vampire continued, "I do have several questions for your scholar."

Norbert took a step closer. "No, you free me. Now."

Casimir's brow arched in amusement, as if a toddler had just stomped their foot and demanded a cookie. He turned to Ignatius as if Norbert didn't exist. "One of my associates tells me you once expressed an issue with those your people would label *dwarves*. I would hear from your own mouth what your intentions are if I release you."

Norbert gaped, shocked the vampire was ignoring him. But after a few seconds, he seemed to conclude he couldn't actually *force* Casimir to obey. Not without another trouncing like he'd received in the corridor—to say nothing of risking that we'd never free him at all.

At the vampire's words, Ignatius glanced my way, one eyebrow rising.

Gods, I wished I could hold his gaze. But I was a coward. I looked away.

"Your associate speaks the truth," Ignatius replied. "Once, I believed how someone was born mattered. That dwarves, by virtue of being smaller than the rest of our kind, must have other deficits."

Clay bristled while a choked snarl left Ozias. The princess put a hand to the bearded man's arm and he stilled.

"I think differently now." Ignatius bowed his head slightly to Casimir, a sign of respect but not so deep as to indicate fealty. "Your citizens are safe with me."

My eyes darted to my friends. Were they believing this? Should I? *Differently* could mean anything.

Safe seemed straightforward enough.

But was I willing to entrust my friends' lives to that?

Or Gwyneira's?

"Ignatius helped me," Niko said quietly. "He protected me from people who... had other ideas."

He didn't quite look at Norbert when he spoke, but Clay clearly read between the lines. "Well, shit. I didn't know Norbert was bright enough to have ideas."

"Clay," Lars started.

Norbert made an angry noise. "What do you know, runt?"

Clay took a step forward, and Dex caught him across the chest with one arm. "Not now," was all Dex said.

At Clay's scowl, Norbert smirked. "Better listen to him—unless you want to be smashed into a muddy paste, *Clay*."

Rage turned Clay's face red. "At least the guy *I* listen to isn't letting women and kids starve."

Norbert growled, starting forward.

"Enough," Dex snapped. "We need to focus, remember? Or do you think that glamour Casimir cast will last forever?"

Everyone stopped, even the imbecilic Norbert. I just wanted to curse—at myself most of all. "Dex is right," I said. "We're wasting valuable time."

"Agreed," Ignatius replied.

I tensed. Wait. Agreed? He *agreed*?

Gods, I wanted to look up and study his expression to determine what the hell that could mean. But damn me, I still couldn't meet his eyes.

"If I take this off of you," Casimir asked Ignatius, "will you assist in harnessing the magic necessary to control this gateway?"

"Yes."

"Very well." For all the firmness of his voice, I still caught a moment's hesitation before Casimir reached out.

I braced myself, praying this was the right decision. Because if we were wrong and Ignatius endangered the princess...

I'd kill him.

Ice shivered through my gut while Casimir wrapped his hand around the metal. Gods help me, I really would kill him. I had no doubt in my mind.

Anyone who threatened that woman would die.

And by harming another scholar, I'd prove once and for all that I'd never been worthy of my vows.

Hell was how I'd lose either way.

Barely breathing, I watched Casimir. Pain tightened his face as his magic worked its way into the mechanism. Hissing between his teeth, he closed his eyes against it.

Clearly the magic in that band didn't like him any more than it liked us.

The vampire whispered something under his breath. His hand quivered, but nothing else changed. He whispered it again, harsh and fast.

"What's wrong?" Norbert demanded. "If you're too

weak, then let your girl do it. She got the thing off the runt here."

A shudder went through Ozias. His lips peeled back with the beginnings of a furious snarl.

Norbert didn't notice. "Hey, I—"

"Said nothing that will be necessary," Casimir interrupted icily as the lock clicked and the manacle fell from Ignatius's wrist.

I braced myself.

Ignatius gasped as the metal hit the ground. He stumbled to one side, catching himself with a hand on the cavern wall.

I didn't move a muscle, waiting for the attack.

"What'd you to do him?" Norbert protested, retreating like Ignatius had the plague.

Standing several dozen yards away at what I could only assume he thought was a "safe distance," the duke recoiled as well. "Are you well, scholar? Did this *king* harm you?"

Ignatius shook his head quickly. "No. No, I... I'm fine." Wonder and grief filled his voice as he dropped to a whisper. "It's been so long."

"Great," Norbert snapped. "Me next."

No one listened.

"Hey, I said me next! Or are you keeping all the *strong* giants trapped while you let that half-dead bastard go?"

Gods, why had no one attempted to murder this bullying fool?

"Your supposed strength has nothing to do with it," Casimir replied coldly. "When we are ready to leave, you and the others who have threatened my people will be released."

"What? You told the king that we would—"

"Deter Ensid is *not* the *king*," Ignatius interrupted, his voice so harsh, it made Norbert's mouth snap shut with shock.

I took a step back, my hand going out to shield Gwyneira.

The scholar drew another deep breath, straightening. "He will not be the king until he stands in the holy waters of Syloria and takes the vows of leadership before the gods. Your father knows this, and you should too."

Norbert snarled, taking a step toward Ignatius. "Watch it, old man, or I'll..."

The stone beneath Norbert's feet suddenly liquified, and into it, his boots sank. A panicked cry escaped the giant, but before he went more than calf deep, the shifting stopped.

Gods save us, we'd been fools. This was it. Ignatius was about to show everyone here who he *really* was.

The scholar smiled at Norbert, no kindness or humor in the expression. "Make note of the one to whom you speak, young one. I've tolerated your nonsense and your cruelty for long enough. It's time you learned to show others respect."

Clay's and Lars's eyebrows shot up, their expressions pleased. But they didn't know Ignatius like I did.

Even full-size giants in the Order had known to dread *that* expression.

Ignatius turned to us. To *me*. "Shall we leave this wretched place, scholar?" he asked mildly.

I froze. What had he just called me?

Gwyneira nudged my hip, snapping me from my shock. "Uh..." I cleared my throat, scrambling for an appearance of self-control. "Yes, of course."

Ignatius nodded. "Then let us begin."

Gods help me, what was happening?

"The..." I drew myself up straighter. "The Zeniryan king will be the one assisting you."

I tried to make the words seem unremarkable, but Ignatius's brow still furrowed with confusion. "As this is Erenlian magic, I would have expected you to be the best choice for assisting me."

Best choice?

"I was tutored by a scholar of the Order when I was younger," Casimir cut in smoothly. "Helorian was his name. Perhaps you were familiar with him?"

Ignatius regarded me a moment longer before turning to Casimir with a nod. "I knew him, yes. He taught advanced levels of spellwork, did he not?"

"And how strict he was." Casimir smiled, gesturing for Ignatius to precede him toward wherever the spell was waiting.

The scholar wasn't fooled by the distraction. He didn't move. "I must confess, Your Highness, I am surprised to see you and your citizens here. I was given to understand that Zenirya was lost to the Wild Lands at the start of the Witch War decades ago." His eyes narrowed. "And that vampires were servants of their creators from the empty realms, those creatures known as the Voidborn."

Oh... fuck.

Magic surged under my skin. He wouldn't hurt Gwyneira. I didn't care what I had to do or what he might do to me. I wouldn't let him—

"Zenirya did fall, yes." Casimir's voice was as pleasant and unruffled as ever. "To vampires, in point of fact."

What was he doing? Did he not see the threat here?

"However," the vampire continued, "my lineage is rather unique, and my magic is as well. This allowed me to escape the fate the vampire witch planned for me and to counteract the madness the Voidborn inflicted upon their creations. My lovely companion has found her own way of doing that as well." He smiled again. "I assure you, neither of us are servants of the Voidborn. Quite the opposite. Now if you would be so kind...?" He gestured for Ignatius to accompany him to the nascent gateway magic.

I couldn't breathe. For a long moment, the scholar didn't move except to turn that questioning look on me yet again.

He was far from satisfied, I could tell. Was he still going to attack? Use magic to hurt Gwyneira or Casimir?

Ignatius's head dipped in a small nod. "Very well." Motioning for Casimir to accompany him, he turned to the gateway spell.

A shuddering breath left my lungs as I started after them. I felt like we'd just escaped the guillotine.

And we'd only begun.

"Hey!" Norbert shouted when even his henchman friends followed Ignatius. "What about me?"

"Oh, we'll get around to you, Norbie," Clay called over his shoulder. "*Maybe.*"

Norbert roared with fury.

"The gateway is here." Ignatius pointed to a collection of stones.

My footsteps slowed. Gateways were strange spells. An inversion of space, in a way. It was often possible to come upon one and not know until you were close. And if they were not set up correctly, stumbling into one meant you may never be seen again.

As escape plans went, to attempt such a thing had been bold, given how risky gateways could be.

"So, um, what do you need to do?" Lars glanced at us, questioning.

"If the Zeniryan king would please direct his power here..." Ignatius pointed. "Then with my power and his, we may have enough to finish the spell."

Casimir came up to the scholar's side, looking far more confident than I would have. The duke's henchmen retreated, still watching us but clearly not interested in getting caught by any magic.

Maybe they had some measure of intelligence after all.

Casimir's power rose, extending out toward the stones. In my mind's eye, I could see it. A glow like sunlight on gold. A heartbeat later, Ignatius's magic swept in like a landslide. I gasped, but it didn't crush him. Instead, his power surrounded Casimir's energy, funneling it and maneuvering it as required for the spell.

"Impressive," Casimir murmured.

That was one word for it.

Ignatius smiled, but it was a distracted expression, his gaze locked intently upon the stones and the spell I could see strengthening there.

But to say gateways were tricky was an understatement.

The magic began to buck and twist, fighting the two men like a thrashing rope made of light. Sweat beaded on Ignatius's brow, dripping down his stone-like cheeks like condensation in a cave. Casimir's breaths came short and fast between his clenched teeth.

My friends noticed. A worried sound came from Niko before Ozias grunted to shush him.

I couldn't take my eyes from the spell, my heart racing. Gateways gone wrong were the stuff of nightmares. Tales of swaths of cities erased from existence. Of people found with half their bodies just *missing*. What it would do in this cave was anyone's guess, but I doubted the possibilities included our survival.

To build a spell beneath all the suppressive magic in this mine would be difficult on a good day, and for a scholar who'd been bound away from his own power for decades...

A choked grunt of effort left Casimir as the magic bucked again.

They were losing control of the spell.

Taking a step forward, I sent my magic rushing toward them, pouring into and around their power. My gift was energy, and theirs needed support if they were going to stop this looming disaster.

"No!" Casimir cried. "Don't—"

Crystalline light swelled in my mind's eye. Shimmering brilliantly, it rushed over and through me like a winter breeze at my back, cold and crisp, bright as the moon on snow.

My breath caught, and I started to turn.

"Focus!" Ignatius snapped.

I flinched, and instinctively, my training kicked in, marshaling my attention back where it was needed.

But that was the princess's power I felt. Her beautiful energy pouring into me as if it was perfectly natural for it to join with mine.

A desperate sound left Casimir, and his magic faltered as if he wanted to pull back. But a warning grunt from Ignatius stopped him.

Apprehension bit at me. Was this what Casimir worried would happen?

Another magic joined hers. Darker. Hard like stone that had never seen the sun.

Ozias.

How was this possible? She—

An icy wind swept around us as the gateway suddenly opened, swallowing the stones in darkness greater than a mere lack of light. Voices murmured in my mind as if from a tremendous distance.

My stomach clenched. Gateway demons.

"Ooh, look. The Nine are here." The voice was pleased but insidious, like a snake twisting around its prey.

My breath caught. The Nine? I... I'd heard that. It'd been carried on a breeze, nothing more than a whisper on the wind, back when the Voidborn were chasing Gwyneira through the forest and we were trying to find her. I hadn't been able to place the term at the time. Even now, its meaning danced beyond my reach—the fragment of something I'd read that I couldn't fully recall.

My eyes darted to Ignatius. Did he know what it meant?

His attention was locked on the gateway, incredulity widening his gaze. He seemed speechless.

Which likely meant yes.

"*Mm,*" another gateway demon said, pulling my attention back, "*they look tasty.*"

"*Should we eat them or let them through?*"

Chuckling followed.

Casimir spoke up, his voice strained. "Do we have permission to pass?"

The gateway demons made considering noises. "*We really* could *eat them,*" one commented as if to another.

"*Bye-bye, prophecy.*"

The demons cackled.

Shudders racked me. My body ached, my magic still pouring into the spell because, until these beings agreed, all my strength was needed to help hold the gateway open. But the princess's power was fading too.

And if our strength failed, the destabilization could be catastrophic. Our only hope would be to close the gateway before the blowback could kill everyone here.

Including *her*.

Desperation pressed the air from my lungs. Damn me, I should have listened to Casimir.

But there *was* another means by which I could close the gateway before it was too late.

The icy chill of certainty settled in my veins again. If worse came to worst, I could throw myself into it. Let my

magic erupt with my death. The power would be chan-
neled into the gateway and should be enough to shatter
the spell before it could destabilize or drain her fully.

The syphoning force grew stronger. There wasn't
much time left. I—

Roan stepped past me. His body rippled and
changed, the demon emerging and making him grow
taller and broader.

At the edge of the gateway, he stopped. A low growl
rumbled from his chest, and his claws flexed on each
finger.

Angry noises came from the gateway demons. *"You
don't threaten us, stygiaterros. You—"*

Ruhl flowed like smoke next to Roan and then
reformed into a massive shadow wolf. His growl made
the hairs on my arms stand on end.

"What? How is that *thing here?"*

"Nyxvarg? How'd a nyxvarg *get—"*

"Do you think he *sent it?"*

Their cries overlapped only to cut short when Roan
snarled. "Let us through."

Silence fell for a heartbeat.

Roan growled. "Now."

"Fine, fine," one of the gateway demons grumbled.

"Impatient, isn't he?"

"Stygiaterros. More like cranky-a-terros."

Laughter came from the other gateway demons.

"Just don't all go through at once, eh?" one said. *"Those
big guys are heavy."*

Casimir nodded jerkily. "Agreed. You have our
thanks."

"Pfft, we should've just eaten you." In sing-song voices, they taunted, *"Mirror, mirror, broken now it lies. Bold are the Nine who shatter the skies."*

They laughed harder, the sound fading into the distance as if they were leaving.

"Good luck, Nine!" one called.

Another chimed in, *"You're gonna need it!"*

Suddenly, the tug on my magic vanished as the sense of depth and darkness from the gateway stabilized, becoming like a tunnel rather than a cliff.

Air raked my lungs in gasping breaths. I turned immediately to check on the princess. Ozias had his arms around her, holding her up, and the rest of my friends had drawn in to surround them, shielding her from view of the giants.

Gods, she looked pale. Weakened drastically by what had just occurred. To let her feed here was impossible, because all hell could break loose if the duke or anyone else saw.

But she'd need strength to use the gateway, and in this condition—

"The Nine?" Ignatius whispered.

Oh *gods*. And then there was that.

Whatever the hell it was.

Ignatius stared, his gaze running back and forth across us like he was trying to make sense of what he saw. "I..." He wetted his lips. "The wolf is not among your number then, I take it. Of the Nine, that is."

Confused, I started to ask what he meant, but before I could, Ruhl huffed as if to dismiss the very thought.

Which was... odd. But then, everything about that creature—or nyxvarg, whatever that meant—was odd.

Gods, I was floundering like an initiate on his first day of training.

Casimir cleared his throat. His skin was ashen and his face gaunt from hunger, but when he spoke, his voice was steady and controlled. "Gateway demons are notorious for playing tricks. We have little time for fairytales."

Fairytales...

"We're not the *Nine*," I blurted.

Casimir cast me a sharp look as if telling me to be silent. I clamped my mouth shut, but I could feel my cheeks heating.

I always had flushed red as a ripe apple when embarrassed.

But what they suggested was *absurd*.

"I understand your reluctance," Ignatius said. "Being told you're the only hope of this world is not something any sane person would wish to hear."

Surprised noises came from my friends, while I just felt sick.

"But regardless," Ignatius continued. "I must ask you stay with us when we reach the other side of the gateway. Whatever your plans may have been, for your sakes and for the sake of the world, you all must return to Erenelle immediately."

28

GWYNEIRA

"You're not serious," Lars said, putting words to the alarm on the faces of my men. Even Casimir appeared dumbstruck—though in his case, a strangely simmering rage seemed to be the reason why.

I wanted to ask what was wrong, but I was too stunned by what the scholar had said. It was insane. We couldn't be the whole hope of the *world*. That was what a crazy person would believe.

"I understand why you might be hesitant to return," Ignatius said.

I sincerely doubted that.

"But if the gateway demons speak the truth—and I cannot see why they would lie about this—then as the Nine, you will need the help of the magic within Erenelle to protect this world. The prophecies are clear. You must—"

"Is the gateway finished yet?" the duke called impatiently from over a dozen yards away.

My jaw clenched against the urge to snarl. That man cared nothing for what his scholar just risked, only that he hurried along like a servant running late.

Not to mention the ten-ton boulder of nonsense the man had just dropped on us.

Ignatius ignored the duke, but he cast a wary look at the man's henchmen. Though they'd stayed back while the spell was activating, now several of the bullying giants were inching closer to the gateway like children urging one another to jump into a pond.

"Unless you wish to die horribly," the elderly scholar called, "I recommend patience until we can remove the Aneiran devices from your wrists."

The henchmen retreated.

Ignatius turned back to us, lowering his voice. "We can discuss these issues more once we pass the Erenlian Wall. But please, I beg you, come with us. You will need the power of Erenelle for what is coming."

Giving a final insistent look at us all, he strode toward the duke. "Yes, we should be ready shortly."

"Well, uh..." Clay blinked. "*That* was cryptic and insane. Anybody else planning to head anywhere *but* Erenelle once we get out of this place?"

Ozias grunted in agreement.

"Casimir," I asked softly, "are you okay?"

His attention flicked to me, his expression still tight with what definitely looked like rage. "Are *you*?"

I hesitated, and before I could answer, he made an irritated noise, seemingly aimed at himself. "Apologies. I am fine." He paused. "*Hungry*," he added in a lower voice. "But fine."

I nodded, trying for a reassuring smile that didn't flash too much of my fangs.

But gods, hungry barely covered it. Every last bit of my energy had been taken by that spell.

"*If* Ignatius is correct about where the gateway lets out," Byron said like the words were being dragged from him, "then when we emerge, we will be trapped between the Wall of Erenelle and hundreds of miles of potentially hostile Aneiran territory in any other direction."

Niko nodded. "It's too risky to run. All of... whatever that was... aside, we really do need to stop the queen. If there is even a *chance* something in Erenelle could help us do that and keep—" he twitched his head toward me ever so slightly. "—safe, then we need to take it, right?"

Scowls crossed Ozias and Roan's faces, but Clay just shook his head. "No. *Hell* no. We do *not* need to be trusting these fucking—"

"Niko's right," Dex cut in, looking vaguely ill. "Byron too."

Clay gaped at him. "You've got to be kidding me. These are the same bastards who tried to kill you. Oz and the pair of us too. Deter Ensid would sell out a *baby* if it gave him a scrap of greater power. And now the scholar who wasn't fond of dwarves thinks *we're* the saviors of the world?" He shook his head incredulously. "The last thing we need is to walk our happy asses back into their fucked-up nation and bring Gwyn—"

Lars slapped a hand over his brother's mouth with a frantic look.

Clay blanched. "Oh, shit," he mumbled behind Lars's palm.

"The last thing we need is to panic," Dex replied firmly. "Right now we have limited supplies, no backup, and no way out. Once we get through the gateway, only one of those issues is solved, but not the others." He sighed. "I'm not saying we need to believe what Ignatius said, but if stopping inside the border of Erenelle helps us address our problems, we need to do it. *At least briefly*," he stressed when Ozias started to growl in protest. "But we stay alert, and we never let down our guard, got it?"

Ozias looked away, but Lars and the others nodded.

I did the same, and Dex gave me a pained look. "If I had a way to keep you out of danger..." His mouth tightened as he left the rest unsaid.

"Your Highness," Duke Ensid called imperiously. "What of our bargain?"

"Pound of gold to whoever stabs that fucker," Clay muttered when Lars uncovered his mouth.

Casimir said nothing, striding toward the duke and the other giants.

I fidgeted nervously as I followed him—and then cursed myself silently for the slip of self-control. I couldn't show tension. Not with that tyrant watching us.

But gods, I could see the problems with this plan. Going to Erenelle aside, if the duke went through the gateway first, he could destroy it before we had a chance to cross.

And then we'd be trapped. Again.

"I would see my people unbound immediately," the duke said without preamble, extending his wrist when Casimir came closer.

"Of course," my vampire agreed, but he didn't move, his eyes twitching to Dex and the others.

"I will remain with our Zeniryan friends until they are ready to cross," Ignatius announced suddenly. "For the good of Erenelle."

The duke turned a surprised and indignant look on the scholar. Ignatius met his eyes flatly.

Relief tangled with worry inside me. From what I could tell, the duke needed Ignatius. Desperation coupled with the duke's supercilious attitude and abuse of authority should have long ago pushed these people to riot. But Ignatius's respected position and calming influence had helped mitigate those pressures and gave validity to Duke Ensid's contemptible "rulership."

The man would be an absolute fool to risk losing Ignatius, not until he had the crown firmly on his head— which meant he probably wasn't going to destroy the gateway and trap us here if the scholar stayed until everyone else was free.

"Our people would be better served by you crossing first," the duke countered. "In case anything endangers the other end of the gateway. We wouldn't want it to destabilize and leave anyone behind, after all."

I bit back a growl as my vampire side wanted to lash out. That was very nearly a confirmation of what I'd feared he would try.

Ignatius made a mild noise of disagreement. "Surely your younger companions are far more suited to ensuring the gateway's security than me."

Duke Ensid's brow arched. "Are you disrespecting my orders, scholar?"

"I would never disrespect the throne," Ignatius replied.

The duke's eyes narrowed. He could hear the distinction Ignatius made just as clearly as I could.

Ignatius smiled. "I simply wish to make certain that our relations with Zenirya remain as you would wish them."

The duke was silent for a moment. To insist would be to imply that he didn't want relations to go well, which would be a mistake considering his magic was still bound and he needed Casimir to release him—which meant Ignatius had backed him into a corner.

Gods, I'd never realized how like politicians the scholars were.

"Indeed," the duke said. "Erenelle values all advantageous partnerships." He extended his wrist to Casimir. "Shall we get on with it, then?"

Casimir gave a slight sideways nod that communicated both agreement and the fact he was only consenting because he chose to do so. It was a movement I'd seen my father use numerous times with impetuous lords and rulers of other kingdoms.

A tight feeling took up residence around my heart. Casimir was born to be a king. Trained too, of course, but some things couldn't be taught. They were character and temperament—something the duke could only fake.

When this was over, would he come back with me to Aneira? Or would he return to Zenirya, where there were only empty halls and a forest of ghosts?

Wrapping his hand around the manacle, Casimir whispered those words under his breath again, same as he had for Ignatius. The spell moved faster this time—or perhaps he'd simply figured out what steps worked best —and soon, the lock clicked and the metal band fell to the floor.

Tension mounted among my men as we braced for what the duke might do.

A shudder ran through him. "My loyal supporters next." He nodded at his henchmen.

Casimir's brow twitched up, but he didn't say a word. Reaching over, he freed the duke's men.

But I could see the tiny shivers running through my vampire. The increasing way his hand shook with every metal band he grasped.

He truly was starving. I was too, but he was pushing himself too hard to continue using magic like this.

All while surrounded by giants who could make the pain of starvation go away.

Tension quivered through me as I walked over to him, ignoring the questioning and alarmed sounds from my men. "Here." I put a hand to Casimir's arm. "Let me."

"No."

"I can help—"

"Not needed."

Gods, what had gotten into him? First Byron with the gateway, now me.

Still trapped in stone, Norbert called out. "What's wrong with your king, girlie?"

A short growl slipped from Casimir, and the giant he was freeing recoiled with alarm.

This was madness. He was losing control of himself. And yes, so was I, but surely we could trade off helping? I knew removing those manacles hurt like hell. The force and magic it'd taken for me to rip one of these off Niko's arm had been excruciating. But that didn't mean I'd leave Casimir to bear this alone.

Barely holding back my own growl, I stalked over to a waiting giant. The giant gave me a wary look as I extended my palm, waiting for the woman to allow me to grasp her metal band. She towered over me by several feet, so large she made me look like a doll. But still she looked afraid as her eyes darted from me to Casimir.

"Pri—" Casimir bit off his protest with a frustrated noise.

I ignored him. "I won't hurt you," I told the woman.

Anxiety drove her to pause a moment longer, but finally eagerness to be free overrode her concerns. She extended her wrist.

Pain stabbed my hand like needles the moment I placed my hand on the metal. The surface was cold, but it burned like acid. With every second, the agony grew stronger, until it was all I could do not to scream.

Gods, how was Casimir enduring this over and over?

Gritting my teeth, I fought to force magic into the band. I'd been panicking when I freed Niko. Driven by pure terror that I would lose him. But vaguely, I recalled twisting the energy coming from me a certain way. Tearing it into the lock just... like...

Click.

The pain drained as the metal band fell. I lowered my hand, my body shaking, while the woman stared at me in wonder.

"Thank you," she murmured.

Before I could respond, hands took my shoulders, pulling me aside. "That was *not* necessary," Casimir growled.

"Neither is you bearing all the burden of doing this your—"

"Do you understand what it does to your men to see you in pain?" he hissed in a tone like I'd never heard from him. It was low. Furious.

Desperate.

I stared at him. His gaze held a feral hunger, and his attention twitched toward the side of my throat every few seconds before jerking away.

My eyes shot to Dex and the others. Ozias was shuddering so hard, it was all he could do not to shift. Roan's teeth were bared, his skin taking on the decidedly gray hue of the demon. Clay, Lars, and Niko looked sick, while Dex's hands were white-knuckled fists.

And Byron was so pale, his red hair looked like blood on his head. Short, sharp breaths made his chest rise and fall with jolts like he was about to suffocate.

Oh gods.

"Go," Casimir ground out. His furious tone softened ever so slightly. "Please."

Nodding, I hurried back to the others. Dex's hand took mine the moment I came close, yanking me back into the thick of their group. Ozias grabbed me away from him, his hands shaking, and he didn't let go. Without a word, Dex nodded and turned away, putting himself between me and the duke's line of sight.

Like a bodyguard.

Peeking past my men, I cursed silently at the curious, considering look in the duke's eyes.

"Is your woman well, Your Highness?" the man asked with blatantly feigned concern.

Clay muttered insults under his breath.

"Your people need my concentration, Duke Ensid," Casimir replied tightly. "Not my conversation."

The duke's brow rose, but he didn't appear remotely offended. More like amused, and the sight sent quivers of rage through me. Gods, what I wouldn't give to just *fix* this.

But then, that was the vampire side of me talking.

I might agree with it, though.

"*Stay. Put*," Ozias growled like he'd read my mind.

Eternity passed until the last metal band hit the ground. With more self-control than I could fathom, Casimir drew himself up and walked calmly back to us. "Now," he said to the duke, "for your part of our arrangement."

The duke's lip curled, coming dangerously close to a smirk. "Indeed." He twitched his head at one of his men, never taking his eyes from us. "Go. See what the other end is like and then return with a report."

Nodding fast, the man strode toward the wall. Like a rock dropped into a pond, the darkness rippled and swallowed him, stilling a moment later as if nothing had happened at all.

Clay whistled low. "Creepy."

A noise of agreement came from Lars.

I couldn't take my eyes away from the darkness.

Whatever lived in that space was invisible, but I still swore it was watching us.

"So, uh," Clay continued. "How long do we wait? If he doesn't make it, I mean?"

Norbert scoffed. "Worried, runt?"

"Please. That's big talk from a guy whose foot is trapped in a rock."

The giant snarled at Clay, jerking his leg in an attempt to break it free.

"If the boy has any intelligence at all," the duke said, "he will return shortly. We have only to wait a few more—"

The darkness rippled. The man stumbled back into the cavern. "It worked," he gasped. "It's... Gods, it's beautiful."

Like he'd unleashed the floodgates, the other giants rushed forward, clamoring to leave.

"One at a time! One at a time!" Ignatius called. "Please! We must be careful not to—"

Duke Ensid and his henchmen strode through without a backward glance.

The darkness rippled so hard as it swallowed them that it seemed like ink about to splash over the cavern walls. A quiver ran through the stones beneath my feet, and my gut twisted like a rope was tugging on my insides.

And my magic.

I stumbled while giants cried out and retreated from the gateway.

"That damned fool!" Ignatius cried.

A growling sound came from the darkness. The sense that *something* was watching us grew stronger.

"Um..." Clay pushed me behind him as he backed away. "You're sure those demon things aren't related to the Voidborn, right?"

I doubled over, the pull on my insides growing stronger. The growl felt like it was all around me. Like the darkness was reaching out invisibly to surround us all.

"Please," I whispered, not even sure what kind of creature I was begging, only that certain death was in that power.

There was a reason these creatures were called gateway *demons*.

"Please." My head shook. "Please don't..."

The darkness paused. I barely dared to move.

"*Mirror, mirror,*" a deep and angry voice growled. "*Broken now it lies...*" A hungry, cruel chuckle carried from the darkness. "*Doomed are the Nine who shatter the skies.*"

My lips parted with breathless shock. "What?"

"*Well...*" I swore something in the darkness grinned. "*Maybe.*"

Confusion made me falter. Maybe? What did that—

"*Cross, little doomed one. She's coming.*"

The tugging sensation vanished like a rope had snapped. I lurched backward.

Clay caught me. "Are you okay? No, stupid question. But you were talking to yourself and—"

I looked up at him, baffled. Talking to myself? "Didn't you hear that?"

Wary glances passed between the others. Clay's head shook. "Hear what?"

My eyes darted over the cavern. Up ahead, the darkness had stabilized again, becoming as still as a black pool.

And my men weren't the only ones staring at me.

I wetted my lips, trying to regroup. I had no idea what just happened or if that voice in the darkness was trustworthy.

But everything in me swore I knew who *she* was.

"We need to go," I said. "Now."

29
MELISANDRE

A hush lay over the city.

Over the entire land.

The lords had returned to their cities, and steadily, they brought their people under my control. Valeria was in the tunnels now with the rest of my servants, awaiting the next stage of my plans.

And Gwyneira remained in her trap.

"All is right with your world, is it, pet?" Alaric asked from the soot-smeared reflection of a broken windowpane.

I smiled. Let him jab all he liked with silly little comments. I'd accomplished more than he could imagine.

And I was hardly done yet.

Still smiling, I strolled along the silent streets of Lumilia, listening to the frightened heartbeats of the few citizens who remained in its walls. Most of the populace were my servants now, either by being bitten or by doing the biting themselves with apples. Only a few holdouts still hid from me, caught up in the laughable illusion they could escape my plans. Meanwhile, those who resisted were dwindling daily, through surrender to the inevitable or because they lay dead in the pits outside the city.

When the wind was right, the scent of their decay was like the finest perfume.

"This death and destruction is hardly sufficient proof of your victory," Alaric commented from the reflection of a puddle.

What did he know anyway? The Voidborn were *reveling* in this. I could feel it. Destruction had always been their goal, but in every instance before, it had taken the form of annihilation. The complete eradication of a land, a world, an entire realm with nothing left behind, not even a blade of grass or the breath of a breeze.

They'd never taken the time to savor every stage of it the way they did now.

"Your vision is so *limited*, pet."

I spun, glaring at a fallen metal shield. "Or *yours* is."

The metal was pockmarked and smeared with soot, but still those smears shifted like his smirking face lurked behind the grime. "I've watched entire realities die. You've seen a mere *city* burn."

Seething, I turned away. A flash of a pale and frightened face caught the corner of my eye. The woman tried to run before I could see her.

As if the patter of her frightened heartbeat wouldn't give her path away.

I strode after her, a grin tugging at my lip for the thrill of this little chase.

"It doesn't have to end here," the bastard continued, his voice tracking me from fragments of glass and metal debris. "My power is in you. Do you have any idea what you could accomplish? How many realms you could rule?"

I slowed. The woman's heartbeat faded as she ran down an alleyway.

No matter. I'd send the Voidborn or my servants after her later.

"Rule?" I repeated carefully.

"You know what to do, pet. You're already almost there."

My brow furrowed. What did he mean? I—

Magic surged in the west.

I gasped, my head snapping toward the electrifying sense of power. A rattling hiss came from the Voidborn as my lips pulled back from my fangs. This... this was not possible. My plan had been perfect. Fail-safes upon fail-safes from which she couldn't escape. And yet still—*still!* —a damned heresy came to life among the ley lines.

A gateway.

Through the darkness of my kingdom, a piercing sensation lanced, a needle-like light stabbing at the corners of my senses. Like moonlight on frost, it glimmered brighter as it grew.

I bit back a snarl. Gwyneira couldn't form a *gateway*. To do so required a level of control that only witches like myself or the highest levels of the Jeweled Coven possessed.

Other magic pricked at my senses.

Oh, that little bitch. Those were Erenlian powers. A multitude of them, like multicolor fragments of wool someone had attempted to weave into a rope of energy. It shouldn't have been possible. The restraints I'd crafted for those brutes should have kept them from coming anywhere *close* to their own powers. And even if they had managed to cling to a trace of magic beyond their shackles, the prison I'd created should have caged them entirely.

Yet the prickling offense of their magic grew stronger.

How the *hell* had she managed to break them free?

Around me, the whispers of the Voidborn turned to a frenzy. They wanted to consume that magic. To swallow it whole until it joined the glow of destroyed realms burning inside them. They wanted to snuff out every trace of that power, until not even embers would remain.

But I had a much better plan.

Alaric's chuckle came from a fragment of glass. "Silly child, isn't she?"

A smile curving my lips, I made a noise of agreement. "Indeed." My smile grew. "*That* was a mistake."

30
GWYNEIRA

o one argued, for once. In moments we were at the cusp of the gateway, ready to follow the giants through.

It felt like standing at a cliff, beyond which was pure darkness. And we were about to dive over the edge.

"Brace yourselves," Casimir said as the last of the other giants passed through the gateway, leaving only Ignatius, Ruhl, and the nine of us on this side of the portal.

I nodded. Unlike Duke Ensid and his men, the rest of the giants had passed through individually as the gateway demons requested. Gods willing, they'd made it safely to the opposite end.

"Well—" Clay grinned, but I could see the apprehension in the tight expression. "See you on the other side."

The grin faltering, he turned and walked into the gateway. The darkness rippled and swallowed him.

"I will make sure he is well met on the other side," Ignatius said.

The portal swallowed him too.

One by one, Ruhl and my other men followed. Soon only Ozias, Byron, Casimir, and I remained.

"Now you," Ozias said to me.

"Byron should go with her," Casimir spoke up quickly.

"What?" Byron gave him a confused look. "You heard the demons. That isn't—"

"You are not the same size as the other giants. She is smaller still. It will be fine."

I didn't move. "Casimir, what's going on? You're acting strange."

His mouth thinned. "Later. You said it yourself, there is no time. Go." His eyes flicked to Byron, including him in the order. "Now."

I frowned, but there wasn't anything for it. He was right about that at least.

With Byron behind me, I walked toward the gateway. At the edge, I glanced back, a sudden thought occurring to me. "Will you be okay?" I asked Ozias. "The... you know, bond. If I'm too far—"

"Go," he said calmly. "I'm right behind you."

Praying that would be enough to keep him safe, I nodded and stepped into the darkness.

Instantly, up and down vanished. Everything did. If Byron was beside me, I couldn't feel or see him. My senses warped as noises rushed around me, indecipherable, soft then loud, then soft again, like I was being buffeted by invisible waves coming from every direction.

My heightened vision was useless. The darkness rendered even my own body invisible.

My vampire side rebelled, overwhelmed by the waves of noise and the absence of sight. It surged up within me as if to take control and fight the chaos.

"Can you believe it?" An impish chuckle came from the madness. *"She actually crossed."*

The gateway demons were here.

"Aw, I was betting the big one would scare her off."

"No, he liked her, didn't you hear? She's doomed.*"*

Pleased laughter followed.

I shuddered. The big one? Did they mean the dark and hungry voice from the gateway a short while ago?

Gods help me, it seemed accurate. The owners of these voices did sound somehow *smaller* than the owner of that voice.

And it *liked* me... because it thought I was doomed.

That couldn't be a good thing.

"Should we let her through?"

"Hmm, maybe we should eat her."

"We talked about this."

"I know, I know. But she looks tasty."

Gods, where was the end of the gateway? I couldn't tell if I was moving, let alone in which direction I was heading.

Had they eaten my men?

My vampire side pressed harder at my control. I'd kill these creatures if they had. I'd find a way to hunt them down and—

"Ooh, she's getting mad, can you see that?"

Another demon giggled. *"Maybe she wants to eat us! Wouldn't that be—"*

The gateway demon cut off with a frightened gasp. Suddenly, the chaos felt emptier, as if the invisible presences had scattered like terrified children. Even the waves of noise rolled away.

"Well, well..."

I tensed, terror shooting through me. I knew that voice. It wasn't the demons. It wasn't even the so-called *big one.*

"You made a mistake, Gwyneira."

Melisandre.

"You came back to the dark. Don't you know I own it all?"

Panic gripped me. My stepmother sounded wrong. Like herself but twisted, as if her voice was accompanied by someone else's, like a sibilant echo. And she was gaining on me. I couldn't even tell where I was or what direction I was moving in, but I swore she was—

"You keep dancing so close to the edge of this realm. Mere inches from the abyss. And if I reach *just right...*"

On the back of my neck, icy fingers slid against my skin like they were about to wrap around my throat.

And then a strange pressure gripped my hand and yanked me forward, hurtling me through the darkness like a meteor shooting across the sky.

"Flee, little doomed one," came the low and growling voice of the larger gateway demon. A bright thread of light appeared in the distance, growing larger and larger as I rushed toward it. *"And when the time comes, call."*

The gateway demon's grip on my hand vanished as

the light rushed around me. Gravity suddenly took hold, sending me tumbling across uneven terrain.

"Whoa!" New hands grabbed me.

I shrieked and started to shift, but then reality caught up to my panic. Shaking hard, I stared up at Dex, stunned. Beyond him, my other men were watching.

All of them. Even Byron, Casimir, and Ozias.

The latter strode right at me, taking me from Dex's hands and engulfing me in his arms. Waves of his relief and fear poured through our connection.

Shivers coursed through me. Gods only knew what he'd felt when I was in there. "I'm okay. I'm sorry. I—"

"No apologies." His grip tightened. "I just need you here."

I nodded against his chest. "I am."

He held me for another moment, and then he grunted like he was regaining control of himself. He released me except for one hand that stayed planted on my back like he needed to keep touching me.

Or keep me from being stolen away.

"What happened?" Dex asked. "You were gone longer than any of us."

I shuddered, looking around but finding no sign of the gateway. The terrain was a rough mix of small hills and exposed boulders between patches of snow beneath a blue sky devoid of threats.

I hoped.

"My stepmother. She—" I cast a tense look at the larger giants. They were staring too, but none of them were close enough to have heard. "She was there."

Ozias snarled, pulling me closer again.

"Are you okay?" Dex demanded.

I nodded. "Fine. I—" My fangs suddenly ached, Ozias's scent somehow reaching me even if my breath was gone.

Hunger returned to hit me like a boulder to the head. All thought of finishing the sentence vanished.

Gods, Ozias smelled amazing. Even through my sweater and coat, I could feel his warmth. My ears pricked at the steady thud of his pulse and the quiet rush of blood in his veins.

My lips clamped shut on a whimper. The vampire side of me wasn't happy going back into a cage inside my mind, not after the chaos of the gateway.

It was hungry. *I* was hungry. The monster inside me wanted out.

It wanted my mate.

I couldn't stop shaking. I'd struggled with the urge to feed before, but after the gateway it felt as if every stopgap between me and absolute starvation had fallen apart. My fangs *ached* to bite him, and my muscles were tensed like a spring ready to release.

My eyes flashed to Casimir. His gaze was locked on me, intense. Ravenous.

Oh gods. Neither of us was going to make it much longer.

I looked around quickly, seeking a way out. The terrain rolled in gentle hills of leafless forests draped in snow. Mountains rose in the distance, more rounded and softer than the peaks on the west side of Aneira. Though snow covered their slopes, the pristine blanket was marred by dark, jagged lines with strange growths around them.

"More apple trees," Dex said, following my gaze. "Byron says they're following the ley lines."

A keen of hunger choked out any response I would have given. But what did I care about apple trees right now?

I needed to bite someone, dammit.

But where to go? The other direction only held a wall of gray fog that interrupted the forest and blocked any view of the sky and all that lay beyond.

The Wall of Erenelle.

That was no help.

Drumming panic clogged my ears. My men's voices came from a distance, their words unintelligible. Hunger had too strong a grip for me to comprehend something as advanced and unnecessary as *language*.

Suddenly, Ozias was in front of me. His hands gripped my shoulders. Calm poured through our connection like an avalanche.

My mate, trying to calm me as only he could.

A whimper escaped me. I could think again, but words were still so complicated. It was all I could do not to attack him right now.

"Help me," I whispered.

He smiled. "Always."

31

GWYNEIRA

With one hand, Ozias pulled me around, giving a brief glance to Dex. Though not a single word was spoken, the former soldier seemed to immediately understand my mate. "Roan, guard them." Dex twitched his head at the rest of my men.

Roan nodded.

Holding me between them, Ozias and Dex started away from the giants, striding fast for the safety of the forest. Casimir stalked after us, his eyes trained on us all like a predator stalking prey.

Willing prey, but prey nonetheless.

The mere thought sent shudders of need radiating through me.

"Where are they going?" the duke called behind us.

I threw a worried look back. If he followed...

My vampire side growled with the urge to remove the man from being a problem.

"Not your concern," Roan replied, crossing his arms and placing himself in the duke's path. Byron, Niko, and the twins all joined in, forming a barricade of silent support on either side of Roan.

"If this is some kind of trick," the duke snarled, motioning for his henchmen, "I'm warning you, I will—"

Roan shifted fast, the demon surging to the surface and stopping the giants in their tracks. "You will *stay put.*"

Anger flushed the duke's face while his henchmen just backed away. Nearby, Ignatius watched us go, saying nothing. I couldn't read the look in his eyes.

"Focus, little mate," Ozias murmured, pulling my attention back to him. "They won't disturb us."

I bit back another whimper. The vampire inside me didn't care about disturbances. It needed blood and didn't care whose it took.

But I did. Gods help me, staying in control wasn't the half of it. Feeding was so intimate. I didn't want to share that with anyone but my men.

"Please..." I begged Ozias as the forest continued on, unrelenting. "Are we..."

"Just a little farther."

I clung to the words like a rope to save me from being pulled beneath a bloody, ravenous sea.

The trees came to an end in an open space of snow and leafless bushes. The remains of a massive fallen tree lay across the middle, its gray and weathered trunk split as if by a lightning strike. It must have been hundreds of feet high when it was alive, so large it blocked enough light that nothing much could grow around it, and when it fell, it left a clearing.

But suddenly, the clearing started to change. Vines twisted up through the snow, weaving together at high speed. Each tendril moved with a will of its own, darting between its neighbors in an intricate dance that spread around the clearing, climbing higher and higher until they formed a green and luscious wall that surrounded us completely, shutting us away from any giants who might have tried to follow.

A ripple spread through the snow like something beneath it was moving. Blades of grass appeared, pushing against the white blanket covering them in a wave, like the forest itself was shrugging off its carpet of snow.

"What—" I spun, searching for the source of this magic. It didn't look like something my stepmother would have done.

It wasn't trying to kill us yet, for one thing.

Tiny pink blossoms suddenly peeked out from between the vines, and I froze. I recognized those. Niko had grown them for me when I first came to the giants' cabin.

Dex smiled. "I take it Niko's making sure we stay safe." He gave Ozias a brief questioning look, and the other man twitched his head in silent agreement.

"Good." Dex turned. "Casimir?"

The vampire was on him in an instant, bearing him to the ground with his fangs buried in the side of Dex's throat. Beneath him, Dex groaned, pain and desire in the sound.

Paying them no mind, Ozias turned me to face him. Moving his hair and then his beard aside, he bared the side of his neck. "Feed, little mate."

My eyes locked on his throat, my vampire side surging up to fracture my control. But memories suddenly flashed through my mind too.

The forest past the Wild Lands. The cave where I'd run. Ozias's body on the ground, his chest going still because I'd taken too much.

"I-I don't want to hurt you like I did before," I whispered.

"You won't."

He couldn't know that.

"You are my mate. My life is yours."

I whimpered.

He took a step closer to me. His hand came up to unfasten the collar of my coat and blouse, drawing them aside.

Cold air bit at my skin. I barely felt it. Every bit of my focus was taken up by the effort of not attacking him. "What..." Gods, words were difficult. "What are you—"

His fingers brushed the four thin lines above my breast where his claws had cut me to form our mate bond.

Pleasure shuddered through me in a hot, molten wave, making my knees weak and scattering my concentration.

The vampire in me seized the opening.

My fangs were in him before I realized what was happening. The heat of his blood flooded my mouth and throat, rushing straight into my veins and making my pussy flutter to life. Gulping him down, I moaned as his hands slid around me, holding me in place, supporting me as I clutched his shoulders and drew deeper on his veins.

"That's it, little mate," he murmured. "That's it."

Carefully, he eased us both down to the earth. Never releasing his throat, I crawled on top of him, pinning him. While I dragged on his veins, he lay beneath me, stroking my sides, my back, continuing to murmur encouragements.

Fuck, I... I wanted him. Needed him. Needed—

His fingers brushed the scars again. My pussy spasmed instantly, making my hips rock into him, seeking release. But the surge of that different need also brought me back to myself. Quickly, I pulled away, sealing the wound.

Ozias smiled up at me. "Good girl." His eyes went to the four little scars above my breast. "Come here."

That smile never fading, he helped me extract myself from the rest of my coat and blouse, and then he pulled me closer. His lips sealed over the scars.

My eyes rolled back in my head. "Holy..." Pleasure coursed through me like he was stoking a fire that would consume my soul. "H-how is this—"

"Mating mark." He drew back again. "Proof of our bond."

I wasn't sure how that was an answer, but I also didn't have time to ask. Desperate sounds came from my left. Casimir had finished feeding, but the men were by no means done. Dex lay on his back, Casimir on top of him. Their clothes were gone, tossed aside in their hurry.

Pressed together, they kissed passionately while their cocks ground against each other.

My core throbbed. Oh gods, that was arousing. How had it never occurred to me how enticing it could be to watch as well as join in?

Dex gasped, his head tilting back and his hips jerking as his release overtook him. Gripping his shoulders hard, Casimir buried his head against the giant's chest and groaned out his own orgasm.

I shuddered, wet as hell, my gaze riveted on them both.

Ozias made a pleased noise and then took my chin, drawing my eyes to his. "Your men will be with us momentarily, little mate." Hunger rumbled through his voice. "Shall we get you warmed up for them?"

I'd no sooner nodded than he flipped me so that I was on all fours with him poised above me. His hands made quick work of my breeches, and in only a moment I was bare, my wet core exposed for the three of them to see.

Rock melted around my hands, pulling me several inches down into the earth and then reforming. Eyes wide, I looked back at Ozias, questioning.

"You've been testing us, little mate." He stripped down and tossed his clothes to the side. Hard as stone, his cock stood ready. "Risking yourself over and over, when it's our purpose to protect you."

My mouth opened to protest.

His palm struck my ass, and I choked on a startled cry. Pain blossomed, hot and sharp.

But impossibly, my breasts and pussy tingled too.

What the—

His palm connected again, making me gasp. "Are you done challenging our need to keep you safe?"

I couldn't find words. Intoxicating arousal coursed through my body at the hot, dark, and *desperate* look in his eyes. I could stop this. Easily. He knew that. But that also wasn't the point.

My mate's dominant streak craved this claim over me. Casimir and Dex did too. All three men were alpha predators in their own right, in charge of their domains.

And each was secretly terrified of losing me.

My vampire and my soldier stalked closer, their gazes fixed on my naked body. Already, their cocks were getting hard again. Dex's hand flexed like he couldn't wait to turn my flesh a darker pink, while Casimir gave a low growl, the sound wild and hungry.

They needed this dominance. This submission from me, even if only in this moment.

But that didn't mean I had to make this easy on them.

Shuddering with anticipation, I turned back to Ozias. "No."

His growl turned my insides molten. His palm collided with my ass again. Once, twice, a third time, making my flesh burn and my hands jerk in the stone restraints.

But my hips rocked back on instinct too, my core seeking just the right impact to send me over the edge.

"I feel how much you're enjoying this, little mate." His hand struck again. "I think your soldier should have a turn, don't you?"

Dex circled behind me. He drew his rough palm over my ass, cupping my soft flesh and making my skin tingle in a new way. "You remember the night you gave me your virginity? How you begged me to fuck you? How you called me sir?"

Oh gods…

I quaked with need, breathless. "Yes?"

He leaned in close. "Your sir wants to hear you beg again."

Holy—

His palm struck my ass. Hard.

I gasped, my hands lurching in the stone restraints. But he didn't stop, and as his hand kept going, tears welled in my eyes. The pain was real, but it was doing strange things to my body.

And between my legs, my core was on fire.

Casimir bent down in front of me. "Are you going to be good, my little fucktoy?"

I shook my head, too overcome to form words.

His brow arched. "Is that so?" Reaching down, he caressed my breasts.

My awareness scattered between the alternating sensations of his hands massaging my breasts and Dex's palm striking my ass. What was he doing? Why—

A grin flashed across Casimir's face. He glanced up at Ozias and Dex, and at whatever he saw, he nodded.

His fingers pinched my nipples like twin clamps.

The fresh spike of pain unleashed my orgasm like a chain reaction of lightning. I convulsed, my vision blacking out. I lost all awareness of where I was or why. I was nothing but the tangle of pleasure and pain, the combination so overwhelming, I couldn't do anything but feel.

I returned to my senses on the ground, my restraints gone and my body throbbing where it pressed to the earth. Footsteps sounded behind me, and when I opened my eyes, I saw my men striding across the clearing, visibly surprised.

Ozias reached me first. Gathering me into his arms, he brushed the soil from my skin. His release clung to him, wet and sticky, but he paid it no mind as he sat on the ground and held me close.

I nestled against the dark hair of his chest, my body still thrumming with the aftershocks of what they'd done. "You... you came just from what we were doing?"

A low rumble carried through his chest, the sound radiating satisfaction. "When your pleasure overtook you like that, it was..."

"Exquisite," Casimir filled in, brushing a strand of my hair away from my face.

Dex nodded, his eyes locked on me. "Beautiful."

I quivered. "Thank you..." A smile tugged at my lips. "Sir."

His gaze heated. Bending down, he kissed me deeply while Ozias held me in his arms. Casimir sank to the ground beside us, stroking his fingers along my ass and sending little tingles of residual pleasure-pain through my veins.

My mind was spinning when Dex leaned back again. "Do you think anyone, um..." I glanced in the direction where we'd left the giants. "Anyone heard?"

"You shifted before you made any sound, my precious little fucktoy," Casimir assured me. "There was nothing to hear."

Relieved, I sighed. The last thing we needed was the duke, Norbert, or any of their buddies knowing I'd just had the orgasm of my life. As it was, we'd probably already left Niko and the others for too long.

Though, on that topic...

"Casimir?"

"Yes, lovely?"

"What's going on between you and Byron?"

His pleased expression went still.

"I know something is wrong. You've been... strange about him for a while." I hesitated. "And me."

Sighing, he sank back onto the grass. "I take it you haven't noticed." At my silence, he continued. "Your magic."

Oh.

He read my expression. "Or perhaps you *did* know?"

I could feel Dex's and Ozias's eyes on me. "It's okay. It's just—"

"It is *not* okay," Casimir cut in. "Your magic and Byron's have merged somehow. You are connected, and if any harm should befall to him, you could die."

I froze.

"What?" Dex shoved up from the grass. "How the hell did that happen?"

Rage and dread flooded my link to Ozias.

"Gwyneira's a vampire," Dex continued. "Aren't you both essentially..."

"Immortal?" Casimir filled in.

Dex nodded.

"Vampires can still be killed, my friend. Her life and Byron's are tied through their magic. It is a different connection than a mate bond." He nodded to Ozias in acknowledgement. "It is life force. And near-immortality or not, if his life ends, hers will as well." He turned to me, his expression becoming apologetic. "I have been searching for a means to break that bond without killing either of you, but until I discover a safe path forward, it is imperative you both exercise caution." Tension flashed across his face. "Please."

I couldn't find words.

"I will find a way to fix this," Casimir assured me. "I swear it on my life. And until then, I will protect you both."

"We all will," Dex added.

Ozias just pulled me to him, his body warm amid the cold air. A low rumble carried through his chest, a growl for the thought that I could be taken from him.

I squeezed my eyes shut, praying Casimir's efforts would be enough.

"We should get back," Dex said. "We can't leave the others for too long. Especially if Byron..." He left the rest unsaid.

"Agreed." Casimir rose to his feet.

Ozias's arms tightened on me, his worry more than clear through our connection.

Why couldn't the link between Byron and me have been like this?

Except, of course it wouldn't have been.

I scowled at myself. Byron wasn't interested in me sexually. He admitted I was his treluria, yes. But his vows came first. I had to respect that. And for him to be able to feel how I stupidly still wanted him even when I knew we could never be...

I pushed the thought aside, climbing to my feet and collecting my clothes. What happened between Byron's magic and mine was a mistake, and one that, with Casimir's help, we'd fix. That was all.

The men made short work of the vine wall, and together, the four of us headed back through the forest. Apprehension hung in the air like a heavy cloak, and when we neared the clearing, voices carried through the trees, just on the edge of hearing.

The giants were arguing.

But so were my men.

"What is it?" Dex asked.

"Something's wrong," Casimir said, hearing the same thing I did.

"Fuck." Dex took off.

I tore after him, my vampire speed more than making up for my shorter stature. We broke past the trees to see a crowd gathered in the distance at the base of the wall. Past the giants, I couldn't see my men, though Roan still stood by the edge of the forest as if to keep anyone from heading our way.

"—and now you're going to fucking do *this*?" Clay's furious voice carried over the crowd.

Alarm joined my dread. My feet sped up as I hurried toward Roan. "What's happened?"

"It's complicated."

"Short version, then," Dex demanded.

Roan's jaw muscles clenched. "Duke Ensid has forbidden us from entering Erenelle."

32
MELISANDRE

A gateway demon ripped Gwyneira away from me, and then she passed beyond the edge of the gateway itself.

In the darkness, I screamed with rage.

I'd had her. I'd been within inches of snuffing her life out forever, and then that *damn* amorphous *thing* had the audacity to intervene.

"We should make him pay, don't you agree, pet?"

Snarling inarticulately, I ignored him. Alaric was only a trick played by the Voidborn—though how the hell he'd managed to be here in this place too, I couldn't imagine. The gateways weren't the empty realms, nor were they my realm. Not precisely, anyway. A middle space just beyond reality but still attached to it, weaving through the gaps between what *was* and what *wasn't*, they should have been beyond the reach of Voidborn trickery.

But the creatures who called this place home certainly weren't beyond the reach of *me*.

Stretching out into the darkness again, I whipped my power through the between-space that formed the energy of a gateway. Tearing into it as if with claws, I didn't stop until something caught, something writhed.

Something screamed.

I grinned. In my grip, the little gateway demon thrashed and squealed like a trapped piglet made only of energy. It wasn't the larger wretch that had saved Gwyneira.

But it would do.

I shredded the shrieking gateway demon into nothing but ephemeral fragments of energy and dust.

"Well, that hardly satisfied," Alaric commented dryly.

An irritated sound escaped me. "Be quiet."

"You didn't even catch the one responsible for thwarting you."

"I did enough." Irritation swelled. I shouldn't be answering him, especially after he just ignored my command to be silent.

The arrogant bastard needed to *fear* me, not receive encouragement for disrespecting me.

He chuckled. "Do not misunderstand, pet. It is impressive that you can use my power to capture a gateway demon with your 'bare hands,' hypothetically speaking. But is that truly the limit of what you want to do? Frighten a few ethereal mice, when you could terrify lions?"

I didn't respond.

His voice held his smile, even if I couldn't see him. "Peer past the edge of the gateway, pet. Let me show you what *could* be yours."

Damn the bastard for being so tempting. But that was the point, really. He would have me bend—even just a little—to his wishes, when in reality he was dead and gone. Nothing but a game played by the surviving Voidborn.

"Unless," Alaric continued casually, "you'd rather hide from your true greatness and cower in your own little realm like Smelly Melly the pig farmer's daughter once cowered from the village girls who terrified her?"

Rage twisted in my gut, hot and biting. How dare he use my past to taunt me?

"Is that who you really are, pet? Smelly Melly... or a queen on her way to becoming a goddess?"

How *dare* the bastard think he could speak to me this way?

I flung my power at the edge of the lingering energy of the gateway. All around me, the space shuddered, cracking and tearing, unable to withstand my might.

Shrieks came from the tiny beings who still hid within the darkness, hoping they were too small for me to notice them. They burned as the blurred space of the gateway splintered and let in light from my world and darkness from the empty realm beyond.

Alarm tried to interrupt me at that, chattering that perhaps this was a mistake, but that was a mere distraction. Those cracks were nothing. A testimony to my strength and nothing else.

The rippling effects of my strike faded, leaving the

energy of the gateway hovering around me like the fraying threads of a rope on the verge of being severed completely. Tendrils of light and sound seeped in behind me from my world, plucking at my awareness like annoying fingers trying to pry me back from the edge of greatness.

But before me lay a profound and eternal darkness. I could see it past the gaps I'd created in the gateway energy, as if the fractured space of the gateway was a cliff overlooking something so much deeper than mere *night*.

Shudders crept through me, unstoppable. My eyes couldn't leave the darkness, the pure and utter emptiness in which nothing so small and fragile as *life* could ever hope to survive. The sheer weight of it, the enormity and inescapability of it, had given rise to countless warnings from the witches and scholars. They all believed that without precautions and protections, it would drive their lesser minds utterly mad.

But I'd been here once. Seen this once, when Gwyneira had escaped being sent here as a sacrifice in my place. Alaric had taunted me that I hadn't survived it unscathed, but I didn't believe him. He was a fiction made by the Voidborn to torment me.

Or... he was now. But back then, he *had* been real. At least before I killed—

"Do you feel it, pet? How it calls to you?"

I growled in irritation. Damn that bastard and his persistent attempts to destabilize me. I wouldn't crack in the face of him *or* this place. "I hear nothing."

"Now, that is a lie."

"What would you have me perceive, you dead, irrelevant bastard?"

"The possibilities."

"What?"

"Look closer."

Fear bubbled at the edge of my mind, and Alaric chuckled, contemptuous, as if he could tell.

Rage took its place, crushing any paltry trace of cowardice as completely as this place wanted to crush me. That bastard sounded closer now. Practically like he stood at my side, but that was madness and I wouldn't succumb to such a thing.

I peered deeper into the darkness as if I was leaning over the edge of a cliff. But I would not fall. I only sought the better vantage point I deserved.

The darkness before me changed. Pinpricks of light glimmered in the distance, glinting like stars. Clouds of myriad colors slowly became visible, dancing between some of the stars while others shone all on their own, surrounded by nothing but darkness. Like a glistening land beyond a fathomless sea, they all lingered on the far side of the darkness, whispering. Waiting.

Alaric's voice came again, thoughtful and quiet, almost as if he was standing by my side and musing upon this sight. "The highest ranks of scholars and witches have only glimpsed what you now see."

I nodded distantly, staring. I'd heard this described. Gleaned details from what little those vain bitches in the Jeweled Coven had mentioned in my presence, years before when they thought me nothing more than a carbon witch barely worthy of being a servant let alone capable of achieving anything great.

But to *see* it…

"Countless realms," Alaric continued. "Realities upon realities, all of them marring the beautiful darkness with their pollution of noise and life and light."

I blinked at the description. "Marring?"

"Well, think on it, pet. What would you call all this power and possibility left to just… *be*?" He made a rude sound. "The energy of those realms *could* be used to serve us—to serve *you*. Yet they continue to simply *exist* as if you don't matter. As if you are *nothing*."

I shuddered. That… Was that a good point?

It rather felt like one.

I leaned closer, ignoring the plucking fingers of my realm as it tried to pull me back from the abyss like an annoying child seeking my attention. From across the emptiness, hints of the whispers that carried on the clouds of energy reached my ears.

Whispers of truth that entered the other realms as myths. Legends.

Fairytales.

"You can hear them, can't you, pet?" He hummed low with awe. "All those worlds where *your* story could be told."

Anticipation shivered through me.

His voice became a murmur, as if he stood at my ear. "You know what you need to do. Let this realm die. Let it burn and light the way to your destiny."

Yes.

Wait... no.

"What?" I straightened, pulling back from the abyss. "I am the rightful ruler of this realm. I am its *queen*. What good does it do me as ash?"

Alaric was silent for a moment, but the strangest awareness of movement prickled at my senses, as if the insufferable bastard paced a thoughtful circle around me.

A vexed noise left me. That wasn't possible, and I wouldn't allow him *or* this place to make me think otherwise.

The light and sound of my realm tugged at me, and this time, I let it draw me back.

If only for now.

"You seek to distract me," I spat at Alaric as the ruins of a city street in Lumilia appeared fully around me once more. Burned buildings lined the road on either side, soot and fading bloodstains smudging the crumbling walls. By contrast, my velvet dress and fur-lined cloak glistened in the thin rays of sunlight that pierced the smoky, overcast sky, their color all the more vibrant for the darkness from which I'd just come.

Slivers of warped air floated around me.

My breath caught. I lifted an arm, staring.

They weren't slivers of warped air. They were... nothing. Hair-thin spaces beyond pure darkness, in which light and substance simply didn't exist. They floated away from me like dandelion seeds on a breeze.

"I don't seek to distract you, pet," Alaric said calmly.

I looked up. In the glass fragments of a broken

window, he smiled, wisps of this same endless darkness dancing around him. "I only seek to help you become what you were always meant to be."

33
GWYNEIRA

"He *what*?" I stared at Roan. "How can he not let you into Erenelle?"

Roan glowered in that way I swore only he could, glaring in the direction of the duke as if he would personally wrap the man in darkness and leave him screaming for all eternity.

And quite frankly, I approved. After how my giants had debated and agonized about returning to their home country, for the duke to *forbid* them...

"He says we're a 'security risk,'" Roan growled with disgust.

"A security..." A breath left me, cold certainty suddenly taking the place of my shock. I'd seen the way Duke Ensid looked at me when my giants took me into the forest. "Or is it that *I* am?"

His glower dimmed into a wince. "Not just you. All of us. Because we're dwarves and you and Casimir are 'outsiders.'"

"Ah, a bigot *and* a nationalist," Casimir commented dryly. "How lovely."

Roan's eyes twitched to him, a look on his face like he both agreed and *hated* agreeing with the vampire, all at the same time.

"No." I shook my head, starting into the crowd of dwarves. "I'm not letting him lock you out after all of this. We all know what's out there hunting for us, and if we're trapped against this wall for hundreds of miles..."

I couldn't finish. The thought of my stepmother sent chills down my spine. She'd come so close to grabbing me in the darkness, and if not for the gateway demons...

I shuddered. She hadn't followed us out of the gateway. I wasn't even sure she'd truly been *in* it, or if she'd done something with magic to only make me think she had been. But either way, that still left those apple trees out here, along with humans and monsters and the gods only knew what else. We'd already taken too much time fixing my hunger and Casimir's. If there was even a chance an answer lay in Erenelle, we needed to take it.

The crowd stared as I strode through it, Casimir and my giants surrounding me. These people had seen my fangs—honestly, it'd been foolish to hope I could hide them when my hunger had been so intense. But from the whispers I heard as I passed, some of these people knew what I was and what that meant.

"—and as the highest ranking Erenlian royal still alive, *I* decide who has the right to enter my lands." The duke's voice rose over the crowd, and as they pulled back, I could see him towering arrogantly over Clay and Lars. The misty wall that shielded Erenelle lay only a few yards beyond them like a gray swath of fog that brought an end to the world.

"But I am telling you, my lord," Ignatius insisted like he'd been arguing this point for some time. "It is *imperative* these people enter Erenelle. If you have ever trusted me for anything, I ask you to please trust me now."

The duke scoffed. "You forget your place, scholar. The sanctity of Erenelle is *my* domain, and I will not have our precious land sullied by the likes of—"

"What is the meaning of this?" Casimir demanded, cutting the bastard off.

Duke Ensid looked down his nose at us all. "Our alliance is at its end, *king*. You and your honorary citizens are free to go."

Clay choked on a scoff. "*Free to go?*"

"Erenelle is our country too." Dex spoke up, his voice tight. I could only imagine what the words cost him, given that he'd run for his life from Erenelle as a child. "Every Erenlian has the right to enter its borders. That's the law."

"It *was* the law, dwarf," Norbert spat, still brushing away dust that clung to his leg from where it'd been trapped in the cavern floor. "That was before the royals made the wall."

Casimir turned to Byron and the twins with a questioning look.

"Turns out the Wall of Erenelle is keyed to the royal family." Clay bit off the words. "It won't open except to someone of their blood. And anyone who tries to get through without a royal paving the way will die."

He jerked his head toward the base of the wall, where

a few pieces of leather and metal rested inside a pile of ash and dust.

Duke Ensid shook his head with a pretense of sorrow so false it was nauseating. "Even my trusted subjects could not restrain their impatience to return home."

Casimir cleared his throat, pulling his focus from the dead giants to Clay and Lars. "But this man is your uncle, is he not? So your blood should also be sufficient to—" At a negating noise from Lars, he cut off.

"Deter is family by marriage, not blood," Lars said. "His sister was one of our biological mother and father's partners."

My heart sank. Giants commonly took multiple mates, unlike in Aneira where only one man and one woman could ordinarily marry. So of course the duke could be family but not blood.

"Indeed." The duke smirked. "And as I am descended of the royal line, it falls to me to decide who may enter our beloved homeland." He lifted his chin, raising his voice to the crowd. "Erenelle will never again be threatened by an invasion of outsiders. Of this, you have my word!"

"I say we just rid ourselves of those outsiders right now." Norbert started toward Byron and the twins.

My heart hit my throat, but Ozias was already moving. Shifting fast, he stepped between my men and the oncoming giant, a snarl ripping from him that made the hair on the back of my neck rise.

"Hold, son."

The duke's command was nonchalant, despite the fact Norbert was easily within range of Ozias's ability to kill him. When Ozias pushed Byron and the twins back, making them retreat back to where we stood, his smile only grew. "These Zeniryans are within their rights to gaze upon the power of our nation, knowing they cannot overcome it. Because that is our truth, isn't it?" He raised his voice to the crowd. "The Wall of Erenelle is my solemn promise of safety, entrusted to me by blood and birthright! By that authority, I keep us safe from criminals and invaders, from usurpers and spies."

My skin crawled as he smiled at me like he was labeling me with that description.

"I spare us the unpleasant business of executions and court proceedings because I understand that above all, the citizens of Erenelle need to feel safe!"

As Byron and the twins reached us, Ozias shifted again, putting himself between me and the duke. Nearby, Dex grabbed Byron's arm.

Byron made a startled sound. "What are you—"

"Stay here." Dex pulled him to the rear of our group. "Do *not* move."

"But—"

At high speed, Dex whispered what Casimir had told us about how the scholar's powers and mine were linked. A gasp left Niko when he overheard.

"Oh, gods." Byron sounded nauseated.

Watching us all, the duke smiled like a cat with a mouse between its paws. "But if anyone should disagree with my decision to protect Erenelle—" he leveled a pointed look on Ignatius, "—they are welcome to stay behind in Aneira with the *honorary* Zeniryans and their king."

Worried murmurs raced through the crowd. Nearby, Clay muttered something about bigoted assholes, and Dex had already turned his attention to scanning the terrain like he was plotting the best way out of here. Shaking his head with disgust, Niko looked at the misty wall like he couldn't believe what the leadership of Erenelle had become.

"You forget," Ignatius said tightly, "you need my blessing on the waters of Syloria to establish the legitimacy of your rule. The magic there has chosen every king and queen for a thousand years. You swore when I agreed to support your position as de facto king in the mines that once we returned to Erenelle, that tradition would be honored."

The duke leaned closer to Ignatius, and my vampire hearing picked out his murmured words. "I think you will find, scholar, that the puddles at Syloria and your pretensions of authority are irrelevant now. I am already *more* than legitimate to these peasants. I freed them, after all. I control the barrier that will let them go home and that will make them feel safe against the scourge of Aneira. I hardly need you or your precious temple at Syloria to tell these commoners I'm their king."

His contemptuous sneer made me sick.

"So your first act upon escaping imprisonment—" Casimir raised his voice just loud enough that the crowd could hear without ever seeming like he was doing it on purpose. "—is to reject the traditions of your people and scorn the magic that declares who is fit to be their ruler? Moreover, you would make an enemy of the very nation that helped free you?" He shook his head, a cautioning look on his face. "You should know I have a *very* long life-span, Duke Ensid. If you go through with this, I will never forget or forgive how you treated my people."

More murmurs passed through the crowd, apprehensive and displeased.

Duke Ensid arched an eyebrow. "I *could* have left you to die in those caves, Your Highness."

"Without our assistance, you would have died right along with us."

"And yet you think that gives you the right to dictate our border policy." The duke scoffed. "I have the blood of the king, my dearly departed cousin—"

"Third cousin," Lars pointed out coldly.

"And thus the wall of our nation will answer to me," the duke continued like he hadn't spoken. "This proves my legitimacy!" He drew himself up taller, looking down on us like we were scum beneath his boots. "Erenelle is done with the cowardly approach of compromise with other nations. We are done letting foreign powers and foreign values influence our decisions. We have seen where that leads. Imprisonment! Torture! All while those who were born *lesser* than us think they can tell us what is right and good and— Wait, what is the dwarf doing?"

I spun.

Niko was walking toward the wall.

"Berinlian preserve us," Ignatius gasped. "Stay back, boy! It will kill you!"

Ignoring him like he couldn't even hear the scholar, Niko lifted a hand.

Terror shot through me. "Niko, stop!"

I lunged after him, shifting fast.

But not fast enough. His palm came to rest on the misty surface.

A deep and resounding *gong* rang out. It reverberated from the wall like a massive bell whose chime was so low, it became more sensation than sound. The gray fog rippled like water, radiating away from his hand.

The fluctuations grew until the surface bucked and roiled like waves on the high sea. Green tendrils of light spread from beneath Niko's palm, twisting through the colorless fog like radiant emerald vines. Around them, the pale blue of the bright winter sky began to peek past the mist.

And then white joined it, closer to the ground. Flecks of brown and green too, here and there.

I gasped. That was the snowy terrain on the other side of the—

Like ice melting beneath the sun, the mist before Niko faded away, creating an opening tall and broad enough for even the largest of giants.

Silence hung over the crowd.

Niko turned. "It told me what to do," he said quietly.

I stared. "How? It—"

"This is a trick!" the duke shouted. "A dwarf lie!"

Niko shrugged. "Or we just don't need royal blood after all." His smile faltered when he saw our stunned expressions. "Right?"

"That... that's not it, boy." Ignatius shook his head. "This means you're descended of Erenlian royalty too."

34
CASIMIR

As a child, I'd watched council meetings from hidden spots in the upper levels of our royal meeting halls. I'd witnessed the shouting matches between all manner of people.

Those paled in comparison to the chaos that broke out at the scholar's words.

"How can the dwarf be royal?" someone in the crowd shouted.

"Does that mean Duke Ensid isn't next in line?" another cried.

"What's the boy's parentage?" a third demanded.

"We can't be ruled by a *dwarf*!"

My royal training was all that held my disgust in check. Bigotry always betrayed its allies, robbing them of the chance to make wise choices and rendering them instead as utter fools. It was blatantly obvious that Duke Ensid and his henchmen had taken more than their fair share of food and left these people to starve. For the gods' sakes, the man looked healthier and more well fed than the *children*. Yet these fools would rather he remain as their leader instead of a young man of honor and compassion, purely because of superficial physical traits.

It was idiocy. They panicked because Niko didn't look like they thought a leader should, as if *that* said more about him than anything.

The duke barely acknowledged them, though. As the questions and protests came from every direction, the man simply stared at Niko and then at Ignatius, his eyes slowly being consumed with rage. "How *dare* you claim this boy could be *royalty*."

Norbert stormed toward Niko. "I'll fucking crush your skull, you pathetic—"

Ruhl and I moved simultaneously to intervene, but there was no need.

"*Enough!*" Ignatius roared.

Even the duke stopped.

Shaking with rage and tension, the old giant drew his threadbare robes around him as if they were as imposing as a judge's cloak. He scanned the crowd, pinning them all with his gaze before turning lastly to the duke. "We have a challenge to your claim on the throne. It will be honored."

Shouts and protests rose all over again.

"*I said enough!*" Magic thrummed through the air, amplifying Ignatius's words. When the shouts quieted, he continued in a calmer voice. "We are less than a day's journey from the temple of Syloria. If Duke Ensid truly is meant to be our king, then let there be no question of it.

The waters there will settle this dispute, as has been our way since the dawn of the Order of Berinlian itself."

I scanned the crowd, reading the body language of each giant I could see. Some were opposed, grumbling of traitors and dwarf tricks. Some were swayed, murmuring their approval for the old ways.

Watching them too, the duke scowled, only to bury the expression quickly. The man was a narcissistic bigot, but he was no fool. He needed the support of the people here if he wished to claim the throne and restart the war with Aneira.

Because I had no doubt he would do *that* as soon as possible. The proud giant had spent years as a prisoner to an enemy nation. He was champing at the bit for payback—likely no matter the cost.

Gods, we had to keep Gwyneira's true identity a secret, if only to protect her from this man rallying his people for retribution.

By my side, Ruhl let out a growl so quiet, only a vampire could have heard. His green eyes flicked over, meeting mine.

I'd wager half my kingdom the shadow wolf was in full agreement with my unspoken thought and would be damned if he let anyone try to harm us.

"We must obey tradition, must we not... your lordship?" Ignatius prompted the duke pointedly.

With meticulous decorum and restraint, the duke nodded. "Of course." He gestured sharply at his bullying allies. "To the temple!"

The giants began walking, passing one by one through the opening in the wall.

I glanced at Niko. He'd retreated from the opening, and he didn't make a sound as the giants passed by. Moreover, he looked as if he'd been hit by a plank, and now he could only stare in shock at everything transpiring before him.

Curses ran through my mind, even as my heart went out to him. Unlike him, I'd grown up knowing I would be the heir to the throne of Zenirya. I imagined Gwyneira's life had been much the same as mine, at least in that regard. But to learn of a potential royal inheritance so suddenly, and in such a dramatic fashion had to be a monumental shock.

But he was surrounded by a combination of outright enemies and those who did not know what to make of him. He could not appear unequal to this situation.

Not if he wanted to survive it.

Nearby, Gwyneira watched him as well, a hint of pity on her face for the dumbstruck nature of his expression. Keeping an eye to the duke and his allies, she walked over to Niko.

I did the same, Ruhl pacing along at my side.

When we came closer, the young man blinked as if surfacing from a daze. His eyes turned to Gwyneira and me with blatant desperation. "What do I do?" he whispered.

The princess put a hand to his arm. "Breathe," she said. "Start there."

A deep lungful of air rushed into Niko's chest, but he still looked shaken.

"You must ground yourself, my friend," I murmured. "Use your other senses to stabilize your emotions.

Silently name what you smell, what you hear. Allow your body to catch up with the moment. These people are stunned as well, but they will look for your stability to gauge whether you can be trusted, so you must present that to them."

Taking another breath, Niko closed his eyes for a moment. "Okay."

"Now," I continued, "I have found that when one does not know what to say, silence is often the best choice. Allow the other party to fill the gap and reveal themselves, as it were. And quite often, they will, whether that is with their fears or with what they desire. This gives you an opportunity to assess your next move more fully."

"Stay quiet to buy time, you mean?" He stared at me, wide-eyed.

"Precisely."

He nodded like I'd thrown him a lifeline to stop him from drowning. "I can do that." His eyes twitched to the duke. "But if he tries to do something to stop there from even *being* a test at these waters Ignatius talked about..."

My respect for Niko grew. Clearly, he saw the potential trouble that lay before us.

I also knew he was right. The duke was not the type of man to allow *chance* to play into his machinations for power. He would try to kill Niko at the first opportunity. Us too, most likely.

My fangs tingled with the urge to descend and resolve this problem. These men mattered to Gwyneira. To me as well.

Erenlian blood would not harm me the way human

blood could, and *removing* that blood from certain individuals would solve a number of our problems.

I exhaled slowly, keeping my vampire nature in check. "Do not worry, my friend. If the duke or his allies try to harm us, they will live to regret it—if only for the brief time it would take to make them cease being a threat entirely."

Gwyneira met my eyes, and my heart swelled to see the cold resolve in my Aneiran beauty's gaze. She was kind and gentle, it was true. A merciful and understanding ruler. But when it came to protecting those she loved, she was as fierce as an Aneiran Huntsman and infinitely more deadly.

And for that and a thousand more reasons, I loved her.

She smiled like perhaps she could see the emotion that had stolen over me, but worry infiltrated her gaze when she glanced toward the duke. Beyond the opening in the wall, he stood amid his group of lackeys, calling out to the Erenlians still waiting to pass through. A beneficent smile was fixed upon his face, with nothing but charity in his bearing.

Given the contrast between his condition and that of his starving people, the behavior was despicable.

"I, um..." Niko started to wring his hands together and then stopped himself, forcing them down to his sides. Exhaling sharply, he straightened a bit, though his skin still held a pallor of shock. "I'm going to go see if anyone needs help."

"Excellent plan," I replied, but past his turned back, I gave Dex a pointed look.

The former soldier was intuitive as well as intelligent. He read my glance immediately. With Ozias at his side, he moved to join Niko when the younger man started toward the crowd.

"Two of us should stay with Niko at all times," Gwyneira murmured, watching them go. "Possibly more. We're going to be in their territory, and the duke has too much to lose. We can't risk even a second where he could get past us to hurt Niko."

I loved that she, too, perceived our need for a strategy to protect the boy. "Agreed."

Ruhl gave a low growl as if voicing his agreement as well.

I glanced at him. There was no longer a question in my mind that he understood us. There never really had been.

But those creatures of the gateway had recognized him, calling his species *nyxvarg,* a name I'd never heard. For that and so many other reasons, my questions about this strange companion of mine only multiplied.

"And," the princess continued, "no matter how this test goes, we need to be ready to get Niko and ourselves the hell out of here."

"We will," I assured her. "I promise you."

She nodded as if hanging onto my words, and silently, I swore I'd do whatever it took to make them be true.

35
NIKO

This was not happening.

Clinging to Casimir and Gwyneira's instructions on how to *not* look like a floundering fool on the verge of drowning, I made myself keep breathing as I walked toward the crowd of giants. The vampire was right, I knew. The Erenlians didn't need to see my doubts or fears. They needed me focused. So I had to keep my thoughts centered and grounded and not panic about the fact all I'd wanted to do was protect my treluria, not inadvertently nominate myself for a *crown*.

Never mind that the wall itself was a *bit* hard to ignore.

Whispered pleas came from the magical barrier. They hadn't stopped once since we left the gateway. But the voices didn't speak with words, exactly. Just strangely distant cries of pain and murmurs of sorrow that somehow communicated what they needed—and what I needed to do.

Except now I realized I might be the only one hearing them.

Which *surely* meant this wasn't actually happening.

I did my best to smile at the giants as I approached, but it didn't seem to help much. They glared or eyed me with suspicion, or sometimes avoided my gaze entirely. Which made sense, really. They didn't trust me. Animals in nature were rarely friendly to anyone they didn't trust. Why should giants—or humans or witches or anyone for that matter—behave differently?

But gods, maybe that meant this really *was* happening.

I swallowed hard and reminded myself *again* to keep breathing. "Is there anything I can do to help?" I asked an Erenlian woman who was struggling to quiet the crying infant in her arms.

She tensed with a soft gasp. Her dark skin was faintly marbled with swirls of tan and golden brown, and her clothes were as threadbare as the blanket she tried to wrap around the baby. Nervously, her amber eyes flicked past me to someone near the wall. "N-no, thank you." She bundled the baby closer. "We're fine."

Retreating quickly, she disappeared into the crowd.

Gods, was she scared of me?

I glanced over my shoulder.

No, not me. Not exactly. More like she was scared of anyone thinking she wasn't loyal to the duke—same as probably every other giant here.

Because near the opening through the wall, Norbert was watching me, Brock at his side. The former smirked and said something to Brock, while the latter just stared at me without the slightest hint of a reaction to Norbert's words.

Both were making it abundantly clear I was under their scrutiny, and so was anyone who spoke to me.

A giant shoved past Ozias, sending him rocking back and nearly colliding with my side. "Move it, dwarves." The giant glared at us as he strode onward, heading for the duke with a swagger in his step like he knew he'd just proven his loyalty.

Ozias growled, but a cautioning noise from Dex kept him still.

I fought to give no sign of how my heart sank. Gods, I knew our options before now hadn't been good, considering Duke Ensid intended to leave us in Aneira. But I'd definitely made things worse.

I wasn't royal. I was a guy who'd grown up as far from *that* as one could get. My home in the forest had been nothing more than a cabin built into a hillside, with moss hanging from the rafters and dirt for a floor. Marnira had decorated with rocks and flowers, and every spring, we'd needed to patch holes in the walls and ceiling to keep mud from getting in. Until Clay came along with his skill for magically crafting clothes, I'd worn baggy homespun shirts and rough leathers I fashioned by hand. Even now, I was more comfortable in a forest than a crowd.

No one could look at me and think I should be nobility, let alone *king*.

"Come on," Dex said as the duke stepped through the opening. "We don't want him out of our sight for long."

And then there was that.

At the heart of the group with Gwyneira at my side, I followed them, trying desperately to find a bright side to keep myself from suffocating under this madness.

But then, maybe I was overreacting. After all, this whole thing really could be some kind of mistake. Maybe some distant ancestor of mine, twenty generations removed, had been royal. Maybe everyone here had a distant ancestor like that too. So if one of my friends had touched the wall instead, *they'd* be the ones standing here because some thimble-full of royal blood still lived in their veins.

The thought was calming.

But it didn't do much for how the giants continued staring at me or murmuring among themselves with distrustful looks on their faces.

At long last, the final few Erenlians made their way through the gap, leaving only us. Keeping me at the center of their line, my friends trailed the giants, protectiveness radiating from them like predators on high alert.

They were behaving like bodyguards—for me and Gwyneira both—and I appreciated it beyond words, at least where she was concerned.

My own safety was nothing compared to protecting her.

The wall whispered louder as I passed through the gap I'd somehow made. So many voices overlapped each other from within its gray fog, it was impossible to understand any words. The murk was at least six feet thick, smooth like glass, not that I dared touch it again. A tingling sensation rushed around my skin in a wave when I stepped through to the other side, the prickling there and then gone.

And then we were in Erenelle.

I looked over my shoulder as the tingling faded. Behind me, the opening in the wall was sealing shut, but the gray murk didn't look the same as it had on the other side. Instead of fog obscuring my view, there was opalescent glass, through which I could see the expanse of Aneira stretching away beneath the blue winter sky.

I stared. It was as if we stood inside a shimmering soap bubble so massive, it could surround the entire nation. The wall stretched away from me on either side as far as my eyes could see, and it rose into the sky higher than birds could fly, until at last it curved back toward the heart of my nation.

"It's beautiful," Gwyneira whispered.

I would have agreed, if not for how it still whispered with far-off cries of pain.

"Can you hear them?" I whispered back.

Her confused look was answer enough.

"Never mind." I ducked my head, hurrying away from the wall.

From the corners of my eyes, I saw the curious looks my friends gave me, but they didn't press for more. Falling in around me like bodyguards again, they turned their attention to the giants and the terrain.

Not that the latter presented much of a threat. Yes, I picked up on a few larger animals here and there—a pack of wolves, some elk, and something that felt like a bobcat quite a distance away in the forest—but none were interested in approaching a group as numerous as ours. Other than that, there were only sleeping plants resting beneath the winter snow and small creatures who might run or might willingly be food.

But no people.

"Anybody else feel like we're walking in a grave-yard?" Clay whispered.

Murmurs of agreement passed among my friends, while up ahead, the larger giants huddled together with pained or apprehensive expressions. Even the duke seemed on edge. Nature had flourished in the years since the wall rose, and I could only assume some strange twist of the spell allowed sunlight, snow, and the wind to penetrate the barrier even if nothing else could. But if anyone had survived the war within our nation's borders, they weren't anywhere my magic could perceive.

"Do you think they're hiding?" Gwyneira asked, her voice low like the silence of this place made her nervous.

Dex glanced at me, an unspoken question in his eyes.

"I'm only picking up on animals," I admitted. "No people."

Grim looks settled on my friends' faces. "Let us know if that changes," was all Dex said.

Ignatius slowed his steps. "I take it you have an affinity for nature?"

I supposed there was little point in hiding it, given what I'd just told my friends. "Yes."

"And your companions?"

The others hesitated, but finally, Dex sighed. "Growth." He twitched his head at us.

"Wood," Roan said.

Ignatius's brow rose. "Possibly some form of demonic fire too, I suspect?" At Roan's shrug, he made a thoughtful sound. "Interesting. Flame and its fuel. Yet did you know that some of our oldest stories speak of wood that will not burn, even when surrounded by a blaze? I've always understood that as a metaphor for life that persists even at the heart of that which should have consumed it. Quite the inspiring image."

When Roan said nothing, he merely smiled and turned to Ozias. "And you?"

"Stone."

"Water," Clay said at the same time Lars spoke up, "Fire."

Ignatius chuckled. "Fate has a sense of humor, doesn't it?" He glanced at Byron. "If I recall, your mentor Dathan told me you had an affinity for... what was it?"

"Energy." Byron's voice was like ice.

"Ah yes, lightning and the power of the sun and so forth."

Byron didn't respond.

"What of your vampiric friends?"

I could feel the tension rise like static on the air.

Casimir gave the scholar a measured smile that could have meant anything. "Legend has it, my family is descended of angels. My gifts incorporate aspects of those powers."

Ignatius made an impressed sound. His eyes went to Gwyneira.

Fear gripped me. What did we say? The giants needed to keep believing she was Zeniryan. But if we mentioned witches, would it make Ignatius question that story?

Gods, I didn't know enough about Zeniryan history to have any idea what the right answer could be.

Gwyneira smiled, and when she spoke, her words were as calm as a windless lake. "My mother was a diamond witch."

"Truly?" His brow rose and fell. "I knew several of their number. They were as honorable as they were powerful."

Her polite smile communicated respectful gratitude and nothing more, like a work of art whose calm I could never hope to match.

"But I don't think I learned your name, dear," Ignatius continued.

Gods, how the tension rose around me. Could the old scholar feel that? The way every single one of us suddenly became like an animal torn between bolting and attacking?

"Snow," Byron said suddenly. "Her name is Snow."

I scrambled to hide my incredulity. Had he honestly just named our treluria after the first thing he saw?

Admittedly, it did sort of fit her.

I damn near scoffed at myself. That hardly mattered. I mean, yes, fine, *Snow* seemed like a good nickname for her if nothing else. But Byron was a brilliant scholar. Surely he, of all people, knew Ignatius would see through the blatant ruse and demand to know her real name.

But the elderly giant only smiled. "How lovely."

Gwyneira said nothing while I tried to remember how to breathe.

"The Nine are balanced between so much of this world," Ignatius continued. "Fire and water. Wood and stone and nature itself. Even the energy of life and magic, and with links to the angelic and demonic realms." He shook his head as if marveling. "In their joined strength, the power of the wielder at your center must be incredible."

Forget breathing. Or blinking. Or knowing what the hell to do.

"Joined strength?" Casimir repeated.

"Wielder?" Clay added, looking like he'd never heard of such a thing.

"Well, yes." Ignatius seemed surprised. "While there have been few studies published concerning the legend of the Nine, the most highly regarded interpretation is indisputable on that point."

"*What* point?" I asked carefully.

Ignatius looked like it was obvious. "That the powers of the Nine are as one, joined to their very core around a central member for the sake of saving the world."

36
BYRON

I'd read hundreds of books in my lifetime.

Apparently, I'd missed one.

"Are you unfamiliar with Hidgerson's *Treatises on Pre-Cumlerian Understandings of the Legend of the Nine*?" Ignatius asked Casimir.

"I will confess," the vampire said carefully, "that particular title was not part of the Zeniryan royal libraries."

Ignatius's brow rose. "But you are the central wielder, yes? As the descendent of angels and as king, you would be the logical choice."

Casimir bobbed his head in a way that could have meant anything. "Logical indeed."

While another giant might have taken the answer at face value, Ignatius had spent too many years around politicians and other dissemblers to be fooled by the response.

Unfortunately.

"And yet I do not hear that as a confirmation." Ignatius's quizzical look included me along with the vampire.

And as ever, I was a coward. I ducked my gaze away, doing my best to hold a neutral expression while I fought to regain my mental footing. But, gods, it wasn't easy. Implications were tumbling down on me faster than an avalanche on an icy slope, bombarding me with more realizations than my mind could handle.

Joined powers. That could mean anything.

But if there was a chance in hell that it meant what happened between me and Gwyneira *wasn't* a catastrophic mistake the likes of which could kill her...

"Surely you have a central member of your joined powers?" Ignatius continued.

Casimir sighed, seeming to realize—like I did—that there wasn't a way around the scholar's question. Lying wouldn't help us, not in the long run.

Telling the truth was the only choice.

"As I said," Casimir admitted, "I am not familiar with that book. Nor, I believe, are any of my companions. We have not intentionally joined our powers."

I noted how carefully he placed the word *intention-ally*—and prayed Ignatius might overlook that.

But please, gods, if what happened between my power and Gwyneira's *wasn't* a mistake...

Hope overwhelmed me, making it hard to concentrate on the conversation. When Dex told me that my life and hers were tied, that my death could mean her end as well...

Horrified didn't come close. To think that I'd been on

the cusp of throwing myself into the gateway to save her, when I would have been damning her instead... it was more than I could bear.

My heart pounding, I cast a glance at the duke. He was too far ahead to hear, but the way he was buried in talks with his henchmen made apprehension join the elation racing through my veins. He likely thought we were plotting his demise, so he was returning the favor by plotting ours. Little did he know we were instead listening to lunacy that might still be the best news imaginable.

Well, best except for the part about needing to save the world.

"—don't you agree?" Casimir turned to me.

I blinked, scrambling to recall his question. "Y-yes."

Gods, let that be the right answer.

Casimir's eyes narrowed slightly, but he buried the reaction with speed as he returned his attention to Ignatius. "So any information you have would be most appreciated."

The scholar stared at us both. "If this is true, then it is even more important that we reach Syloria with all speed. Tell me, what do you know of the threat the world faces? Do you know why you've been called forth now?"

This conversation felt like quicksand, and any misstep could send us plummeting into its depths.

"Thus far," Casimir said carefully, "the primary threat we've faced has been from a species known as the Voidborn."

Ignatius straightened. "Oh dear. So it happened, then."

Did I sound like this when I talked to my friends? Like I was speaking in maddening riddles and half-told stories?

Gwyneira cleared her throat politely. "Forgive me, but I'm unfamiliar with the stories you mentioned or what information you may have regarding the Voidborn and Syloria. Could you please share with me what you know?"

Her voice was decorum itself, and her words were phrased as skillfully as any scholar could have achieved. With that single maneuver, she carefully sidestepped the fact that *none* of us knew what the hell he was talking about and prompted the man to provide exactly the information we needed.

Gods, I loved her.

I stumbled, thrown by the sudden and overwhelming thought. My cheeks burning, I steadied myself, muttering, "Sorry."

Thank Berinlian, no one commented.

"Of course, miss." Ignatius tilted his head in acknowledgment. "My apologies. Given that Zenirya was lost to the Wild Lands so long ago, may I ask: are you familiar with Aneira's war with Erenelle?"

"I am."

Gods, her face didn't even flinch. Nothing in her bearing showed the slightest reaction to the question.

Ignatius nodded thoughtfully. "Excellent. Well, when it began, I admit, our King Archerias and many of his advisors—of which I was one—were quite confident we would win. With our military might, physical strength and size, and our natural magic, we were certain we would be more than a match for Aneira."

His mouth tightened briefly. "Or so we thought. But as the war dragged on and nothing we did could stem the Aneiran tide, it became clear that the force we faced was more than merely human.

"It may come as a shock—or perhaps not, given what you and your king both are—when I tell you that the queen of Aneira is also a vampire. She was one of the first in our world, turned by Voidborn prior to the start of the Witch War."

A small nod was Gwyneira's only reaction, and her voice revealed nothing when she replied, "I've heard this, yes."

She was incredible.

"In that case, perhaps you also know that the Voidborn wish to destroy reality. They have various means of doing this, but one possibility is that they would consume and destroy the ley lines and nexuses of magic throughout a realm. And though the Aneirans themselves have a... shall we say *strange* relationship with magic, King Archerias and his advisors—including me—came to believe that ultimately, the Voidborn would use the queen of Aneira to remove anyone who could protected the nexuses and ley lines, both here and in every other nation. Thus they would destroy our world."

He sighed. "With the king's blessing, we kept this to ourselves, not even sharing it with other scholars in the Order. The king felt that the people of Erenelle faced enough threats without learning their enemy might devour reality itself. But in secret, we worked with the king to devise ways to protect our world."

Regret closed his eyes for a moment. "So many of our plans failed, and in the end, we only had one last. The creation of the Wall of Erenelle—a final, devastating spell to avoid annihilation. We'd already seen the Aneiran Warden Wall. We knew that magic, though we'd never been so desperate or so heartless as to undertake it ourselves. But it was the opinion of the king that the impending doom of our nation left us no choice."

Gwyneira's eyes darted to me, and I could see her questions. "You say *heartless*," she said carefully to Ignatius. "Why heartless?"

"Because the spell to create the wall is a brutal form of magic. Yes, it renders a land untouchable to outside magic. Yes, if one does not possess the key—in our case, the blood of the royal family—it is nearly impenetrable. But to create it requires a special form of fuel. Death on a horrifying scale."

"The crying," Niko whispered.

I gave him a confused look. He never took his wide eyes from Ignatius.

"You hear them?" the scholar asked.

Niko nodded.

"The king refused to take that final step as long as he could. Even when he knew we'd lost, he tried to buy time to come to another solution. But then the Aneirans laid siege to the capital." Ignatius closed his eyes, shaking his head with sorrow. "I wasn't there for the end. Aneirans captured me about a week before the final moments of the war, marching me off to a camp beyond the Aneiran border. But from what other prisoners have told me over the years, it seems the king ordered our people to flee in those last days. Ships of refugees took to the western ocean, seeking safe harbor elsewhere. Others fled via gateways to the farthest reaches of the land."

"Like Dathan," the princess said.

"Last I heard before I was captured, he'd been stationed at the palace itself. Since he still lives, he may well have been one of the final ones out. Because once the magic to create the wall was unleashed..." His brow rose and fell. "Anyone still alive within the borders of Erenelle would have been fuel for the spell."

Suddenly, the silent countryside around us felt infinitely more ominous.

And full of ghosts.

"But the..." Gwyneira started. If one didn't know her, she might have sounded calm. But I could hear her tension. "The Warden Wall. The one around Aneira. It didn't kill everyone. So that must mean she didn't..."

She trailed off, and when Ignatius shook his head, a sickened look crossed her face.

"Aneira had the luxury of time," he said. "And sadly, a lack of concern for life. We had neither of those. But the spell requires lives to be sacrificed, and it's likely the queen accumulated that power by killing those no one would miss."

Gwyneira looked away. "That... that does seem likely, yes."

I ached at the tight pain I could hear suppressed in her voice. From what we'd shared, I had memories of her stepmother. Of Melisandre's cruelty and the way she twisted truths to hide her lies—not that Gwyneira had understood that when she was a child.

But that was the benefit of hindsight. Or sometimes, the curse of it.

"We never knew how many were killed to create the Aneiran wall," Ignatius said. "Only that the queen has trafficked in the death of others for years, starting from the decimation of the Jeweled Coven down to the start of the war and the creation of the so-called Warden Wall. And her masters want more death still. The destruction of the world itself. King Archerias was determined for our people to survive. In the end, the only way to ensure that was sending away as many Erenlians as possible, and then creating the wall to make certain the queen could not reach the nexuses and ley lines within our borders. Thus the king and every giant left in Erenelle, along with all the Aneiran soldiers within our borders, lost their lives."

"They died to save the world," Niko whispered.

Ignatius nodded. "But when the war ended, the queen did not do what we'd expected. Rather than grant the Voidborn entrance into our world immediately, she seemingly resisted them and maintained the pretense of being the 'human' queen of Aneira instead. No attack on the ley lines came, nor any nightmarish apocalypse unleashed by the Voidborn. For all those years I endured in the mines, I never could figure out why."

No one spoke, and gods, *no* one looked at Gwyneira. But we all were aware of the answer.

The queen had been waiting to turn her stepdaughter into a vampire and sacrifice Gwyneira to the Voidborn in her place.

"But," Ignatius finished, "now you all are here, so I take it that has changed."

Dex studied the scholar briefly, evaluations running behind his eyes. "Did you see the fissures on the Aneiran mountainsides when we left the gateway?"

The giant nodded.

"Those fissures are surrounded by apple trees, corrupted ones that bear fruits that steal the will and that force whoever eats them to attack any who do not."

"They turn people into puppets for the queen," Roan added. "They even speak in her voice."

"Berinlian preserve us," Ignatius murmured, taken aback.

"How can the magic of Syloria help?" Casimir asked.

Ignatius drew a breath, regrouping. "Legend says the strength of the Nine is united around a central member, one whose gifts will focus and refine that magic into a weapon against their enemy. I assume that will be the Zeniryan king." He nodded in brief acknowledgement to Casimir.

None of us reacted. But gods, was I the only one who knew to his *bones* that the scholar was wrong? There was only one center for us. There always had been. And even now, she walked at the heart of us all, protected and surrounded by those who'd give their lives for her.

Our treluria.

"Regardless of who the gods and fates choose to be your center," Ignatius said, "as you have not yet joined your powers, the magic of Erenelle can help you with that process. Syloria is one of our most holy sites. The waters there are steeped in the magic of our ley lines and our land."

Dex managed a nod, and Casimir did the same.

The rest of us seemed too poleaxed to speak. Gods knew I was.

"But—" A hint of pleading entered Ignatius's eyes. "—I am well aware *other* matters may interfere with what you need to do." His gaze didn't quite go to the duke, but the implication was clear, and I thanked the gods the man was still distracted.

Admittedly, he seemed distracted by the fact he was plotting with his henchmen, and we should probably do something about that soon, lest he get us all killed.

But at least he wasn't listening to this insane conversation.

"I swear," Ignatius said, "I will do all in my power to help complete the rituals for joining your powers. But I beg you, if the question of royal inheritance should go a certain way, do not abandon us. No matter how strong the wall remains, sooner or later it will not be enough. Not if the entire world falls. Erenelle cannot stand on its own forever... no matter what some may believe."

Worried looks passed between my friends and the vampire king, but Gwyneira showed no such hesitation. "We won't. Erenelle will be free and safe. You have my word."

Underlaid by iron, her voice brooked no compromise.

Ignatius regarded her for a moment. "You remind me of the diamond witches of old. Rufinia the Wise. Eira the Brave."

At her mother's name, Gwyneira tensed slightly. A heartbeat passed before she softly said, "Thank you."

He nodded. "And if all does go well and the Nine prevail—" He turned to me and it was all I could do not to freeze. "—then perhaps together you, I, and any other survivors could restore the Order of Berinlian as well."

I faltered. "T-together? You would ask me to—"

"There are so few of us left who know the old ways and swore our oaths within the Halls of Magic. And your friend tells me you've held true to your vows and observed our traditions all these years. That faith is a testimony to the loyal scholar you've proven yourself to be. If I were to let my old prejudices stand in the way of rebuilding the Order, it would be the height of foolishness, would it not?" He smiled. "In Syloria, we will start over. With hard work and dedication, you and I will see the Order rise again."

My body was numb. Blood rushed in my ears. Acceptance like this was all I'd ever wanted. More than that, even. This was a level of honor and respect I'd never *once* dreamed I would receive.

So why did I feel like I was falling from a great height, all the world spinning and tumbling around me?

Gwyneira's voice came from far away. "That is an incredible honor. The Order means everything to Byron. So what must we do to protect Erenelle and make that a reality?"

Speechless, I turned to her. Did she want that? For me to leave?

She wasn't looking at me.

"The other nexuses in this world must be freed," Ignatius replied. "The ley lines as well."

I wanted to laugh, but it wasn't funny. *Insane*, but not funny.

Gods, did no one else feel the world falling to pieces?

"They all must be purged of the Voidborn poison," he continued, "until you claim even the queen's own power center in Aneira."

"Lumilia," Dex filled in.

Ignatius nodded. "I believe so. Apples have been the symbol of the Aneiran queen for countless years. The capital city reportedly even has a royal apple tree at its heart. That those are the vehicle of her corruption seems rather like a calling card for where she might have started her campaign."

"Or like a cruel joke," Gwyneira murmured bitterly.

"Indeed. Considering that to claim Aneira, she killed the previous queen Eira and blamed the murder on us, the sadism of her choice is most pointed." A shrewd look entered his eyes as he studied Gwyneira. "I must say, you seem rather familiar with that nation."

Panic choked me, but the princess didn't even blink.

"Only compared to some," she replied, as if it was neither here nor there that her carefully chosen words could mean anything.

Gods, she was brilliant.

My mouth opened, teetering on the verge of telling her that. She was incredible. Breathtaking. I'd never once let myself see the truth this clearly, and the stupidity of that oversight stunned me.

"Nevertheless," Ignatius said, "your knowledge is

impressive. Did you also learn from the scholars assigned to Zenirya?"

She smiled at me. "Byron is the first of your Order I've met. It is *his* knowledge that has always impressed me."

Her words were polite. Her expression too. The compliment seemed designed to warm me, but it felt wrong, like a cup of tea gone too cold. Her tone and bearing radiated a benevolent gentility that spoke of friendly respect and nothing more.

The combination was a noose around my throat.

My mouth clamped shut, icy pain strangling me. I was a fool. I couldn't blurt out the truth of what she was and expect that to change anything. Not after I'd spent every waking moment since we met showing her exactly what she'd seen in my memories. A man who was first and foremost a scholar.

A man who, if made to choose between her and his studies, would leave.

"What else do you know about how we might fight the queen and these Voidborn?" Casimir asked, and I flinched, jarred from the realization rolling like an avalanche through my entire being.

Gwyneira was fine with how things stood between us. She had no need of me.

"The queen and the Voidborn won't go easily," Ignatius said, oblivious to my world crumbling. "I suspect you will still need help. Tell me, what allies have you gathered? How might you rejoin them?"

"We are not sure," Dex admitted. "Those who might help us are... scattered."

Ignatius blinked, reevaluating. "Oh dear. I will think on that. But you will have my assistance, regardless." A grim, haunted look flashed over his face. "Too many of our brethren died to save this world for me to refuse to help you now." He gave me a nod as if acknowledging a pain we both shared.

Instead of driving home the truth that was killing my soul.

For years, I feared I might be the only scholar of Berinlian left in the world. Yet in all that time, I'd held true to my vows not merely because of how Ignatius and others had said I would fail, but because I honestly believed what those oaths stood for. I'd sworn my heart and soul to the Order. I'd been willing to give my life for it, without hesitation. And to now have the chance to bring back that beauty and mystery to which each scholar dedicated their lives...

It was overwhelming. All I'd ever wanted.

Except...

Gwyneira smiled at Ignatius, her entire being a picture of nobility. "We would be most grateful for anything you could do to help."

Except I loved her.

And it felt like I'd lost everything.

37
GWYNEIRA

Byron was going to leave.

Every ounce of royal training kept my face still and my bearing straight. I smiled at Ignatius. At Byron too. Nothing in my manner would give anyone the slightest hint of how my heart was breaking.

Especially since I knew it shouldn't be.

"How long will it take to reach Syloria?" I asked Ignatius, my voice held at the pleasant, neutral tone my tutors taught me to use for diplomatic functions.

"Half a day's travel," he answered, "assuming the path has stayed clear."

After which, we'd probably see little of Byron or him.

I tried to ignore the thought. Byron had never offered to stay around forever. He'd never misled me about exactly what he could give. I liked to think we were friends, of course. But friendship didn't need constant proximity. And I knew what Ignatius's offer must mean to him, possibly more than anyone else here. To have the chance to rebuild the Order had to be beyond his wildest dreams. Gods, anyone could see he'd been too dumbstruck to even say yes.

So I would support him. Encourage him like a friend should.

And I'd never let him know how much it would hurt to see him leave.

I took a steadying breath, locking my eyes straight ahead on the rough terrain. A questioning feeling brushed across my mind from Ozias, the careful sensation tinged with concern. I sent back reassurance, praying he'd leave me be.

Because I was fine. Why wouldn't I be? Honestly, it was silly to feel upset when I hadn't actually lost anything. My friend had simply gotten something he'd always wanted. If anything, I should be happy.

A glint of discarded armor caught my eye, the dented chest plate nearly lost beneath the bushes.

Well, maybe not *happy*. Not here where every place I looked felt inhabited by ghosts. But I should be... something.

Clinging to that resolve, I strode onward, determined to exude calm, just as my tutors and my father would have wanted.

Gradually, the curve of the Wall of Erenelle faded into the distance. Silence reigned everywhere we went, with only the rare cries of distant birds and the rustling of small animals in the bushes to challenge its supremacy. Occasionally, stones would peek out from amid the snow or grass, each one too flat and regularly placed to be anything but the remains of a road beneath our feet.

But the remnants of the war were everywhere.

Armor and weapons lay scattered and abandoned, half-buried in dirt and snow. Lonely chimneys stood with no homes left to warm, while crumbling walls overgrown by moss lingered in forests where nothing remained to guard.

"The borders were the worst hit in the war," Dex murmured as we passed the moldering ruins of a home. "Aneira and Erenelle had been at peace for years. No one expected an attack."

"Folks in the capital didn't believe it when they heard," Lars added. "They thought it was some kind of mistake."

I shivered, at a loss for what to say.

"We'll rebuild." Niko's quiet voice made it sound like a certainty. "Or they will." He twitched his chin at the larger giants up ahead. "The living always rebuild somehow."

Byron shifted his shoulders. "Excuse me." Not waiting for anyone to respond, he walked faster, going to join Ignatius ahead.

I exhaled slowly. The task ahead of him was immense. It had to be hard to even fathom how to rebuild the Order, on some level. But I'd find a way to help, either with resources or reparations or the gods knew what. Yes, Aneira was falling apart as well now, thanks to my stepmother. But somehow, I'd do it. The gods knew my people owed the Erenlians for this horror.

And he was my friend. That's what friends should do.

Time slid by, and the terrain became rougher. Outcroppings of stone broke through the snow, gradually growing to enormous cliffs. Dried creek beds carved paths through the landscape, forming canyons overhung by icicles.

The giants followed the trail of a dried-up creek, eschewing the leafless forest that climbed over the sheer cliffs on either side. Far above us, trees clung by their roots to the rocky ledges, casting our path in shadow. Fewer signs of the war surrounded us here, the evidence likely washed away by a river that probably returned in springtime.

But the silence remained, and the feeling of being an intruder in the land of ghosts did too. A cluster of deer stood atop a cliff, staring down at us with no sign of knowing they should be afraid. Beneath a scraggly bush, a fox studied us without fear before spotting Ruhl and then disappearing quickly back into a rotting log.

The stone walls of the chasm drew in closer and closer as the hours went on, making our footsteps echo from cliffs rising several hundred feet high. The ground began to slope upward, until we were scaling the side of what might have once been a waterfall. There was no sign of the river, no hint of any water flow, but the snow still conspired to turn the rocks slippery.

Gripping a large stone for balance, I pulled myself up the slope. Our path seemed tiered in a way that reminded me of massive stairs. Occasionally, rotted stumps of wood stuck out from the rocks, their placement too regular to be natural, hinting that perhaps a banister had bordered this route in the past.

Yet even with that assistance, I couldn't imagine how the giants could have used this as a reasonable access to Syloria—to say nothing of invading Aneirans. Even the larger giants were in danger of slipping, and that was without a waterfall soaking everything.

But then, maybe there was another access route elsewhere. Or maybe the rough path meant soldiers couldn't have come this way.

Ahead, the other giants slowed as they reached the top. Murmurs passed among them of worry and wonder. Their eyes were locked on something beyond the edge of the cliff, and even Byron barely glanced at us when we climbed up to his side.

"Wow," Clay whispered.

Beyond the missing waterfall, the ground turned into a massive basin surrounded by rough cliffs and rocky slopes. Nestled at the far end, an enormous building rested against the side of a mountain. Its gray walls merged into the landscape as if the structure was a natural outcropping of the stone slope. The central part of the structure rose at least a hundred feet high, with marble columns flanking where massive doors once stood. Twin wings of the building stretched away on either side, both of them three giant-sized stories tall with countless remnants of glass glinting in their windows.

But that was not what stole my breath.

Above the structure, stone had been fashioned into the shape of an enormous waterfall tumbling down hundreds of feet from the mountainside onto the temple. Metal tiles glinted along its length, creating an imitation of the shimmer of water, while veins of minerals in the stone did the same.

When the enormous sculpture reached the roof, the artistry continued. The stone and metal spread out and curved, pouring over the edges of the building. In shimmering rivulets, they threaded between the windows and columns, flowing down the walls and pooling at the base, until the temple appeared embraced by the water-like stone.

"Syloria," Ignatius whispered like he'd come home.

I stared in wonder. Secluded as it was, the temple had not gone untouched by damage over the years. Patches of metal tiles seemed to be missing on the massive stone waterfall, creating dull spots in the glimmering cascade where time or the weather had torn them down. Likewise, the wall of one building wing had cracked and crumbled when boulders from a nearby cliff had fallen against them in an avalanche. Some of the windows were broken, letting rain and snow reach whatever lay inside.

But if the war had found Syloria, I could see no sign.

Dumbstruck, I followed the giants toward the temple. The ground of the basin was rough, with little evidence of grass or plant life at the deeper center, though where the terrain sloped upward to the edges of the valley, gnarled trees clung to the earth.

"This isn't right," Niko murmured.

I looked over at him. "What's wrong?"

He blinked like he didn't realize he'd spoken out

loud. "No, sorry. Just... Clay?" He turned to the blond giant. "Is this what I think it is?"

"A lakebed," Clay confirmed, eyeing our surroundings with a wary look. "Or it should be."

Niko nodded like that was what he'd been thinking.

Oh no. "But if we're supposed to be here because of the waters of Syloria..."

"Yup." Clay scuffed his boot on the gravel that should have been at the bottom of a lake. "Where's it gone?"

Dread sank over me. Whatever came of the fact Niko was currently in contention for a crown—gods help us— we'd traveled all this way because Ignatius thought Syloria could help against my stepmother.

But if the magic was gone...

Up ahead, Ignatius scanned our surroundings with a perturbed look. Every so often, he bent to scoop up a rock, turning it over in his hands before setting it back among its brethren. Walking on his own ahead of us, Byron seemed tense as well. His head twitched left and right like he was checking for a threat.

Even the duke was surveying the terrain with suspicion, and occasionally, he'd glance back from where he walked in the lead to give Ignatius or us an accusatory look.

What did he imagine we'd done? Raced ahead to do away with the magical resource he believed would confirm him as king?

The rest of the giants didn't seem to catch onto the problem, though. His henchmen strutted along they were an honorary royal guard. Norbert only smirked at the terrain as if planning to use it for his advantage somehow.

Ozias's hand slipped around my side. Comfort radiated through our connection. "Breathe, little mate," he murmured so softly, most of the others wouldn't hear. "And later, tell me what hurts you so I may destroy it."

I hesitated, but he wouldn't accept a no and I knew it. Nodding, I drew a breath as he asked.

"Good girl," he murmured, making a frisson of heat twist in my insides.

Squeezing me briefly, he gave me a tiny smile and then let me go as we came closer to the temple. Broad marble steps led up to the massive door, and above its arch, the stone was engraved with words in a language that looked like Erenlian but not.

"Knowledge Above All," Byron murmured, a twist of bitter irony in his tone.

"The credo of the Order of Berinlian." Casimir gave him a sympathetic look. "It reads beautifully in the old Erenlian, does it not?"

Blinking, Byron seemed to pull himself from his thoughts. Nodding curtly to Casimir, he followed Ignatius up the steps, never looking back.

My heart ached.

"Scholar," the duke called from the top of the steps. "Are there traps my people should expect within these walls?"

Furrows lined the older giant's brow. "There were once many layers of magic on this place. It saturated the ground and the walls. But now..." He shook his head. "The residual effects have sunk into the earth, obscuring what lies beneath, but I cannot feel any magical traps. And any physical ones would likely have been tripped by animals long ago."

"So the temple might be safe but the earth beneath it could be a giant trap?" Clay commented. "Fantastic."

The duke ignored him, while Norbert just sneered.

"Good enough." Duke Ensid gestured imperiously to his henchmen. "Open the doors."

Dex cast a glance back at us, twitching his head slightly. In silence, my giants retreated down several steps, bringing me and Niko with them.

Putting distance between us and the temple... just in case.

Byron stayed where he was, barely seeming to notice we'd moved at all.

The double doors swung wide, revealing a mix of deep shadows and dim twilight, as if the sun had gained entrance to the temple somewhere up ahead too. Drawing himself up proudly, the duke gestured again, silently ordering his men to precede him through the door.

From the nervous looks that passed between the henchmen, it hadn't escaped their notice they were his test subjects, proving it was safe.

"Move it, you fucking cowards," Norbert spat, hanging back with his father.

"He's one to talk," Clay muttered.

The henchmen inched toward the opening. When they came close, two of those at the rear moved fast, shoving the pair ahead of them through the doorway.

With a startled cry, the giants stumbled into the shadows and twilight.

Nothing happened.

Anxious chuckles left the pair, relief obvious on their faces. "Guess it's good?" one offered with a shrug.

"Move, scum." Norbert strode past them. "We've got a king to crown and a dwarf to handle."

Niko tensed beside me, while I fought back a growl from my vampire side.

"Stay close," Dex murmured. "If anything happens, you know what to do."

His brief glance went to Casimir and Ozias, both of whom nodded, and I frowned. When it came to protecting Niko, I wholeheartedly agreed. But when it came to risking themselves just to remove me from danger...

Gods, these men had the audacity to call *me* stubborn?

Shaking my head at them, I scaled the massive stairs. The larger giants were filing inside and staring around themselves in awe at whatever lay beyond the door.

My steps slowed. Sometimes I felt small around my own giants. I felt smaller still around the larger Erenlians. But as I approached the doorway, I felt like a child's toy come to life, suddenly walking about in a building meant to impress people many times my size.

And impressive it was. My boots scraped on the grit overlaying a white marble floor striated with gold, where the tiles were as big as bed mattresses. My lips parted in wonder at the sculptures towering on either side of the entryway, each of them a hundred feet high at least and depicting wise scholars in robes with books and crys-talline orbs held high in their hands. Marble pillars held up a ceiling so high, it felt like it should reach the gods.

An enormous archway brought the entrance hall to an end, its edges lined by the same symbols as I'd seen on Ignatius's robes. Beyond it, a sprawling central room waited, tiled by the same white-and-gold marble as the entryway. At its center stood a fountain shaped like a stone flower surrounded by a walled basin. Railings lined a gallery level above, though the brass banister was tarnished and sections were broken, left to dangle over the ground floor below. Overhead, segments of the roof were inlaid with thick glass, but some panels were blocked by debris, while others were cracked, affording only a blurry view of the stone waterfall above the temple. Still more had broken entirely, falling to the floor far below and leaving gaping holes where the elements could enter.

And enter they had. Moss grew over the large basin surrounding a fountain at the center of the room. Several trees had started growing between the tiles beneath the biggest breaks in the ceiling. Their roots had cracked and shoved up the marble flooring, like even those massive stones wouldn't stop them from reclaiming this build-ing, piece by piece. Sheltered here from the cold winter outside, they thrived, with red berries clinging to their branches and a lush sheen to their dark green leaves.

"So, uh, Niko," Clay started, eyeing them. "Those aren't... you know, anything like the fucked-up trees in Aneira, right?"

Niko shook his head. "Just normal ones. Azurine

holly trees, I think. They grew in secluded spots in the forest where I grew up too."

"They're beautiful," I said softly, and Niko smiled.

"Well, scholar?" the duke called, surveying the ruins of Syloria with a look like the temple should take care not to fail him. "We are here. Commence the test."

By the fountain at the center of the room, Ignatius didn't respond.

Impatience twisted the duke's expression briefly. *"Scholar?"*

"The waters have run dry." Ignatius turned from the fountain, a pained look on his face. "There is so much decaying magic here, I cannot tell what caused it."

"Excuse your lazy ass?" Norbert demanded. "My father traveled all this way because you insisted these waters had to make him king."

"*Not* what he said, dumbass," Clay muttered, rolling his eyes.

"Then I propose we see this as a sign from the gods," the duke said. "If they wanted the waters of Syloria to speak, they wouldn't have let them dry up. Thus—" My skin crawled at the cruel look he turned on us. "—I say we do away with this stalling and settle things in the manner of the ancients. Trial by combat. Me versus the dwarf."

Protests came from Lars and the rest of my men. Near the front of our group, Roan rolled his shoulders like the demon was fighting to get out, while Ozias growled and made several of the nearest giants back away.

"Like hell," Clay spat. "You come near him, I swear to the gods I'll—"

"Before we decide that's necessary—" Casimir's voice cut through noise, "—I suggest we check the location of the water's source. Perhaps after all these years, there is simply a blockage. Unless you think the gods would choose a ruler who would expect *them* to do all the work?"

I hid my smile—and my relief. Casimir was impressively good at this. Yet again, he'd backed the duke into a corner.

Duke Ensid turned a look on him that could have poisoned an entire village. He didn't respond immediately, but I could see his jaw muscles clench beneath his stone-like skin. His eyes flicked to his people and then to the temple itself, skimming over the walls and then the floor as if evaluating the situation.

He paused, his eyebrow twitching upward ever so slightly.

It made me freeze. My father's tutors had stressed that I should study the faces of nobles to learn all the things they wouldn't say. Giants were harder to read, it was true. But right now, that skill was telling me the duke was... *amused*. Intrigued, too.

That couldn't be good.

After only a heartbeat, he scoffed and buried any trace of that strange reaction. "Zenirya wishes to force the good citizens of Erenelle to labor for the obvious truth, I take it? And so soon after we escaped the Aneirans' labor prison too."

Unbelievable.

When none of us rose to the bait, the duke continued, "Or is this merely a cowardly attempt to forestall the inevitable?"

Casimir kept his expression neutral. "How is seeking to aid you in honoring the traditions of Erenelle *stalling*? Unless it is you who fears the truth once it is done?"

Anger simmered in the duke's eyes, but he didn't respond. He'd walked squarely into that trap too, and he knew it.

"I will see to the water's source, as the Zeniryan suggests," Ignatius said. "We'll start with the underground canals and work our way along from there. But I may need assistance, depending on what the issue is." He turned to Byron. "If you would accompany me?"

Byron nodded. "Of course."

I held my face still, not looking at either of them. There was no reason to be upset. To think about how this was a prelude to when our little group would fall apart.

I was being ridiculous and emotional, and the last thing I needed was to draw attention or make anyone question why I thought something was wrong.

Ozias's concern reached through our connection like a gentle hug anyway.

"Hold on." Norbert kicked aside a chunk of marble. "So we're just gonna let the so-called *Zeniryans* screw up the water and steal the throne from a *true* Erenlian? Fuck that. I'm going too."

A shudder went through Ozias. I could feel him fighting back the urge to attack at the man's bigoted words.

He definitely wasn't alone. Every bit of my royal

training was struggling against the need to claw Norbert's eyes out for how he spoke to my men.

But then the duke cast a sharp glare at his son, and it brought me up short. Duke Ensid looked like he was *seething* at Norbert, yet he didn't say a word.

Casimir regarded the duke for a moment, obviously studying the man's reaction too. But when the duke said nothing, the vampire's brow twitched up slightly. In a meticulous tone, he said, "Surely you trust your own scholar to make certain nothing untoward happens while we're attending to the water's source?"

The duke tugged his attention away from his son. "I trust Erenlians of *worth*, Your Highness. No one else." He glanced at the larger giants. "Brock. Take those five and accompany them." He jerked his chin at several giants nearby.

Norbert smirked at us. Nearby, Brock looked between the duke and the giants he'd indicated, something odd in his eyes.

"Brock?" the duke snapped.

The blond giant nodded once and then turned to go.

"*Guards,*" Niko muttered with contempt.

"What was that, dwarf?" Norbert stalked toward him. "You say something?"

Instantly, Ozias, Roan, and Dex stepped between us and Norbert, never saying a word. Ruhl flowed around them, reforming into a wolf ahead of our group with his teeth bared.

"Aw, are the dwarves worried about their little fake king?" Norbert mocked, but I didn't miss how he came to a stop far shy of Ruhl.

Rage shivered through me all the same. I knew I shouldn't draw attention, but this bastard just *wouldn't* stop.

But before I could speak, Niko stepped past Ozias and Dex. My heart hit my throat.

"We would never ask these Erenlians to do anything we weren't willing to do ourselves." Niko's voice so calm it made me pause. "If seven of your people go with Ignatius, then it's only fair that seven of mine do as well. Or would *you* wish to give rise to rumors that you manipulated the results out of fear that a dwarf would win?"

It took real effort to suppress my smile this time, no matter how worried I was for him. Even my other men seemed taken back, and Clay gave a low whistle like he was impressed.

But the duke didn't react with anger this time. Instead, his lip curled ever so slightly and he looked almost *pleased*.

My skin prickled with apprehension. Why had Niko's response caused *that* reaction?

But a heartbeat later, the duke's satisfied expression vanished behind a supercilious arrogance that even the marble sculptures in the entryway couldn't have rivaled. "Very well. Seven giants and seven dwarves." He made the last word drip with insult. "But you cannot be among them, boy. I would not have dwarf duplicitousness steal my people's chance at being ruled by a *true* king."

Niko paused only a moment. "No one could steal the answer that the magic of Erenelle chooses to give. But I will not let your fears rob my people of their faith. I will stay here."

Gods, did Niko realize how good he was at this?

The duke definitely did. Anger flashed through his eyes again. "Get on with it." He jerked his chin at his people. "Fix the water's flow and let us be rid of this dwarf's false claim."

"We'll see about that." Niko's voice radiated calm assurance. Without waiting for the duke's response, he turned to us, his bearing like he was utterly at peace with how the interaction had gone. But when his back was fully to the duke, the expression cracked, apprehension showing through. "Is that okay?" he whispered. "I didn't mess anything up, did I?"

Clay choked back a small chuckle. "You realize you can't ask us that if you're king, right?"

Niko's eyes widened.

"He's joking," Lars assured the younger man quickly.

"Uh, I kind of wasn't," Clay countered.

"Then you're not helping."

"Enough." Dex cut the brothers off before they could keep arguing. He met Niko's eyes firmly. "Yes, it's a very good strategy."

Gratitude flashed over Niko's face. "Thanks." The worry returned. "Except it *does* leave Gwyneira and me on our own up here."

The others exchanged a wary glance.

"The duke is up to something," Casimir said quietly into the silence. "I cannot determine what, but his face offers hints of his true reactions, and they are... strange, given the circumstances."

"I noticed," I murmured.

Respect showed in Casimir's eyes as he nodded at me.

Lars shifted his weight with discomfort, but his voice was striving for optimism when he said, "The old bastard was always up to something. It's not surprising he's still trying to scheme now, right?" He directed the last to his brother hopefully.

Clay frowned, not taking his eyes off the duke. "Yeah."

"We'll keep an eye out," Dex assured them both. "But Niko's got a point too. If it's just him and Gwyneira up here—"

"Take the wolf instead," Roan cut in. "I'll stay."

Niko's worried look returned. "They're expecting seven of us."

"They're not going to complain if there's one less dwarf," Roan countered. "And the wolf can do plenty of damage if needed." He gave Ruhl a pointed glance, like he was ordering Ruhl to do exactly that.

Ruhl's head tilted ever so slightly, almost as if agreeing.

"Good enough." Dex nodded. "But don't let Niko or Gwyneira out of your sight, understood?"

"Wouldn't dream of it."

Dirt and debris crunched as Ignatius walked closer. "If your people are ready," he said, directing the words at Casimir and Niko alike, like he was being careful to address both the king and the *potential* king in our group. "We can head down into the tunnels that supply the fountain now."

Niko nodded, and the others did as well.

"There used to be sleeping quarters in the east wing," Ignatius continued, pointing. "If you and your friend—" I could hear the slight pause before he called me Niko's friend, and it made me tense. "—would like to find a place to stay down there, you're more than welcome."

"Thank you," Niko said.

"Yes," I added. "Thank you."

Ignatius bowed his head in acknowledgement.

Maybe it was my imagination, but the nod seemed a bit deeper than any he'd given the duke.

Interesting.

"This way." Ignatius started toward the far end of the enormous room.

Dex exhaled slowly. "Watch your backs," he ordered my men quietly.

Trepidation quivered through me as the others murmured agreement and started after Ignatius into the belly of the earth yet again.

Gods, this had to work. They had to stay safe.

The vampire inside me wouldn't let the duke survive if this went otherwise.

38
ROAN

"They'll be okay," Niko murmured to Gwyneira as Casimir and the others disappeared down a side hall after Ignatius.

They damn well better be.

I kept my thoughts to myself as my eyes slid to the duke darkly. The arrogant bastard was watching us, ignoring his son and nephew as they left the room. The rest of his loyal henchmen were around him, and while the looks on their faces were as sadistic as ever, *his* expression was just strangely satisfied.

What the hell was he after?

The demon growled in my mind, echoing my question with a hefty dose of bloodthirsty threat thrown in. If Gwyneira asked for him to return, he was more than happy to oblige—*especially* if it meant he got to remove that bastard from our list of concerns.

"I guess we should head this way, then?" Niko prompted.

I barely restrained a scowl. Clay wasn't wrong. If this went a certain way, then Niko would need to stop *asking* people what to do and start *telling* them instead.

A smirk twisted the duke's lips. The demon growled louder in my mind.

Gritting my teeth, I forced myself to turn away. One problem at a time. First I needed to keep Niko and Gwyneira alive and safe.

Then we could worry about how many of these bastards we might need to kill if our lives decided to go sideways *yet* again.

"Come on." My voice was curt and cold, but it was the best I could do. Jerking my chin at the two of them, I kept my eyes on the duke as we walked away.

Thicker shadows closed in as we left the main chamber behind, and all of them made the demon want to take control, if only because they might hide something to threaten us. There weren't as many holes in the roof here, keeping any trace of light from entering from the outside. But in a number of rooms, the windows were shattered, letting leaves and dirt in to cover everything.

A squeak came from the shadows, and my eyes heated with the demon's flames as my gaze snapped toward the sound. My night vision improved immediately, picking out more shapes in the darkness.

Paralyzed, an opossum stared at me, one pink paw hovering in midair as if it had frozen halfway through a step.

I let out a breath of relief, but inside my head, the

demon still growled. It didn't trust that the harmless, terrified creature wasn't a trap anyway.

Idiot.

Behind me, Niko shooed the poor thing onward, murmuring reassurances. I swore the little creature actually squeaked like it was thanking him for saving it before its paws finally scrambled through the debris and it bolted away.

Figured, though. I was the monster. Niko was emphatically *not*.

Nature knew that.

My stomach twisted, the thought bringing up the anxiety I'd been trying to ignore all day. Last time I saw Niko, it hadn't gone well. *Catastrophic* was probably the better term. All the secrets I'd kept had come home to roost, and while yes, the others had since forgiven me, Niko had been so hurt, he'd left. He'd gotten captured by Aneirans.

And he'd suffered the gods knew what kinds of torture until we could finally rescue him.

I tried to breathe through the worry as I kept walking, the grit of years of accumulated dust and debris crunching beneath my boots. If Niko needed to have it out with me, I'd let him. Hell, I'd do anything he wanted if it'd make this up to him. Gods knew *sorry* wasn't enough for what he'd gone through.

The shadows grew deeper as we left any trace of the main chamber's light behind. The corridor became a winding maze full of dark corners, doors that were rotting from rusted hinges, and crumbling reading nooks. I'd never been in a temple of the Order before, but like everything else built by full-size giants, the proportions of the whole place were wildly too large. Three of me could have strode side-by-side through any of the doorways, and even the books scattered on the floors were so big, I'd need both hands just to lift them. It took me a moment to realize the rooms around us were actually bedchambers and not oddly separated libraries, given that most of the beds in question were moldering piles of cloth and wood lost beneath heaps of books. But when I finally spotted an intact frame and mattress, even those were large enough that several of us could have fit there with Gwyneira easily.

Not that I was thinking about that.

Scowling at myself, I came to a stop halfway down the corridor. This had to be far enough away from the main chamber to give me warning if the duke or his people tried to sneak up on us. Plus, the room to my left was more intact than the others, if only because its roof and windows remained in place and the entry still had a door solidly attached to its hinges. The bed hadn't crumbled, though mold and dust obviously coated its blankets. There was even a candleholder fallen by one leg of an unbroken table with a wax candle lying nearby.

I glanced at Niko. He was frowning at the bed.

Fuck, what now? Yeah, it was moldy but—

Oh.

"Do you think you could do something about that mold?" I asked, my voice so much sharper than I intended because of my nervousness.

Dammit.

But he didn't react like he was offended, merely

nodding and walking into the room. "Give me a second." He extended his hands over the bed and closed his eyes.

A moment passed. The colors of the blankets grew stronger. Shades of brown and green and blue that were muted before now became, if not bright, then at least more noticeable.

Niko exhaled as he lowered his hands. "Done."

I hesitated, torn between my own awkward discomfort and the demon's sudden insistence that *we* needed to do something for Gwyneira too.

Which was dumb.

Also probably accurate.

Niko started to look my way.

Fuck.

I turned and strode back down the corridor, caving to the demon's demands. Anxiety—on my part and the demon's—fueled my muscles as I dragged several of the massive doors around, layering their corners atop each other across the width of the hall.

If anyone came this way, they'd have to step on those, making enough noise that I'd hear them coming.

When I came back down the corridor, Gwyneira and Niko were standing by the doorway, staring.

"Wow," the princess whispered.

"What?" I faltered, glancing behind me.

Oh. Those were huge. That shouldn't have been possible for someone my size.

Shit.

Don't you dare try to take control now, I snarled at the demon as I gestured for Niko and Gwyneira to go back into the room.

The creature didn't respond.

Bastard.

I shut the door behind us all. There was only one entrance, which was good, and the debris in the hallway would serve as a warning if anyone approached from that direction. The windows could still be a problem, though.

Harpies being able to fly and all.

Scowling, I crossed to the window and glared out at the landscape.

"So, Roan..." Niko began.

Fuck.

"I wanted to say I'm sorry."

I froze. That... that hadn't been what I expected.

When I finally managed to make myself turn, I could only stare incredulously at the regretful expression on his face. He... Holy fucking gods, he actually meant that.

"What the hell are you sorry for?" I demanded.

He shrugged. "I shouldn't have lashed out at you." Niko's eyes went back and forth between me and Gwyneira, including her in the statement. "Either of you. It was wrong of me, and I—"

"You had every right to be angry at me," I blurted, too shocked to stop myself from interrupting him. "I lied. Risked her." My head twitched toward Gwyneira though my eyes couldn't leave Niko. "I owe *you* the apology, not the other way around."

He was quiet for a moment. "Still. I'm sorry."

My mouth moved. Gods damn me, how... how was he so *good* all the time? So kind and generous and *nothing* like I could ever—

The demon twitched inside my head, almost like he was smacking me in an effort to pull me out of my thought spiral.

It was a weird feeling.

But damn that creature, it also helped.

"I... I'm sorry, too," I managed to say. "For... Well, like I said. All of it."

Niko let out a breath as if relieved, and he smiled.

Fuck, he really meant it, didn't he? He was sorry and he was okay with me being sorry too.

He glanced at Gwyneira.

"You already apologized to me," she said as if reminding him. "And it's okay. Really."

His smile grew.

I stared, still stunned. When it came to me and my friends, Niko was pretty much the kindest and most forgiving of us. But everything I'd done still felt like it should've been too much for our friendship to survive.

Yet it was also *because* I'd known him all these years that I could see the strain creeping back into his face while I watched him now.

"How are you holding up with all this?" I asked carefully.

Shrugging, Niko looked away. "Fine, I suppose."

I wasn't sure I believed that.

Gwyneira certainly didn't. She reached out, taking his hand. "It's okay if you're not."

Niko sighed. "I just..." A humorless chuckle escaped him. "I guess I'm used to staying in the background, you know? Letting Dex or the twins or you—" he nodded at me, "—take the lead. And now all these people are looking at me like *I'm* the one to lead them and..." He trailed off uncomfortably. "What if I can't?"

Before I could figure out how to respond, he shook his head with a small scoff. "I mean, that's assuming these magical waters even choose me, which they absolutely won't, so it's beside the point anyway." His eyes flicked up to Gwyneira's. "No reason to worry since it's not really going to be an issue, right?"

I glanced at her. Like me, she didn't seem to buy that he was nearly as disbelieving as he was trying to seem. But based on how she stayed silent, she also seemed to agree that pointing that out wouldn't help anything.

Gently, she squeezed his hand with a kind smile.

Relief flickered in his eyes. "I did have a question, though," he continued to me. "Why did you take her away from us?"

I froze all over again, while inside my mind, the demon cringed at the memory of the first time it'd fucked everything up. "It, uh..." Gods, how could I explain this? "It wasn't really me. I wouldn't do that. But the demon is... well, I don't know what, exactly. But it's not me."

Niko gave me a sideways look. "It's not?"

"No."

My voice was emphatic, but then the truth caught up to me. Dammit, I wasn't going to lie to him. Not even by omission. Not anymore.

"I mean... not exactly. We're... Well, like I said. I don't know. But we're not the same." A new thought occurred to me, one that felt almost like a peace offering. "But that's why nature was so strange about me, right? Like you said back in the forest. Because the demon and I are like this."

Niko was quiet for a moment. "Nature told me you had secrets, yes. That there was something odd about you. And it's still saying..." His brow furrowed. "I don't know. *Something*. Like there's almost an echo when I look at you, but... strange."

Gwyneira glanced between us, a worried look on her face. "Do you know what he's talking about?" she asked me.

I shook my head.

"But it's not the demon," Niko continued. "And I don't think it's a threat. I know how that sounds, coming from me. I've said that before and I... Well, anyway, I mean it." He looked at Gwyneira earnestly. "I'd tell you if it did."

The words sounded like a promise, and they made my heart ache.

Fuck, had she asked him about me before? Had he said she could trust me?

Probably.

And then the demon and I proved him wrong.

Niko turned back to me, and I scrambled to focus rather than spiral into self-recriminations again.

"The demon still feels like *you*, though," he said, "at least in a way. Kind of like the two sides of a leaf, you know? Different and sort of distinct, but still the same leaf. Anyway, if there *is* any truth to this *Nine* thing, it wouldn't make much sense for you and the demon to really be two different beings, right? Because that'd technically make us ten and..." He splayed his hands like it was obvious.

Or it meant that I wasn't supposed to be part of their group at all.

I turned away, my stomach twisting into a knot.

"It doesn't mean there's anything wrong with you," Niko added.

I couldn't respond to the obvious attempt at a peace offering. Not when his words had created a whole new angle of awful to this *thing* that the demon and I were.

What if we weren't supposed to be part of Gwyneira's... whatever it was? Because there wasn't a doubt in my mind that Gwyneira was at the heart of this, no matter what Ignatius thought about Casimir and the "center" of the Nine's supposed power.

What if the ninth member of that group was someone else? *Ruhl* or some other fucking thing?

Or just the demon and not me?

There was no stopping the spiral of dread in my thoughts this time. The fucking demon didn't even try. It just sat there in my head, silent, without a single gods-damned hint of what it was thinking.

Bastard.

But did I even want to be part of this *Nine* thing? Did I really believe *I*—or the demon or whatever—was going to play a role in saving the whole fucking world?

Because if we were, then Niko's argument that we weren't really two beings made sense.

And mine didn't.

"Roan?" Gwyneira prompted gently.

I didn't care about saving the world, I realized. Not really. Not like a good person like Niko would.

I wanted to be part of this *Nine* thing because Gwyneira was.

I only cared about saving her.

A dark wave of agreement came from the demon, but it felt strange. Like it came from something else living inside my head... but like an echo of my own too. Like the two of us were closer inside my skin than ever before.

My skin crawled, and internally, I retreated from the sensation. I couldn't trust that. *Wouldn't.* But I understood all the same.

We'd burn the world if that was what it took to protect her.

"Did something I said upset you?" Niko asked.

I shook my head.

The silence stretched.

"It's just..." The words felt they were being pulled from me. "When I was a kid, it did feel like we were more... one, somehow. I admit that. But ever since what I did to my family..." I chafed a hand on my arm like I could rub away the pain of the memory.

"It was easier not to be?" Niko offered.

I glanced back, frowning. The idea was absurd.

But Niko only gave me a kind smile. "Thing is, sometimes in nature, animals get so scared, they sort of disconnect from themselves. I've felt it when a rabbit or deer run from a predator. It's like they're not even *there* anymore. And maybe when what happened to your family... *happened*, the pain and the fear was so much, the you that's *you* and the you that's the demon split just to survive it."

I turned away again. "The demon doesn't..." The words hurt. "It calls me the *broken* one. It doesn't want to be the same as me." Anger coiled hot inside my chest. "And the feeling is mutual."

More silence followed.

I was too damn good at shutting up a room, and it burned. We needed to be getting rest or keeping watch or doing anything besides standing here talking about my fucked-up life.

Footsteps came from behind me. "You're not broken." Gwyneira rested her hand on my arm. "Maybe what happened to you made things go the way Niko says, or maybe the explanation for you two is something else entirely. But you're still not *broken*." From the corner of my eye, I saw her smile. "I mean, you heard Ignatius, right? The wood that wouldn't burn. That's you. And that's strength and power, not brokenness." Her fingers tightened on my arm, comfort and encouragement practically radiating from her. "And even if you feel differently, it doesn't change the fact you deserve to be treated with respect and worth."

The burning feeling changed because her words were so kind and good that they hurt. "I... I don't want to lose myself," I whispered. "Lose the man who loves you to a monster who—" My eyes squeezed shut, and I shook my head. "Who can't even be bothered to understand the most *basic* ideas of consent or willingness or..."

"What do you mean?" She sounded confused.

"Back in the forest. Byron's spell. When—" I glanced

at Niko, suddenly feeling awkward. "When you and the others and the demon..." I bobbed my head indicatively rather than say more.

Her confusion cleared. "Oh. You mean when the demon and I almost..."

Now *she* was the one faltering like she was embarrassed.

And fuck if Niko's eyes weren't fastened on us both.

"Yeah." My voice was terse. "I was there. In... in the demon's head, I mean. I could see you were overcome by that magic. But the demon..." I scoffed, contempt and disgust rising in me again for that damn creature. "I fought him, but even then, the bastard wouldn't relinquish control enough for me to truly stop him." I shook my head. "He can't be trusted, which means *I* can't be. Not when it comes to..."

I jerked my head toward the bed rather than state out loud how irrevocably the demon had messed everything up when she'd laid there before it, legs spread and her skin coated in his cum. All he'd seen was her wet, luscious pussy and not the worry and fear flickering through her eyes, growing stronger with every passing second.

She hadn't been able to stop herself, even if it was clear she'd wanted to, so he damn well should have.

And now thanks to him, neither of us could have her.

The demon twisted uncomfortably beneath my skin, hating that. Wanting to change it.

I gritted my teeth, fighting him back. Outside of life-or-death situations, I wasn't giving him control again. Not if I could fucking help it.

Gwyneira bit her lip briefly. "I *did* want him. The demon wasn't wrong about that."

"You weren't sure, though. I could see that. The demon could smell it in your scent. But that magic was driving you, so you couldn't stop. And since that's damn well not the same thing as being willing, he should have controlled himself and—"

"What if the magic was driving him too? I mean, we all were—" she searched for a word,"—*ravenous*. I couldn't think beyond that. I'm pretty certain Casimir and the twins couldn't either. So maybe the demon was overcome, same as we all were. But he also *did* stop, so..." She shrugged.

My mouth moved, but I wasn't sure what to say.

And it didn't help that inside, the demon was perking up, hope rising at the possibility Gwyneira presented.

That didn't let him off the hook, though.

"Roan, I wasn't worried because I didn't want to be with the demon. I did. I... I *do*. I just worried whether he would be willing to share me with the others. That's all. Because when I first met that side of you—or that other creature within you, or *whatever* he is—he sounded like he planned on keeping me all to himself. And I don't want that. I want all of you."

I floundered, speechless. I wanted her too. Gods, I did. Sharing her with the others didn't bother me a bit.

That wasn't the point.

"But..." She took a step closer. "Maybe I was wrong to worry about the demon this time. Maybe I jumped to a conclusion based on my own fears from the past, when actually, he *would* be willing to share. It wasn't a particularly fair moment for me to have judged him in, since *none* of us were fully under our own control. So maybe..." Her hand took my cheek. "The demon deserves a second chance."

My eyes twitched toward her, but I couldn't hold her gaze for long. Didn't she understand what she was asking? I couldn't *trust* the demon. Not with her. Okay, so maybe the magic had overcome him too. Maybe he couldn't have stopped himself any more than the rest of them. But *I'd* still seen the issue and he wouldn't let me protect her from it.

From him.

He was the problem. He *always* was.

But arguing that—with her *or* him—suddenly felt exhausting.

"You two should get rest." I turned back to the window, trying to ignore how cold my skin felt when her soft, barely warm palm fell away from my cheek.

Silence followed, and then—thank the gods even though they hated me—Niko made a noise of agreement. "Probably, yeah. Since it's been... Gods, what day is it anyway? How long was I gone?"

"Too long," I said shortly. "So go on. I'll keep watch."

A moment passed, and then the two of them finally turned away. From the corner of my eye, I saw Gwyneira's coat hit the floor as she got undressed for bed.

I locked my attention on the terrain.

Inside my head, the demon was watching me. I could feel its thoughts racing in the darkest depths of my mind, but I couldn't hope to tell what it was thinking. It'd gone totally still.

Blankets rustled. A sigh left Gwyneira that made my cock hard and my heart ache.

I gritted my teeth. I wanted her. Gods, I wanted her.

Try again, said the demon suddenly, as clear as day in my head.

Fuck off, I thought back, shoving it away.

Try again. The demon pressed at my skin, urging me to turn around. To join them even though I knew it'd go so gods-damned wrong. *Trust me.*

Never. I squeezed my eyes shut, my head throbbing. *Gods, I hate you.*

The demon went quiet for a moment, his presence sinking back toward the dark. *I know.*

Alarm skittered through me because, as impossible as it seemed, there was a note in his voice that sounded like actual understanding.

His attention returned to me. *But...* I felt him smile in my mind, fangs and all. *What if we made a deal?*

39
GWYNEIRA

Guilt gnawed at me for leaving Roan on his own at the window.

But I also had no illusions about how willing he'd be to sleep while *I* stayed up.

Leaving my outer layer of winter clothes on a chair nearby, I climbed into the bed. Niko quickly did the same, and a grateful sigh left me when he immediately pulled me closer beneath the covers.

"Gods, I missed you," he murmured, wrapping his arms around me. "I clung every day to the faith I'd see you again, but to have you here..."

I nestled against his warm chest, holding him tight. "I missed you too."

His hands slid down my sides, and my breath hitched.

"Sorry," he said, starting to take his hands away.

I made a negating noise, and he paused. For a long moment, he didn't move.

"That wasn't the only thing I hung onto," he murmured. "I promised myself I would make it up to you. How I treated you. How I left things between us. I swore I'd show you what you mean to me."

Drawing me onto him, he nestled my core against the hard length between his legs.

Need pooled low in my belly. "Is that so?"

"Mm-hmm." His hands cupped my ass, pulling me tighter against his cock, but then his eyes slipped to where Roan stood by the window, his back to us and his posture rigid.

Hesitation flashed over Niko's face, and I closed my eyes regretfully. I was wet for my sweet giant already, but it wasn't fair to do this with Roan unable—or unwilling—to join in.

"Between the two of us," Niko asked him, "do you think we could help her sleep and keep her safe at the same time?"

Roan's dark gaze slid to us. "Take her together, you mean?" The demon's hungry growl lurked in his voice.

Niko nodded.

He didn't move, holding himself with tight control, but hunger and longing filled his eyes.

"Give both parts of you another chance, Roan," I urged. "Please."

A tense shudder went through him. "I can't risk hurting you. He wants to try, but if he breaks out and I can't stop him—"

"He won't," I said, putting every ounce of insistence and faith I could into my voice. Meeting his eyes, I tried to speak to the demon within him. "Will you?"

A hint of firelight glinted in his dark gaze. The demon heard me.

But Roan just shuddered. "I can't." His voice became quiet. "I won't risk you."

A breath left me, my heart aching for him. Pushing the blankets away, I crossed to his side. "Give him a chance to prove you can stay in control with me—and that he can too. And if you're right and it turns out he can't be trusted, then..." It made my stomach twist, but I had no doubt Roan needed to hear the words. "Then we can do it your way. Stay apart. Okay?"

The fire flared higher in his gaze, bringing a look of fear with it this time, before Roan squeezed his eyes shut.

I watched him, waiting without breathing to see what he'd decide.

Refusal flashed over his face, and my heart sank.

But then it faded into grim resolve. "One more chance," he muttered.

He definitely wasn't talking to us.

His eyes opened, going to Niko. "But if there is the *slightest* hint that the demon is about to hurt her *or* you, I want your word you'll use every ounce of your power to end us."

I took a step back, shocked. "Roan."

He didn't even look at me. "Your word, Niko. I don't care what it takes. Turn us into a tree. Drop this building on our head. It doesn't matter. If..." He scowled like he was swearing inside. "If I'm even going to *consider* this, then I need you to promise me. Please."

Niko nodded solemnly. "You have my word."

Gratitude crossed Roan's face. He took a breath, seeming to regroup.

I stared at them both. "I-I don't want you to put your *life* on the line here."

"That's not what this is," Niko said.

At my incredulous look, my sweet giant shrugged. "He needs this to feel safe being with you." He looked back at Roan, respect in his eyes. "And he'd rather die than hurt you."

I was speechless.

"That said," Niko continued, still watching Roan, "*whatever* the demon might be, I'm guessing it wants to meet our beautiful treluria's needs, yes?"

"It... He..." Clearing his throat, Roan gave a careful nod. "Yes."

"And her needs include being given as many screaming orgasms as she can withstand, correct?"

Roan's dark eyes were wide and unblinking. He nodded again.

"But—" Niko grinned. "—she won't get as many of those as she deserves unless *all* of us are safe and alive, don't you agree?"

Another nod. "I do." A tight shudder. "W-we do."

A tiny breath left me. I loved Niko. He was actually reasoning with the demon on Roan's behalf.

Maybe even proving—gods help me—that no one needed to *die* for the sake of sex.

"So then, we probably shouldn't keep her waiting, should we? Considering our beautiful princess will probably need..." Niko's gaze slid back to me, his brow rising in implicit question of whether I was okay with this too.

"What would you say, treluria? At least a dozen orgasms before you're ready for sleep?"

My core twisted, hot and needy, and I sent a prayer up to the gods that Roan's condition of *death* would never need to be tested. "I'd like that."

Niko's smile grew. "Guess we better get started then." Extending a hand to me, he beckoned me back to the bed and then gave an encouraging look to Roan. "Right?"

A hint of a low, hungry growl left Roan. With a short nod, he urged me back toward Niko.

I went, climbing across the expansive mattress and beneath blankets sized for a giant.

But when I looked back, Roan wasn't following. His eyes darted to the window, checking briefly, and then to the closed door.

Grunting something inarticulate, he strode over to a massive wardrobe in one corner of the room. Made of solid wood and built like it could house a small family, the thing looked like it weighed a ton.

Shoving it across the gritty tile, Roan moved the entire thing to block the window.

A breath left me, and Niko whispered a soft curse. Clearly I wasn't the only one who thought that—like the massive doors in the hallway—moving that thing single-handedly should have been impossible.

At least... for someone besides the demon.

Maybe there really was something to Niko's theory about those two.

Turning back sharply, Roan pinned me with a hot, hungry look. Slowly, he stalked toward me. I suddenly felt like prey trapped in the gaze of a predator. In spite of myself, I scooted back on the mattress, instinct telling me to flee.

While desire whispered with hope that he'd catch me.

"Uh-uh," Niko cautioned, grinning.

Something brushed my wrist, tearing my gaze from the men.

Vines were growing from cracks in the walls, making their way across the floor and up onto the bed. One caressed my wrist, the green tendril thickening by the second. Another twisted across the bed, heading for my other arm, while two more pushed below the blankets on their way to my ankles.

"She likes being tied up?" Roan's voice was tight and dark with desire.

Niko made a noise of confirmation. "She even liked me fucking her with these." His eyebrow rose. "Didn't you?"

I nodded, short and jerky. "Yes."

A ragged, hungry sound left Roan.

Niko grinned. "Well, treluria. I think my friend wants to see that."

The vines convulsed on the bed, sending the enormous blankets cascading to the floor. Paying them no mind, Niko reached over, lifting my shirt away. My pants and underthings followed, leaving me naked on the bed.

Cold air prickled at my exposed breasts and licked at my bare legs. Need pooled between my thighs, soaking the sheets while Roan's eyes lingered on my core.

"So wet already." His voice was thick with the

demon's growl, but not a single trace of gray ghosted across his skin. The demon was letting him stay in control.

But that glint in his eyes told me it was *definitely* enjoying this too.

Quickly, the vines returned, wrapping my ankles and wrists. Gently, the plants pulled me to the mattress and tugged my legs apart, putting me on display beneath both men's watchful gazes.

Niko made a thoughtful noise. More vines slid over the sides of the bed, winding their way toward me. They slipped along my sides, making me wriggle from how their touch tickled. But before I could tell Niko to stop, they continued over my middle and split, sliding in two directions simultaneously.

Oh, was he doing what I *thought* he was—

Tendrils wrapped my nipples. Others threaded between my folds, twisting around my clit and teasing at my core.

Gods help me, I couldn't breathe. Every nerve felt balanced on a knife's edge, just waiting for what Niko wanted to do to me.

But my sweet giant was as generous as ever—or as darkly kinky. Turning to Roan with a wicked edge to his smile, he said, "You take the lead, friend. Tell me what you want done to her, and we'll see how long it takes to have her screaming."

Holy gods.

A shudder rolled through Roan's tight muscles. His dark eyes took on a sharp, hungry glint, savage with its desire. "Fuck her but don't let go of her clit or nipples while you do."

Niko made an appreciative noise.

I gasped as the vines between my legs twisted together, getting thicker, and then pushed into me. The uneven surface rubbed at my inner walls deliciously. Over and over, Niko's magic drew the vines out and then thrust them back in again. Around my nipples and clit, the tinier vines tightened and loosened rhythmically, sending pulses of pleasure radiating through my body.

"Just like that." I could hear the smile in Roan's voice, but my eyes were locked on the distant ceiling, my awareness scattered and overwhelmed by what Niko's devilish vines were doing to me. "Now…"

From the corner of my eye, I saw him motion, but I couldn't make out what he wanted.

More vines suddenly pushed into my rear entrance.

Oh gods.

I came all at once. Hard. My body convulsed in the grip of the vines, my eyes squeezing shut from the intensity of the orgasm ripping through me.

Panting, I returned to awareness of the room.

Niko and Roan were grinning at me.

"Beautiful," Niko said.

Roan made a noise of agreement, but that sharp, incisive look hadn't left his gaze. "Can you bring her upright?"

My lips parted in surprise, but the younger man simply nodded.

Vines coursed around my torso and lifted me from the bed like I was weightless. The ones around my wrists drew my arms upward, until my hands were clasped above my head. Others wrapped around my thighs, supporting me and keeping the strain from being too great on any one part of my body.

It was exhilarating. Vulnerable and yet safe, all at the same time. Instinctively, I arched my back, my breasts already at Niko's eye level.

He smiled. "You doing okay, treluria?"

My body thrumming from the orgasm and anticipation alike, I nodded.

Roan stepped closer to the edge of the bed. "Someday, I want to spank you for how you torment me, treluria. I want to watch your soft flesh shake and turn pink under my hands."

Holy...

My pussy clenched, empty and needy and so *very* turned on.

His nostrils flared like he could smell what he was doing to me. His lips pulled back in a smile. "But tonight, I want to taste you."

Immediately, the vines lifted me higher, while others pulled my legs apart, positioning me for him.

Bending closer, he drew his tongue along my slit. I shuddered, my nerves tingling.

"Mm..." Roan smiled up at me. "Do you know how good you taste? How there's nothing in the world that compares?" He took my thighs, pulling me to him as he delved back between my folds.

I gasped, my back arching again as his fingers slipped into me, stroking me from the inside while his mouth never stopped.

Watching us, Niko grinned, his vines continuing to play over my nipples, adding to the rush of sensation. "You're incredible, my beautiful treluria."

Roan hummed his agreement against my clit, sending thrills of vibration through me.

It was so much. *Too* much. I cried out as I came again.

Both men paused, but only long enough for me to come back down from the rush of my orgasm before they started licking and teasing at me again. I gasped, inarticulate in my incredulity.

Niko only smiled. "I *did* say a dozen orgasms minimum, didn't I? Or do you think you're ready to sleep yet?"

Gods, even the sweetest of my giants could be so wicked.

But words were difficult to find when Roan hadn't ceased licking me this entire time. "N-no. I mean, yes. I mean, don't—" Niko's vines began twisting across the sensitive bundle of nerves at the base of my spine. "Don't stop. Please don't—"

Niko's smile grew. "I promise, treluria. We definitely won't."

Gods, what had I gotten myself into?

I barely had time to wonder before his devilish vines sped up their strokes across my skin and nipples. Combined with Roan's fingers working inside me in tandem with his tongue, I stood no chance.

Another orgasm shook me.

Followed moments later by another.

Holy gods...

I was limp in the vines by the time Roan finally

stepped away from me and wiped his mouth with the back of his hand. I'd lost count of the orgasms these two had given me, the surges of pleasure chaining one into the other until I was awash in a blur of blissful peace.

"On the bed," Roan said shortly, stripping out of his clothes while his eyes remained fastened on me with intense hunger.

Niko nodded.

Gods, they weren't done with me yet.

Roan climbed onto the mattress, catching me as the vines carefully lowered me. While the plants slipped away from my body and disappeared over the edge of the bed, he drew me on top of him.

"You still up for more, beloved?" he asked quietly, his fingers drifting up and down my sides, waking my body again.

Blearily, I nodded. His hands felt so good on my skin, and his cock was pressed against my hip, hard and warm. "I want you in me," I whispered.

"That's our girl." He smiled and glanced past me at Niko.

I looked over my shoulder to see Niko already stripped down and climbing onto the mattress. Taking my hips, he pulled me up onto my knees, guiding his cock between my legs and then sliding back and forth, getting wet with my slick.

"You just relax, beautiful treluria. Let us hold onto you while we give you enough pleasure to let you sleep so well."

Gods, I was pretty certain I was there already. But I wasn't going to pass up having them inside me.

Or giving them pleasure too.

I rocked my hips as Niko positioned himself by my rear entrance.

"That's it." Roan guided me closer. The tip of his cock eased into my wet center. "We've got you."

I looked back down at him as he slid inside my body, his cock stretching my inner walls even after all the orgasms he and Niko gave me. There was a trace of firelight at the heart of his dark eyes, but that was all. Just a hint that the demon was still here, but nothing to say he was taking over.

Whatever agreement he and Roan had come to, the demon was keeping it.

Niko began easing into my back opening, and my eyes went wide.

"Breathe, beloved." Roan rocked me gently as Niko slid farther into me with a groan.

I gasped a breath down. "I'm just so... *full*."

Niko gripped my hips tighter, pulling out a bit and then pushing back into me with delectable slowness. "That's right, treluria. And you're about to be filled by our cum too."

A shudder of desire rolled through me.

"You look so beautiful like this." Roan thrust up into me. "Like you're exactly where you should be."

Niko made a noise of agreement. "Riding our cocks."

"I..." Gods, I couldn't find words. But whatever I would have said turned into a moan anyway as Roan took Niko's place holding my hips, letting Niko's hands steal up my sides to pinch my tender nipples.

Stronger shudders began coursing through my body.

"That's it." Niko's voice was tense with his own building pleasure. "Good girl."

Roan nodded, but his face was tight with the effort of not coming yet. "You're taking us so well."

A growl escaped him.

My breath caught, but he shook his head fast. "Not... not taking over. Helping." His fingers dug into my hips. "Helping me keep going for you."

Wide-eyed, I stared at him. But my shock couldn't last.

Not with how hard he was thrusting into my body. How he and Niko *both* were.

Gasping cries left me. My hands fisted the blankets on either side of Roan. I couldn't take much more of this, but I wanted my men to come too. Needed to feel them as they—

Niko's fingers slid down my body to circle my clit.

My release unleashed in an instant, exploding through my body and stealing everything in a surge of blinding bliss.

Niko and Roan were right. This felt like exactly where I was supposed to be.

As I slowly came back to my senses, I could feel their cocks twitching inside me, their hot cum filling me and dripping down my thighs.

"Fuck." Roan drew a few ragged breaths. "You're so perfect."

Niko kissed my shoulder, making a wordless sound of agreement. Carefully, he eased from inside me while Roan did the same.

I sank down to nestle against Roan's side. Niko

reached down, taking the blankets when his vines lifted them from the ground. Drawing them over us, he spooned behind me and wrapped one arm around my side.

"Are you okay?" I asked Roan. "The demon didn't...?"

I let the question hang open-ended.

Roan shook his head. "He... he didn't try to take over." His gaze dropped to the side. "He watched, though. If that's o—"

"That's fine." I bit my lip. "Is he okay with sharing, then?"

"Maybe." Roan hesitated. "Yes. He... he says yes."

My mouth moved, but I didn't know how to respond. For Roan to even admit that meant he was trusting the demon on some level to be speaking the truth.

That was definitely progress.

"In that case," Niko said. "Maybe next time, he could join in? That is, if you wish, treluria."

I twisted around to look at him, shocked. "You'd be okay with that?"

Niko shrugged a shoulder. "Forgiveness has to start somewhere, and I can't think of a better place than buried in your beautiful pussy. Besides, the demon is a part of Roan. He deserves to have *all* of him be able to show you how much he loves you, right?"

My heart melted. Reaching awkwardly over my shoulder, I put a hand to Niko's cheek. "I love you." I looked back at Roan. "Both of you. *All* of you."

Niko tucked me tighter against him. "We love you too, treluria."

Roan kissed my forehead. "Always."

I lay my head on Roan's chest, sighing as sleep began to tug me down. "You were right. I did need all those orgasms."

Niko chuckled. "Better get your rest then. Your other men will be back soon, and you know they're going to want to give you more."

I smiled as I closed my eyes, but a tinge of worry wormed its way into my chest all the same.

Inside, I stretched out, feeling for Ozias. My mate had withdrawn as far as he could from my awareness when Niko and Roan started with me—likely because, surrounded by enemies, he needed every bit of concentration he possessed. I'd felt almost nothing from him this entire time.

But even now, Ozias didn't draw closer, and he didn't send reassurance that he was okay either. My questing mental touch met with only a wary sense of vague warning—maybe to stay put, maybe to run.

Pushing away from the bed, I stared in Ozias's direction, questions rising inside.

No answers came.

"Princess?" Niko sat up beside me.

"What is it?" Roan asked, an edge to his voice.

I shook my head. "Something's wrong."

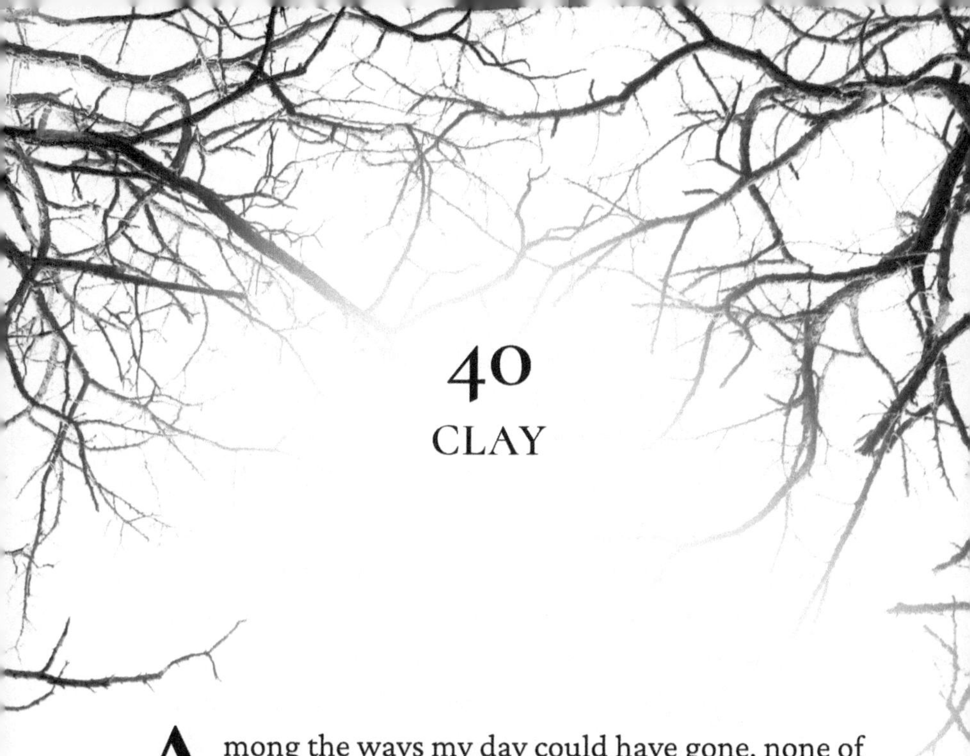

40
CLAY

Among the ways my day could have gone, none of this shit would've made the list.

Hell, none of it had even been in consideration.

Niko was king. *Possibly* king. Of fucking Erenelle, no less, that piece of shit nation that'd kicked out half my friends and tried to kill most of the others.

And now we were trooping through magic-ridden tunnels *in* Erenelle with relatives I'd really hoped were deader than Erenelle itself, all to decide whether my friend or our good ol' uncle Deter would get the throne.

"This is insane," my brother muttered under his breath.

I scoffed in agreement as I side-stepped a fallen boulder. "Hi-ho, hi-ho, down into the earth with a bunch of assholes we go."

He gave me a tired look. "That's not helping."

I returned the glare with a wry expression. "It's true, though."

His tired look deepened, but he didn't respond.

Up ahead, Brock's head turned like he overheard us, though of course the bastard didn't meet our eyes.

But then, that guy always had been a fucking coward. Nice to know some things hadn't changed.

We continued deeper into the tunnel, the seven of us sticking close together in case the bastards tried anything. I wouldn't put it past them, now that they'd had their shiny little bracelets taken off. Dex and the others were equally on edge, though a grin hovered around Casimir's lips, almost as if—after hours of playing politics with these bastards—he was looking forward to the giants trying to make a move.

Damn, I'd love to see that, at least where a few of these giants were concerned. I mean, shit. Giant blood was one of the best ways to keep a vampire from going insane, and here we were surrounded by a bunch who I wouldn't mind inviting to leave this life—especially considering they'd spent years doing their best to make sure Lars and I left it first.

So hey, that worked out fine.

"Your expression is damn near macabre, brother," Lars murmured under his breath.

I didn't take my attention from Brock and Norbert. "Oh, is it now?"

Lars sighed. "Play nice. For Niko's sake, okay?"

My eyes cut to him, but I knew he had a point.

Gods, *king*. Possibly king. Never mind that, honestly, he'd make a great one. He was a dwarf. A dwarf whose treluria was the fucking rightful queen of Aneira, of all things. Everyone and their damned dog would be trying to kill both of them for the rest of their lives, just for that alone.

I didn't think I'd been this angry in years.

Gwyneira and Niko were the fucking best of us. The idea that *they* would be the ones with the target on their backs... all because giants and humans were total assholes about anything that didn't fit in their little boxes...

Gods, *pure fucking rage* didn't come close to describing how that made me feel.

The floor beneath us began to descend at a sharper angle, and I scowled, working to keep from slipping on the steep declination.

This was the problem with giant-made tunnels. To them, this slope was nothing. To us, it made it all the more likely we'd fall on our asses.

To say nothing of the way the place was crumbling all around us.

Scowling, I veered around another fallen boulder, eyeing the crevice in the ceiling where it used to live. Whatever had happened to the lake above us, the magic in the earth beneath Syloria was like soggy, swirled mud caked on the stone. The gods only knew what the original purpose had been for all these spells. Now they were just a mess.

But setting aside the trouble-waiting-to-happen *that* was, I could admit the tunnel itself was impressive. Giants were something of architectural geniuses when it came to the manipulation of stone. Hell, Syloria itself proved that, and it was hardly the extent of what they'd made. Throughout Erenelle, there were cities and villages with half their structures built underground in tunnels and caverns, while others were fashioned straight out of the sides of mountains or grown up from the earth itself. We'd managed something similar with our cabin, but we'd also always built *that* to be able to be torn down if needed.

When it came to using stone, giants built shit to *last.*

But it wasn't just the structures themselves that Erenlians had perfected. Generations of giants had created fairly ingenious ways of making the water supply work too.

Big as it was, this tunnel was actually more like a service access. The aqueducts to hold the water for Syloria were inside the walls around us. Initially carved like channels in the stone, they were then sealed away to be completely watertight except for small access ports along the length of this central tunnel.

Except without anyone here to maintain them...

Shivers crept over my skin. The lakebed above us wasn't the only mystery. The sodden, swirling mud of magic I could feel around us muffled my senses like twenty layers of wet fucking blankets, but the deeper we walked, the more I began to pick up on things.

Thin streams of water still trickled along the bottom of the aqueducts inside the walls, so there was still a water source *somewhere* here. Admittedly, not much of one, given that those little threads of moisture should be flowing like calm, controlled rivers, their erosive qualities offset by the efforts of the giants in charge of their maintenance. But still, that was a start.

Keeping an eye to the bastards up ahead, I concentrated on pushing my magic farther through the muddy magic. While the larger giants probably had heightened skills with various aspects of the natural world, same as the seven of us, one of the few advantages fate had given me and my friends was that we were actually pretty damn powerful when it came to our various affinities.

But it didn't mean that those assholes wouldn't pick up on what I was doing.

None of them turned while I stretched out my power. From the way they were muttering with each other, they didn't seem to notice what I was doing at all.

Which was just as well, because I definitely didn't have enough self-control to stop my face from giving away how I choked in horror when the murky truth slowly presented itself past the fucked-up magic.

"Oh... shit," I whispered.

Lars glanced at me. "What?"

I couldn't find the words. The aqueducts were blocked, yes. Chances were, they had been for years. And while that had been a problem at first, now it was a damn good thing.

Because even I couldn't breathe underwater.

Ozias gave a quiet rumble of misgiving, and my eyes snapped to him. "You picking something up, Oz?" I asked under my breath, praying he had a better answer than *we need to run like hell*, which was all that was going through my head right now.

Except that wouldn't help Gwyneira or Niko or Roan or...

Gods-fucking-dammit.

"You conspiring back there, dwarves?" one of Norbert's buddies snapped.

Norbert scoffed. "Probably. Shut up, runts. Nobody needs your opinions on how to do *real* giant work."

"Need I remind you," Casimir called before I could tell that bastard to go to hell, "that you are addressing the royal advisors of the king of Zenirya? Unless you wish me to inform your duke that you decided to start a war because you thought yourself wiser than him, you will cease speaking immediately."

The two asshole giants glared, while that cowardly bastard Brock didn't say a damned word.

And Ignatius studied us like we were all a math problem he was trying to solve.

Fuck them all. I turned my attention back to my friends. "Oz, what are you feeling?"

A low grunt of discontent left Ozias. "A hundred more yards to the problem."

Problem. Right. That was one way of putting it.

Holy-fucking-shit-we're-dead was another.

"You have an exceptionally strong gift, do you not?" Ignatius asked Ozias thoughtfully.

Not answering, Ozias started walking again. My friends and the larger giants did too, leaving Ignatius to follow.

"You good?" Lars asked me softly.

I huffed out an incredulous breath. Good? Fuck no. I

wanted Ozias to tell me I was wrong. To say he had a plan.

Fucking *something*.

But of course he hadn't said more. On a good day, the guy rationed words like my parents used to ration our food.

Greedy brats. Dwarves don't need to eat three times a day. Give it to Brock. He's the only real *giant here.*

My teeth ground at the memory of ducking their hands when they swung to hit us. Sometimes that'd even worked.

Other times, Lars or I had to hide yet another broken bone.

Because our wounds only proved one more way in which we weren't good enough, and no one in my parents' circle would've helped or been sympathetic to how our family treated us. After all, nobility didn't suffer such petty, common injuries.

"Breathe," my twin brother murmured.

"You breathe."

I didn't need to look at him to feel his exasperated expression. And fine, yes, my response was childish.

But surely he could understand why?

"Gwyneira needs us to get through this," Lars pressed, his voice still low. "She's our future, brother. So don't fuck that up over the past."

He met my eyes firmly. Anyone else would have believed his expression was the calm counterpoint to my simmering fury.

But I could read the pain and anger tightly controlled

behind his blue eyes, and more than anything else, that caused my own rage to drain.

Forget childish. I was being selfish. He was struggling with this too, and I wasn't helping him. "Sorry."

He nodded, accepting the apology. "Now tell me, what are you picking up on?"

I hesitated.

"I know you, Clay. Something's up. What is it?"

My heart pounding, I lowered my voice to a whisper. "We've got more than a *problem* on our hands."

His eyes turned wary.

"Something went wrong with the water supply. Maybe a collapse inside the mountain or because of that avalanche that took out part of the temple. I don't know. But after that happened and the magic here started fucking up because no one was around to fix things, it trapped the water. *All* of it."

"Shit," Lars whispered.

I nodded. "But the water still had to go somewhere, right? So the pressure of the magic pushed *way* more groundwater into the surrounding rock than it could naturally hold."

My brother looked sick.

"I'm not Oz, but from what *I* can tell, the water weakened the stone around us, and now if we try to draw the water out or fucking *touch* this rock the wrong way..." I swallowed hard. "The ground will collapse, the tunnels won't hold, and the destruction could take down everything above us—including the temple."

Casimir's head snapped back toward us with shock. Ignatius paused, seeing our reactions even if he hadn't heard our words, while Ozias didn't turn, though his shoulders pulled up with tension.

So the big guy *did* feel how this place was basically a fucking death trap. Great. Why the hell hadn't *he* said anything?

"Can you do something?" Lars asked me quietly.

Gods, it grated to admit the answer was *fuck no*. Not when we were talking about a sinkhole big enough to turn this whole place into a crater.

He saw the truth on my face anyway.

"Do what you can," he said with a short glance at Dex, as if reading the guy's mind. After all, the words were probably what our fearless leader would have said too. "And if it comes down to it, you focus on a way to stop it from hurting Gwyneira and the folks above us. Nothing else. Okay?"

My mouth tightened, everything in me fighting what I knew I had to say.

"Clay?"

"Yeah, okay."

Gods, that hurt. So did the way he nodded.

But not as much as the way I knew he was right. Gwyneira was up there. Roan and Niko too, and they'd be on board with this. There wasn't a doubt in my mind that they would.

We'd all sacrificed for each other over the years. And gods, we'd do anything for her.

Even drown if it meant our treluria survived.

41

LARS

I may not have said them out loud, but right now, the litany of curses running through my head would have put my brother to shame.

No, forget that. Clay rarely did shame. Likely, he would've been impressed.

And probably agreed with the sentiment behind them all.

My heart pounding, I followed the others farther down the tunnel, wishing there was something—*anything*—my magic could do about the situation my brother described. But fire was useless here, and heating the water until it turned to steam definitely wouldn't fix anything. It'd just give us all horrific burns before we died.

Not helpful.

My eyes twitched to Norbert, Brock, and the other so-called *real* giants. My friends and I had incredibly strong affinities to things like fire and water, stone and wood and nature—more than many Erenlians. I'd always figured that was the gods' way of trying to make up for the obstacles they'd thrown in our paths in other respects.

But right now, it only made me wonder: could these giants tell how much trouble we might be in? Yes, there was magic coating this place. Tons of it, and obviously, that was part of the problem. The various spells were like smeared oil paints, myriad types of magic blending together and making it damn near impossible to tell what the energies *should* have been doing, let alone whatever else might be going on. But surely as we drew closer, the other giants would start picking up on how precarious the situation truly was?

"You think good ol' uncle Deter knew about this?" Clay muttered, eyeing the walls.

A chill rolled over me. "Maybe."

After all, Deter had a water affinity too. That single similarity had made my brother Deter's favorite target, even more than me, when we were children.

Gods forbid a *dwarf* be the only relative to share the affinity of Deter's magic.

But Deter was also Erenlian nobility with the best magical training money could buy, and that meant he was probably second to Ignatius in terms of magical skill among the prisoners—a fact he'd undoubtedly used to his advantage over the years, as much as he could with that manacle on.

But the manacles were gone, and his power was back. If Ignatius didn't have as strong of a water affinity

—or maybe he was just out of practice—Deter may still have picked up on this.

And given how he'd acted right before we came down here... how Brock had too...

My stomach rolled. "Surely Deter wouldn't send *Norbert* down here if he thought this was really going to end badly, though. Right?"

Clay met my eyes with a flat look.

Right. We knew our uncle. When push came to shove, he'd readily sacrifice family for power.

Even his own son.

Besides, the years hadn't been kind to our uncle. The mines hadn't either. Obviously he'd done what he could to make sure he had the most food and the best provisions, but he'd still spent well over a decade in a prison and he wasn't getting any younger.

Deter may not have originally planned to sacrifice Norbert today, but where Brock and these five others were concerned, I was less sure. Brock hadn't ever spoken up against Deter or our parents when we were all kids. Hell, when they told him to, he'd joined in on their "games" of beating us senseless.

But I'd seen the look on Brock's face after Deter gave the order. Something was up. I'd almost swear Brock had seemed suspicious of the old man.

But did that mean I should warn them about this?

"You're looking a bit green, brother," Clay murmured to me.

"What if he wants Brock and the rest to die too?"

"Deter?"

"Mm-hmm."

"Good for him, then."

"*Clay*."

"What?"

I searched for words and came up with nothing. I understood how he felt. I *did*.

But dammit, he was talking about letting people be murdered, and that...

Well, it was *wrong*.

Except they'd happily kill us too.

Should that matter?

I raked a hand through my hair. It shouldn't. It *didn't*. Gods help me, we'd all had this same debate weeks ago when we saved Gwyneira from the snow. We'd spared her because, as Niko pointed out, we couldn't be like the Aneirans who would have killed us on the spot if our positions were reversed.

The same should go for this situation.

Right?

"I don't know what's going through that brain of yours," Clay said quietly as we continued past another curve of the tunnel. "But your face looks like your brain's twisting itself into a knot. There's no bright side here. There's just saving her, like you said. That's what matters. We do what we can to stop the temple from collapsing, no matter what happens here."

Gods, why'd I have to be the optimist of the two of us? "I know what I said, but that doesn't mean we just give up. There has to be something I can do to help you fix—"

Norbert turned, bringing us all to a stop as a collapsed section of tunnel came into view ahead. "What're you whispering about back there, runts?"

"Leave 'em be," Brock grunted dismissively, not even bothering to look our way as he approached the pile of rock that brought the tunnel to an end. "They're just stalling."

I cast an insistent look at Clay.

My brother met it with a wry expression. "They're not going to listen."

"But—"

"But nothing."

I couldn't accept that. "There's a problem with the tunnel."

Norbert snorted derisively.

"See, what'd I tell you?" Brock commented to our cousin. "Just stalling."

Clay scoffed. With heavy sarcasm, he echoed, "See, what'd I tell you?" to me quietly, as if proving his point.

Ignoring my twin, I strode toward the larger giants, though I fastened my attention mostly on Ignatius. "The magic here trapped the water in such a way that it eroded the stone. If we aren't careful, it could bring the whole temple down into a sinkhole."

For a heartbeat, the giants froze, and though it'd been years since I was last surrounded by their type of Erenlian, I could still read the flicker of alarm and—yes —fear that flashed through the eyes of several of them. They'd just gotten free and now this?

But they didn't do what I hoped. Instead of facing the problem and finding a positive solution, they did the opposite. The henchmen scoffed their fears away and rolled their eyes. Norbert muttered about idiot dwarves delaying the inevitable.

Brock just stared at us.

I couldn't believe this. "We need to do something!"

A couple of the giants laughed.

I looked at Ignatius again. His gaze was locked on me with an intent expression I swore Byron must have learned from the monks of the Order, because my friend definitely gave us that same look when he was weighing everything we'd said against the library of information in his head.

Norbert made a derisive sound. "Give me a break. Just admit my father is the king and get it over with. Dragging your feet won't make your little buddy up there any less of a pathetic dwarf trying to steal what doesn't belong to him."

Ignatius spoke up before my brother could open his mouth and, most likely, tell our cousin to go to hell. "Your affinity is to water, is it?"

"His." I nodded back toward Clay.

"Oh, please." Norbert slapped his hand to the wall. "This tunnel isn't going to—"

A shuddering groan went through the stone around us. Dust rained from the ceiling and walls.

"You fucking..." Clay snarled, but his attention was on the tunnel, his eyes wide with horror.

Dex didn't waste a second. "Ozias, support the stone. Clay, do what you can to control the water. The rest of you, help any way you can."

Ignatius, Byron, and Casimir moved to obey immediately, while Ruhl's smoky form spread out against the wall as if to hold it in place. Brock looked between them all and then rushed to help.

"The dwarves did this!" Norbert cried. "They set us up!"

The words were so ridiculous, they left me too dumbstruck to argue. Gods help us, we were going to die here because my cousin was an idiot.

No. No, I wouldn't let that happen.

Forcing myself not to freeze in despair and horror, I raced to the wall to help my brother. I didn't have magic like Ozias or Clay, but by the gods, I was still a giant. I could help them control the rock enough to keep us all from getting crushed.

Hopefully.

"Ugh, get out of the way, runts!" Norbert shoved Byron away from the wall, sending him stumbling. "You're going to screw this up too."

"You mean like you just did?" Clay snapped back. "Keep your fucking hands off my friends, asshole, or I'll let you drown."

Like a bull with the attention span of a gnat, Norbert abandoned the wall and stalked toward my brother.

Fear gripped me for Clay. I knew that look.

"I should've crushed you when you were a kid," Norbert snarled. "You fucking—"

Before I could reach him, Brock was suddenly there, stepping between them both. "Leave him," he said to Norbert.

Norbert's eyes widened. "Did you just give me an order, you piece of—"

The tunnel shuddered around us.

"We need your help to save everyone," Brock pressed, a calmness in his voice I'd never heard before. It wasn't the disinterested tone he'd taken when our parents lashed out at me or Clay. It was... controlled. Level and yet pointed.

Dust rained down stronger than before.

Spinning away from Brock like he didn't exist, Norbert shouted at the giants, "Get to work, you lazy asses!"

Brock's eyes twitched to me. I couldn't read his expression at all.

But there was no time.

Shoving my concerns aside, I put my hands to the stone again. The mysteries of my blood relatives could wait. Right now, I needed to help my *family*.

My magic merged into the stone. I wasn't as skilled as some in this regard. Thanks to our parents, Clay and I hadn't started school for our magic until years after most Erenlian kids. But even with my middling powers over the earth, the problem started becoming clearer after only a few moments.

This decaying magic wasn't just some smeared blur of random spells. No, these were the protective spells cast by the long-dead members of the Order to guard this place. The magic had sunk into the bedrock beneath the temple, and without the monks to maintain it, the spells had merged and twisted and made a bigger problem. But they were still trying to fulfill their purpose.

Protect the temple, whether that was from invaders

or—now—the very waters this place was originally built to enshrine.

But after all these years, they'd gone feral.

I felt the magic condense a split second before a blast erupted from the wall. It lashed out like a tangled crackle of lightning to strike the giant closest to the collapsed section of tunnel farther ahead. A charred hole in his chest, he flew back, crashing into the opposite wall and making it start to crumble.

"Holy shit!" a giant beside Norbert shouted, frantically retreating as another blast built up in the wall.

He was too slow. The magic struck, ripping through him like a thunderbolt.

Another tangle of magic rushed from the wall straight at Norbert. Ignatius raised a hand to intervene, but Byron got there first.

With hurried words, my friend chanted something unintelligible. The blast curved before it could reach my idiot cousin, the power slamming into the stone instead. The other spells rippled as it struck. That wall started to crumble too.

Ozias stepped in quickly, molding the stone around itself, fighting to keep the entire place from crashing down.

"Lars!" Byron yelled to me. "Send your power to me!"

I had no idea what he was planning, but I didn't care. As another blast of defensive magic built in the wall, I let my magic rush out at Byron. In my haste, my power was laced with flames that flickered visibly and charred the dust in the air.

But my friend didn't even blink. His gifts twisted the energy in midair, sending it through the wall and deep into the stone.

The burgeoning blast from the magical defenses suddenly pulled back, not striking out at us but instead chasing his power like an attack dog going after its prey.

"It should read the heat as a person attacking the walls," Byron said. "That'll buy us some time. "

"Good." Dex nodded, though his attention returned quickly to the shuddering walls that Ozias was fighting to support. "Keep it up."

Byron's eyes darted to Ignatius. The older man nodded. "Well done, scholar."

It was a compliment. I knew it was.

But even as he nodded back, Byron didn't look pleased.

Gods, our group was a mess.

I shoved the thought aside. Yeah, a mess that might drown if we didn't concentrate—and thank the gods Byron seemed to know that too. Turning back, he drew hard on my power and sent it racing through the stone like he was throwing glowing balls of heat through the earth.

Creating a diversion just in time.

More defensive spells swelled around us, crackling on the stone walls like lightning. But Byron never stopped. Over and over, he flung bundles of my magic and his back into the rock, while around us, the others worked frantically to keep the tunnel and the temple above from crashing down into a sinkhole.

Time blurred. The air became thick and harder to breathe from the panic around me. The ground shuddered and quivered, and at any moment, I expected the earth to crash down and end us all.

But slowly, the shuddering began to fade.

Blinking sweat from my eyes, I looked around as Byron stopped pulling on my magic.

The tunnel still stood. The giants and the dwarves slowly lowered their hands from the walls, all of them eyeing the tunnel and each other like no one was quite sure what to do now.

I raked a hand through my sweat-soaked hair. We'd done it. Gods, we'd really done it.

But the tunnel was *significantly* taller than before.

I paused. How much rock had my friends and the others needed to pull from the surrounding countryside to keep this place standing? If I went back aboveground, would the hills even be there?

But the walls around us were more stable. I could feel that. The ground overhead was too.

I could even hear water rushing through the aqueducts again.

A breath left me. The magical defenses around us weren't raging anymore, either. We probably had Ignatius and Byron to thank for that. Rather than a smear of muddy paint or tangled lightning, the spells now twisted through the rock like threads of a fine net, supporting the earth and extending up toward the temple.

In fact, now that it wasn't trying to kill us, it was even kind of beautiful. That kind of spellwork wasn't exactly my forte, so I could only pick up on the barest edge of what the scholars had done, but the intricacy was shocking.

"Good job, everyone," Dex said, including Ignatius and, gods, even Brock and the larger giants in his acknowledging nod.

Norbert scoffed. "Bet you learned something from the *real* giants here, didn't you, runt?"

"You fucking—" Clay started forward, but Dex caught his arm.

"Don't," Dex said quietly.

My brother's jaw clenched. He shrugged off Dex's grip, but he didn't start toward Norbert again.

Norbert smirked.

But that wasn't what made me pause.

All around my idiot cousin, discomfort and maybe even *embarrassment* flashed over the faces of the other giants. These were Deter's henchmen. His honor guard of bullies. Yet not a single one of them seemed eager to join in Norbert's mockery. For gods' sakes, Brock looked like he'd just bitten into a lemon.

Well, that was... different.

"We should return to the surface," Ignatius said. Lifting his robes to step over the fallen chunks of rock, the scholar started back down the tunnel. "The lake will be filling again, and the others will likely want to know what happened."

"Indeed." Norbert smirked, his supercilious tone like a snide imitation of his father.

Ignatius's face tightened, but he didn't say anything, simply continuing past us on his way to the surface.

"Oh, and scholar?" Norbert called. "Best you start planning my father's coronation. He'll be your king before the end of the day."

Ignatius didn't respond.

"Not fucking likely," Clay muttered.

Gods, I hoped my brother was right.

42
NIKO

I raced back into the temple with Gwyneira at my side, and I wondered the whole way whether I was making a mistake.

Not where she was concerned, of course. Being with her was the only thing in my life that still made sense.

But everything else...

Dex and my friends emerged from the hall leading to the tunnels just as Gwyneira, Roan, and I reached the main room.

"Everything okay?" Roan asked them immediately.

Behind us, a murmur rose. I looked over my shoulder.

Water trickled from the fountain, the flow growing stronger with every passing moment.

"Fine, freak." Norbert strode past, bumping into Roan and making him rock to the side.

A quiver went through Roan. Quickly, Gwyneira put a hand to his forearm with a cautioning look.

One that was probably meant as much for the demon as my friend.

When no one responded to his jibe, Norbert cast a glance back. An intrigued look flashed over his face to see Gwyneira's hand on Roan. His eyes raked over her body, a cruel smirk twisting his lip like he was imagining doing unspeakable things to her.

My fingers curled into fists, my magic seething to lash out and make him pay for looking at her that way.

The princess didn't deign to notice that bastard in the slightest. "What happened?" she asked, directing the question at Ozias.

"Nothing we couldn't fix," Dex said briefly before Ozias could speak—assuming he even would have. Barring a brief glance of reassurance to Gwyneira, my bearded friend kept his eyes trained on Norbert like he wanted to rip the guy's throat out.

"I'll fucking kill that bastard if he doesn't stop looking at her that way," Clay growled in a low voice, his eyes locked on his cousin too.

This brought Gwyneira's attention around. At the sight of Norbert, her brow arched and she drew herself up, every bit of her radiating royalty.

Norbert spotted it. Contempt replaced his smirk, but he didn't say another word as he continued over to his father's side.

A shudder coursed through me. I wasn't a killer. Not really. But I had no doubt in my mind I'd be right there with Clay and Ozias if Norbert tried to lay a finger on Gwyneira.

As if dismissing the giant from relevance, the

princess turned back to Ozias. "It didn't seem like noth-ing." She gave him an insistent look.

"It's over," Ozias replied firmly. "That's what matters."

She frowned.

"*Almost* over," Lars countered carefully, his attention still on the giants.

I let out a slow breath, trying not to panic. Right. That part.

Dear gods...

I swallowed hard. I wasn't royal. I couldn't be. I was a healer from the Forest of Azurine, and the only honor I wanted to attain in life was that of being a good partner to my treluria. But for Gwyneira's sake—for *all* our sakes—I needed to pretend to be something else now. Animals in nature needed to see the leader at the forefront of a pack in order to believe that pack was strong. If the alpha hid behind others for protection, then preda-tors would see weakness. They would attack.

No matter what, I needed to keep that from happening for as long as I could.

"Everybody ready to run for the hills?" Clay muttered.

"Quiet." Dex's eyes skimmed the room, assessing everything. "Everyone stay with Niko and—" He twitched his head toward Gwyneira rather than say her name.

My friends nodded. I drew myself up as tall as I could—never mind that I was the shortest giant of the seven of us—and started toward the enormous fountain.

Gwyneira never left my side. "Are you okay?" she

murmured, her lips barely moving while she scanned the temple chamber.

I made a confirming noise. "You?"

She nodded ever so slightly. "Mm-hmm."

We rounded the fountain, and my heart sank to see the duke already standing at its side. A host of giants waited beyond him, watching him like a king.

He barely spared them a glance, turning to us with a proud, condescending expression. "Ah, the dwarves finally arrive. We thought perhaps you'd given up and fled rather than continue this duplicitous claim."

Shivers rolled through me. There was no doubt in my mind that the minute this ceremony confirmed he was the king, he'd label us traitors, put a price on our heads, and chase us all the way back to Aneira, where the queen and the Voidborn would make sure we died in the most horrific way possible.

Admittedly, that was the worst-case scenario.

But then again, we'd been running into a lot of worst cases lately.

"Breathe," Gwyneira murmured.

My lungs did as she asked, and slowly, my head cleared. Gods, I was letting my imagination get away from me—and *that* was reckless as hell. Humans and giants were no different than animals, even if they pretended to be. They could sense fear.

But I knew how to handle that.

Drawing on every trick I'd learned to stay calm in the face of predators in the forest, I walked with my friends the rest of the way to where Ignatius and the duke stood. Murmurs followed me in a wave, most of them disbelieving and uncertain. The duke smiled at it all, radiating a confidence I could only pretend at possessing.

Eye contact with a predator was a challenge for a fight, so I locked my attention on the fountain instead. The wall of its basin was half my height, though on larger giants like the duke and Ignatius, it barely came up to their knees. But in the time we were gone, the rushing water had filled the basin nearly full.

"So many bodyguards," Duke Ensid scoffed as my friends and I came to a stop several yards away. "Are you afraid of *true* Erenlians, dwarf?"

Acknowledging a predator could trigger them to attack, so I didn't bother to reply. Keeping my body language neutral and calm, I turned to Ignatius. "What now?"

Ignatius took off his boots and then stepped over the basin wall into the water. "One at a time," he said, "the ones who have stated a claim to the throne will stand within the pool. The waters of Syloria are no ordinary waters. They are alive with the magic of our people. They remember the royal blood that was last chosen to rule, and the power given and taken in this place. They will show us who has the strongest and truest claim to the throne of Erenelle."

Murmurs of wonder ran through the giants. I wished I shared their awe. I was too busy eyeing the water with barely controlled dread.

The *living* water.

I'd never heard of such a thing. Not like this. I knew water had tiny organisms in it. That was a given, as was the fact it sustained life.

But for it to be alive in and of *itself*...

I glanced at Clay. His gifts were closely tied to water. If anything was dangerous about the liquid in that pool, he'd know it.

He caught sight of me, and he seemed to understand my silent question. "Yeah, um... the water's definitely weird."

"Weird *how*?" Lars asked before I could.

Clay shrugged, his eyes returning to the basin. "I don't know. Just... alive, I guess. Like the guy said." His brow furrowed. "It's kind of creepy."

Well, that didn't exactly make me feel better.

The duke strode forward, no trace of worry on his face.

"Boots off." Ignatius held up a hand to stop him. "The Holy Water of Syloria deserves respect."

The duke paused for only a heartbeat before saying dismissively, "You are too impatient, scholar. Of course I respect this water."

Clay snorted with disbelief.

Ignoring him, the duke took off his boots and set them aside. His eyes skimmed imperiously over the room as if checking he had everyone's attention, landing at last on us. A tiny smile crossed his face, one that clearly said he expected to be ordering our deaths soon.

But predators loved to posture. That didn't mean I had to react to it.

His smile soured. My stomach quivered with a perverse sense of victory.

Turning sharply as if to put distance between himself and us, the duke slammed his feet down into the pool.

Water splashed us, making Ozias growl and Clay mutter more curses.

I tried not to shudder at the thought of living water again, turning instead to check on Gwyneira. "You okay?" I whispered, looking her over quickly.

"Fine." She smiled, but there was an edge to it. Her eyes never quite left the larger giants. "A little water never melted anyone."

Norbert chuckled. "Gotta watch out there, dwarves. You might drown."

My temper flared, only to falter at the strangely uncomfortable looks that flashed over the faces of Brock and the five henchmen who'd gone down into the tunnels.

What was *that* about?

I had no time to ask. Striding to Ignatius's side, the duke spun, sloshing water around, and faced the room like he was already imagining everyone bowing while he sat on the throne. "Let the proof of kingship begin!"

Expressionless, Ignatius extended his hands over the water and began chanting words I couldn't understand.

"He's asking the spirits to show us the strength and truth of this one's claim to the throne," Byron murmured, translating.

"If anyone feels like praying for those holy waters to drown Deter's ass," Clay muttered darkly, "now's the time."

Roan and Ozias both looked wholeheartedly in agreement, while Dex's eyes just scanned the room, constantly checking the exits.

Gwyneira reached out, taking my hand with a tiny smile. A small measure of my tension faded.

But then a murmur went up from the crowd, yanking my focus back to the fountain.

A shimmering glow was rising from the water. It hung above the surface like the ghostly lights that sometimes lit up the northern night sky, glistening with red and orange like the memory of a sunrise.

And then they grew stronger. Darker, taking on the color of blood.

The murmurs around the room became cries of surprise.

"Well, fuck." Dread filled Clay's voice.

I stopped myself from nodding, even as my heart sank. It was impressive. Admittedly disturbing, yes, given the fact it looked like blood hanging in the air. But the crimson glow seemed a clear sign the duke was tied to the throne.

Gods, how quickly could we get out of here?

I glanced at my friends, wishing I could ask. But to do so would only provoke the predators among the giants to attack us, never mind how my friends weren't even looking at me anyway. Dex's eyes darted across the room like he was running every possible escape scenario through his mind, not liking any of them, while most of the rest of my friends appeared on the edge of grabbing their swords, prepared for the fight we all knew had to be coming.

But Byron's eyes were narrowed. He didn't seem impressed at all. More like he saw something other than confirmation of the duke's claim to the throne in that blood-red shimmer.

Confused, I pitched my voice as low as I could and whispered to him, "What's wrong? Why do you—"

"The waters speak," Ignatius called, cutting off my question. "This one does indeed have a claim to the throne."

Never mind then. But I swore the older scholar's voice was tight, like he wasn't any happier with this answer than we were. Even the duke seemed to hear that, his eyes sliding briefly to Ignatius as if making note of the tone.

"The dwarf!" someone in the crowd shouted. "Test the dwarf!"

Cries of agreement ran through the room.

I swallowed hard and then cursed myself silently for the brief show of nervousness.

But here came the moment I'd *never* been waiting for.

Duke Ensid drew himself up, that smirk returning to his lips. "Indeed. Let us prove this little dwarf's claim to be false with our precious Erenlian waters."

Dex's jaw muscles twitched. A low, displeased rumble came from Ozias, while Roan cracked his neck like the demon was fighting to get out.

But what would happen when the waters really *did* prove that?

Gwyneira's hand squeezed mine gently. "It's going to be okay," she murmured. "No matter what."

Utter certainty was in her eyes, and it stilled my breath. Gods, I loved her. Marveled at her. Wanted to spend the rest of my life worshipping her. She'd come so far from the frightened princess who once collapsed in exhaustion inside the cabin of seven strangers, and no matter what, she would always be my queen.

Gods, please don't let this be the last time I saw her...

"We're with you," Dex assured me, his eyes on the giants.

I nodded, trying to look confident when I felt anything but.

Yet, in nature, animals would puff themselves up when they were scared, pretending courage although they were secretly terrified.

So that would be my choice too.

And with any luck, the Erenlians before me wouldn't know the difference.

"You've got this, buddy." Clay flashed his bright, joking grin, the one I hadn't seen in a long while.

Right now, it looked like a shield on the battlefield. Turning to face the giants, he stood shoulder to shoulder with Dex, while nearby, the rest of my friends did the same, until they all formed their own wall between me and the crowd.

A small shiver coursed through me, one made of gratitude and love for the incredible family I had. Yes, I knew we'd all be running for our lives in a few minutes, but I'd still be worthy of their faith in me.

Holding myself as if I feared nothing, I took off my boots and then swung my legs over the lip of the basin. Noises of amusement came from the crowd to see me hoisting myself past the ledge.

Nearby, Ozias growled louder, the sound bordering on feral.

And honestly, even that helped. Yes, it was odd to know he could make that sound because he wasn't exactly Erenlian like I was. But when I glanced back, his eyes were on the crowd and his body language radiated that death was coming for whoever mocked me.

Resolutely, I dropped into the basin on the other side of the wall, bracing myself as the water splashed up around me. On the duke, the liquid had barely risen above his calves. On me, it was up to my hips, soaking me with its cold touch.

And it felt *strange*. Tingly, but so faint it was only the barest hint of a sensation.

Living water...

Doing my best to ignore that, I forged onward to Ignatius's side. With a calm expression, the old scholar gestured for me to face the rest of the room, and so I did, drawing myself up and trying not to shiver at the cold.

In the crowd, more than one giant didn't bother to hide their amusement.

"Looks like a lil kid, he does," someone commented.

"Ignatius's grandbaby," another replied.

Several people snickered, and the duke's smirk grew. By the basin, Gwyneira glanced away from the giants to peer over the top of the wall as if checking I was okay. Nearby, Clay shifted position like he was fighting the urge to respond to the taunts and Ozias rolled his shoulders like he was doing the same.

I gave Gwyneira the best smile I could manage. But maybe it was for the best if the water decreed that I didn't belong. That this was all some weird mistake, never mind what I'd felt by the barrier wall. After all, as

Clay would say, who needed this kind of bullshit? In the end, it really would be best if we could just go back to the mountains and rebuild the cabin and live in peace where no one cared what we looked—

The water began tingling stronger around me. *Much* stronger. I glanced down in alarm, but I couldn't see any reason for the change.

But gods, the tingling sensation was pressing in on all sides like needles prickling over my skin.

"Begin," the dude called imperiously, like he was already the king officiating this entire ceremony.

"Ready?" Ignatius murmured to me.

I pulled my attention from the water. "Uh, yeah." I cleared my throat. "Yes."

Gods, I needed to sound more confident if I wanted to hold the predators at bay. Kingly, or even just like a powerful giant who knew he belonged.

Rather than a worried young man who *definitely* didn't want to get his friends killed because he'd been foolish enough to listen to the sorrowful cries of a glowing magical wall made out of dead people.

Gods, what had I been thinking?

Solemnly, Ignatius turned to face the crowd again. He extended his hands over the pool, murmuring the same words as before.

A heartbeat passed. Another.

Maybe this all really had been a mistake. Maybe it—

The tingling pressure started to swirl around my body, coursing across my skin through my sodden pants. The water began to glow.

Around the room, the chuckles stopped.

A red shimmer rose from the water, but it wasn't alone. More shades followed, shining like those night-time lights in a northern sky—red and orange, gold and green. Blue as well, and deep purple. The rainbow emanated from the entire pool, like the water itself was made of light.

Shocked gasps came from the giants.

For a moment, I thought they were for the glow around me. But when I tore my eyes from the light, the crowd was staring at something behind my back.

Warily, I looked over my shoulder. Out of the shimmering mist, a shape was forming like a ghost. It looked like a giant, like a man. Clad in chain mail and armor, he stood with an enormous sword in one hand and a golden crown atop his head.

"King Archerias," one of the giants cried. "That's King Archerias."

Suddenly, the apparition moved, its free hand lifting.

Coming to rest on my shoulder.

Alarmed cries broke out around the room. "The king claimed him! The king claimed the dwarf!"

I couldn't even breathe. There was no weight to his hand, only a stronger tingling like my shoulder had gone numb. And as for the man himself, he was obviously a giant, not a dwarf, but his eyes... his nose...

Were they familiar somehow? Maybe even sort of like mine?

My gaze darted faster over the figure as my heart raced. Even made of light, there was a suggestion of brown in the giant's skin, as if the stone-like flesh would have resembled brown marble in life.

A slightly darker shade of my own olive tone.

I couldn't breathe. This wasn't possible. Was I really related to this man? This... gods, this *king*?

The apparition's head tilted downward slightly, his gaze dropping toward me, though his eyes weren't focused and his eyes stared through me.

But it felt like he was looking at me all the same.

"Welcome, my son. Welcome, heir to the crown and throne of Erenelle."

The words boomed out over the room, though the figure's mouth didn't move.

A hushed wave of surprised and alarmed murmurs from the giants greeted the words, but I could barely make them out over the rushing of my own blood in my ears.

Son? Heir? Had the figure of the *king* just called me his son and heir?

The apparition's head rose again, his gaze leaving me, and his other hand moved, lifting the shimmering sword. I tensed, trying not to recoil as he tilted the blade forward.

But he didn't strike. He pointed.

Straight at Roan.

"Welcome, son of his mother. Welcome, brother to the crown."

Roan froze. I did too. He... That wasn't... He couldn't mean Roan was my...

Oh. I knew what this was. I must be dreaming. Honestly, I couldn't believe that hadn't occurred to me before. I must have hit my head in the mines, and this all was a fiction my brain had concocted to cope with the trauma and swelling that would probably kill me if left untreated.

So I needed to wake up. Any minute now, really. I obviously needed medical assistance, so any second now would be—

The sword moved, the tip pointing at each of my friends and Gwyneira. "Welcome, the Nine."

Oh, gods, not that again. Even my dreams couldn't stop telling us we were in danger.

The apparition drew the blade back, returning the sword to its upright position in his grip. "The shield of Erenelle stands ready to defend this world." Tilting his chin higher, his expression imperious and solemn, the king stared into the distance as if all our futures played out before his eyes. "The skies shall fall."

The glow on the water faded, taking the figure of the king with it, until only the empty air and the ruins of the temple remained.

Silence reigned supreme.

"King Archerias has spoken," Ignatius announced, his voice a bit faint, as if even he was shaken. "The waters of Syloria have spoken. By the laws and rites of our people, their word will be obeyed. All hail King Niko of Erenelle!"

Chaos really was too mild a word for the giants' reactions.

People shouted. Others stared like I'd suddenly sprouted three heads. Several more had the strangest expressions of relief, like maybe they'd secretly hoped I would be chosen and not the duke.

And I *still* hadn't woken up.

"It's a fucking trick!" Norbert yelled. "The dwarves did something to the water! To the spell!"

Brock stared at us. I couldn't read his expression at all.

Ignatius's shout carried over the cries of the crowd. "That was not all King Archerias said!"

The noise dwindled, though it definitely didn't die. Rumblings of confusion still came from the giants, while Norbert and the duke glared like they wanted to peel the flesh from my bones.

"This young man isn't *only* the heir of our late king," Ignatius announced. "The time of the Nine has come. And if *anyone*—" he fixed his eyes on Norbert and the duke briefly, "—should harm the heir or his friends, they risk our entire world."

"The hell I do," Norbert snarled, yanking out a knife he'd gotten from the gods knew where.

He charged straight at me.

43
ROAN

I didn't think. Didn't wait.

I just let go.

The shift roared through me in an instant, transforming me into the massive form of the demon.

Yet unlike every time before, the demon didn't shove my awareness into a dark and foggy abyss. Instead, I remained at the forefront, the demon riding with me behind our shared eyes. We were distinct, yet joined. Two personalities, two minds within our changing body.

And both of us agreed this bastard Norbert needed to die.

"Protect the king!" Dex called behind me. The others drew in, bracing themselves to defend Niko.

My brother.

The thought made me shudder, but there was no time to let it sink in. Raising a short, rusty knife, Norbert lunged with a deranged battle cry.

My claws shredded his arm. My other hand shredded his throat.

Giant or not, he was no match for what I'd become.

Norbert's weapon went flying as his bloody corpse toppled to the ground. The crowd screamed.

"Monster!" The duke snatched up the blade that had clattered away from the idiot who tried to hurt my brother.

Oh, gods, I had a *brother*...

My chest ached, my longing for that to be true so strong it was physically painful. But now that entitled asshole was—

Brock crashed into the duke. With a swift motion, the younger man disarmed Duke Ensid and took control of the knife. Spinning it smoothly in his grasp, Brock slammed it through the man's heart.

Duke Ensid stopped cold, his mouth gaping. His hands rose, clutching at Brock's tight grip on the weapon buried hilt-deep in his chest. "Y-you... you..."

Brock's face was like ice, and his tone was too. "To disrespect the king is punishable by death." With a jerk, he yanked the blade from the duke's chest, sending the dead man toppling to the ground.

The duke's few remaining henchmen skidded to a halt. Their eyes darted from me to Brock and then to my friends. Quickly, they held up their hands. "H-hail King Niko," stammered the one in the lead. His buddies echoed the words, suddenly appearing eager to be anywhere but here.

Brock looked past me at Clay and Lars, but since the

demon and I both struggled to read people on a good day, neither of us had a chance in hell of interpreting his expression now.

Meanwhile, my friends just seemed stunned.

And behind them was... my *brother*.

My entire body shuddered. How could Niko be related to me when I was *this*?

I wanted it to be true, though. Gods, I *needed* it to be. I'd lost my childhood family, and I'd spent years fearing that, if the truth about my nature was revealed, the new family I'd built with my friends would be destroyed too. And when my beautiful, precious treluria Gwyneira came along, that fear had only grown.

But things had changed. I'd learned I could stay in control. My demon side and I *both* could. Right now it even felt like the demon was taking our bargain one step farther, letting me stay in control and at the forefront of our shared mind in this form. Like it was giving me a peace offering, trying to prove it really *could* be trusted, even when we were like *this*.

And meanwhile the gods I'd always thought hated me had rewarded me with a *brother*.

Discomfort flashed over Niko's face as I stared at him.

Oh, fuck me. I was a moron in either form. What about how *he* must feel about this? Yes, he and I had come to a truce. Quite a good one, since he was willing to share Gwyneira with me.

But that didn't mean he'd be happy to find out I, of all people, was actually *related* to him.

His mouth moved like he was searching for words, but nothing came out.

My stomach turned to lead. Oh, this was bad. And here I was, standing around like an idiot in demon form, probably making it all worse.

At least this time I had pants on. I should thank Clay for that.

I was stalling.

With a shudder, I tried to shift back, but the demon didn't want to go. It agreed that, yes, this was awkward. Excruciatingly so, in point of fact. But we had higher priorities here, namely that we were still surrounded by potential enemies who could hurt our treluria.

So what if I was a monster with blood coating my hands? That was a good warning to anyone who'd consider fucking with what was ours.

Embarrassment gnawed at me. Yeah, okay, the demon had a point. Except there were plenty of regular folk here too, and *gods*, they were staring.

I looked around, feeling a bit frantic. If I'd been in human form, my face would have been burning brighter than a cherry because of how badly I was messing everything up. As it was, I faltered with indecision and then bent to dunk my hands in the pool. It was probably disrespectful as hell to get blood in the holy water, but what else was I supposed to—

Gwyneira's hand came to rest on my side. "Demon?"

Oh gods, how did I explain *this*? My mind, his body, and neither of us with the slightest fucking clue about how to handle anything at all.

"Breathe," she whispered.

My eyes darted to her, and gratitude tangled with the confused panic inside me. Her smile was like a lifeline, saving me from drowning.

Saving us both.

Beyond her, the others were gathering, making sure that even if I was distracted she stayed safe among these giants.

My gratitude only grew, and after a heartbeat, the demon decided that, okay, perhaps we could let down our guard—a *little*. As long as I swore that if anyone tried to hurt her, he could come back and unleash fucking murder.

A rough breath left me. *Deal.*

My body shifted back to my Erenlian form.

"You okay?" she asked softly.

My mouth moved soundlessly. I was great except I might be awful. It all depended on whether Niko thought being related to me was the worst thing that could have ever happened to—

Small splashing sounds brought my thoughts up short. From the corner of my eye, I saw Niko walking closer, Ignatius following.

Shit, I couldn't even breathe.

"Okay, wait, hold on." Clay's urgent words snapped my attention back around.

Oh, fuck. Brock was starting across the room toward us, the knife still in his hands.

The demon surged inside me again. We shouldn't have shifted so soon. We'd been fools to let our guard down so—

"Easy," Dex cautioned in a low voice.

Was he talking to the others or me?

Brock stopped far short of my friends. With his hands out to his sides, he dropped to one knee. Placing the knife on the floor, he pushed it away, letting it skitter across the gritty marble tiles to our feet. "On behalf of myself and those close to me, I pledge our loyalty and lives to King Niko." His jaw muscles clenched briefly. "And I offer my apologies to my brothers."

"What the fuck…?" Clay whispered.

Brock's eyes flicked up to the twins. "I'm sorry. I was a child but still a coward, and I should have stood up for both of you."

Clay's brow climbed. Lars blinked, speechless.

"I won't ask your forgiveness," Brock continued, his gaze dropping back to the floor. "Only that if you decide to ask the king for retribution, you would spare my family and only punish me."

The twins turned in unison, unspoken *what-the-fuck* looks passing between them. "F-family?" Lars asked.

Brock glanced over his shoulder, nodding to someone in the crowd.

A woman emerged from among the giants. Her stone-like skin was the color of dark brown marble, with whorls of amber and tan through it in a beautiful pattern. Her moss-like hair was deep amber, and her eyes were as well. Covered in a threadbare scrap of blanket, a small form lay curled in her arms.

At Brock's murmured reassurance, she walked closer. Her eyes darted across all of us like she was torn between running and fighting to defend her family, and I didn't miss how many times her wary gaze landed on me.

The monster who looked like a man.

"This is my wife, Fleur, and our daughter," Brock said.

Fleur carefully lowered herself to one knee beside her husband, keeping her little one carefully secured. "Your Highness," she murmured to Niko. "Thank you for trying to protect Nadine and for saving us from the mines. I'm so sorry Brock couldn't speak up to help you sooner. Duke Ensid made him a part of his inner circle on the basis of blood, but he held our lives over his head. Had my husband showed even the slightest sign of *disrespect*..." The word held an edge of old and bitter pain, even as she trailed off with a wince.

Niko blinked for a heartbeat. "I-I understand," he said, sounding stunned.

But then, we all were. Even Casimir seemed frozen, only his eyes moving as they bounced from Niko to the twins to the family before us. Gods, I didn't think *any* of us knew what to do.

Except Gwyneira.

A warm smile spread over her face. She walked closer to them, ignoring a strangled *what-are-you-doing* protest from Clay. "No one will harm your family, you have my word." She cocked her head at the baby. "May I see her?"

The woman pulled aside a corner of the blanket, revealing an infant with a tousled crop of amber-and-gold hair and wide eyes.

"Her name is Clarissa," Fleur said. "Brock chose it, as a mix of their names." She nodded briefly at the twins. "To honor the brothers he lost."

Gwyneira glanced back at Clay and Lars, her lips parting in a silent *O*.

"Well... fuck." Clay's voice was thick with emotion. "That's just—"

Lars elbowed him, his eyes never leaving the baby. "We're uncles now. You've got to clean up your language."

Gwyneira gave a soft laugh as a choked "yeah, okay" came from Clay.

I retreated while the others drew closer to the family, my gaze darting around the crowded room. There could still be enemies here. One of us needed to keep an eye out. For the gods' sakes, a *baby* was involved now. We couldn't risk someone hurting us *or* the little one.

And yeah, never mind that I felt like I was dog-paddling in the ocean, unable to keep my head above water with the speed at which everything was—

"Roan?" Niko's voice was hesitant.

Fuck.

I cleared my throat. "Yeah?"

"Um..." He looked around like whatever words he wanted might be hiding somewhere in the temple. "About what King Archerias said..."

Fuck, fuck, *fuck*...

"Did you know about that?"

I gaped at him, incredulous. "Did I—" What the hell? "*No.*"

My voice was sharp, and I didn't mean it to be. But Niko just nodded—seemingly mostly to himself, and then turned to Ignatius. "How is it possible? Roan and I —" He faltered. "I mean..."

The elderly scholar regarded us both like he was examining every inch of our features for similarities—which was insane. Yes, okay, Niko had dark eyes like mine. Maybe a little bit of the same face shape. But most days, I looked like death warmed over and there wasn't a damn thing I could do about it, while he looked...

Well, *alive*.

"There was a woman," Ignatius said. "Her name was..." He searched for a moment. "Jessora, yes. That was it. Beautiful girl. Pitch-black hair. Dark eyes. She was not of noble birth, but she had a... an almost *otherworldly* quality about her. A sadness, too, as if she'd lost something precious. Rumors whispered that it may have been a lover or a child, but to my knowledge, she never confirmed any of the stories. She came from a village in the mountains, where the king met her on a hunting trip. From the moment he laid eyes on her, he was enamored."

I had so many questions, I couldn't sort them into words. My adoptive parents always told me my biological mother was a girl from another village. That she'd been young and alone, too scared to raise a child by herself. So she'd given me up, and when my... well, *other side* revealed itself years later, no one could find her again to ask what I was.

But this...

"What happened to her?" Gwyneira asked as she came up beside me, her hand returning to my arm in a gesture of comfort.

And gods, the small contact helped.

Ignatius sighed. "King Archerias's position was

complicated. He had enemies in the royal court, and they did not want him making a strange, quiet village girl his queen. So, one winter's night, they kidnapped her. The king was enraged. He ordered a search of the entire kingdom, and eventually, his loyal soldiers found the ones who took her." Ignatius's mouth tightened. "I was present for their questioning. They were... nearly incoherent. Shaken so badly, yet none would say why. Even after days of interrogation, they gave us no answers." He shook his head. "But Jessora was never seen again."

Gwyneira's fingers tightened on my arm, her expression radiating support, and damn, I loved her for it. Loved her too for how she reached out to Niko, taking his hand and squeezing it in silent comfort.

"There were rumors, however," Ignatius continued, "that she was with child when she was taken. And if that was the case, and she had the babe while in the custody of those scoundrels..." His brow rose and fell as he regarded Niko.

"So," Niko said like he was trying to find his voice. "If it *was* a child she'd lost before meeting the king, and then if she was pregnant when the kidnappers took her too..."

He stared at me. "*That's* what the echo was. The thing nature has been trying to tell me over and over, even after we found out about the demon. I just never imagined it could mean you're my..." He smiled like this was sort of amazing. "My brother."

"But—" My voice was choked, and gods help me, I didn't want to make him think I hated this idea. I just...

I wasn't used to *hope*, even now.

"But I'm *this*," I managed to say. "A monster, and you're not, and—"

Gwyneira's hand slid up my arm, and when my eyes found her own, her expression was achingly kind. "Who says Jessora couldn't have fallen in love with a monster?"

My fears and doubts broke at her gentle question, melting down into a molten craving to hold her, have her, never let her go. She brought stability to my world and light to my darkness. What could I have ever done to deserve someone like her?

Nothing, that's what. Gwyneira defied logic and description.

And she was mine.

Ours, the demon pointed out.

Yes, that.

"There is, however, the matter of the Nine," Ignatius started. "And the impending doom to the world that has been foretold."

All my doubts and anger came rushing back. Oh, for the love of the gods, couldn't we stop for one damned minute? The twins had a niece, I had a brother, the duke and his son were dead on the floor, and Ignatius wanted to talk about the end of the fucking—

"Tomorrow," Gwyneira told the scholar, her voice calm but firm. "Please."

Gods, I loved her.

Ignatius looked ready to argue.

"She's right," Niko cut in before he could speak. "Whatever all of this means, we can talk about it later. The end of the world can wait for a few hours."

Ignatius frowned, and every old anxiety I had knew

why. Apocalypses didn't wait. They happened whether we liked it or not.

But dammit, I couldn't handle much more of this, and from the looks on the faces of all my friends, I wasn't alone.

I just hoped the gods would give us time.

44
MELISANDRE

Every nation was mine.

Except one.

Seated on my throne with shadows hanging thick all around, I listened to the distant lullaby of screams and whimpers, whispers and shouts elicited by my pawns throughout the world. They occupied every neighboring nation now. Every province. They'd even stolen into the Wild Lands, seeking any stragglers mad enough to flee in that direction. My apple trees were there too, following the contortions of ley lines beneath that cursed territory, draining its volatile magic into me.

I felt it all. *Saw* it all.

"It is practically like being one of the gods, is it not, my pet?"

My teeth clenched. "Silence."

He chuckled. "True, it's not *quite*. The gods wouldn't be thwarted by a silly little thing like the Wall of Erenelle."

Beneath my hand, the golden arm of the throne cracked.

"Oh well," he sighed. "Perhaps you weren't meant to be anything more than *mostly* a queen."

I shoved to my feet, stalking away from the broken throne. Slivers of nothingness wafted away as I moved, scattering in the air and drifting up through the windows and out into the city to spread throughout the land.

"After all," Alaric mused, his voice following me as if he paced right at my side. "You can't precisely say you rule the world when somewhere like *Erenelle* still resists you."

"Erenelle is *nothing*," I growled.

"Exactly, pet. It *is* nothing. A fallen nation of ghosts and burned cities. So why haven't you been able to over-throw it?"

I snarled, inarticulate with rage. I was sick of his goading. Of his taunts and jibes. He wasn't even *real*, just a trick played by the Voidborn to twist my mind.

My footsteps came to a stop.

He... he was just a trick of the mind, wasn't he? Of *my* mind. Which meant my mind was the one taunting me. Goading me. My mind was doing all of this.

So wasn't it *more* mad to argue with it? With... myself?

"Those bastards," I whispered. "They... they want me to doubt myself. To resist what *I* want myself to do."

It was so obvious. So clear that I couldn't believe they'd succeeded in deceiving me about it for so long.

I looked down, flinching a bit to find the grotesque

sword Alaric had once claimed now gripped in my hand. In the blade, my own face stared back at me, damn near dumbstruck by the obviousness of the truth. "I am the queen of this world. *Me.* Every ruler is dead or hiding or mine now. I've bent every one of their nations to my rule."

The image blurred strangely, and now Alaric's face stared back at me. But since he was my own mind taunting me, I wasn't sure that mattered either way.

"All but one, pet. Or can you not feel the change in the air? The shift in the wall that says not all is as it seems anymore?"

What the hell was he babbling about?

I scowled. If Alaric was simply a representation of *me*, then I already knew what he spoke of. I had only to concentrate and the answer would become...

My breath caught. It was true. Far to the south of my trees, I could feel how the energy of that damned barrier *had* changed. Parted, at least briefly, only to close again.

Someone had passed through the Wall of Erenelle.

How had I missed that?

"It occurs to me," Alaric commented idly. "That your stepdaughter is still missing." In the blade, he regarded me pointedly. "Or is she?"

No.

A shriek of rage tore from me. "That is *not* possi—"

"Anything is possible, pet. Or have you already forgotten all the realms I showed you? Trust me when I say all the permutations of reality and possibility exceed even *your* wildest dreams."

"Gwyneira could not—"

"Maybe it's not her. Maybe it's someone else. But the point remains the wall *has* been breached, and not by you." He shook his head with such theatrical sadness, I wanted to murder him again. "Powerful queen you may be, but someone out there is obviously more powerful than even you fancy yourself to be."

I made a furious noise. "It's not enough to taunt me, now you have to *rhyme* as well?"

He chuckled. "Why not? If you're going to fail, I might as well find another way to entertain myself."

"I am not failing!" I flung the blade away. It hit the wall hard enough to send chips of stone flying before the metal clattered to the marble floor.

My entire body shook. How *dare* this bastard—this damn creation of *my own mind*—speak to me like I wasn't queen of this whole realm?

"*Almost* the whole realm." Alaric's tiny voice came from the blade by the base of the wall.

I spun away, striding toward my throne again. That was a better place from which to think anyway.

Proudly, I took my seat once more.

I *was* queen. Of Aneira and Gentresqua and the entire damn world.

There was no one more powerful than me.

"Then why do you hold yourself back?"

I raised my hand to knock aside the silver throne to my right, only to pause. The brushed metal held a strange shadow, like more than his face was present in the dull reflective surface.

Like a shadow of his body was there as well, seated idly beside me.

I shuddered, lowering my hand. I was striking at shadows when I'd already confirmed it was my own mind speaking, not the ghost of a dead bastard I'd defeated.

But he—*I*—had a point. "How am I holding myself back?"

He chuckled, the shadow moving like he'd shifted position on the throne to converse with me. "By not taking full advantage of what you've already made. Think about it, pet. You have all my power. You've created these beautifully toxic apple trees throughout the land. And if you simply let those trees of yours dig *deeper* and spread *farther*, you could do more than twist the ley lines. You could shred that wall, conquer what remains of this world, and reach out into all the other worlds beyond this one as well. You could conquer so much more than one silly little realm."

I eyed the strange shadow. "That would tear this world apart."

He scoffed. "And you're meant for more than this anyway. You always have been. You don't need to limit yourself to only *this* petty world. Not when you could rule over so many more." The shadow leaned closer. "You could be an empress. A goddess. *The* goddess, above which none can stand. Surely that's better than restraining yourself to being a mere *queen*."

I was silent, my eyes narrowing with suspicion at his pretty words. But was that all they were? Mere flattery designed to manipulate me?

Or was my mind speaking truth to me instead?

"I can do both," I said. "I *will*. I can destroy the wall

and take those realms, but still rule as a goddess from this one as well."

A trick of the light made it seem as if his metallic teeth glinted in the air, grinning.

"Prove it, pet."

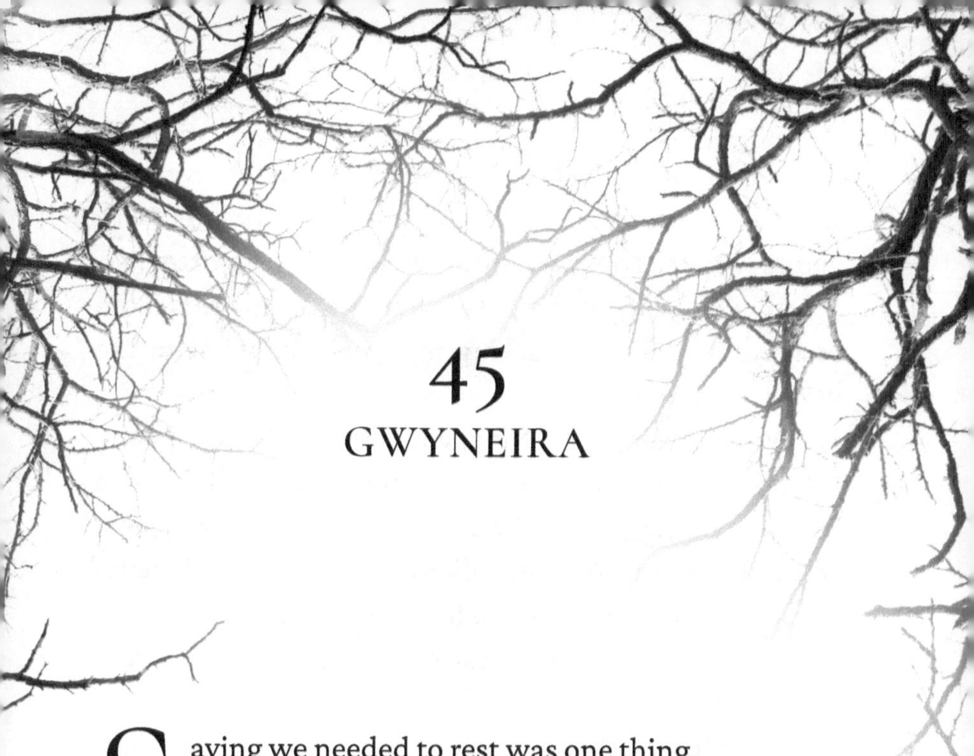

45
GWYNEIRA

Saying we needed to rest was one thing.

Actually doing it was something else entirely.

Lying on the bed I'd shared with Niko and Roan, I stared at the cobwebs dangling from the mottled tiles on the ceiling. It was quiet in the temple now. Most of the giants had retired to various abandoned rooms to sleep after the madness of the day. The sun had set some time ago, and barring the few candles we'd found to break the gloom, most everywhere was shrouded in darkness. In a room down the hall, Clay and Lars were talking with Brock and his family, getting to know their niece and sister-in-law and trying to make peace with the brother they'd long thought was dead. Niko and Roan were still in the main area of the temple. From what I'd heard of their conversation before I left, the two of them were piecing together stories they'd heard of King Archerias, along with what little they knew of their mother. Meanwhile, Ozias was keeping watch over this wing of the temple, while Dex and Casimir met with giants who Ignatius and Brock said were trustworthy.

All while I spent the past few hours pacing this room or lying in this bed, racking my mind for what in the world to do now.

We couldn't be the Nine, whatever that truly meant. I knew what I'd heard and seen, but truthfully, the idea that we were some prophesied collection of warriors just seemed absurd. Yet, regardless of labels and fanciful names, I knew we still needed to stop my stepmother. We had to keep her from destroying whatever was left of my nation.

Or, at least... *I* did.

Apprehension gnawed at my stomach. Niko was safe, and despite all odds, we'd gotten him out of the mines alive. My seven giants had returned to Erenelle, and even though the duke eventually did try to kill him, we'd come out of that with Niko as king and with new allies instead.

My men were safe. Maybe safer than they'd been their entire lives. Clay and Lars had a chance to rebuild with their brother, and Roan and Niko had discovered they were blood as well as family. Dex was already stepping into the role of general for the new king, and the gods knew Casimir would be an incredible help in advising Niko about ruling as well. Byron now had a chance to return to the Order of Berinlian and even to restore one of their temples, while Ozias—

A questioning feeling came from my mate, one that

said he knew my thoughts were spinning me in circles and he wanted to know why.

Quietly, I cursed to myself before silently trying to reassure him I was fine. The last thing I wanted to do was distract him.

I was distracted enough for both of us.

Because I didn't know how to save my nation and make sure the men I loved survived.

Huffing out a breath, I glared up at the ceiling tiles. In books it seemed so easy for generals and soldiers to come up with battle plans. For kings and queens to wage entire wars. Every textbook and tome I'd read laid out each grand strategy as if it had been handed down by the gods. Worry, doubt, and second-guessing never seemed to cross anyone's mind.

Being a leader was easy, if the books were to be believed. Funny how they never talked about what happened if your plans went poorly, and the people who mattered to you died.

I squeezed my eyes shut. This whole time, we'd just been surviving. Running from cabin to mountain to forest to temple without any chance to slow down—and certainly never reaching a place where we could stop for good. That we'd face my stepmother and the Voidborn together had been a given, even if I'd struggled to know how we'd manage that on our own. But now that we were here and, for once, no one was trying to kill us, it suddenly seemed cruel to ask these men to go to battle.

When they could stay here and have a home.

The bed rocked slightly. I opened my eyes, alarmed

because Ozias hadn't left the hallway and I hadn't heard anyone come in.

Ruhl stood on the mattress watching me.

I let out an irritated breath. "What?"

The wolf's eyes narrowed, turning into glowing green slits.

"Please just leave me be. I don't..." Gods, why was I talking to him? It wasn't like he'd ever replied.

Shaking my head at myself, I looked back up at the ceiling. Any other allies I might claim were scattered, to say the least. Valeria and her people were most likely dead—a fact that hurt all the more because I'd hoped one day to call the woman a friend. Meanwhile, Lord Thomas only had farmers for soldiers all the way on the other side of Aneira, and whatever allies I might have among the Jeweled Coven were on the opposite end of the Wild Lands.

Really, *scattered* was a laughable understatement. I didn't even know how to communicate with them, let alone gather them together to mount an offensive military campaign.

Which left us. *Just* us, with no army and no soldiers, and no plan worth—

Ruhl's head butted into my side.

I jerked away from the pillow. "What?"

He huffed—which wasn't exactly an answer.

"I *said* just leave me be. I can't understand what you—"

He huffed again and jerked his head toward the door.

I froze. "Is something wrong?" I whispered, stretching out my senses for Ozias immediately.

Confusion came from my mate, while Ruhl just cocked his head at me.

A wolf should not have been able to look that wry.

"Then what is it?" I demanded.

He stepped closer, bending down.

"What are you—"

Ruhl yanked the pillow from beneath my head.

I shrieked, startled.

Tossing the pillow off of the bed, he gave me another wry look and then hopped down from the mattress. Huffing again, he threw a glance over his shoulder at me before walking to the door.

But unlike times past, he didn't flow around it. Instead, he just turned and sat down.

"You're waiting on me, is that it?"

He didn't make a sound.

"You're not going to let me stay here and think, are you?"

A slight huff that definitely sounded amused.

And also like *no*.

For a moment, I didn't move. I was being ordered around by a wolf, which was patently ridiculous. But equally ridiculous was the fact I doubted he'd leave me alone if I didn't follow.

He jerked his head at me, practically proving my point.

"Fine." I swung my legs over the side of the bed and got up, splaying my hands at him. "Now what?"

Another amused huff. This time he flowed around the door.

"Unbelievable." Shaking my head, I followed.

Ozias stood at the end of the corridor, and when he saw me, another questioning feeling came through our connection.

"Ruhl seems to think we need to go for a walk," I explained, keeping my voice low.

Ozias had no trouble hearing. Agreement radiated from him, and in the darkness, he nodded once to Ruhl like he appreciated the wolf's decision.

Which was just irritating, really. "I didn't say I agreed with that—"

"Go." His voice was barely a murmur. "This area is secured, and movement may help calm your mind."

"I am calm."

"Says the predator tearing itself apart from the inside."

I scowled.

"I can feel your tension, little mate. *Move.*"

Ruhl nudged me.

"You're both so stubborn," I muttered.

Ozias chuckled, a warm and loving feeling coursing through our link. "As are you."

Shaking my head at both of them, I buried a smile. Gods help me, I couldn't stay annoyed, not with his love flowing into me.

What would happen if I lost that?

Biting back a groan at myself, I turned and strode down the hall, turning corners and ignoring Ruhl while he paced along at my side. Maybe Ozias was right, and I really was tearing myself apart. But who wouldn't when everyone they loved was at stake?

And when they had no way to make sure the people they needed would survive?

My eyes swept the open doorframes as I walked, my mind too distracted to truly register what lay beyond. Decaying furniture. Broken windows. Pages from books scattered across the floor, their ink destroyed by rain and time.

Meanwhile, I was no closer to a solution than I'd been while lying in bed staring at a ceiling. Movement wasn't helping. How was I supposed to protect anyone if I couldn't even—

Ruhl flowed in front of me, bringing my momentum to a halt.

"*Now* what?" I demanded.

His wry look gone, he didn't react to my sharp tone, but simply nodded his head to the side. Frowning, I followed his motion.

And froze. "Oh."

The massive wooden door was intact, though it stood ajar, affording a view of the space beyond. While most of the rooms I'd seen were obviously the chambers where scholars slept, there was no bed or chests for clothes in here. This wasn't a bedroom or apartment.

It was a library.

My irritation forgotten, I walked slowly past the door. Beyond the rows of dark wooden bookshelves, moonlight poured through tall windows that miraculously still had their stained glass intact. More dark shelves lined the walls multiple stories high, and every few levels overlooked the ones below by way of galleries with brass railings. Enormous chandeliers hung along the distant ceiling, dust and cobwebs dangling from crystals that glinted dully in the moonlight. Here and there, books lay scattered on the marble floor, some with their pages falling out. But hundreds more still sat upon the shelves, covered in dust but intact.

"It's beautiful," I whispered. I turned to Ruhl. "Did you know this was here?"

A movement rolled through the wolf's smoky body that I swore looked like a shrug.

"Thank you."

He lifted his chin as if motioning me to go on.

Giving him a smile, I walked deeper into the library. Unlike so much of Erenelle, this place didn't feel haunted by ghosts. There were too many books for that to happen. Too many stories and ideas and memories here, living on between the pages.

Books were immortal in their own way. Time itself couldn't change that.

With a sigh, I paused beneath one of the massive chandeliers, turning a slow circle as I took in the beautiful space. Nearby, Ruhl sat on his haunches, his eyes on the stained glass window and the darkness outside.

I couldn't say why, but somehow, I swore there was sadness in his bearing.

Curiosity tugged at me. Quietly, I walked over and sank down onto the tile at his side. "Are you okay?"

He huffed, something dismissive in the sound.

I didn't believe him. "Why are you here, Ruhl? Really?"

This time, he was silent, never looking away from the window.

"Casimir told me that your pack simply showed up one day, several years after Zenirya fell. He never knew where you'd come from or why, just that you helped hold back that corrupted magic in the Wild Lands somehow. But I know you can communicate with me. You showed me your home when we were at Lord Thomas's castle. A land of fire and darkness, yes? And you were searching for something?"

His head turned a bit, though he didn't look at me.

"What is it?" I pressed. "What did you come here for?"

For a long moment, Ruhl didn't move, his eyes on some middle distance like it held secrets only he could see. But finally he turned and lifted one massive paw, letting it hover above my knee almost as if asking permission.

I nodded.

Gently, his paw rested on my leg.

Images and emotions flooded my mind, transporting me into his perspective. I was surrounded by a place of endless fire and darkness, of sheer black cliffs and pits made of flame. Yet I had no need for fear. Those flames and shadows weren't a danger.

They were home.

But as beautiful as it was, the one I longed for, the one whose essence called to my pack... she wasn't there.

We needed her. Craved her. Everything in us hunted for her, and we dreamed of the day our search would come to an end.

But we couldn't leave. Not home nor this place with

its bitter cold and wild magic. Our oaths bound us even now.

And some nights, we feared we'd never find her.

I gasped as Ruhl's paw left my leg. Tears burned my eyes from the overwhelming desperation choking my throat.

His desperation. And gods, his pain.

Swallowing hard, I tried to find my voice. "You could go now? Search for her?"

Ruhl sighed and shook his head like a man.

"But what oath is keeping you here? Surely we can find a way to help you fulfill it so you could—"

"Princess?"

Gasping, I threw a startled look over my shoulder.

Byron stood behind us, staring. Half a dozen enormous books were in his hands as if he'd been in the process of relocating them. "What are you doing here?"

I hesitated. The last time Ruhl communicated with me this way, it'd seemed like he didn't want me to share what he could do with anyone.

And this time, he merely rose from his sitting position, turned, and walked away.

Which was no help.

Trying to gather myself, I pushed to my feet and brushed my hands down my breeches to buy time. "I was just, um... talking."

Byron's brow twitched down. "Ah."

He didn't move to leave.

I fidgeted, overcome with awkwardness. "Okay, well. Have a good night."

Ducking my gaze away, I headed for the door.

"Princess."

I stopped. It took a moment before I could turn back and know my face didn't reveal reluctance or the fact I was internally swearing up a storm.

It hurt to wonder if the others would go.

I already knew Byron was going to.

"Yes?"

He exhaled, taking a step closer. I tensed, fighting not to retreat.

"I should apologize." Propriety seemed to wrap around him like a cloak. "I did not realize that what happened with our magic was—" A frown creased his face briefly as he searched for words. "How it might have been a risk to you."

I blinked, confused. "You *saved* me, Byron. What happened from then on wasn't your fault. And besides, you heard Ignatius. Maybe it's fine."

He shook his head. "I should have been more careful."

I really didn't want to argue with him. Not when it was just the two of us here, maybe alone together for the last time before we faced my stepmother, *hopefully* survived, and then he left for good.

"Apology accepted, then." I turned away again.

"Gwyneira."

I bit back a curse. Why did it hurt to hear him say my name?

Footsteps crunched on the dirty tile. His hand caught my arm.

"Are you angry at me?" Surprise and worry showed on his face. "I swear to you, whatever I've done I—"

"It's not you."

It was everything.

The concern in his eyes was almost more than I could bear.

"What is it then?" he asked, his voice gentle.

And that gentleness hurt more than cold propriety ever could.

As if seeing my heartache, he looked around quickly and then strode over to a wooden chair. Dusting off the seat, he brought it back and urged me down into it. Crouching before me, he took my hands between his own. "What's wrong? Please. Tell me."

His emerald gaze transfixed me. Why did he have to choose tonight, of all nights, to behave so compassionately?

But it pulled the truth from me. "I'm worried." My voice came out barely stronger than a whisper.

He only nodded, urging me to go on.

A tiny, desperate breath left me. "I've studied strategy. War tactics going back for centuries. My father and my tutors did everything they could to train me to be a good queen." I shook my head, unable to look away. "And I don't know how to *begin* taking back my throne. Even now, even after all these days and weeks... I don't. Not without the risk one or all of us could die."

Shame finally shattered the hold his gaze had on me. "And even if we do succeed, that'll only mean it's time for you to leave."

He was silent.

My shame grew, burning in my chest like it would

devour me from the inside. Pulling my hands from his, I rose from the chair. "I'm sorry. I should go."

I started away, making it almost to the door before his voice came from behind me again.

"Princess, stop. Please."

My feet came to a halt, but I didn't turn. "The Order needs you, Byron. More than maybe they know. You're honorable and wise and..." Gods, this hurt. "And you deserve to reap the rewards for how you've held true to your calling all these years."

I started to move.

"And if I can't do that?"

My footsteps stopped at his words.

"If Casimir's worries were right and the tie between us causes pain if we're too far away from one another?"

My eyes closed, a sad smile crossing my face even if he couldn't see it. Always thinking, this incredible scholar. Always doing the right thing even if it cost him. "You'll find a way to break it and keep us both safe. I have faith in you."

"And the prophecy of the Nine?" There was a note of desperation in his voice. "Everything Ignatius said? What of that?"

"Perhaps it's not what we think. Perhaps the prophecy counts Roan and the demon as two, and it was never meant to include you." I let out a breath, clinging to my resolve. "Take your place in the Order, Byron. Please."

I started toward the door again, my heart hurting. Niko must have been wrong on the math. That was all.

But regardless, I couldn't ask Byron *not* to be who he was.

I loved him for who he was.

"Roan and the demon," he muttered behind me, my vampire hearing picking out the gritted words.

Before I could look back in confusion at the frustration in his tone, footsteps crunched on the debris. A hand caught my arm, turning me around.

"Do you want me to go, Gwyneira?" he demanded, a pained fury in his voice I'd never heard before.

My mouth moved, but there wasn't another answer to give. "No. But you have your vows and I don't want to cause you any pa—"

He pulled me forward so fast, I couldn't react.

And then his lips were on mine.

For a moment, shock froze me. But my body caught up faster than my stunned brain, moving my hands to his sides, blurring my thoughts with desire. Shock melted, turning into heat that rushed through my blood and bones and core.

Holy gods... Byron was kissing me.

His hands gripped my arms, holding me to him with such force it would hurt us both if I tried to pull away. But I had no desire for that.

Only for more of this.

Even if it violated everything he'd sworn to uphold.

The reality of that began chewing into my desire like a rot that was determined to destroy everything about this impossible, amazing moment. Because this couldn't last.

It shouldn't even exist.

That reality seemed to catch up to him too. Breathing hard, he broke from my lips, his body shaking. "I..." He cleared his throat with effort and released me, taking a step back. "I'm sorry, Princess. I shouldn't have—"

"Indeed."

The voice came from beside us, sending ice shooting through my veins as Byron froze entirely.

Trembling, I turned.

Ignatius stood in the library doorway.

46

BYRON

Words failed me, leaving only a sensation of falling. Like, in an instant, I'd run straight off a cliff after suicidally concluding I didn't need the ground after all.

And now as I stared at Ignatius, the taste of Gwyneira's lips still on mine, I was left with only one truth—one so simple its description was worthy of Clay.

I was fucked.

"It's not what you think," Gwyneira said, fear and urgency in her beautiful voice. She knew what this meant, perhaps more viscerally than anyone else could, considering our shared memories. She knew what I'd just lost.

Ignatius didn't say a word.

Never taking my eyes from the larger giant, I took Gwyneira's arm and pulled her behind my back. It wasn't that I actually believed she was in danger from the scholar. The reaction was instinctive, a need to protect her that transcended any rational evaluation of the threat.

No, the scholar wouldn't harm *her*.

Me, he would eviscerate. Not with swords or knives, but with words and disgust. With excommunication. Because no matter what respect he may have shown me in the past few days, I'd just violated all my vows and become exactly what scholars like him had always said I was.

Weak.

Incapable of honor or integrity.

A shame to the Order.

"Please," Gwyneira persisted, using her vampire strength to pull away from my grip and move into view of the old scholar once more. "He's never broken his vows, and he wouldn't—"

Ignatius raised a hand, his eyes never leaving me, and despite the fact she was nobility and outranked him, my beautiful princess fell silent, casting an anxious glance in my direction.

It hurt. I never wanted to cause her to worry, and yet she did, all because of what I was about to endure.

Gods, I'd send her away if I thought she'd go.

"Do you believe in the Order?" Ignatius asked me, his quiet words nevertheless seeming loud in the silence of the ruined library.

I refused to tremble. To cower. "With all my heart."

A brief chuckle left him, the corner of his lip rising. It was not a kind expression. "Do not lie, boy."

My jaw clenched. A new feeling simmered below my worry, my dread. It was hot. Burning. It had no name, no shape. But it chewed up from my gut into my chest, scorching everything to ash.

"I don't lie." I bit off the words.

Ignatius was silent.

It was worse than any insult.

"I served." Fury thickened my voice. "*Every. Single. Day.* Even when I thought I might be the only scholar left in the world, I kept the rituals. The ceremonies. I held true to my vows because I believed—"

"Enough."

"No!"

Ignatius's brow rose at my shout.

"No," I repeated in a lower voice. "You spent years making my childhood hell. Denying me even the most *basic* respect because of how I was born. And only now that there is *no one else left* do you offer me the respect that should have been mine all along." My body quivered with rage as I nodded to Gwyneira, never taking my eyes from him. "This is my treluria. We were chosen for one another by fate and the gods themselves. I love her with everything I am. But because I gave into that love for one *fucking* moment, you'd strip away everything I've fought to uphold for my entire life and disrespect me *yet again.*"

Ignatius's expression didn't change. "One moment is all it takes for the truth to emerge."

Outrage burned me alive from the inside, turning my voice into a snarl I barely recognized. "I could have served a *thousand* lifetimes, and it still wouldn't have been enough to prove my worth to you."

"No."

The agreement was simple. As plain and honest as the sun in a winter sky.

And to hear it out loud...

Something snapped around my heart, falling away like the metal shards of a restraint I'd kept in place for far too long. "*You* are the disgrace to the Order." Contempt filled my voice. "Not me."

Taking Gwyneira's hand, I started for the door, determined to shove past him if that was what it took. I was done with this wretched old man who, like so many others, had driven me to doubt myself for so many years. I was done with the belief I only needed to work harder, do better, in order to earn something they *never* would have truly given.

"I agree."

Ignatius's even response stopped me in my tracks. I turned, staring. "What?"

"I was the disgrace. Not you."

What was he playing at?

As if seeing my shock, his brow rose and fell with tired irony. "Twenty years in a cage will teach you a few things, son. Things about others. About yourself. I held so many ironclad beliefs before the Aneiran war that were misguided." He paused, and chagrin crossed his face as he amended, "*Bigoted*. I used my supposed learning to convince myself and others that you were lesser, when in truth, it was myself who was the lesser."

This... this was a dream. I'd had ones like them as a child, when the pain of rejection and bullying became too much to bear, and my mind would try to comfort itself with fantasies.

But I never believed I'd experience anything like them in real life.

Old regret filled Ignatius's expression. "Character is everything. It transcends appearance, station, and circumstances. It defines more about a person than any other factor in their lives, and yet I could not see that. I thought the outside defined the inside, when in reality, the inside holds the power. A person can be born in the lowest of circumstances and have greater integrity, honor, and trustworthiness than the highest person in the land. To judge someone on what you *think* they are rather than seeing them as an individual and having the humility to believe you *don't* actually know everything..." He shook his head. "It is the definition of ignorance. Berinlian would be ashamed that I dared to call myself his scholar."

I stared, utterly speechless.

"And the... the mines taught you this?" Gwyneira said as if carefully choosing her words.

Ignatius's gaze turned briefly to the corridor as if looking past the walls to the other giants.

Or perhaps to the giants who'd lived and died here long ago.

"Over and over again, yes. In the mines I learned more than I had in decades with the Order—perhaps most importantly that I, esteemed scholar and keeper of the wisdom of Berinlian, was in reality little more than a frightened old man who had been a fool for far too long."

He turned back to me. "And I am sorry."

I was speechless.

"In that case," my precious treluria began carefully,

as if testing out a political opponent in court. "Once the threat of the Voidborn is gone, may he take his place with you and rebuild the Order?"

Even as my heart ached for how she so relentlessly supported me, I braced myself. Throughout my life among the scholars, I'd learned not to immediately put faith in a monk's kind words.

They could too easily be a lure designed to make me miss a coming trap.

And as certainly as the sunrise broke the grip of night, Ignatius's mouth tightened with misgiving. "I believe he has a new calling now."

My heart sank. That was it, then. One brief moment, and the faith around which I'd built my life would no longer recognize me as its own.

"The most secret and precious of Berinlian's teachings spoke of the legend of the Nine," Ignatius said. "Of the warriors who would rise up to save our world. But the hearts of those warriors must not be divided because of their own internal conflict. For this reason, my son, your time with the Order must end."

"But the prophecy isn't forever," Gwyneira protested. "Surely he could—"

"No." Ignatius's brow rose in a pointed look. "But that also doesn't mean Byron's place with us is gone."

My pain turned to confusion. Beside me, Gwyneira's expression reflected the same.

"Destiny calls each of you to become the Nine," Ignatius said. "Of that, I have no doubt. And your heart calls you to her. To fight against your heart while also fighting for the fate of the world..." He made a soft sound of disbelief. "Thus, just as I needed to change, so too does the Order's understanding of the vows Berinlian told us to swear. After all, how true is a pursuit of knowledge if it requires us to seal ourselves away from the fullness of life itself?"

I trembled. "We seal ourselves away for the purpose of focus. Of dedication."

Gods, I didn't know if I was pleading for him to prove or disprove what I'd believed all my life.

A rueful smile touched Ignatius's face. "Seal anything away for too long and it becomes weak, not strong."

"So," Gwyneira said as if wanting to hear it with her own ears. "Byron can explore this side of himself and stay in the Order too?"

Ignatius nodded. "He will be Berinlian's strong sword arm in this fight, for you and for all of us." His gray eyes met mine firmly. "You will always have a place in the Order, Byron. Our doors will always welcome you as a brother. But you are now the *champion* of the Order, not its monk. You and your allies are the hope of this world. Your heart need no longer be divided."

I couldn't breathe. This couldn't be true.

Oh gods, let it be true.

"Th-thank you." I fought to hold my voice steady and mostly failed.

Ignatius bowed his head. "And thank you for enduring despite a foolish old man's bigotry."

I couldn't speak.

Smiling a bit, he started away and then glanced back at Gwyneira. "Come find me in the morning. I have some ideas on how to reach your allies and marshal your army."

Her mouth fell open, soundless, but before she could say anything, he walked out of the library, carefully closing the door behind him.

Barely feeling as if my body itself was real, I turned to Gwyneira.

She was smiling, the expression a mix of hope and happiness for me.

Yet questions were there too. The ones I'd seen live and die a thousand times in her eyes.

Was I okay? Did I want this? Did I want her?

I knew exactly how to respond.

47
GWYNEIRA

Byron reached out, his fingers brushing my cheek. "Would you do me the honor of staying the night with me, my beautiful treluria? Of allowing me to worship every inch of your beauty?"

His words made my core quiver. But still I stared up at him, searching his green eyes. "Are you *sure* you're okay—"

"Without question." His brow rose. "Are you?"

I nodded quickly, and his lip twitched.

"Before we go any farther, though, I want to say something."

Apprehension made me tense.

"It's nothing bad." His hands rubbed my arms. "It's simply that, as you could probably guess, I..." His brow rose and fell. "I've never lain with anyone before. To be honest, I never understood how others craved the experience. Being close in that way..." He gave a tiny chagrinned scoff. "It held no appeal." His green eyes locked on me. "Until I met you."

He took my hand. "What I'm trying to say is that I love you. I've loved you since before I could admit the words. Since before I even understood what I was feeling. You're the only one for me, Gwyneira. And even if my body betrays me by coming too quickly to bring you pleasure this time, I swear I want to do this again and again until I can spend hours making you scream my name."

Gods. "We... we can start slow? Give your body time to—"

He shook his head. "I'm done with slow. I've spent my whole life thinking, analyzing, staying controlled. I don't want that with you."

Confidently, he pulled me against him. The hard length of his cock pressed to my stomach, making my breath hitch and my insides turn molten.

"I've studied countless books and scrolls, princess. But I can say with utter certainty that *you* are what I want to study for the rest of my life. How to bring you joy. How to be what you need in bad times and good." He smiled. "How to make you fall apart with pleasure... starting now."

Bending down, he crushed my lips to his.

Holy...

My body pressed to his, melding against him. My fists clenched on his sweater while he slipped his hands down my sides, feeling me through my clothes. He nipped at my lips, urging me to open to him and then devouring me when I obeyed.

Tingling need coursed through my body, bright like pinprick stars dancing in my veins.

His magic...

I gasped as he broke from my lips, his mouth exploring down the side of my neck. I could feel his power like a cool breeze pulsing around his skin. My own rose instinctively to meet it, tangling with his until I couldn't tell where one of us ended and the other began.

Frost shimmered in the air around us like diamond dust beneath moonlight.

My eyes widened. "Byron."

He paused, catching sight of the display. A smile lifted the corners of his lips. "We were made for one another, even in our magic." He looked back down at me. "My treluria."

"You... you felt that about us?"

He nodded.

"Is it why you called me Snow when Ignatius asked for my name?"

A hint of embarrassment crossed his face. "You've always felt like snow and starlight to me. And in old Aneiran, *white snow* is the etymology of your name, so it... fit." He hesitated. "Did I offend you?"

I shook my head. "I like it."

Relief took the place of his chagrin. He drew me to him once more. "Then I'll call you that, even if just between the two of us. My beautiful Snow."

He bent lower, gently exploring my lips, my neck, and the gap where my blouse was unbuttoned at the base of my throat. "I confess," he murmured between kisses. "I do have a question, though."

Making a noise of encouragement for him to ask, I fumbled to unfasten my blouse, my pulse racing.

His lips ghosted across my collarbone. "You've read so many love stories. But I have not. All I know of how to please you is what little I saw in your memory. So tell me, princess. What would the heroes in those books say to you now?"

Confused, I paused with my fingers on a button. "What?"

He drew back, his eyes like molten emeralds. "Let the books you love be my teachers. Tell me what they say. What dark and delicious things you read that make your beautiful body tighten with need." A decidedly wicked smile pulled at his lips. "I want to know what fantasies those books gave you. What secret desires live in your incredible mind."

Holy gods above...

My body lit on fire and my mind went blank as the snow for which Byron had named me. I didn't know what to say, strange embarrassment turning my cheeks red.

Was this really happening? My younger self never would have dreamed I'd have the love of men like Byron and his friends, let alone that I could give voice to the fantasies from my books.

His smile softened. "Think on it. I want to make all of them come true with you. But for now, just tell me something they would say."

"Perhaps..." I wetted my lips. "Perhaps that they liked to kiss me... down there?"

I twitched my chin toward the apex of my legs.

"Mm." Nodding thoughtfully, he kneeled. His fingers found the ties of my breeches. "And would they say that your beautiful cunt is the altar at which they'd worship until the day they died?"

My jaw went slack with surprise. "I—"

I gasped as cool air brushed my wet center when he pulled my pants away.

A hungry, needful sound escaped him. Gently, he traced his fingertips down the crease of my hips, making my skin pebble and my core throb. "Rose petals," he murmured.

I started to ask what he meant, but then his fingers brushed across my clit, making me buck against the bookcase at my back. My hands gripped a shelf, holding me in place while his thumb circled my sensitive flesh again.

Gods, I was going to come from this alone.

Carefully, he slid a finger into me, rocking it in and out as if testing the feel of my channel and then crooking it gently. Pleasure thrummed through me in time to his motions, and my legs trembled. "Byron…"

He didn't take his eyes from my sensitive core. "And what else would they say?"

"Th-they—" Gods help me. "They'd say how they liked my, um… my breasts?"

His other hand slid across my abdomen and up beneath my blouse. But his motions weren't quick or rushed. No, he guided his palm along my torso like an explorer mapping every inch of my skin, until at last his fingertips traced over the curve of my left breast.

My nipple hardened, and I whimpered with need.

He made a pleased sound. "And would they say these gorgeous peaks are more beautiful than any mountain? That you are all they want to come back home to every day?"

Any attempt I could have made at a response was lost as his hands began working in tandem, his finger crooking inside me while his other hand tightened around my breast and pinched my nipple tightly. Staring down at him, I couldn't even find words to plead for release.

He watched my desperation intently, a red-haired devil with eyes like dark emeralds. His gaze lingered on my face like he was drinking in what he did to me, before tracing over my body again like he was noting every reaction. "And tell me, princess. Would they taste you?"

I nodded. "Y-yes."

Humming thoughtfully, he leaned closer. His tongue slipped between my folds once. Twice.

A groan escaped him. "Would they say that the nectar of the gods could never taste as good as you?"

Without waiting for my response, he returned to my core like a man possessed. Fervently, his tongue delved between my folds, flicking and licking at my sensitive flesh while his hands and fingers never stopped their movements.

I gripped the shelf so hard, I felt the wood crack. Pleasure coiled hot and tingling between my legs, nearly stealing my balance. My head fell back against the bookcase while my hips rocked into him over and over, totally out of my control. "Oh *gods*, Byron..."

A cry left me as I came, my core clenching around his

fingers. Keeping up his motions, he didn't stop until I sagged against him, my body shuddering with the aftermath of my orgasm.

"You…" I swallowed hard, trying to find my voice. "You're a quick study."

He looked up at me, his face wet with my slick, and he grinned. "I've always been a good student."

Breathlessly, I laughed. "I'll say."

His grin turned hungrier. Rising to his feet, he kissed me, the taste of my release on his lips.

And gods, that was arousing.

He drew back again. "I need you, Gwyneira. I've needed you my whole life, and I was just enough of a fool to think I could live without you."

My heart tumbled over itself. "You have me."

"Not yet." His grin returned. "May we see how long I can last in that intoxicating cunt of yours, my treluria?"

I managed a nod, my clit throbbing with desire. "Please."

Swiftly, he shucked his breeches. Taking my hips, he hefted me up like I weighed nothing, hoisting me above his cock.

My legs wrapped him on instinct. Between my thighs, I could see his length, thick and veined, ready to enter me. Shivers of need went through my core as his tip hovered at my entrance.

When I looked back up, wonder filled his eyes. "Gods, I love you," he whispered.

I started to respond, only to cut off with a choked gasp when he lowered me down and my pussy stretched around his thick cock.

He froze, tension flashing over his face. "Are you okay?"

I nodded fast. "Yes." Wiggling my hips, I tried to take more of him. "More, please. *Please.*"

Chuckling, he smiled. "Greedy girl. What was that about going slow?" He sank in deeper and groaned. "Fuck..."

"Yes," I begged. "That. Now."

A huff of amusement left him, but when I succeeded in pushing my pussy farther down, it quickly turned into another groan. "Berinlian save me."

With a grunt, he pulled out a bit and then drove himself back into me, deeper.

I moaned as he began thrusting into me. Gods, he was so big, I could feel every inch of his cock. My body burned with the delicious pleasure-pain stretch of taking him. Over and over, his thick girth stroked across my inner walls, stoking my need higher.

But when I leaned back to see his face, his eyes were wide.

"Are you—" I started.

"Fine." Breaths came fast through his nostrils. "Who..." Another choked huff of amusement came from him. "Who knew the... focus techniques... of the Order... could be used to last longer... for you?"

My mouth moved in surprise. But my words turned into a startled whimper when his hands clutched my ass, crushing my clit against him.

"Gods..." he groaned. "Fucking *gods*..."

I nodded. "Remind me—" I bit back a moan as he

rocked against my clit, "—to thank you for studying those focus techniques."

He gasped out a short laugh. His thrusting sped up, making my spine bump the bookcase. But before I could hit it again, he spun me away, supporting my weight while his thick cock kept pounding into me.

I clung to him, every nerve in my body lost to what we were doing. But gods, why hadn't we stripped down completely? My breasts were scraping against my blouse and not his chest. My hands gripped his sweater and not his skin. My flesh burned with the desire to be completely naked with this amazing man.

Because once, he'd been so restrained.

Now he was ravenous.

"Tell me." His fingers teased at my back entrance as he kept thrusting into me, sending whole new waves of pleasure coursing through my veins. "What do you need? What does this beautiful body crave?"

My muscles tightened, my entire being chasing a release just beyond my reach. "You." My head fell back. "I... I need you."

"You have me. Forever."

The word stole my breath. I squeezed my eyes shut against the burn of tears of relief and desire.

He grunted with desperation. "Come, princess." He shifted his grip on me, shoving one hand between us and flicking my clit. "I want to feel you... when I..." A choked groan escaped him as his hot cum hit me deep inside.

Fire roared higher in my core. It tangled between my legs like a ball of lightning and exploded in a rush of sheer ecstasy. My legs clenched around his hips. My hands and pussy clamped down on him at the same time. In a white-hot rush of pleasure, my release washed over me, blinding me to the world.

Rivers of light coursing beneath us. More rivers in the distance, but dark vines wrapped them, poisoning them.

And the dark vines were starting to head this way.

I lurched back, my eyes flying wide. The vision faded, leaving only my shaking body and the feeling of Byron gripping me while my pussy milked his cock of the last of his cum.

His eyes found mine. "Did you—"

"See that?" I finished at the same time.

He nodded. "The queen's magic is coming."

48

OZIAS

We had too many enemies in this temple that was anything but silent.

Invisible in the shadows, I scanned the corridor. Small creatures crept through the debris. Stones shifted and settled, sending dust whispering to the ground. Far below my feet, water rushed along, newly freed of its prison in the earth.

And down the hall—in a library, from the smell of it—my mate was finally finding peace with my obstinate friend.

I adjusted my aching cock, breathing slow and steady while sunrise began to lighten the dark sky beyond the window at the opposite end of the corridor. I was happy for my mate and my friend. Of course, I *also* would have liked to join in. But I understood giving them both space while they addressed the tension that had been building between them ever since the seven of us met our beautiful treluria.

Not to mention *someone* needed to protect them while they attended to their needs.

I could be patient.

Ruhl's glowing green eyes lit the shadows briefly, floating near the door of the library. I swore the wolf *smirked* at me.

Damn that infernal thing.

I returned my attention to the corridor, determined to remain focused. I could wait to—

My mate's release rolled like an earthquake through our connection, and I bit back a groan with effort. This close, I could smell traces of her in the hall, and the combination was... gods...

I shuddered and straightened, avoiding giving that damned wolf the satisfaction of acknowledging his existence. Let him smirk. I could handle their—

Alarm shot through my link to my mate.

I lunged from the shadows, running for the library door. With distant satisfaction, I noted the wolf recoiling in surprise. But the creature regrouped quickly, flowing after me as I yanked open the door and charged into the library.

At the sight of me, Gwyneira came to a stop. "The queen's magic is coming this way," she said without preamble. "The power that made those poison-apple forests are heading for the wall."

Fuck.

I jerked my head back the way I'd come, and then took off. My beautiful mate didn't need further explanation, racing after me.

The others lurched awake when we raced past their door. "What's wrong?" Dex asked immediately.

Quickly, the princess relayed what she'd told me.

"We need to warn someone," Niko said.

Byron and Lars nodded, but I didn't like the idea. Warn them of what? We didn't need to debate or think through possibilities, and gods knew that was what some of my friends and that scholar Ignatius would want to do.

We needed to stop this, keep the princess safe, and fucking annihilate anything that dared to threaten her again.

From the corner of my eye, I saw Roan shudder. His eyes met mine, except I could see that strange glint that I now understood was his demon too.

I suspected that creature agreed with me.

"We find Ignatius," Dex said. "We go from there."

I suppressed a growl. Fine. I headed for the door, not bothering to wait for the others. They would catch up or they would debate, but I didn't care.

That queen would die.

"I guess we're going then," Lars said.

My mate was already on my heels.

Gods, I loved her.

Moving fast, I tracked Ignatius's scent through the winding halls, coming to another section of the temple where the larger giants had found sleeping quarters.

When I rounded the corner, Ignatius was walking out of his room, a stack of dusty books beneath one arm and another book open in his opposite hand.

He came to a sharp stop at the sight of us. "Something is coming, isn't it?"

The words were a question, but clearly, he already knew the answer, because a heartbeat later he simply said. "Come with me."

Turning quickly, he retreated into his room.

Not letting down my guard, I trailed him, keeping my mate safely at my back. Candles burned in wax-covered holders in random spots around the room, casting wavering light. The windows were dusty and covered in dirt, obscuring the hints of sunrise outside. Along one wall, books were stacked in haphazard fashion, as if they'd been moved out of the way—but with more care than I would have shown.

I didn't trust those things.

Ignatius strode past them though, heading for a tall wooden table on the opposite end of the room. Made of a warm, golden wood, it was carved as if from one massive log, no seams to be seen, and it stood tall enough that the princess would struggle to see over its top. Assorted pieces of metal gleamed on its surface, looking almost like components of a disassembled clock. In the center of the mess, a mirror reflected the room from within a brass frame that had more bits of metal sticking out from its sides, as if it was in the middle of being repaired.

Byron's brow rose. "A magic mirror?"

Ignatius nodded. "I've almost got it working. With the help of the kings and you, scholar, I believe I should be able to get a message past the wall."

Warily, Lars glanced between us and the older scholar. "Uh, who are you contacting?"

"The witches," Gwyneira said before Ignatius could respond. "Right?"

The old man nodded. "If they are still alive out there, they need to know what's coming."

"Well, great." Clay rubbed his hands together. "Let's do it already."

"As impatient as a tidal wave," Ignatius said, not unkindly before turning back to the table.

Clay glanced at us with confusion like he couldn't understand the comment.

In spite of myself, I buried a smirk.

A fizzling sound came from the mirror. The reflection of the room wavered like a pond would when a rock had been dropped through its surface. Invisibly, a wave of magic emanated out from it like a chilled breeze.

My beast's hackles rose with distrust for the sensation.

The reflection stilled, but it showed only murky gray.

"It may take a few minutes," Ignatius said. "Not only are we crossing the Erenlian wall, we also have the Wild Lands with which to contend. If we can bypass that magic, we should be able to—"

"Hello?"

A garbled voice came from the mirror. It sounded like a man, but no image appeared to identify the speaker.

Ignatius turned back quickly. "Hello, yes." He tapped on the mirror frame. "Can you hear me?"

"—said hello?"

A frustrated sound left the scholar. He fiddled with the bits of metal on the side of the mirror.

"—sure who this is—" The voice suddenly became

less garbled and the murky fog cleared into the image of an elderly giant in a candlelit study with walls that looked like they belonged in a cave.

The elderly giant gaped with shock. "Ignatius? Is that... How is this possible? Where are you?"

Relief showed on Ignatius's face. "I am in Erenelle, old friend. The temple of Syloria, to be specific. And—" He motioned to Byron, waiting until the younger man joined him. "I have your former mentee and his friends to thank for it."

Dathan smiled. "Are you well, Byron? Did the glass box work to protect the princess?"

Oh... fuck.

My eyes darted to Ignatius. The elderly scholar frowned and then turned.

He looked straight at Gwyneira.

"It, um... yes." Byron stammered. "Listen, we need your help with—"

"Princess," Ignatius said like he was filling in a blank. His brow rose, his eyes never leaving my mate. "There is a reason you thought the apples were a cruel joke, is there not? And why you know so much about Aneira."

Gwyneira was silent.

"You have more than the look or power of Queen Eira. You are her daughter."

I braced myself to lunge if he *dared* look like he wanted to hurt her.

Ignatius nodded to himself. "That makes a great deal of sense." Without another word, he turned back to the magic mirror. "We have need of your assistance, Dathan.

Tell me, are you still among the witches of the Jeweled Coven?"

I stared at Ignatius as he continued explaining the situation to Dathan. That was it? It made sense and... nothing else?

I didn't trust it.

Gwyneira's hand slipped along my back, calming reassurance coming through our bond. For some reason, she seemed as if—beyond her initial alarm—his reaction hadn't surprised her.

I eased out of my tense posture ever so slightly, but I still watched the scholar. I trusted my mate, but where her safety was concerned, I could never be too careful.

"—really are the Nine, then why has their magic not joined as the oldest interpretations say?"

My jaw clenched at Dathan's words. And then there was *that* risk to her...

"Syloria may be able to help with that," Ignatius said.

"Setting that aside," Dex cut in before Dathan could speak. "The priority right now is the attack the queen is sending toward the Wall of Erenelle. It may be some distance away still, but that only means we need to use that time to prepare. Because if that destroys our defenses, we'll have too much on our hands to worry about any prophecy or whether our enemy plans world domination."

"Yeah, mostly because we'll be dead," Clay chimed in. "So how does this help us with that?"

Ignatius gave the blond giant a wry look. "The wall is only half the issue. Tell me"—he turned to Niko—"when we first met, you thought you were in the mines outside Lumilia. Why is that?"

My friend faltered at suddenly being the center of attention. "The, um... the soldiers brought me to see the queen first."

"What?" Gwyneira exclaimed. "You never mentioned that."

He shrugged. "It didn't really matter. I mean, she wanted to..." Hesitation flashed over his face as if he was reconsidering his words. "Okay, well, she tried to have one of the Voidborn take me over, but it—"

"Niko!" The princess reached out, gripping his arm in her shock.

"I'm fine. It didn't work."

I definitely wasn't the only one staring at him in confusion.

"Didn't *work*?" Byron repeated carefully.

Niko's eyes went to Ignatius and Dathan, questions starting to rise in his gaze. "There was a, um... like a weird crystalline feeling and then the Voidborn just kind of... you know, died."

"Holy shit, friend." Clay gaped at him. "You think you could've mentioned you're Voidborn-proof."

"I have no idea why it happened," Niko protested. "Maybe there was something wrong with the Voidborn she ordered to attack me." He hesitated. "The queen seemed pretty shocked, though. And angry."

Clay scoffed. "I bet."

Niko frowned.

"Shield of Erenelle," Byron murmured.

Roan turned to him. "What?"

Blinking like he didn't realize he'd spoken out loud, Byron glanced around. "Um, what the king said. Or, rather, the magical representation of the king."

"Precisely." Ignatius nodded.

In the magic mirror, Dathan smiled and nodded as well.

I bit back a growl of irritation, but Clay got there first. "Someone want to fill us in?" he prompted.

Ignatius smiled. "The wall is the shield of Erenelle. Its power responded to King Niko—and it appears it extended to protect him even in the castle at Lumilia."

"Perhaps this is what joining their powers truly meant," Dathan told him.

Ignatius nodded. "To share the protection of Erenelle."

I glanced at the others, wary at my own hesitation, because I was no scholar. Who was I to question? I hated books.

But I loved stories. Their winding tales coursed through twists and turns like prey determined to flee. Yet when all was said and done, the predator always hunted down their meaning and caught them in the end.

And true, *this* was no story, just the random path of real life.

Yet somehow, the scholars' conclusion didn't quite track.

"Whatever it means," Dex said with all the incisive logic of a general determined not to let hypothetical musings make him lose sight of the war. "At best that only protects the nine of us, and only for as long as the wall still stands. We need a strategy beyond merely trying to outlast the queen's current attack."

Ignatius sighed, nodding. "I agree. Syloria is the safest place in Erenelle right now, given that the waters are flowing and fueling the defenses here again. But that and the wall itself are only half the battle. As I've said before, Erenelle cannot stand on its own forever. We must reclaim the nexuses. Starting with the princess's home in Lumilia."

"Um, why Lumilia?" Lars asked warily.

"Because I suspect Queen Melisandre has made that her base of power. She has twisted Aneira from the start, and to take bend the nexus beneath its capital would be too irresistible a victory to resist. But Lumilia was Queen Eira's home as well, and the home of Princess Gwyneira's father's ancestors for generations." He gave Gwyneira a pointed look. "The magic there knows you, just as the magic of Erenelle knew King Niko. Of any nexus in the world, you'll stand the best chance of reclaiming the one beneath your home."

Casimir scrubbed a hand across his chin thoughtfully. "Reclaim the nexus, reclaim the throne. Fate is efficient for once."

At my mate's worried look, Casimir gave a small shrug, sympathy in his eyes.

"Indeed it often is," Ignatius agreed, "even if it doesn't always appear as such at first. And now it brings together the representatives of reality itself. Each of you were drawn from three nations that—in their own ways —both possess strong magic and are fighting to be resurrected from death because of it. It makes sense that you are the ones chosen to fight for our world."

I had no idea what he was talking about, but I also didn't care. Gwyneira had turned away, her eyes on the window.

Shame suddenly filtered through our connection, coming from her.

"What is it?" I asked, confused. The worry, I understood. But shame?

She remained quiet.

"Princess?" Niko urged. "What's wrong?"

"It's just..." She closed her eyes. "You talk of strong magic, but I'm no match for my stepmother. She has decades of training, strength from the Voidborn..." The shame deepened. "Her power has been hunting me, and every time it's found me... I've almost died. And that was without me *intentionally* seeking her out. Even in the gateway, she almost..."

My mate trailed off, the worry inside her mixing with a questioning feeling that also made no sense.

"What?" I urged her.

Exhaling, she turned back to us. "I don't know how to stop her. Not really. I tried and she just came back from the empty realms stronger. But I think the gateway demons want to help. Or the, uh... the *big one* does."

Clay made an incredulous sound. "Big one?"

"It told me when the time was right, I should call."

Ignatius's brow furrowed thoughtfully.

"Call..." Byron said like his mind was running the simple word through a maze of meaning. He cast a glance back at the magic mirror.

Dathan nodded as if answering my friend's unspoken thought. "Gateway demons often have more than one meaning to their words."

"So there was more than one meaning to 'eat us', then," Clay commented. "Wonderful." At his twin's tired look, he gaped at him. "What? Those things wanted to devour us. I say we tell the witches what's going on and let *them* deal with crazy ol' Queen Mel."

Lars frowned. "I know you're not a coward, brother."

Clay's dismissive attitude faltered, cracking into barely suppressed anxiety. "That bitch could *kill* Gwyneira."

Dread settled over my friends' faces, mirroring what I was damn sure was on mine.

"She's wanted me dead since the moment I was born," Gwyneira said into the silence. "That's not what worries me." Her eyes darted across all of us, and I could only too easily read the truth.

Losing *us* was what scared her.

"But Dex is right," she continued. "We need a plan, and I think, Ignatius, you were on the right path with reaching out to Dathan." She looked at the elderly scholar in the magic mirror. "We're going to need *anyone* who will help us if we're going to stand a chance of stopping my stepmother. So if the gateway demons agree, do you think you could convince the witches to take a gateway and meet us in Lumilia? Perhaps in the old apothecary district to the west of the castle? I know magic isn't exactly popular in Aneira"—wryness filled her voice at the massive understatement—"but that still seems like a place the witches might know."

Dathan nodded. "Rufinia has spoken of it, yes. I will tell her." He smiled. "And I will join them."

"Good. Thank you. Then while you're doing that, we'll take a gateway to the wall, have Niko help us past that, and then take another to meet you there."

The elderly scholar smiled. "I'll see it done, your highness." He glanced over at Ignatius and Byron. "And Berinlian willing, I'll see you both in person when this is done."

His image disappeared, the mirror becoming nothing but a reflective piece of glass once more.

Resolutely, the princess turned to us. Her bearing was straight. Her face calm. But I could still feel how her nervous worry bubbled inside. She doubted herself, even now. Even when, standing here between us all, she looked every inch the warrior queen she'd been born to be.

She wouldn't face her stepmother alone. I'd die before I let her do that. But *no one* should doubt her strength.

Especially not Gwyneira herself.

My mate's eyes flicked toward me. She could feel my confidence in her. I wasn't hiding a scrap of it.

But still, she worried.

"Okay, but, um... one thing?" Niko straightened a bit, clearly trying to overcome his own apprehension. "If there's something about me that will protect Gwyneira —that will protect *all* of you—then I think we need to try that too before we go anywhere. Especially before going *there*."

Dex was frowning, but he nodded. "What does that require?" He directed the question to Ignatius.

The scholar looked around at all of us, and my beast growled, apprehensive at the hope and confidence in his gaze.

Anything that protected Gwyneira was good in our eyes. But that didn't mean either I or my beast wanted to risk her by undertaking strange magic.

But the scholar only smiled. "Come with me. The joining of the Nine shall begin."

49
GWYNEIRA

Drawing his robes around him like a suit of armor, Ignatius strode past us, heading for the main chamber of the temple.

Apprehension tangled in my stomach as I followed him. Did all leaders feel this gnawing worry on the eve of battle? This fear that, with the plan they'd set in motion, they just signed the death warrants of everyone they loved?

My father hadn't. Not that I could truly tell. His generals certainly had not.

And now I was going to lead a siege against the very kingdom they'd fought and died to protect.

As we walked, Ozias bent down, growling in my ear. "You're not alone, little mate."

That was part of the problem.

I tried to let him feel my gratitude for his attempt at reassurance, rather than my dread, but this link between us meant I was doomed to fail from the start. The *problem* was that on my own, I didn't have a clue how to stop my stepmother. And if my men were with me, it only meant they might die too.

Consternation came from Ozias. I didn't have the first clue how to ease that either.

Up ahead, Ignatius motioned for Byron and Casimir to join him as he continued across the temple's main chamber and past the fountain. His murmured words reached my ears, but it was merely a list of book titles and magical references I couldn't follow.

Which only proved the point that I wasn't prepared for this.

Exhaling sharply, I tried to push down the doubt gnawing at me like a rabid dog. In the end, Ozias really was right. Not simply that I was with my men—that still made me nervous as hell for them—but about the fact I wasn't alone. We'd go through the gateway, we'd find the witches and Dathan, and *they* would come up with a way to stop my stepmother.

And maybe no one would die.

At a section of the main chamber's far wall, Ignatius stopped. The stone surface bore an ornate carving of giants beneath a rainstorm, but bore no door or opening I could see.

Pressing his fingers to specific points on the carving, Ignatius murmured a spell under his breath.

A click sounded from inside the wall.

The door swung open, revealing a dark tunnel sinking down into the earth.

"This way." Ignatius hurried into the shadows.

None of us moved.

"We good, Oz?" Clay prompted. "Byron?"

My scholar nodded, but Ozias took a moment longer before grudgingly doing the same. At my questioning look, he growled, "Strange magic in there."

I swallowed down my worry. "We could just go back and—"

"Not if this protects you," Dex interrupted, his voice brooking no argument. "Come on."

He followed Ignatius through the opening, and one by one, most of my men did the same, until only the twins, Ozias and I remained.

And Ruhl.

By the entrance, dark black smoke gathered and coalesced into the shadow wolf. He took one look down the tunnel and then sank onto his haunches, giving no sign he intended to follow.

"Aren't you coming too, buddy?" Clay asked.

The wolf didn't move.

Clay sighed. "Great." He headed after Lars down the tunnel.

I didn't take my eyes from Ruhl. "Is this safe? Really?"

A small huff left the wolf, almost like a scoff. But then he twitched his jaw toward the doorway as if motioning me to go onward.

It wasn't exactly reassuring. But I also trusted the wolf enough to know if this was *truly* a danger, he'd stop us.

For his part, Ozias eyed the wolf distrustfully, but with his hand on my shoulders, he started toward the dark tunnel.

The air grew warmer as we descended. Damp

surrounded us and moisture dripped from the stones overhead. Glowing moss and fungi clung to the rocks, emanating soft blue and green light.

"What *is* this place?" Niko whispered.

No one answered.

The tunnel came to an end, opening out into a shadowy grotto where stalactites covered in bioluminescent plants clung to the distant ceiling. The majority of the floor was taken up by a natural stone pool of water that shimmered in shades of blue and green from other glowing plants that grew beneath its surface. The water didn't seem too deep. Barely more than a few feet and clear as the purest glass. But the glow of the plants within made it shimmer like it was alive, casting dancing shadows and light across the cavern and illuminating gold symbols inlaid in a ring into the stone walls. A ledge of stone ran around the pool, emptying into a recessed area beyond it, where low stone blocks formed seats and glimmering moss covered the ground like a carpet.

"Gods, this is beautiful," Lars said softly, sounding taken aback.

I nodded, speechless.

Ignatius smiled at the cavern like he was greeting an old friend. "All magic done here is contained and amplified by the protective spells placed upon these walls. It is a sacred space for our most potent, powerful endeavors." Turning, he bowed his head briefly to us. "If ever there was a place in Syloria to help with joining your powers as one, it is here. When you are done, come back to my chambers. We will go from there to prepare the gateway."

Without another word, he started back the way we'd come.

"Wait, that's it?" Clay looked around, incredulous. "You're not staying to do *whatever* we're doing here?"

"I am not one of the Nine," the scholar said as if it were obvious. "I suspect this is why your strange wolf knew to stay on the surface as well. All who are here will be joined by the spell."

The scholar disappeared up the tunnel.

"*What* spell?" Clay called after him. Turning back to us, he appeared flabbergasted. "Okay, did this guy honestly just drop us off in a magical cave with a fucking *to-do list* and no idea how to even—"

"Quiet," Casimir said, his eyes locked on the water. "Can't you feel that?"

Byron nodded immediately, watching the glowing pool too. "We need to be in the water." He tugged his sweater over his head and tossed it to the side.

Wary looks passed between most of the others, but Dex merely turned to Casimir. "I'm assuming full nudity isn't required?"

"As appealing as that sounds," the vampire replied. "I suspect not."

Clay turned a wry look on Lars. "We'll be counting on you to dry us out when this shit is over, then, brother."

Lars didn't react, his eyes on the water.

"Everybody in," Dex ordered.

Heart pounding, I removed my boots and then pulled off my sweater before slipping over the stone edge into the water. Soft leaves of glowing plants brushed my legs as I walked forward. The rocky bottom of the pool was rough, but not enough to scratch the soles of my feet, only to give me purchase. Glimmering lights like stars scattered around me when I moved, as if the disturbance of my presence caused something in the water to light up. But the water itself was neither hot nor cold. If not for the way it darkened my breeches and the bottom of my undershirt, it almost wouldn't seem to be here at all.

"Okay, yeah, this is weird." Clay turned around, his hands moving back and forth through the sparkling liquid. "Even the water up top didn't feel like this."

"Everyone okay?" Niko asked as the others spread out to form a rough circle around the edges of the pool. Around the walls, the symbols of the Order reflected the glow in dull gold.

Lars frowned. "So far."

"Princess." Byron motioned me forward. "If you would come to the center?"

I hesitated. "Why?"

Casimir smiled. "Because, as Ignatius told us, the Nine have a singular member at their center. I do not think my friends would disagree when I say you have been and will always be our heart."

Around the pool, my men nodded in agreement.

I bit my lip, searching for words. "And you all are mine."

They smiled, so much love in their eyes that it stole my breath. I wanted this moment to last. To never end.

"Go on, baby." Clay nodded to the center of the circle.

An urging feeling came from Ozias. "It's you for us, little mate. Always."

Nervousness fluttering in me like a trapped bird, I walked forward. The rough surface of the natural pool helped me keep my feet, even as the strange water rose to just beneath my breasts.

"Ready?" Byron asked Casimir.

The vampire nodded.

Lifting their arms, they watched each other carefully and began to speak. I didn't recognize the language. It sounded like Erenlian, yet not quite.

But the effect on the pool was immediate. The sparkling flecks of light stirred by our presences grew in number, spreading out like threads of glitter radiating from us through the strange water.

My lips parted. I... I knew this. What this looked like. It...

"Ley lines," I whispered.

I looked up, realizing I'd spoken aloud. Byron and Casimir continued chanting, and the others were still watching the water. But Ozias heard me. Meeting my eyes, he nodded.

I kept my voice low. "We're like the nexuses."

"The world," he murmured back.

The glittering threads radiating from us came in contact with each other. Prickling feelings suddenly spread across my skin, bringing with them a tingling in my veins.

My eyes darted to the others, landing last on Niko straight ahead of me. We all appeared unchanged, except somehow they seemed... more *real* to me in a way that had nothing to do with sight. As if, when I looked at them, their gifts and their strength and their doubts and fears and *everything* were in my mind too. It wasn't exactly like my link to Ozias, where he and I shared an awareness of each other's emotions. It was like I stood at the center of an eight-pointed star, and each of them were those points. Like we were distinct and yet united, and when I looked at Niko, I had only to reach out in my mind for—

Awareness of the moss and bioluminescent plants suddenly flared to life like a tapestry of life and color. Their essence whispered without words, and somehow I knew that all I had to do was ask and they'd respond.

Gasping, I looked away, retreating from the sensation. It faded.

My eyes landed on Lars. Tentatively, I stretched out in my mind.

Heat coursed through me, and when I lifted my arm from the water, the air wavered above my skin.

I pulled back, but it was harder this time. Like even when I retreated, his power was still there, ready and waiting for me to draw upon it. Niko's too, now.

All of my men's gifts were.

My lips parted. Did they feel this from me? From each other? Casimir and Byron were still chanting, their arms raised, while the threads of glittering light emanating from all of us merged completely together.

Like we were all one.

Byron and Casimir's words came to an end. Slowly, they lowered their arms. The glittering threads in the water faded away, but the sense of them in my mind remained, linking me to my men and their power.

"A-are you all feeling this?" Niko asked. "The..."

"Starlight," Lars whispered.

Byron nodded. "The princess's magic. We're tied to her power now."

Their eyes landed on me.

"But..." I looked around the circle again. "I feel all of you. Fire and nature and... *all* of you."

Questioning looks passed between my men, but there was no worry or fear in their gazes. Just intrigue.

"So this is like the connection between her and Byron, then?" Lars asked. "But for all of us?"

Casimir shook his head. "That was accidental. Half-formed, I think. This is..." He seemed to search for words, finally settling on, "something else."

Dex cleared his throat. "Okay." He looked like he was trying to keep himself focused on the task at hand and not the question of what the hell this really was. "What about Niko's protection? Can you..." He looked between me, Byron, and Casimir, and he gestured in lieu of continuing.

Consternation passed over the vampire's face. "If it was going to work, I would have anticipated the spell to cover that as well."

"Maybe," Byron countered.

Worry bubbled up in me. Desperate, I stretched out in my mind, feeling for... something. Whatever the power of the wall might be like, in this form.

Gods, don't let it kill me... or any of us.

A moment slid past, and then suddenly, my awareness of Niko butted up against a strange sense of crystalline hardness.

My breath caught. In my mind's eye, it was beautiful.

Like quartz beneath moonlight. Yet beneath it was a wealth of emotion that stole my breath—loss and sorrow and confusion, but threaded through with traces of hope that maybe, just *maybe*, this pain could still lead to something good. Something right in a future where those who came after could be safe.

This magic could protect us, yes. But it had been bought at a horrific cost, and not all those who paid had chosen freely to do so.

I squeezed my eyes shut. "I'm sorry," I whispered. "I'm so sorry. I know I have no right to ask, but... please. Help us stop her so this can end."

The feeling of hard quartz suddenly moved toward me, passing around me and sending shivers over my skin. A shimmer of opalescence swept across my body, spreading out until it hovered all around me.

Slowly, I let out a shaky breath. "Thank you."

Turning my focus to the rest of my men, I concentrated on urging the shimmer to pass through my connection to them. My shivering crested and then faded away like the power making me quiver was rushing out from me along channels I couldn't see.

The shimmer of opalescence flared to life before the men and then ghosted over each of their bodies, translucent and breathtaking.

"Whoa," Clay whispered.

Eyes wide, Lars nodded, watching the light.

For a moment, it hovered around them before slowly drawing in, sinking into their skin and fading to invisibility.

But somehow, I could tell it was still there, ready and waiting.

A second slid by. "So," Clay said. "I guess that's... it?"

Several of them looked at me, questions in their eyes, while Byron and Casimir glanced at the walls like they were trying to read something from the stones.

"Perhaps?" the vampire allowed.

My head shook.

"What is it, princess?" Dex asked carefully.

I couldn't explain. A strange sense of *knowingness* had me in its grip. An awareness that, somehow, *something* still wasn't complete.

My gaze landed on Lars, and I let myself reach toward his power again, my hands rising as if I could simply take it in my grasp. But when it flooded into me, instead of keeping it inside me, I stretched my other hand out to Casimir on the opposite side of the circle.

Lars's power flowed through me like a river and Casimir gasped. Heat made the air waver above the vampire.

"Holy shit," Clay said. "Is that what I think it is?"

I turned to Ozias. Urging and consent came from him, and so I reached out again, drawing in his power, sending it to Niko.

My sweet giant's eyes went wide. "Oh *gods...*" He stretched out a hand, and the stone ledge of the pool rippled.

"Don't stop, princess," Dex said. "Do that—" He faltered as I sent Clay's power to him. "Oh, damn." Water coiled up in twisting droplet-ropes when he lifted his hand.

Exclamations of surprise and wonder came from the others, but I could barely breathe. I wasn't *giving* the power to the men, exactly. Each magical gift still belonged to its original owner. But with only a thought, I could direct them to another member of our circle for them to use too.

Yet my heart raced. Even now, I had the strangest sense this wasn't enough. Wasn't done.

Their words and sounds of alarm washed over me, but my focus was on the power flowing between us. Drawing on their gifts one by one, I sent the energy first to one man, then another, around and around.

With each pass, my men became quieter, until there was only the soft, desperate sound of our breathing in this grotto deep within the earth. Only the glow of plants illuminating our wide, stunned eyes. Every time I transferred their power, it felt like a filament of a magical bond tying us closer together, as if I was a weaver sending the shuttle of my thread back and forth... back and forth...

Until there was no space between us at all.

I trembled, my hands lowering. We felt like something new. Something stronger than we had been, reinforced by one another, and connected in a way that transcended definition.

"The Nine are as one," Casimir said quietly.

Exhilaration bubbled inside me, tugging at my lips with a smile. Turning a slow circle, I met my men's eyes. Magic coursed through my veins, the feeling as sharp and bright as starlight on a winter snowfall. The presences of my men hovered in my mind like pinpoints of blazing light, connected to me by cords of power so very like ley lines. The world around me felt more *solid* than ever before, like every drop of water and fleck of stone, every trace of plant life and each glimmer of light and heat was so *real*, it was practically a part of me.

And something out there wanted to destroy that. I could feel that too. It was still some distance off, stalking across the land like a predator with all the time in the world. But it was coming with the intent to shatter everything. And we couldn't—*wouldn't*—let it.

But the nine of us were still too far apart. We *were* one. We needed more than this.

And my men felt that too.

Together, they came toward me. Ozias's hands took my shoulders, turning me toward him. His eyes blazed with need as his gaze locked on my lips. All he could say was, "Please."

I nodded breathlessly.

That was all it took.

Instantly, he tore my undershirt away and tossed it aside. Lifting me up, he slammed his lips to mine while other hands—those of Dex and Lars—pulled away everything else covering my body. Clay and Niko took my breasts, massaging my soft flesh, while Byron, Casimir, and Roan hovered beyond them, their eyes trained on me.

My legs wrapped around Ozias, and I clung to him while he fumbled with one hand quickly, unfastening his breeches. His thick, hard length pressed to my core.

I moaned against his lips.

"I want you, little mate," he growled. "But I need you

relaxed first." His eyes went beyond me, a smile pulling at his lips that was decidedly wicked. "So each of us will take a turn at that, stretching that delicious pussy of yours until your monsters take you last."

His words sent a surge of craving and need rushing through me, but I had no time to say a word before Ozias spun me and handed me off to Clay.

My blond giant was already naked, and when my legs encircled his hips, he grinned. "You want this inside you, baby?" He rubbed his hard cock against my slit.

Taking his cheeks in my hands, I nodded frantically before crushing my lips to his. He kissed me deeply for a moment before lifting me up, positioning me. In a long, slow stroke, he drew me down onto his length.

Another moan left me. Immediately, I started rocking against him, desperate for the friction that would bring me release.

He made a hungry noise, thrusting harder. Water splashed against my hips, my back.

But it didn't stop. The liquid only climbed higher.

I broke away from Clay's lips, gasping. Rivulets were coursing up my sides, twisting over me like watery versions of Niko's vines. A shiver rippled through me as the water turned cold like fragments of ice tracing deliciously over my skin.

But like my body couldn't make sense of the sensations, somehow the cold shivers sent quivers straight down to my pussy, making my channel clench around his hardness.

When I looked back at Clay, he was staring at the water, surprise in his eyes.

We *were* different. I could feel it. My men had always been strong in their relative powers. But now, somehow we were fueling each other. Supporting each other in a way that left our magic absolutely overflowing.

Clay looked back up at me, grinning. "Have I ever fucked you in *my* element, baby?"

The water froze against my nipples, sending a shock of sensation through my sensitive flesh. But a moment later, it became as warm as a caress.

Still grinning, he started thrusting harder while the water never stopped. Ice chilled me and made my clit throb. Heat made me tremble while my pussy melted into pure need.

"Deep breath, sexy." Clay drew me down with him beneath the surface.

Hot water coursed over me, *into* me around his cock. Icy water froze my nipples, making me jolt with a sudden shiver of pleasure. Tiny waves pulsed against my skin, massaging and stimulating every sensitive place I possessed.

The effect was overwhelming, instantly throwing me over the edge into my release. Water streamed from my skin as Clay lifted me back above the surface. I clung to him, shuddering with pleasure. His hands dug into my ass, his body thrusting raggedly as his cock pumped out his cum.

I barely had time to catch my breath. Dex's dark eyes insatiable with need. Behind him, my other men watched us, naked and hard.

With a smile, Dex said, "Ozias is right, little one. We're all claiming your pussy tonight."

50
GWYNEIRA

I gasped as Dex hefted me away from Clay, taking me from my blond giant's cock and bringing me to him. "Do you have any idea how hot you are? How incredible you look, all wet and ready for us to fuck you?"

His cock impaled me before I could even hope to find an answer.

"Do you know how good it feels when you clench around me?"

His thickness stretched me so well, it sent pleasure radiating through my core. Immediately, he began thrusting, hard and rough, a counterpoint to the calm way he delivered his dirty words.

"Does your hungry little pussy want to come again, princess?"

I moaned out something that I hoped resembled a yes. He was hitting me so deep inside, over and over, it was like all the control in his voice couldn't make its way to his body. Like he needed to come every bit as badly as

I did, no matter that he sounded like he had all the time in the world.

"F-fuck me, sir," I begged, nearly incoherent. "Oh gods, please."

A groan left him, any trace of control breaking down. His thrusts sped up. At the waterline, our skin slapped together with the water in an obscene sound.

I cried out as I came, and his hands dug into me when he did too. His cock pulsed inside me, driving his cum deep into me with a rush of warmth.

A pleased sound came from beside me. "Exquisite, as always."

Casimir's hand slid over Dex's shoulder. Bending briefly, my giant kissed the vampire and didn't resist when Casimir lifted me away.

"Do you see your men watching you, my little fuck-toy?" Casimir murmured. "Can you see what it does to them, witnessing you come in the arms of all your lovers?"

My eyes darted to the side. The others *were* watching. Niko grinned when I saw him, while Byron was studying me intently, as if making detailed note of every twitch of muscle and hint of expression. Lars was beyond them, nodding and smiling as Clay whispered suggestions for more ways to make me scream with pleasure. Ozias and Roan stood at the edge of the group. My mate's eyes were intense with echoes of the pleasure still shuddering through me.

Roan's gaze held traces of flame.

My breath caught, but there was no fear in his eyes.

No worry or question of what the demon inside him would do.

Just a confidence that made my core melt with hopeful anticipation.

Casimir chuckled, seeming to see my reaction. "That's it. Shall we give your delectable men a show?"

I started to look back, but he moved with lightning speed, his fangs sinking into the side of my throat only a moment before his cock plunged into my pussy.

The spike of pain from his bite mingled with the feeling of him filling me. Gasping, I bucked against him as pleasure ricocheted through me, chaotic and blinding. My hands clung to his shoulders, my legs gripped his waist, and I could only rock on him as he drew on my vein in time to the thrusts of his cock.

My thoughts turned fuzzy. It never ceased to be amazing, being with him like this. Feeling him drawing me into his body even as he thrust into mine.

Limply, my head fell back, and I moaned.

"Holy *gods*," Clay murmured. "So fucking sexy."

A smile tugged at my lips. I felt delirious with pleasure in my vampire's arms, my heart galloping from the combined impact of him drinking from me while pounding into my pussy.

Extracting his fangs, Casimir closed the wound quickly and then reached between us, supporting me with one hand while the other found my clit.

The sensation was overwhelming after the rush of his feeding, and I shrieked at it, jerking me forward. Instinct took over, my vampire side unable to process this much pleasure without acting.

Lunging forward, I sank my fangs into his neck too.

His blood filled my mouth like an intoxicating ambrosia. My entire body bore down on him, my pussy clenching hard around his cock while my hands dug into his shoulders and my mouth locked on his throat.

Casimir groaned loudly, his grip tightening on me. "Yes. Oh gods yes, my little—" He snarled, abandoning his massage of my sensitive flesh in favor of thrusting into me harder.

My release hit like a hot and tingling wave. I barely had enough rational thought to make myself seal the wound on his neck before it engulfed my world.

His pleased murmur was the first thing I heard when my senses returned, and when I opened my eyes, he smiled.

"I shall never tire of watching you come apart in my arms or theirs, my precious little fucktoy." The teasing confidence in his eyes melted into something softer, warmer, and full of wonder. His gaze traced over my face before returning to meet my eyes. "I love you, Gwyneira, queen of my heart."

His lips brushed mine, stealing my tiny breath of awe at the heartbreakingly vulnerable promise in his voice. When he drew back again, his mouth curved into a smile. "Your men await you." He lifted me, that unshakable confidence returning to his gaze. "And your luscious pussy isn't done being filled yet."

A thrill went through me, even as the joints of my legs burned. The pounding I'd taken already made my hips ache, the feeling somehow mixing into both pleasure and pain.

Casimir merely glanced to the side, his expression turning suggestive. "Your highness."

I followed his gaze to find Niko nearby. Beyond a short breath to brace himself, he didn't react to the title, merely nodding at the vampire. "Highness."

Casimir grinned like he was proud of my sweet giant for the response.

Niko smiled. "Come here, my beautiful treluria."

My vampire handed me over.

Moving us through the water, Niko kissed my lips, one hand supporting me while the other extended behind me. A moment later, my back bumped against the rocky edge of the pool.

But the surface wasn't rough.

Breaking from him briefly, I glanced over my shoulder to see glistening moss covering the stones now, cushioning my back. Green lights glimmered like tiny trapped stars amid the dense carpet of plants. The water wasn't as deep here at the far end of the cave. It barely came up to my calves. But underwater plants still stirred around my legs and feet to massage my skin like gentle fingers.

Carefully, Niko lowered himself to his knees, taking me with him.

My breath caught. The water lapped around my midsection, and my position gave the plants greater access to me. The long fronds drifted between my legs, brushing against my sensitive skin, but they didn't move like they were trying to work me into a frenzy.

More like they were trying to soothe my tender flesh.

Niko hitched me higher on his hips, his tip hovering

at my entrance. But he made no move to enter me yet, letting the plants continue their massage.

When I turned back to him with a questioning look, he only shrugged. "They have medicinal qualities, and I thought you might appreciate that." A wicked look came into his kind eyes. "Gods know my friends and I still want to keep fucking you."

The ache from the others pounding into me slowly faded between my legs.

I stared at him in wonder. "You always take such care of me."

His smile returned, pleased. "You're all I ever wanted. Why wouldn't I treat you like the treasure you are?"

Whatever I could have said was lost to a gasp as he lowered me onto his cock. The delicate leaves of the underwater plants pulled back to twist around my ankles and calves. Others drifted around my hips to tease along the curve of my ass.

Holding me securely, he drew out and then eased back into me again and again, gentle and slow. "I want to spend a lifetime exploring how to make you come, treluria," he murmured to me. "Everything nature can do to help you find all the pleasure you deserve."

I gripped his shoulders, my eyes squeezing shut against the emotions rising in my chest. "I love you, Niko," I whispered.

A happy sound left him. "I love you too."

The plants climbed higher, brushing the sensitive spot at the base of my spine and making my eyes roll back in my head. Grunting, Niko held himself tense with the effort of restraining himself from driving into me faster.

"More, Niko," I urged. "Please."

A gasping sound left him. His grip tightened as his restraint broke.

The combined impact of his thrusts and the soothing touch of the plants dazed my senses. I was relaxed and yet tense, calm and yet aroused. And in only a moment, my orgasm hit so strongly, it sent me lurching forward to wrap my arms around him, hanging on as the waves of it crashed over me.

Niko clutched me tightly, his hips jerking in a ragged rhythm before finally slowing again. His cock twitched inside me, and his arms held me every bit as closely as I held him.

"*Gods*, I love you," he whispered like he was repeating himself.

I drew back, but only far enough to find his mouth for a kiss.

He smiled against my lips. "Your men aren't done. Are you?"

I shook my head quickly. Niko's grin grew.

"Out of the water, then," Lars said behind me. I looked back to find him eyeing me up and down. "Because as hot as you are, I don't want to accidentally heat this pool to pure steam and burn us all."

Clay chuckled.

"Yeah, definitely not," Dex agreed wryly.

I grinned.

Taking my hand, Lars led me up the stone slope from the pool. My legs were wobbly beneath me, but he didn't let me struggle for long. As my feet left the water and the ledge leveled out beneath us, he drew me close. His hands held me secure, stabilizing me, while his blue eyes burned with desire.

"Having you all to myself..." He made a pleased sound. "But I don't need to be greedy." Quickly, he turned me, pressing my back to the stone wall and caging my body with his. "I know they'll all still want to see your gorgeous face when you come."

Taking my waist, he lifted me. My ankles crossed behind him, pressing my clit to his hard length. Past his shoulder, I could see my other men climbing from the pool, water streaming from their naked, muscular bodies. Their eyes were locked on us.

I bit my lip as Lars eased into me. Warmth spread over my skin, licking away every water droplet and keeping away any trace of a chill. But even as the moisture faded, the hot air remained, flitting across my skin like tiny invisible fingers.

Shuddering breaths escaped me as he thrust deeper into my wetness, one of his hands supporting me and the other bracing him on the wall. Tiny tongues of heat teased at my nipples and twisted around my throat, stoking the molten need in my core.

"I'll never get enough of this pussy," he grunted out. "Gods, beautiful. How can you feel this... this fucking *good*?"

Leaning my head back against the rough stone, I could only smile as my breasts tingled with my rising need to come. "That's my question for you too."

He chuckled, but the sound was breathless and lost swiftly under the quickening pace of his thrusts.

Gold light flickered at the corner of my eyes, unexpected. I rolled my head to the side, searching for the source.

The symbols inlaid into the wall were glowing.

I stared. "Lars."

"I know. I can feel it." He grunted with the effort of restraining himself. "It's taking the overflow of my magic."

"But..." I winced with pleasure, unable to stop myself from grinding harder against him. "Is that—"

"It's... okay. I don't think it'll hurt..." A desperate sound left him. "*Fuck.*"

He turned suddenly, his grip on me tightening. His back slammed into the wall while his free hand shoved between us, flicking my clit with fingers that burned hotter than the rest of his skin.

The sensation was a jolt to my system that sent me straight over the edge into an orgasm. My forehead fell against his chest while my eyes squeezed shut. Overwhelming pleasure made a sudden rush of moisture pour from inside me.

My eyes flew wide with surprise, but Lars only flashed me a grin. The expression quickly turned to a grimace, though, as his cock jerked inside me and his cum suddenly flooded me too.

Behind him, Clay whistled low. "Fire guy makes our girl gush. *Nice.*"

Lars's grin returned as his orgasm faded. "Pretty sure I had you and the others' help with that, brother." His expression turned teasing when he met my eyes. "But as for seeing our beautiful princess's face when she comes, I guess I am greedy after all."

A blush burned my cheeks, but then a glint of bright gold caught my eye.

The symbols were still glowing on the wall.

I tensed. "What *is* that?"

Lars glanced over his shoulder at the gleaming symbols. "Not sure."

"Opportunity," Byron said, coming closer and twitching his chin briefly at Lars.

The blond giant nodded and let my scholar take me into his arms.

"What's that mean?" I asked, holding onto Byron tightly.

His green eyes slid over the symbols thoughtfully before he turned me, resting my back on the stone wall again. "It means"—he groaned as he slid into my wet core—"Lars's power and need charged these symbols, and now I get to show you more of what my training from the Order can do."

At the corner of my eye, the gold light changed as he started to move inside me. I glanced over my shoulder, and my lips parted in silent shock at the threads of gold light tangling out from the symbols and down through the stone, all of them heading for where my back was pressed to the wall.

And when they touched me, tingling pleasure began to pulse through my body. "Oh... oh gods," I gasped.

Byron's expression was intently focused, one hand splayed on the wall and his eyes on squeezed shut. But his lips still curled into a smile at my exclamation. "I cannot wait to explore a thousand ways to make you come, my beautiful Snow. Berinlian willing, this is only the beginning."

I couldn't form words to respond. The energy thrumming through me was overwhelming. Every inch of my body felt hypersensitive, like the same force that made my clit tingle with pleasure now lived in my skin.

It was too intense. Too *much*. And it was building toward a crescendo that I wasn't sure I could withstand.

His hand tightened on my ass.

The grips unleashed an orgasm that ripped a scream from my lips. Pure ecstasy shot through me like I'd been struck by lightning, every vein and nerve crying out with utter pleasure. I lost the cave, the gold light and the glistening water.

And when I returned to my senses, I was in Ozias's arms several yards away from where I had been. The rest of my men were on the low stone seats surrounding us, while Ozias held me on the moss that covered the ground like a dense rug.

Sticky wetness clung to the skin of his lower abdomen.

Blinking, I looked up at him, still dazed. "You came from...?" I twitched my head toward the moisture rather than try to form the rest of the question.

Sitting on a stone block behind him, Clay grinned. "Oh, Oz has been losing it like a teenager since the rest of us started getting you off, baby."

Tossing a glare over his shoulder, my mate growled a

brief warning at the blond giant while Lars elbowed his brother.

Clay's unabashed enjoyment of the situation didn't fade a bit.

Turning back to me, Ozias seemed to dismiss the others from his mind as he brushed a strand of my hair behind my ear. Even though he'd clearly come already—several times, if Clay was to be believed—I could feel Ozias's length beneath my ass, growing hard and ready again. "I think you're relaxed enough for me now, little mate. Yes?"

A breath left me. My men and this marathon sex might just leave me sleeping for days.

His eyes narrowed as he felt my reaction. But he didn't seem offended.

More like amused.

"I can help with that," he murmured.

His fingers left my cheek to stray down to the mating mark on my chest.

Arousal washed through me and my eyes went wide as his fingertips teased across the tiny scars left by his claws. Nearby, a hungry sound came from Roan, like he could see what Ozias had just done to me.

"Take some of my hunger for you, little mate. Let it fuel what I want to do with you."

Moaning with renewed need, I let him turn me around and put me on my knees in the center of my circle of men. Picking me up a bit, he held me motionless for a moment, teasing the tip of his enormous cock against my swollen flesh..

Noises I didn't recognize escaped me. Desperate, needy, whimpering sounds. "Please. *Please...*"

He chuckled and then eased me gently down onto his massive cock.

I gasped as he stretched me, the sensation of his thickness penetrating me feeling all the more obscene for how we both were sitting. My back was to his chest, my legs splayed as wide as I could make them around his massive thighs. Every inch of what he was doing to me was on display for my men. Every thrust of his cock and slap of his balls against my wetness was visible for all to see. But I could only rock and moan as he splayed one hand beneath my breasts and slipped the other between my legs, rubbing his fingertip in tiny circles around my clit.

Appreciative noises came from several of the others.

"Gods, I'm about to come all over again just watching this," Lars murmured.

Niko made a ragged noise of agreement. "We need to watch her getting taken like this more often."

"Every fucking day," Clay seconded. "No, twice a day."

My breasts bobbed with Ozias's thrusts, and Casimir's grin was feral as he watched them. "It makes me want to bite her again," he agreed.

I leaned my head back, resting against Ozias. My lips curled into a smile. I *was* small compared to my mate, and surrounded by the others, he'd put me fully on display.

But gods, I felt so powerful. Held tight by his hands, my body splayed out, I still held all of these incredible men riveted, the sight of me getting fucked mesmerizing them.

It was intoxicating.

"She loves your eyes on her," Ozias growled to them. "I can feel it."

Rough sounds of desire and surprise came from the others.

"Fuck, baby, is that true?" Clay rasped.

I nodded, words failing me. Pleasure tingled through my veins, getting stronger with each of my mate's thrusts. Between my legs, tension built like everything Ozias was doing was concentrating tighter and tighter around the spot where his fingers circled.

A grunt left him. Swiftly, his other hand slid past my breasts to press down on the mating mark on my shoulder.

I gasped, pitching forward as the tension between my legs suddenly released in an explosion of ecstasy. Ozias's grip on me was the only thing keeping me upright as he jerked his hips harder, driving his massive cock so deeply into me, it made my insides throb.

Panting, I hung in his grasp, limp.

Pale skin and dark hair caught the corner of my eye. I looked up to find Roan kneeling on the moss before me.

My core twisted with desire, but gods, I was exhausted. Spent and ready to sleep for days. Yet still my body craved the last of my giants.

And the demon he hid inside.

A smile lifted the corner of his mouth as he took my cheek. "Don't worry, beloved. I have a proposal for you."

51
ROAN

Sex-dazed and breathless, my beautiful treluria stared at me. The demon's heightened senses could smell her renewed arousal, even over all the scents of sex, cum, and her release around us. Even now, she wanted me. Us.

But she was like a beautiful waif at a feast, fuller than she'd ever been in her life yet still trying to figure out how to have more.

My friends and I had fucked her in groups before. For gods' sakes, the others had worked together to have her in veritable orgies.

But we'd never had her *this* way. Never all of us together, one after the other with our powers on full display, fucking her until the soft skin between her legs was flushed red from taking so many of us.

She'd be lucky to be able to walk after this.

Inside me, the demon rumbled. It would fix that. It would fix everything.

If I would let it.

"What proposal?" my beautiful treluria breathed, blinking at me. Ozias had damn near split her open with that massive cock of his, and that was after Byron and the others used *every* trick they could think of to show her how much she meant to us all.

Now it was my turn.

With a careful glance at Ozias to confirm his beast was willing to release her, I waited for his small nod before I lifted her away from him. Laying her down on the carpet of moss Niko had made thicker for us all, I traced a finger along the curve of her pink cheek. "Let me tend to you."

Her brow wrinkled in adorable confusion. "But"—her hands reached between us for my cock, a noise of frustrated desire escaping her—"I want you."

I stilled her hands. "Use this connection between us first. Draw on my magic. My energy." I took a breath, pushing myself past the doubts that still clung to the edges of my mind like old habits refusing to fully die. "And the demon's."

Her eyes widened. Murmurs passed among the others.

But they didn't protest. Not enough to make me take my eyes from hers while she absorbed what I'd said, anyway.

She bit her lip. She was so worn out that I worried exhaustion would pull her down into sleep before she could agree.

But suddenly, the cool, bright feeling that I knew was her grew stronger. Ever since the spell Casimir and Byron cast over us all, it was like a window opened in my mind, allowing ghostly moonlight to pour into the darkness of my soul.

I couldn't understand how I'd ever lived without it.

And we'd all already learned that when she focused, when she wanted to do so, the brightness could grow, as if she'd blown aside a curtain to let her true brilliance fully shine through. Feeling it now, my own magic rose instantly to meet it, and the demon's did too, both of us relishing the sense of merging our powers with hers.

Because joining with her light felt like coming home.

Her eyes widened, our energy flooding into her, renewing her strength and stamina. Someday, it would be exhilarating to test how far this could go. How long we could keep her sexual appetite fueled before we all collapsed into a puddle of postcoital exhaustion.

But for now...

"May I, princess?" I asked, tracing a finger down between her breasts.

She nodded, her eyes clearer and wide with desire. "Fuck me, Roan. I want your cum in me too."

Gods, I loved hearing filthy talk from her. Desire drove a growl from me that had precious little to do with the demon. Lowering myself over her, I let my hips push her legs wide.

I sank into her wet heat.

And that, too, felt like coming home.

Her inner muscles clenched around me like her pussy was eager to follow through on everything she'd said moments ago. My fingers dug into the thick moss as I pulled back slowly, savoring the feeling of her slick heat stroking my cock. When my tip hovered just inside her entrance again, I reversed course, driving back into her and watching her eyes squeeze shut as she moaned.

The brilliant light of her presence tightened around me at the same time her pussy did.

I groaned, fighting with all my strength not to come right this second. But holy *fuck*...

Her hips rocked against me, tiny pleading noises coming from her.

There was no way I could leave her wanting.

My fingers ripped through the moss, and my teeth clenched. I grunted with desperate effort as I thrust into her soft heat.

A shudder passed through my body, and my skin prickled. The demon was here, but he wasn't fighting for control.

We will last as long as she needs, he growled in my mind, his strength fueling my thrusts.

I simply nodded because gods help me if I could form a single fucking word.

She felt too good for that.

Beneath me, our treluria gasped, frantic little noises leaving her as her pussy began fluttering around my length.

In my mind, the demon groaned at the feeling of it.

"Come for me, beloved," I gasped. "Come like the good girl you—"

She cried out as her inner walls clenched down hard and pulsed with waves of pleasure.

The demon and I didn't stand a chance.

A shout tore from me as I came, my voice thick with

the demon's growl too. My eyes squeezed shut, my cock pumping for all it was worth to fill her.

Mate her, the demon snarled, just as overcome as I was. *Breed her, fill her with cum until she swells with our young.*

Breathing hard, I rested my head on the moss for a moment as my instinctive thrusting slowed and stopped. *Yeah... you know that's probably not going to happen, right?* I told him silently.

The demon made a dismissive sound in my mind. *We shall see. Either way, we will fill her with cum and bring her pleasure, yes?*

A small chuckle left me, breathless. *Definitely.*

I could feel him smirk arrogantly, fully confident he could accomplish whatever he wanted, even breeding a vampire, as long as she was on board with it too.

Beneath me, my beautiful treluria stirred. Pulling out of her, I shifted position quickly to keep from resting my weight on her too heavily.

She smiled up at me. "Thank you."

I smiled back. "Thank *you*, beloved."

Her hand reached up, taking my cheek, and a question filled her eyes. I knew what she was going to ask before she spoke, and I tensed in spite of myself.

"And the demon?" Her brow rose hopefully.

The monster within me shuddered with need. But rather than rush forward, rather than steal control, his fiery gaze only turned to me, waiting for my answer, every bit as hopeful as our princess.

At the edges of my mind, the old fears still lingered like ghosts unwilling to fade away.

But that didn't mean I had to continue living my life by them.

Dropping my gaze from hers, I squeezed my eyes shut. *Promise me,* I said silently to the demon. *Promise me on both our graves you'll never hurt her.*

Drawing himself up in my mind, the demon regarded me like the proud king and dethroned god he'd always believed himself to be. But there was no malice in his appraisal. None of the judgment I'd felt for so many years. Only something that left me stunned speechless.

Respect.

I swear, unbroken one, he replied. *I swear.*

52
GWYNEIRA

oan let out a shaky breath, opening his eyes. When his gaze found me again, fire lived at the heart of it like the core of a dark star.

"He..." Clearing his throat, he tried again. "He wants to mate bond you. *His* way."

My lips parted, speechless.

"He thinks it'll be good for you. Be good for all of us, really. Helpful or... something. And, I mean, he's definitely got an ego so maybe that's not—" Roan winced and I wondered what protest the demon had just made. "Look, I'm not saying you're *wrong*," he started, not sounding like he was talking to me anymore. "I just—"

I put my hand to his chest, and he cut off, his gaze returning to me. "Yes."

The fire in his eyes flared brighter.

"If," I continued, "it won't damage my connections to anyone else."

Roan shook his head immediately. "He swears it won't."

My eyes darted around, but Ozias's consent was more than clear and I found only curiosity on the faces of the rest of my men. "Okay, then." I nodded. "What, um... what do we..."

A breath left Roan. "He might be too big to have you like... like this." He nodded toward where his cock rested against my thigh. "But if you're willing, he still wants to try. And if it hurts, he swears he'll stop and just"—his shoulder rose and fell in a small shrug— "give you pleasure with *other* parts of himself. Is that okay?"

Clay made an appreciative noise only to cut off as Lars jabbed him with an elbow yet again.

My amusement couldn't quite beat out the tangle of apprehension and desire coiling in my core.

"We won't do this if you don't want it, princess," Roan cautioned, drawing back a bit like somehow he could tell what I was feeling.

Though maybe it was the demon scenting that, like Roan once said.

My fingers took his arm, stopping him. "I want it. This." I looked deep 'into his eyes, praying the demon could hear me. "You."

For a heartbeat, Roan didn't breathe, and then his head moved in a small nod. "Okay."

Again, somehow, I didn't think it was only me to whom he was speaking.

He drew back, a shift coursing through him. His muscles and bones grew. Wings erupted from his back and claws lengthened on his hands and feet. Blazing fire consumed his eyes, leaving only a dark pinprick at their core. His long, sinuous tail lashed the air, and his sharp, vicious features curved into a fanged smile while he regarded me on the ground below him.

Even if Roan had just come, it meant nothing for the demon. His thick, ridged cock jutted out between us, hard and leaking glistening pre-cum.

"My mate," he growled, tracing his fiery eyes over my naked body. He glanced at my men, his gaze landing last on Ozias. "*Our* mate."

Ozias tilted his head in a small acknowledging nod.

The demon grinned, turning his eyes back to me. "Share you. But only with them or only with ones you choose." His brow arched. "Deal?"

Swallowing hard around the lump that had risen in my throat, I nodded. "Deal."

His grin broadened. Bracing himself with one massive, clawed hand beside my head, he straddled me with his knees on either side of my hips.

I stared up at him. He really was *huge*.

His tail thrashed the air for a moment, only to curl past him and slide along the inside of my thigh. "Begged me to put this in you once, yes?"

My core throbbed. Desire soaked me. "Yes."

His tail dragged along my slit, making me gasp and buck beneath him. "Liked my cum soaking into your soft, beautiful skin, true?"

Gods... "True."

His grin turned hungry. "Good. You will like it even better inside you."

Twisting between my folds, the tip of his tail coiled

around my clit. My back arched involuntarily, the jolt of pleasure making me cry out.

He made a pleased sound. "Always so responsive." His tail slipped farther down to tease at the edge of penetration, like he was testing something. "Other mate stretched you wide for me. Other men left you soft and ready to take my cock. They are satisfactory mates for you." He rocked back, his hard length replacing his tail. "And so am I."

The tip of him pushed into me, each ridge stretching my entrance just to get through.

I gasped, my eyes going wide. Gods, he was thick. Huge, even. Pleasure and pain mixed, inextricable from one another. The vampire side of me rose, almost as if to drive me to escape, only to become equally transfixed by what was happening.

The demon was every bit as much of a predator as Ozias. As Casimir.

As me.

And the feeling of his cock entering me made me want to bite him and mewl at the same time. Inch by inch, he eased deeper, moving just slowly enough to make me think maybe, just *maybe* I could take him.

If I didn't break something first.

"Good mate," he crooned as desperate little noises escaped me, involuntary and beyond my control. " Good."

He traced his claws between my breasts. I fell silent, shuddering as my attention scattered between the strain of being penetrated by his cock and the scrape of his deadly claws on my skin.

"Now..." He stilled inside me.

My heart racing, I lay beneath him, my pussy stretched to the point of breaking but slowly—gods, so slowly—starting to adjust to his girth.

"You are such a good mate," he murmured again. "You take my cock so well."

His words made heat coil low in my belly. My fangs pricked my lips, aching to bite him, taste him.

But between my legs, a new need started to build. Whimpering sounds left me, becoming wild and pleading for something I couldn't capture with words.

"You are okay, my good mate?"

My head moved in a jerky nod. "I... I..."

He made another satisfied sound. "You wish me to begin, don't you?"

My mind was reeling. I needed that. Gods, I needed that. "Y-yes. I... please."

"Good mate."

Slowly, he eased back. Each time a ridge of his cock drew past the entrance to my pussy, a throb of pleasure went through me that tore a moan from my lips. At the cusp of pulling out entirely, he reversed course, slowly thrusting back in.

My eyes swept the cave ceiling, unseeing. My hands fumbled wildly before finding his broad forearms and clutching them tightly. I didn't understand what this was doing to me, to the vampire within me either.

But the pressure in my core was becoming overwhelming.

"I..." Begging sounds escaped me before I could find

words again. "I need to come. Please, I... please, Demon, I need to..."

His satisfied sound was more of a growl this time. His thrusting sped up, and his tail whipped through the air only to dive down behind him.

I cried out as the tip of his tail thrust into my rear opening, filling me so full, so tight, I couldn't have stopped my orgasm if I tried.

I screamed as I came, my body gushing again around his massive cock. I jerked with the force of it, my muscles no longer under my control.

The demon roared as his own release overtook him. Hot cum, scorching cum filled me, making me gasp and jerk forward, clutching my belly.

Exclamations of worry and alarm came from around me, but curled in on myself, I couldn't react to them. My vampire side wasn't trying to flee. It reveled in the burning, in the claiming.

And the burning sensation was already fading, like the bite of incredibly hot water right before your body adjusted to its touch. Soon, there was only the tingling feeling of pinprick heat surrounded by a delicious sort of warmth.

"I'm... I'm okay." I opened my eyes, still hugging my middle, but now because of the warmth that made me feel so full and sated inside.

My men quieted. Inside, my vampire side rested, soothed on some deep level I couldn't define.

Leaning back, the demon regarded me, his cocksure smile radiating satisfaction. "Mine."

I looked up at him and nodded.

His smile spread. He lifted one hand, his black claws glistening in the light of the glowing plants around us.

Flames surged up from his palm to dance around each claw.

My eyes went wide. "What are you…"

His eyebrow arched like it was obvious. "Mate mark you." He lowered his claws over my skin. I could feel the heat radiating from them. "Brand you."

At my silence, he paused, a hint of concern flickering in his dark eyes. "Yes?"

I swallowed hard. This was going to hurt. I knew it would.

But my bond to Ozias had changed my life. My bond to these men had made us stronger. My vampire side was practically preening and purring at the idea of bearing the demon's mark too, but in a way that didn't feel dangerous somehow. More like the idea of his mark soothed something.

I nodded, my eyes on the demon's. "Yes."

The outer edges of his claws came to rest on my chest, opposite of Ozias's mating mark.

I choked on a scream, but the demon moved fast. With his other hand, he scooped up some of his cum leaking from me and smeared it onto the wound.

The pain vanished almost as quickly as it had come, turning into a strangely tingling throb that left me stunned and blinking on the ground.

Trembling, I looked down.

Four blackened ovals formed an arc with a fifth below them. Specks of orange light glimmered inside like embers trapped in my skin.

The demon brushed his fingertips over the marks.

My body quivered and arched toward him instinctively.

He smiled. "So responsive. My good mate." His gaze went beyond me.

I felt Ozias coming closer. A rumbling sound left him, satisfaction radiating through our connection, and he crouched down beside me, the movement fluid and effortless.

His beast was close to the surface. Its hunger and desire lurked in his eyes as he traced his gaze over my naked body. With a glance to the demon, he lifted an eyebrow, some unspoken question passing between the two predators.

As one, they pressed their hands to their individual mate marks on my chest.

Pleasure hit me like a bolt between the eyes, whiting out my vision and making me arch away from the ground, instantly overcome. My hands flailed blindly for something to hold onto while my pussy clenched and fluttered, burning with the intensity of this sudden orgasm.

When the wave finally passed, I sagged back to the ground, limp, wrung out, and panting.

But I wasn't the only one.

Blinking, I looked around to find my men on their knees, breathing hard with their cocks in their hands and their release on the stone and moss beneath them.

"Holy *fuck*," Clay gasped.

I stared. "What..." My voice was raw. "What happened? You felt that?"

Casimir made a rough sound like an incredulous scoff of confirmation.

To his right, Byron nodded. "Your starlight. It... It used your connection to Ozias and the... the marks, and it transmitted the impact to..." He shuddered, seeming unable to find any more words.

"He means yes," Lars translated.

"*Gods*, yes," Niko added emphatically.

Dex reached over, brushing my hair from my face. "Your pleasure was ours, little one."

Ozias nodded. Everything I could feel from him said he didn't mind a bit that I'd involuntarily pushed our connection out to the others, albeit only when I came. It had only lasted as long as my orgasm, and it hadn't changed a bit of what the two of us still shared.

Seated beside me, the demon simply smirked, pride and satisfaction practically radiating from him. "I said it'd be good for all of you if I matebonded our beautiful treluria, didn't I?"

Clay chuckled in breathless agreement. "You all know what this means, though, right?"

I twisted a bit to see him. "What?"

He grinned. "When we make it through this, we're going to need a *much* bigger bed for fucking you. Like, huge. Bigger than giant-sized. Because we're *all* going to want our hands on you when that simultaneous orgasm thing happens again."

A laugh burst from me and his grin broadened.

Dex's hands returned, drawing me away from the ground into his arms. I nestled close to his chest, resting but no longer exhausted. Warmth pulsed through me now, not just from the blood I'd taken from Casimir or the way Lars's magic had licked away any trace of a chill.

It was the power Roan shared with me, and the thrum of the demon's bond still quivering through my body, both at the same time. Where his claw marks had left brands on my chest, a small current of energy continuously fed me his strength.

Gingerly, I reached out in my mind, tracing along the threads of sparkling light I could feel more than see. My links to my other men glistened in my mind's eye, binding us together and giving us all strength. The brilliant ties radiated out from me, and even if it wasn't like the empathic bond Ozias and I shared, it still let me know where each of them were and if they were well.

But when I looked closer, my breath caught. Tiny orange embers coursed through those connections too, but not coming from the demon.

From me.

His power flowed to me, and out from me to them.

Further strengthening us all.

I looked over at where he still sat nearby. His fiery eyes met mine, and though he still held himself with pride and arrogance, there was something else in his gaze.

Love.

My lips moved, mouthing the words silently. "Thank you."

He nodded once, regal and yet kind. The dark star at the center of his fiery eyes grew larger as he reached out and took my hand, his gray palm engulfing my fingers.

"The unbroken one and I will always protect you," the demon said. "This we both swear."

My lips parted in surprise, a warm, pained, but happy feeling swelling in my chest at the words and the title alike.

The *un*broken one.

A shudder rolled through him, and the demon shifted back into Roan, but the look on his face didn't change. My somber giant only nodded like he was echoing the demon's sentiment.

Dex tightened his arms around me. "We all swear it."

Sounds of agreement came from my men.

My eyes prickled with tears. "And I'll always protect—"

A cascade of light suddenly rolled across the symbols inlaid in the walls. A clang like a gong being struck reverberated through the air.

Straightening fast in Dex's arms, I stared around in shock. "What is that?"

The hard crystalline sense of the wall that I'd spread to all of us shuddered inside me.

And I had the answer to my question.

"Oh gods," Niko whispered.

I nodded. "My stepmother's magic is attacking the Wall of Erenelle."

53
GWYNEIRA

In clothes frantically conjured by Clay, we ran from the grotto tunnel. At the entrance, Ruhl waited, already on his feet with tendrils of black smoke rising from his fur. From the far end of the chamber, Ignatius raced toward us, Brock and a collection of giants on his heels.

The scholar skidded to a stop. "The wall—"

"We know," Dex said shortly.

Brock bowed briefly to Niko. "My wife is leading the children and those too sick or weak or scared to fight to a more secure location within the temple. The rest of us are yours to command."

Behind him, the other giants made noises of agreement.

Niko nodded gratefully. "Thank you."

From the quick way they glanced at one another and drew themselves a little straighter, I wondered how often any of them had been thanked for anything in the past.

Another gong-like sound reverberated through the air, prompting a few muttered curses. Ruhl's head whipped from one side to the other, his green eyes sweeping the walls. His fangs peeked past his lips as he hovered on the edge of a growl.

Ignatius's hands splayed briefly, his gaze darting across the walls too like he could read something from the stones. "Syloria *will* hold," he said like he was willing the temple to obey. "But we must go." He nodded to the decorative wall that had already swung shut behind us, concealing the tunnel to the grotto. "If I may, Highness?"

To his credit, Niko barely blinked before nodding his approval and stepping aside.

Ignatius hurried past him, lifting his arms and already whispering spells under his breath. Byron and Casimir followed him.

Staying close to my men, I walked after them. Apprehension tangled in my stomach as my scholar and vampire nodded to Ignatius and then began the spell.

This had to work. Had to be a good idea.

Gods, please let us all survive it.

A shiver rolled over my skin as Byron and Casimir's powers called upon the gateway spell. The magical link between us thrummed, sending them my power and, through me, the strength of the others as well.

The decorative wall suddenly blurred, the stone carvings swallowed by shadows that hadn't been there a moment before. Deepening quickly, the darkness took on a sense of extending so much farther back than it possibly could go. Farther than merely the length of the temple, or even of Erenelle itself.

Maybe even deeper than the world.

And for a few moments, the darkness seemed empty. Vast and containing nothing at all. But then nervous awareness prickled over my skin.

A shiver quivered through my middle. This must have been how ancient humans felt on moonless nights when they could just *tell* a predator was watching them from beyond their campfires. Because while I couldn't see anything, every instinct I had screamed *something* was there.

And its eyes were on me.

A low, hungry chuckle came from the darkness. *Ah, little doomed one. We meet again.*

When I tensed, Dex cast a quick glance at me. "Is it here?"

I nodded. I didn't bother asking why he couldn't hear it and I could. Making sure this massive, invisible predator wouldn't eat us was a more pressing issue.

"We need your help," I said, determinedly holding my voice steady. "We need to reach the apothecary district in Lumilia. Can you take us there?"

The gateway demon made a considering noise. From the edges of the gateway's darkness, distant laughter echoed, cackling and somehow sounding *smaller* than the other creature to whom I spoke.

Ooh, the Nine, came a taunting voice. *Aren't they shiny with all those little links between them?*

My heart sank. The other gateway demons were here

too. The ones who *did* seem smaller, but who liked to threaten to eat us.

"Please," I said, trying to focus on the so-called *big one*. "You told me to call when the time came." I braced myself. "I'm calling now."

Noises of sarcastic surprise came from the smaller demons. But the larger one was silent.

From the corners of my eyes, I could see my men glancing warily at each other and at me.

A deep, wry chuckle rumbled from the gateway, like I'd amused the creature somehow.

Oh gods, please don't let this be a mistake...

Very well, the larger gateway demon said. *But only if you can get past the barrier of magic the dead king made. To cross it is... itchy.*

And annoying, a smaller demon chimed in.

And it might kill you! another added gleefully.

A breath left me. "We can. Thank you."

I could hear the larger creature's smile in its voice, even if I couldn't see a damn thing. *Never thank a demon, little doomed one.*

The smaller demons cackled, but ahead of me, the darkness stabilized.

Clay gave us all a wary look. "I take it we're good, then?"

I shrugged. "I guess."

"We must go," Ignatius said. "The witches and Dathan will be waiting for us." Another reverberating gong rang from the walls, making him scowl briefly. "And this must end."

The scholar stepped into the gateway. Brock and the other giants bowed to Niko before doing the same.

"See you on the other side, my friends," Casimir said, the corners of his lips curling with a hint of a confident smile. But his expression turned solemn when he met my eyes. "Be safe, my queen."

He disappeared into the gateway.

One by one, my men did the same, until only Roan and Ozias remained with me.

"Deep breath, little mate," Ozias said. "See you soon."

I stepped into the gateway. Darkness swallowed me instantly. I couldn't even gasp. The momentum crushed air from my chest as my body rushed forward, making my stomach pitch and roll.

As fast as the darkness came, it vanished again. Ignatius and the other giants were ahead of me, and my men were on either side. We stood on a rocky hillside beneath an overcast sky, yellowed grass and frozen dirt crunching beneath our boots.

But directly ahead, the shimmering soap bubble of the wall sparked with light. The Erenlian side was unharmed, but the Aneiran side was another matter entirely. Cracks tore the earth on that side for as far as my eyes could see, with twisted apple trees growing and spreading from them like nightmarish rot. Around the base of the barrier, fallen apples steamed in the cold air as they decayed into blobs of putrescent flesh. The branches clawed at the surface of the wall, and where they struck, crackles like lightning radiated across the magical barrier like they were trying to tear straight through it.

"Fuck," Roan swore when he emerged from the gateway, his eyes on the destroyed terrain of my home nation.

I could only nod, dumbstruck.

"Those stones should be good for a gateway." Ignatius pointed to a collection of boulders just beyond the barrier. "If we can reach them."

Dex nodded, scanning the terrain like he was mapping out a strategy at lightning speed.

"The minute we get beyond this wall," Clay warned, "you know that crooning lullaby shit is going to start up again."

"Then we move fast," Dex replied. He started for a section of barrier where there were fewer trees and cracks in the earth. "Come on."

The rest of us hurried after him. The air buzzed with energy the closer we came, and sparks flew from the far side of the wall in crackles and pops, making me flinch. Whispering cries rose and fell in my mind like distant waves, carried on my invisible bond to the others.

But Niko heard more. His teeth gritted, he pressed his hands to his ears. "It's *screaming*. The... the spell sustaining the wall. It—" He winced. "*Gods...*"

Worry flashed over the faces of several of my men, but Dex simply pulled Niko around, his expression like stone. "Can you do this?" He sounded like a general assessing the battle hardiness of his soldiers.

"I... fuck..." Taking a sharp breath, Niko nodded. "Yes."

Dex nodded back. "Get ready," he ordered the others.

Niko stretched out a hand, his face twisting in a grimace. With his eyes on the sparks flying from the wall, he whispered a count under his breath, as if timing the impacts.

And then he pressed his hand to the magical barrier.

A gap opened in the wall. Crooning sounds rose like a blanket of sodden, icy wool trying to engulf our minds.

"Go!" Dex ordered.

The energy of the wall crackled around us, making the hairs on my arms rise. But the cracks in the earth were already diverting our way before we even passed the barrier.

The trees thrashed. Globs of poisonous apple hurled through the air at us.

Roan shifted fast, and fire roared out from the demon, burning the rotting fruits into ash. "Lars!" the demon called.

"Got it!" Hands outstretched as he ran, Lars split the streams of flame in midair, sending them after more trees and apples.

The crooning sounds fell back, growing quieter as the trees nearest to us burned.

"Hurry!" Dex shouted at Ignatius.

Nodding, the scholar skidded to a stop before the boulders. My connection to Byron and Casimir vibrated as their magic surged up to join his in crafting the gateway at high speed.

A shout came from my left. I whirled to see a giant stumble. A tree branch skewered his side, continuing to grow even as he tried to hack at it and escape.

"Move!" Brock yelled, swinging a sword larger than I was.

The blade crashed through the branch, splintering it into kindling. But the giant staggered, the wood embedded in his side still growing. His body thrashed for a moment, and then he screamed as a new tree suddenly burst through his skin.

I choked in horror.

"Fucking *hell!*" Clay exclaimed. "Demon!"

Flame hit the tree surrounded by the giant's remains, turning it to ash.

A thumping sensation went through the air. I spun to see the darkness of a gateway swirl to life behind us.

"Go!" Dex yelled. "Now!"

We ran. Darkness swallowed us, yanking away the forest of nightmarish trees and sending me hurtling forward. I couldn't hear my gasping breaths or feel the horror still gripping me.

But this would work. The apothecary district was ahead, and the witches would help us. We only needed to get to—

The darkness began to shudder.

Oh, gods.

I twisted frantically, searching for my stepmother. Magic tangled in my veins, still connecting me to the others even here. But I couldn't find—

The shaking grew stronger. Cracks split in the darkness around me, but light didn't pour through.

I'd thought this was as dark as anything could be.

I was a fool.

The darkness around me poured into the cracks like

smoke being sucked out of a room. And everything was going with it. The gateway. The whisper of noise around me. All of it fell into an emptiness more profound than even this magic could survive.

Hurry, little doomed one, urged the large gateway demon.

Something whipped me to the side, sparing me from colliding with a crack of oblivion directly ahead of me.

She... the...

The gateway demon's voice came in fits and starts, like something was cutting into the sound, swallowing it with silence.

Your realm is dying. Its deep voice was suddenly much closer, as if the creature was right beside my ear. *We cannot cross that which no longer exists.*

The shaking around me grew worse. Screams came from the darkness. It sounded like the smaller gateway demons.

It sounded like my men.

Desperately, I strained to reach them in the darkness. But everything was fracturing, and I couldn't find a single place to hold on to as I tumbled faster and faster toward cracks that were dragging everything into—

Light flared ahead of me and something shoved me from behind. I hurtled through the blur of light like I'd been pushed from a cliff.

Gravity caught me. Reversed. Slammed me down onto my back atop something rough and scratchy.

Air rushed from my chest, and I gasped. Overhead, the gateway hung in the air, split through by a fissure so much more horrifying than the gateway itself.

Pure *emptiness*. A space my eyes couldn't make sense of, because *nothing* was there. Not even air. Not the sky beyond it.

Just nothingness that had never heard of such a thing as darkness or light.

The empty realms.

Holy gods, what had my stepmother done?

In an instant, the tear in reality started to eat into the gateway. A shudder went through the spell.

Like a great force was ripping it safely away from my world, the gateway opening vanished, leaving only blue sky.

And the fissure, which was spreading wider with every passing second.

Scrambling to my feet, I backed away from the gash in the sky and looked around frantically.

I wasn't where I should have been. This wasn't the apothecary district of Lumilia. Instead, I stood all alone in the northern garden of my castle. The hardy winter plants were withered and dying in their beds. The castle wall was ahead of me, obscuring any view of the city or the countryside. Meanwhile, the air to the west felt strange. Tingly like what I'd felt among the witches of the Jeweled Coven, which hopefully meant that they'd made it here.

But as for my men...

My heart in my throat, I stretched out in my mind, searching.

Relief hit me a moment later. Somewhere deep in the earth beneath my feet, Ozias was moving fast, heading toward the castle. A vague sense of presence told me

Niko was there too. The rest were behind me, but not close.

I turned.

And froze.

The castle that had been my childhood home looked like something out of a fever-fueled nightmare. The walls were crawling with black fungus-like vines. Gray, gnarled branches stabbed out from between the stones of the walls, like the poisonous apple trees were growing from within the walls themselves. Dried and blackened leaves encrusted with yellowed pustules of rot hung half-dead from their ends.

My heart ached. I'd been away for so long, and this felt like returning only to find everything I loved had been destroyed.

Or *almost*.

I pushed down the pain as best I could. There had to be a way to stop this. Reverse it. *Something*.

We just needed to find it.

And each other.

I started toward where I could feel Ozias.

A door banged against the wall on the far side of the garden. Hulking figures with green skin and tusks strode through the opening. Their eyes glowed, and when they saw me, they growled like hungry predators.

Oh gods.

One of them pointed. When he spoke his voice held a strange hissing-clicking quality, like it wasn't just *his* voice but something else speaking as well. "There she is." He grinned. "Get her."

I ran for my life.

54

OZIAS

Tumbling like a rolling rock in an avalanche, I crashed out of the gateway and onto rock that didn't soften itself to cushion my fall.

And *fuck*, that hurt.

Seething against the sharp pain, I struggled upright. Nothing felt broken, but I'd probably have some colorful bruises soon.

Assuming I survived this.

Shoving the rest of the way to my feet, I scanned the shadows quickly. I was in a tunnel, the ceiling low like it'd been crafted by humans who didn't come close to my height. There seemed to be a torch burning beyond the next turn because I could smell its smoke. The thin traces of its light stopped the darkness from being absolute.

But the stench of rot surrounded me, sickening to my senses, and cold dampness clung to the air. In the wall, the stones were worn down, their mortar chipped and crumbling. Dark fungus crawled like black vines from their gaps all across their sides, clawing toward the surface. The tangled corruption was unlike anything I'd seen in the earth before, but it wasn't what gave me pause.

My mate was not here. Her presence was utterly gone, and sheer panic gripped the beast within me to realize we could not feel any trace of—

In a rush, my awareness of her returned, as if she'd suddenly flared to life like a candle in a darkened room.

But she was above me, not down here. Her fear and pain radiated through our connection, spiking higher for a moment before fading into a persistent sort of horror.

Shuddering with rage, I scanned both directions of the tunnel, my senses racing to determine the fastest way to her side. Where the others were, I didn't know, but every one of them would agree saving her was the first order of any business.

The sound of growling came beyond the turn to my left.

Monsters were here.

My lips peeled back from my teeth. Very well.

The shift tore through me as I took off, moving fast. My bones realigned. My joints jerked into new configurations. In only a few strides, it was no longer a man racing down the tunnel, but another monster.

And not a moment too soon.

A wolf charged around the turn, fangs bared. It was larger than an ordinary one of its species. Nearly the size of Ruhl, wherever the hell that shadow creature was. But the glowing red light burning in its eyes told the truth of what was truly inside the beast.

That didn't make it any harder to kill.

Twisting fast, I evaded its teeth and slashed with my claws. A yelp of pain was followed a thudding crash as the wolf collided with the tunnel wall.

I spun. The wolf was on the ground, its side torn open. Its chest rose and fell in short, sharp breaths. It was already dead, its mind and body just hadn't caught up to that fact yet.

But something else had.

A curl of smoke wafted up from the wolf's back. Contorting in the air like snake that could fly, the Voidborn surged forward, racing for my chest.

Grabbing my ax, I swung the blade around, but the confines were too tight, the damned human tunnel too small. My ore-lined blade couldn't move fast enough.

The Voidborn slammed into me.

And began screaming.

Stunned, I retreated, blinking fast as the strange sensation of glistening light faded from the corners of my eyes. My body felt encased in cold stone, radiant like quartz in the sunlight, but even as I registered that, the feeling already began to melt away. Where I'd been standing, the creature hung in the air, thrashing and writhing as if it was being tortured. The sound of its scream was like metal grating over stone, high-pitched and piercing my ears.

But even that faded, almost as if it was being dragged away into the distance to be swallowed in silence.

The Voidborn's body turned to dust and disappeared.

I blinked. Well. That worked, then.

A groan came from the dying wolf. Except... it wasn't

a wolf any longer, but instead a man lying on the stone floor. His blond hair was matted into thick braids, and blue ink stained his temples and forehead. Sticky and red, his hands grasped his bare midsection, doing little to stem the tide of his blood pulsing away.

Barely focused, his light blue eyes found me. He coughed, struggling to make a sound. "Thank... you," he rasped, his accent so thick, it nearly obscured the words.

His body sagged back to the ground, the life leaving his eyes.

Huh.

Turning, I took off down the tunnel again. The scent of damp fur, pungent smoke, and anxious sweat hung in the air. The first was likely from the creature behind me and the last one—

A chunk of wood swung at my head, accompanied by a panicked cry.

I ducked, and the wood splintered against the corner of the tunnel.

"Sorry!" Niko emerged from behind the turn, gripping the piece of wood with embarrassment coloring his cheeks. "I thought you were a— Never mind."

I straightened again, huffing out an irritated breath. He looked mostly intact, though one cheekbone bore a bloodied scrape that was starting to swell. It didn't look like a cut from claws. More like he'd crashed into the stone wall or floor, possibly when the gateway spit him out.

Regrouping quickly, Niko dropped the wood and retrieved a torch that was wedged into a sconce on the wall. "Any idea how to get out of here?"

My nose twitched, testing the air again. Grunting, I jerked my fanged jaw toward the tunnel beyond him.

He nodded quickly, and because he was a smart man, he stayed behind me when I set off again.

My claws would protect us both.

Especially since the thought of doing magic in these close confines, surrounded by this climbing rot, seemed like a terrible choice, somehow. These tunnels were *wrong* in a way that made my skin crawl.

We hurried onward, tracking the tunnel as it curved in an erratic path through the ground. "Something bad happened down here," Niko murmured as if in an echo of my thoughts.

I grunted in agreement. The earth felt... split. Like two tectonic plates had slammed into each another, causing one to buckle and be pulled beneath the other. But... not in a physical sense. An energetic one.

It made my head hurt.

Up ahead, a stairway came into view beyond a small archway. The steps were worn down and nearly lost in shadow, but the stone was still stable.

I slowed anyway, sniffing the air.

"What's wrong?" Niko peered past me. "Oh."

I glanced back at him.

He met my eyes resolutely. "I'll guard our backs. You take care of anything coming down at us."

I didn't move. Those steps were a bottleneck. I couldn't smell anything coming, and the asshole gods knew I couldn't feel another way out of this place. But we'd still be vulnerable.

"We've got this," my eternally hopeful friend assured me.

We'd see.

I strode onward, taking the short, human-sized steps three at a time. Niko jogged after me, the torch clutched in his fist. The firelight played across the walls, casting strange shadows from the blackened rot climbing the stones even here. But I trusted my nose more than my eyes to warn me of threats, and it said we were alone.

Barring this gods-forsaken rot.

Eyeing the vines warily, I kept climbing. Nothing in me wanted to let my fur come anywhere near those things. Up close, they really did look like a fungus. Slightly furry fungus that glistened strangely in the firelight and pulsed like veins in a living being.

But nothing about those things spoke of life to me. I didn't even need to ask Niko. This wasn't nature.

This was death, and it had come for Aneira—and through Aneira, the world.

The stairs came to an end in a small wooden doorway with rot climbing over its frame.

My lips peeled back in a displeased growl. Why did humans have to build things so *small*?

Shuddering, I shifted back to my Erenlian form. My skin prickled at the chill hanging on the air, and gods knew I was still too large for this place. But at least this form stood less of a chance of brushing up against that fungus.

"Are we okay?" Niko asked behind me.

"Yes. Just—" I gestured to the door and then decided

it wasn't worth trying to explain. "Doesn't matter. Come on."

Pausing to sniff the air, I waited until my senses confirmed there was no one on the opposite side of the door and then pushed it aside, taking care not to touch the rot. We were at ground level from the feel of it. The princess was somewhere to my right. Based on her speed, she was definitely running from something, and it made me want to race to her side this instant.

But the castle corridors made the tunnel seem tame.

"What the..." Niko said behind me.

The rot was here as well, but tree branches were as well. They stabbed out from the gaps between the stones of the castle walls like they'd grown from within the building itself. Blackened leaves encrusted with pestilent growths hung from them, many on the verge of falling and others already on the ground. Where they'd dropped, more rot spread, like the growths on the leaves had exploded to release spores.

I didn't take my eyes from the branches and rot. "Can your magic—"

Niko was already making an *oh-hell-no* sound. "This... whatever it is... It's *angry*. Raging with hate. If I try to touch it with my magic..."

"Bad."

"Uh-huh."

"Then stay behind me."

Ax in hand, I set off. The halls were wider than those in the tunnel, but with the branches sticking out everywhere, it still made for careful going.

Footsteps came from up ahead, shivering through

the stones of the floor. The scent of my friends reach my nose.

Dex and Byron raced around the corner, skidding to a stop at the sight of us. "Oh, thank the gods," Byron said. "This place is—"

He cut off as a blur of smoke swept around the corner, transforming swiftly into Casimir. "Strange, yes?" the vampire finished.

Byron gave a brief nod.

I frowned, scanning the corridor. "This way." I strode past them. My mate was moving fast, but she was still up ahead, and I needed her back with us.

Immediately.

"Any sign of anybody else?" Niko asked as he and the others followed.

"Witch magic is on the air to the west of us," Casimir confirmed. "It is different than what fills this place. Hopefully that means our allies fared better with the gateways than we did."

I scowled. Even if they had, the witches wouldn't do a lot of good out there, and we had no way to tell them we were in here.

Dex seemed to come to the same conclusion. "Okay, once we find the princess, we need to get a signal to—"

A roar shook the walls.

"Shit." Dex took off running, but before he made it half a dozen steps, two green-skinned creatures with tusks came barreling around the corner.

They looked like they were running for their lives.

At the sight of us, their glowing eyes went wide. They tried to halt.

My ax cut them down. The Voidborn within them tried to flee only to meet my blade as well.

The floor quivered with heavy footsteps. Crouched down with his wings tucked into his sides, the demon stalked around the corner. Irritation twisted his gray face, the expression growing more pronounced when he spotted his prey already on the ground.

But he didn't comment on the fact I'd killed his quarry. He merely kicked one of them and then harrumphed when they proved well and truly dead.

"Demon," Dex said. "Take the lead. Ozias, you're the second line of defense behind him. We'll find the princess and then we signal the witches."

"What about the twins?" Niko asked.

"We'll find them."

My friends nodded. I hefted my ax, staying well enough back from the demon to hopefully keep from hitting him if I had to swing the weapon.

The demon only scowled. Awkwardly, he turned around. "These stupid hallways are too small," he groused.

I grunted in agreement. "Princess straight ahead."

We took off after our mate.

55
GWYNEIRA

I raced through the corridor, monsters on my trail. I'd lost them briefly when I slipped into one of the servants' access halls, but the reprieve hadn't lasted long. Their running footsteps shook the ground. Their growls spurred me onward. All around, branches reached from the walls like skeletal hands. Rotting leaves fell in my wake, the growths upon them sending plumes of black spores into the air when they hit the ground.

And then more vines would begin up the walls.

Gods, if I survived, this *absolutely* would haunt my nightmares.

New growls came from up ahead. Three green-skinned monsters charged around the corner, cutting off my escape path. I skidded to a stop and tried to retreat, but there was nowhere to go.

Panic gripped me. I could shift, but if these possessed creatures touched me, would it have the same effect as the Voidborn?

I couldn't lose my humanity *here*.

The monsters stalked closer, grinning. I backed away, my mind racing. I couldn't—

The wall at my side rippled like water. Where a moment before there'd been nothing but stone and tree branches, suddenly a door appeared.

What the...

Shoving aside my shock, I took the opening. The monsters roared as I yanked the door aside and then slammed it at my back.

The surface rippled again. Now only unbroken stone remained.

My heart pounding, I stared at the blank wall of stone. There were no branches. No rot. Everything was so dark only my vampire night vision stood a chance of piercing the gloom. But as I turned around, slowly scanning the corridor in which I found myself, I couldn't recognize where I was at all.

To say nothing of the fact a magical door had led to this place.

Warily, I started forward. If this was a trick of my stepmother's, it seemed a strange one. She wouldn't save me from the Voidborn.

So who did?

Cautiously, I stretched my hand out, letting my fingertips trail along the wall. Beneath my touch, the stones warmed, a faint thrum carrying through them.

I stopped. I... I remembered this. I thought it'd only been a dream. When I lay unconscious on the edge of a cliff outside the Jeweled Coven's sanctuary in the mountains, I'd dreamt of walking the halls of my castle.

Of the stones vibrating ever-so-slightly beneath my fingertips.

Welcoming me home.

I pressed my hand to the wall. Beneath my palm, the stones quivered.

Ignatius spoke of the magic in Lumilia being tied to my bloodline. But what about the castle built atop the nexus of that magic, standing strong for hundreds of years while generations of my ancestors lived and died in its walls?

"You know me," I whispered.

The thrumming grew stronger. Around me, the stones moved almost imperceptibly, and suddenly sounds echoed through the dark corridor.

"—take the lead. Ozias, you're the second line of defense behind him. We'll find the princess—"

My lips parted in surprise. That was Dex, but I could feel he wasn't near me. The stones moved again, the change so slight that if I hadn't been staring right at them, I would have surely missed it entirely. Growls carried down the hall, turning into hissing-clicks.

"—she won't be able to get far—"

My stepmother.

I stared at the walls as the stones shifted again, returning the corridor to silence. All those times I'd heard people's voices carry through the halls... all those times I'd joked with my father of a "little bird" whispering secrets to me, giving a name to what I thought were mere oddities of the castle's acoustics...

And no matter how often the servants hung tapestries to deaden those places at my father's orders, others would only appear later on, carrying more secrets to my ears.

Like the castle was trying to tell me something.

I splayed my fingers on the wall, my heart hurting. "But you didn't warn me about *her*."

The thrumming changed, slowing and becoming... sad, somehow.

"You couldn't, could you?" I wasn't sure how I knew, except that it made sense in a way. "You wanted to, but you couldn't?"

The vibrations sped up a tiny amount. It felt like confirmation.

A breath escaped me. Gods only knew what kind of suppressive spells my stepmother put around her quarters for all those years. Melisandre had done everything she could to keep us from learning the truth about her magic. She'd pretended even coming near her power would make our minds lose their grip on reality.

The irony was painful.

"But you saved me back there," I continued. "Thank you."

The thrumming became pulses like infinitesimal waves in the stone.

"This way?" I asked.

The pulses came faster.

"Okay."

I hurried down the corridor, my senses stretching out around me. Ozias was somewhere to my right. Most of the others too. Clay and Lars were somewhere ahead and moving fast, maybe running from something I couldn't perceive.

I sped up. "Can you help us with my stepmother?"

A shudder went through the stone floor, and my heart sank. Somehow, I suspected that was a no.

At least, not more than it already had. Given the way the other halls had looked, overgrown and pierced through with gnarled branches bearing toxic leaves, the castle was likely fighting a battle of its own.

The corridor came to an end in a closed door ahead. Slowing down, I put a hand to the wall again.

"Thank you."

The stone shivered. The lock clicked and the door swung open.

"Holy—" Clay exclaimed.

I hurried through the doorway.

"How the fuck did you just—" Clay stared as the wall shifted back into blank stone again.

"Are you okay, princess?" Lars asked.

I nodded. "The castle helped me."

"The *castle*," Clay repeated. "Okay." He eyed the hallway warily. There were fewer branches here, but thin vines of rot were making their way along the cracks between the stones. "Thank you?" he called skeptically, like he was addressing the walls.

The ground thrummed beneath my feet.

I grinned. "It heard you. I think you're welcome."

He scoffed as if amazed.

"We need to get to the others," Lars said. "Do you think the castle could... I don't know, get us to them faster? We've already run into monsters that don't look too happy to see us."

"Or their puppet masters don't," Clay amended.

"Maybe." I glanced around. "Could you?"

A pulsing quiver carried through the floor.

I nodded. "This way."

We started running. Corridors split off ahead of us, each one veering from a path I knew into a narrow hall I'd never seen.

"How is it doing this?" Lars asked as we ran.

"Uh, magic?" Clay answered like it was obvious.

"Yes, but"—he ducked under a branch as we emerged back into a main hallway—"the actual physical *space* shouldn't—"

I held up a hand, coming to a stop at the sound of running footsteps from beyond the turn. It wasn't my men. They were hurrying this direction, but still too far away.

Clay and Lars took up positions ahead of me quickly, swords drawn.

Valeria rushed around the corner, her braid disheveled and dirt smudged on her face. Behind her ran a curly-haired young woman wearing a stained and torn dress—and at the sight of her, my world reeled.

"Fironia?" I gasped.

My maid choked on a sob when she saw me. "Oh, thank the gods, you're alive!"

"How..." I shook myself, trying to regroup. "Harran told me you were dead! That you killed yourself after my father died."

Fironia cast a quick glance at Valeria. "That's only what the queen told everyone, my lady. I've been locked away this entire time. If not for Valeria finding me, I'd be there still."

"Please, princess," Valeria said, starting toward us, only to stop when Lars and Clay leveled their swords at her chest.

"How are you here?" Lars asked coldly. "Last time we saw you, we'd left you in charge of watching our backs in the mines. That didn't exactly go well."

Valeria grimaced. "I know. I'm sorry. We were captured."

"Yeah, we're going to need more of an explanation than that," Clay snapped when she didn't say anything else.

Her mouth tightened. "The queen had us brought here, and she tried to make us eat those apples. But when we wouldn't, she killed the others. Me, she locked me up. Said she had plans for me." Resolve flashed over her face. "It took me a while to pick the lock, but I got away."

Clay watched her for a moment, and then scoffed. "Never can keep a good general down, eh?"

Warily, Lars lowered his sword.

Her lip twitched gratefully. "We need your help, though. I could get her out"—she nodded toward Fironia—"but there are others. Wounded. Weak. We were scouting a way for them to escape safely when we found you."

Lars looked torn, while Clay seemed on the verge of tucking his sword away. "We'll be quick," Clay assured his brother, starting forward. "We can't—"

"Wait." I didn't take my eyes from the two women as I walked a little closer. I wanted to believe them. Gods, I was relieved to see them alive.

Something just seemed... off.

"Please, my lady," Fironia begged. "The people down there need your help."

I nodded, but I didn't move to follow her.

And suddenly, it hit me what was wrong.

I couldn't hear their heartbeats.

"Stay away from them!" I grabbed the twins' arms, yanking the men backward and then putting myself between them and the two women.

Valeria stared at me. "Princess?"

"Drop the act. I know what you are."

"What?" Fironia looked baffled.

Confused, Valeria started toward me. "I don't understand what you're—"

"I said drop the act!"

Valeria stopped moving. Lost and clearly baffled, she looked between me and the twins like she was seeking something to make my words make sense.

And then she scoffed, the expression falling away like it'd never been. Sharing a wry look with Fironia, she shrugged, her fangs appearing. "Oh, well. Can't blame us for trying."

Fironia grinned, fangs suddenly peeking out from between her lips too. "The mistress told us to have fun with you before draining you. I was *so* looking forward to leading you down to the pit where the mistress's servants live, *princess*." She twisted the word into an insult. "Seeing the shock on your face when you realized there wasn't anyone to save. Savoring your cries of horror when we pushed these oafs over the edge."

Valeria gave a dramatic sigh. "Guess we'll just have to skip ahead to the feast."

They lunged.

A door beside us suddenly swung open. A bucketful of water erupted from within, splashing Valeria and Fironia. It turned to steam when it hit them, reeking of garlic and making the women shriek in pain. Turning instantly to smoke, they writhed in the air for a moment and then fled down the hall out of sight.

"Oh. Goodness, that was dramatic." Clutching the bucket to his chest, Harran emerged from the doorway. "The books were quite right about garlic."

"B-books?" I repeated, staring at the thin, gray-haired man. Despite our surroundings, his livery was as spotless as ever. When he turned to me, he quickly smoothed a hand over his balding head as if surreptitiously attempting to straighten his few silver hairs back into place.

"In the royal library," he confirmed. "Accessing it without permission was inappropriate, I am aware. Once matters return to normal, I shall chastise myself quite thoroughly and accept whatever punishment you decree. But since your stepmother returned, I felt it necessary to educate myself on the... the *situation*."

He huffed out a ragged breath and then drew himself further upright. "My apologies, Princess Gwyneira. I find myself rather overcome. It..." A quiver of restrained emotion ran through him. "It is *quite* good to see you again."

"Do you know this guy?" Clay asked me as Harran executed a tight bow.

I nodded, dumbstruck. "He's the castle steward."

"You sure he's not a vampire too?" Lars asked.

"I most certainly am not." Harran sounded affronted. "But to prove it to you..." He dripped the remaining garlic water from the bucket onto the back of his hand.

Nothing happened.

Clay's brow rose and fell. "Okay, well, how the fuck are you still alive, man?"

Lars winced at his brother's words. "No offense," he added on Clay's behalf.

"My family has served the throne for seven generations." Harran tucked the bucket down by his side, the same rigid propriety in his bearing that I'd seen every day of my childhood. "We have survived worse than this."

Rot began climbing the walls behind him, while tree branches pushed through the cracks between the stones.

The steward blanched, retreating from it. "Perhaps not *much* worse."

I shook my head, trying to dispel my shock. "Okay, um..."

Gods, how would he react to the fact I was in league with honest-to-the-gods *giants* storming the castle?

Ironic futility rose in me. Like it mattered?

"We need to find something," I continued. "It—" I glanced to the side. Footsteps carried down the hall, but thank the gods, this time it wasn't vampires or monsters. The others were here at last.

My relief faltered when it was the demon, not Roan, who rounded the corner first, my other men on his heels.

Harran gasped at the sight. "Get behind me, princess!" He flung himself between me and the demon.

"It's okay!" I grabbed his arm before he could hurl the empty bucket at the demon. "He's on our side."

Eyes wide, the steward turned to gape at me.

"Harran, this is Demon." I nodded at him. "And that's Ozias, Dex, Niko, Casimir, and Byron. Guys, meet Harran, the castle steward."

The demon's eyes narrowed at him. "You are small and bear a foolish weapon, but you still defend my princess." He nodded to himself. "You should stay behind me too."

Harran blinked in shock.

I gave the steward a wincing smile. "It's a compliment. Sort of." Turning to the others, my relief returned. I longed to reach out to them, but I restrained myself to saying only, "It's good to see you."

They nodded, echoing the sentiment.

"Any sign of the others?" Niko asked.

I shook my head, worry bubbling up at the thought of having lost Ignatius and our new allies among the giants.

And Ruhl.

With effort, I pushed down the fear trying to overwhelm me. We'd find the shadow wolf or he'd find us. But either way, I had to focus.

"We need your help," I said to Harran. "We need to find the place where my stepmother did the magic that caused"—I gestured around me tightly—"this."

"Ah. That." Harran nodded. "At first, they used the

tunnels. But lately, the queen seems to have concluded the royal tree is a greater source of power."

I cursed under my breath.

Harran's eyes went wide with affront. "Princess!"

My men ignored him. "What is it?" Lars asked.

I shook my head, trying to find a way to explain. But it made sense. Of course she'd used the royal tree. I'd thought the apples were a cruel joke, a twisting of the symbol that had defined the Aneiran queen for generations.

But what if it'd been more than that?

My eyes skipped to the walls. The ceiling. The floor. Rotting filaments of fungus were climbing across them all, like a miniature version of the destruction her magic was wreaking on the ley lines and the world.

The castle was steeped in the magic of the nexus. It was saturated with it to the point the building itself was very nearly alive. But with its roots twisting down into the earth itself, how much more saturated by the nexus was the tree?

"She's using the royal tree as a channel to the nexus, using it to create all of this," I said. "The apple trees we saw in the countryside. The fruits that steal people's wills. Even the rot growing in the castle. It's all connected. But if we..." Gods, it hurt to say. "If we kill the tree, maybe that's how we can break her hold on the nexus."

The twins and Niko shared a wary look, while Ozias glared at the walls as if blaming them for this personally. Dex frowned, looking away as if seeking a strategy, and

Byron watched him as if hoping to spot when he came up with one.

"If she's tied her corruption of the tree into the nexus," Casimir said carefully. "Killing it might damage the nexus too. Perhaps irreparably."

I hated that he had a point. "Or it hurts her enough that we have a chance to kill *her*."

"With her gone," Byron said, nodding, "the Voidborn might lose the hold they've gained on this world. Or at least on her magic. We could stabilize the nexus then. Use it to drive them out."

Ozias gave a low sound of displeasure. "Assuming it doesn't devour us first."

"I will not let it," the demon countered dismissively.

He sounded so confident, it pulled a smile from me in spite of everything.

"You're risking *her* on that," Ozias snapped back.

The demon hesitated, a hint of anxiety flashing over his face.

"With our powers as they are now," Dex spoke up. "This might be the best chance we'll ever get, so we need to take it. Agreed?"

Nods passed among the others, but Ozias just scowled.

The demon reached over, putting a massive clawed hand to his shoulder. "You and I will guard our mate, friend Ozias. We will make sure she is not devoured by this contemptible magic."

My heart melted a little.

Gods, please let us all survive. I wanted a life with these monsters and men.

Closing his eyes briefly, Ozias nodded. "We will."

"Okay," Dex said. "Then there's only one other problem."

"The tree is in the courtyard," I filled in.

Clay made a noise of understanding. "Where I'm guessing all the monsters will be waiting for us?" He nodded to himself. "Great."

Ozias hefted his ax, grim resolve coming from him. "Then we kill them too."

A breath left me, and I nodded. "Yeah."

Harran stared around at us. I braced myself for him to protest. Surrounded by my giants, he looked like a frail old man desperately out of his depth.

But after a moment, the steward only exhaled sharply. "I will come with you." Lifting his chin, he hefted his bucket like he bore the weapon of a king.

Dex nodded. "All right. We move fast and we protect the princess. No matter what."

I frowned, but the others only voiced their agreement. Even the thin steward.

"Good." Dex jerked his chin at the demon to lead the way. "Let's go."

56
DEX

It had been years since I last set foot in Lumilia. At the time, I'd only been a teenager swearing allegiance to the king, and I never went inside the castle itself, remaining instead in the courtyard or in the barracks where all the other soldiers stayed.

I sure as hell had never heard anyone say the castle could *change* itself.

With my friends around me and my sword in my hand, I ran through the halls. Our cabin had been alive, in a way. Our magic—mine more than most—had given it a sort of life. So the thought of this place having a similar quality wasn't completely foreign to me.

But given what was happening around us, the castle was currently in a battle for its life—and from what I could tell, it wasn't exactly winning.

Branches grew from the stone walls like they were intent on ripping the entire place apart. Rot clung to everything, chewing into the stones like it was devouring the granite and the magic alike. But worst were the fissures where everything just... ended.

"Gap in the floor, straight ahead," the demon called back. He stepped over the jagged gash of nothingness in the granite, his body hunched awkwardly to keep his wings from hitting the ceiling. "Stupid little one this time."

Clay gave a wry chuckle, enjoying the demon's insults, but I kept my attention on the walls and floor as Ozias and I stepped over the gap as well. The strange fissures had started showing up the closer we came to the outer walls, like they were another form of rot slowly gaining purchase on the castle itself. And they seemed able to spread quickly, or for others to open near them without warning.

We couldn't take anything for granted.

"Here, allow me." Byron hefted the steward over the gap and then set the man back down. I vaguely recalled the thin, graying man from the day I swore allegiance to the throne of Aneira. He'd been rigid. Proper. Seemingly clothed in rules and correct procedures as much as the formal livery of his station.

Even the castle becoming this madhouse of trees and rot hadn't done much to shake that from him.

"Thank you," Harran said with a tight nod. "Much appreciated."

Shaking my head, I kept going. We had to be getting close to the courtyard by now.

As if summoned by my thoughts, an archway waited at the end of the larger hallway around the next turn, sunlight shining down on the flagstones beyond. The demon and Ozias had both stopped short of it, hanging back from the reach of the light.

"Well," Lars said, clearly trying to keep a positive note in his voice when he spotted the exit too. "Here goes nothing."

Cursing silently, I adjusted my grip on my sword and continued down the tunnel, only to pause when I reached the archway.

The courtyard was empty.

Clay made a sarcastic sound. "Oh, no. This *definitely* isn't a trap."

"Now what do we do?" Byron asked, peering past our shoulders at the empty space. Shaped like a pentagon with crenelated walls on three sides and the tall castle walls forming two more, the courtyard spanned several thousand square feet. A tall, barred gateway stood on the opposite end, directly across from us. Broad, gray flag-stones covered the ground everywhere except for where a ring of dirt and dead grass waited at the center of the courtyard. At the heart of that ring stood the royal tree.

Or what was left of it.

For a moment, I stared, my examination of the court-yard faltering at the sight of the twisted thing that had once been the royal tree of Aneira. Generations of Aneirans had tended to it lovingly, and in my memory, the tree had been a beautiful testimony to what humans could do if only they tried.

But now its bark was covered in writhing black veins of rot. Its branches looked like those in the castle, skeletal hands clawing at the air. Even in the depth of winter, countless apples hung from its branches, all of them emanating that same nauseating energy designed to draw us in and make us devour them, never mind that we could die.

An icy, crystalline feeling surged over my skin, dulling the pull.

The magic of Erenelle. It wasn't having any of that crooning nonsense. Even as the chill of its power sank back inside me, becoming almost imperceptible once more, nothing about the apple tree appealed to me.

Except making sure it died.

Returning my focus to the courtyard, my mind raced to calculate the possibilities—or lack thereof. I could see what Casimir had spoken of now: magic lit the sky to the west where the apothecary district lay. Hopefully that meant the witches, the giants, and maybe even the shadow wolf had made it, but it didn't do us much good at the moment. Meanwhile, the windows on the castle were a threat, as were the spaces behind the crenelations. Either could hide attackers, and save for this door, the courtyard exit on the far end, and the main entrance to the castle itself, we'd be utterly exposed with nowhere to retreat from any of them.

Clay was right. Perfect place for an ambush.

And we had no choice but to enter it anyway.

"Surround the princess," I told the others, still keeping my eyes on the empty courtyard. "We move fast and we don't stop until we're across the—"

Rumbling suddenly shook the corridor where we stood. The flagstones on the floor cracked, branches shooting up fast between them.

"Holy shit, go!" Clay shoved us forward.

Branches tore the air, growing so rapidly that in only moments the hallway was choked by them.

Separating us from Harran on the other side.

"Princess!" he shouted. "I-I can't get through!"

"Run!" she ordered him. "Get out of here. Don't let this—"

She cut off with a panicked cry as the branches started tearing into the ceiling and pushing through the outer wall of the castle itself.

Biting back a curse, I spun, my eyes sweeping the courtyard while the steward retreated from the collapsing hallway. As yet, no one had launched an attack, barring the damn branches that had just driven us out into the open.

But that could change at any moment.

"Move," I ordered the others. "Stay together."

As one, we started across the courtyard, the princess shielded at our center. I'd spent years training my friends, drilling them on all I knew about how to fight and survive as a unit. It was the best way I knew to show them I cared, by making sure they could stay alive if worse came to worst.

No matter what else happened, pride in them filled me now.

"Voidborn!" Niko called.

My eyes darted to the side. A dozen of those green-skinned men with tusks were pouring out of the main castle door, massive axes and swords in their hands and vicious lights glowing in their eyes.

"Got more of them!" Lars called back.

On the other side of the courtyard, harpies landed on

top of a crenelated wall, leering down at us like they couldn't wait to tear our flesh from our bones.

"Pick up the pace," I ordered, gauging our distance to the tree. We'd just crossed the edge of the ring of dirt and roots, with only a short distance left to go. "We're almost—"

Like the invisible hand of a full-size giant, something slammed into me, sending me flying. Pain erupted from my shoulder and side as I crashed down, dazing me, and my sword clattered on the flagstones.

Scrambling back up, I grabbed my weapon. My friends were scattered, thrown to the ground same as me. Above us, the harpies were circling, their ear-piercing shrieks of joy tearing the air.

But Gwyneira was on her feet. Unlike the rest of us, she hadn't been tossed down, and she stood only a few yards from the tree.

A massive globe of misty, crystalline glass surrounded her and the tree alike, as if someone had turned a round bowl on its head, trapping her inside.

"Holy shit." Clay shoved to his feet. "Hang on, princess!" He charged forward, sword drawn.

Shrieking, the harpies dove, swiping at him and narrowly missing. He skidded to a stop, retreating as another barreled at him.

Growling, Ozias swung at them with his ax, tearing one down while the others darted away.

The green-skinned men thundered toward us, weapons ready.

Swearing blurred through my mind, but it was background noise to the focus that honed my senses.

Slashing my sword, I sent one harpy spiraling into the flagstones. Spinning the blade fast, I stabbed behind me, taking down one of the green-skinned monsters at my back.

Ahead, the princess struck the wall, shouting without sound behind the thick barrier. Even her vampire strength couldn't crack the glass.

Fuck.

"Take that thing down!" I shouted at Byron and Casimir as I cut through another green-skinned attacker.

"I'm trying!" Byron yelled back.

Turning into smoke, Casimir wove through the battlefield at high speed, coalescing into human form just shy of the glass. Pressing his hands to the barrier, he viciously snarled something I couldn't hear.

Light flared like twin suns bursting to life beneath his palms. The blast roared across the surface of the glass, blindingly bright. Behind him, Byron flung out a hand, shouting something in old Erenlian.

Crackles like lightning crawled over the glass, joining his light. Inside the glass, the princess shielded her eyes. Through the strange connection we all now shared to her power, I could feel her magic pouring from her outstretched hand, aimed at the glass.

"Come on," I urged between gritted teeth, spinning out of the way of a diving harpy. "Break, you fucking—"

An icy wind suddenly whipped over the courtyard, driving me backward. The harpies scattered and the green-skinned men stopped, struggling to stand in the face of the onslaught. Casimir staggered, fighting to hang onto the wall and his spell alike.

The wind faded. A chuckle carried through the silence in its wake.

"Oh, I think that's quite enough."

A thumping pulse went through the glass. Casimir flew backward, thrown from the globe like he'd been hit by a battering ram. Before he hit the ground, he shifted and turned, twisting in midair and then landing on his feet.

The queen paced calmly around the side of the misty globe. "Impressive." She regarded Casimir. "You have the look of the Zeniryan royal family. I'd heard one of my sister witches devoured you all. I didn't realize one of you remained for Gwyneira to turn into a *pet*."

She chuckled to herself like the words were some secret joke. Her blond hair gleamed in the sunlight, but so did her skin, the latter with a faintly silver sheen that made no sense. Her black dress seemed to absorb the light completely, swallowing it whole and letting nothing return. When she smiled, her fangs glinted between her red lips while her blue eyes were as soulless as a doll's.

"Release the princess," Casimir growled.

Queen Melisandre made an amused sound. "Such *loyalty*. Risking so much for my pathetic stepdaughter and her idiotic crusade. As if you'd find any other outcome than simply watching her die."

The demon's snarl tore the air. Claws at the ready, he charged.

Her hand caught him around the throat, stopping him in his tracks. The demon's eyes went wide as he struggled and couldn't break free.

"No, no," she chided. "I have something *special* planned for you."

The air warped. Gaps in reality suddenly appeared between them, tearing across his chest and arms like invisible claws.

The demon screamed.

Metal flashed at the corner of my eye. With a roar, Ozias hurled his ax through the air. The blade spun end over end, flying for the space between the demon and the queen.

A heartbeat ahead of when the blade would cost her an arm, she released him. The demon crumpled to the ground, hunched over the wounds on his chest and arms.

The queen's eyes turned to Ozias. She smiled, the expression brutal in its satisfaction.

Dread gripped me, but she didn't attack. "Keep them here," she said to the Voidborn calmly. "And save the winged one for last. I need to have a word with my step-daughter."

She turned away and walked through the glass like it wasn't even there. Inside the globe, Gwyneira retreated, her eyes locked on her stepmother.

As one, the Voidborn charged.

57
GWYNEIRA

Like something out of a nightmare, my stepmother passed through the glass wall. Her eyes never left me. A satisfied smile was fixed upon her face.

And her eyes were so calm, they made my skin crawl.

"You've run for so long, Gwyneira, desperately pretending to be something you're not. But that ends here."

She walked closer. The light reflected strangely from her skin, as if she was made of scales and metal, not flesh. As she moved, the air warped and rippled, tiny new fissures of darkness shedding from her like feathers falling from a molting bird.

My eyes darted to the demon. Beyond the misty glass wall, he was on the ground but, thank the gods, alive. Niko was with him, sword slashing to keep the harpies and green-skinned creatures at bay.

"Do you want to know what I'm going to do to your allies, Gwyneira? How they'll suffer because of you?"

Shudders rolled through me, but as I pulled my gaze back to her, I tried to fight them down. She wanted to hurt me. Scare me. Get inside my head.

But she wasn't the only one with a goal here.

"You have to stop," I told her, making my voice as level as I could while I backed carefully toward the tree, my arm outstretched behind me. "Send the Voidborn back. They're destroying everything."

"Is *that* what you think is happening?" She shook her head as if amused by me. "You're so limited, Gwyneira. You always have been."

I ignored the jibe, taking another step back while I drew upon the magic link I shared with my men. Let my stepmother believe I was trying to reason with her. Only a little farther, and I would reach the tree trunk.

And then I'd kill the thing she'd twisted into destroying the kingdom it once symbolized.

"I admit," my stepmother continued. "I applaud this little menagerie of allies you've collected. Seven dwarves. A vampire prince with angel blood—or is he king now that the rest of his family line is dead? One of your men even hides a demon." She smiled. "They'll all be *most* delicious when I drain them dry."

Beyond the glass, my men were barely holding their ground against the onslaught of Voidborn. But still their power filtered through to me, answering my call.

"Please, Stepmother," I said, taking another step backward. "I know you want to keep the throne, but you *have* to see the damage you're doing. You can't rule Aneira if it ceases to exist. If the whole *world* does. You have to stop this. There won't be anything left to rule if you don't."

She gave me a patient look. "I'm not going to rule *Aneira,* you silly girl. I'm going to rule *everything.*"

I took another step back, but a shudder went through the soil. Roots snagged my ankle, tripping me. Falling backward, I barely caught myself with both hands on the rough ground.

Pain shot through my palms as the sharp roots tore my skin.

My stepmother merely laughed. "Look at you. Honestly believing that Aneira could be enough for me."

Blood welled on my palms, the wounds stinging and throbbing. The image of that poor giant dying when the tree branches stabbed him flashed through my mind. Desperately, I tried not to think about it.

If she won, I was dead either way.

"But you're *destroying* Aneira," I said, not taking my eyes from her. "You're destroying the entire *world.*"

She scoffed.

Twisting my leg carefully, I tried to extricate my ankle from the roots. "You're doing exactly what the Voidborn want, don't you see that? You're not ruling anything. You're acting like their *puppet.*"

Rage flashed across her face. Her blue eyes snapped to me, more alive than they'd been this whole time. "You pathetic little brat. I am *no one's* puppet."

I paused, searching for something to say that would

keep her talking rather than trying to kill me. I was so close to the trunk. If I could get free of these roots, it was only a short distance more to reach—

Tingles of magic licked across my bleeding palm.

I froze.

"You know," my stepmother said, looking at the battle beyond the glass. My men had been driven back to the main gate of the castle. I could barely see them past the Voidborn surrounding them. "I was going to kill you first. Rid you from my presence once and for all, like that damned Huntsman should have done ages ago. But now..."

She chuckled as Niko stumbled under an onslaught by the Voidborn. Dex raced to his rescue, barely managing to drive the monsters back before more lunged at him. "Now I think I'll make you watch."

Swallowing hard against panic, I strained for the magic I'd just felt. It hadn't been like the corruption my stepmother wrought. It was different. Brighter.

The taste of fresh apples flitted across my tongue.

I tensed, but the flavor didn't turn to vinegar and poison in my mouth. It tasted of my childhood. Of summers spent playing beneath the broad and beautiful branches of this tree.

And it felt like a promise and a desperate, dying plea.

The *real* tree of Aneira was still here, beneath all the poison.

Shivers coursed through me, driven by under-standing that fell over me like snow. My blood was calling to the tree, not just because the generations of my ancestors who'd lived and died in this place, but because...

The prickling magic grew stronger against my palm.

Because the tree and I were the same. The castle and maybe even the nexus too. Each of us had been twisted by my stepmother's magic. Each of us had been forced into being something we were not.

I always had been tied to this place. And what she'd done to us—me, the tree, the castle, the nexus itself—it affected us all. Every time my stepmother had tried to twist my home, every time she'd wrought magic to tear my world apart, it had nearly gutted me. Her power had sent me spiraling into darkness, no matter how far away from here I'd been.

Aneira was more than my nation. Lumilia was more than my city. We were connected. We always had been.

And we were still fighting to survive.

"Tell me, Gwyneira." My stepmother turned back to me. "Here you are, all alone, cut off from your precious men. There's no one left to save you, and nothing you can do but watch them die. So *do* tell me. What was this all for? Some noble delusion of dying for your daddy's throne? A misguided effort to avenge that stupid man?"

I shook my head, never taking my eyes from her. "No."

"Then what was it? Why wouldn't you just crawl away and die like you were supposed to? This whole world was always going to be mine. There's no one left to save you, this world, or *anything*."

I dug my fingers into the dirt, my palm stinging and tingling. "There's me."

With all my might, I sent my magic rushing to join the remnants of the tree's original power. Drawn by our connection, the energy of my men came with it, merging with my own.

Fire, water, stone, and wood. Nature itself and power like the sun. Like the energy of the stars.

And my power at the heart of it all.

"What nonsense is this?" My stepmother's amused and incredulous voice came from far away. "You think you can *take* this place from me?"

Roots climbed over my fingers, my wrist, encasing them like the tree was gripping my hand.

Niko's power surged within me, bringing understanding. The tree wasn't attacking.

It was trying to help.

I smiled, drawing on Dex's magic. "Grow."

Fresh roots ripped through the soil. Spreading fast, they tore into the flagstones, racing for the edge of the glass dome.

"You—" My stepmother spun, flinging out a hand.

Fissures of nothingness shredded through the roots. Pain screamed through me and the tree alike, but then the demon's fire was there like my veins had suddenly turned to rivers of flame. Whipping my palm toward her, I let it go.

Eyes wide, she spun. Her magic caught the blast with a slash of nothingness, devouring it.

But my diversion stopped the attack on the roots long enough for them to hit the glass wall. The wood scaled the misty surface, stabbing it over and over.

And the glass cracked. Groaned. Broke like crumbling frost around us. The roots fell back to the earth, but they didn't stop there. Surging forward, they charged at the Voidborn monsters, tangling around them and yanking them away from my men.

Melisandre stared. "You little... You think this means you're winning? Because one little tree listens to you?" She glared. "Try fighting *this*."

The hairs on my arms rose, a sensation on the air like dark lightning preparing to strike. Her hand flung down, aimed at the dirt and stone.

Magic pierced the ground. Through the roots of the tree, I could feel it racing down into the depths of the earth.

Racing for the nexus.

Our magic chased it, following the roots through the earth. Rot and corruption tangled around us, trying to devour our energy and that of the tree alike.

And deep below us lay the nexus. Like a dark cloud in my mind, my stepmother's corruption engulfed it in a swirling mass of vicious, hungry magic.

Melisandre's power hit the dark cloud, merged with it, drew it in like she was drinking its blood. With every drag she took from it, dark veins rushed out through the earth, pouring more power into the rot climbing over the castle. Shudders shook the ground, making the stone and dirt crumble.

Horror gripped me. The nexus was dying. A few ley lines still ran to it, but their power was twisted and corrupted. Countless more lay around it like severed veins, their uncorrupted magic bleeding out into the earth, never reaching the nexus with sufficient strength to let it fight back completely.

She'd broken this. Torn it to pieces in her battle to take control of it. But at the core of that dark cloud, there was still light.

She hadn't yet claimed it all.

Casimir's magic and Byron's surged inside me, and my vision changed. Where before I'd seen a dark cloud, now there were pieces and fragments of spells. A map of magic, and a puzzle too. I could see places where the ley lines *should* have been, and places where they could still reach the core of the nexus beyond the darkness.

If I did this just right.

With the magic of my scholar and vampire as my guides, I reached out for the severed ley lines.

It felt like wrapping my hands around a bolt of lightning. Worse.

I was burning. Dying. All of reality was ending and beginning and bleeding out, and I was too.

The demon's strength surged through me. Byron and Casimir's skill with magic too. Clay's power cooled me, and Lars's gifts made sure I didn't burn. Dex's energy urged the ley lines to grow while Niko and Ozias fought to hold the earth steady.

I wouldn't die.

Drawing the ley lines with me, I sent my power into the darkness, threading it like a needle through the shifting cloud. Ahead, the light grew stronger and brighter the closer I came.

But the ground was shaking, and despite our efforts,

my body was held in place by the fresh roots of a tree still fighting for its life.

I was running out of time.

"Please," I whispered. "Please hold on."

I drew the ley lines past the dark and into the light.

Magic surged around me, blinding and brilliant, as the ley lines connected to the nexus again. It blasted outward, driving back the darkness, shaking her hold.

She'd broken this to take power over it.

It wasn't broken anymore.

But she wasn't through yet.

My eyes flew open as the earth shuddered so hard, it fractured the roots holding my hand in place.

"You..." Melisandre stood where she'd been, her gaze on the ground like she could see straight through to the nexus. "You little..." A chuckle escaped her.

Of every reaction she could have had, *that* chilled me the most.

Her voice became a snarl. "This world is *mine.*"

"No, it isn't. Stepmother, you have to stop—"

"It isn't?" Her eyes snapped over to mine, and another tiny laugh left her. "You think you can just say it... it *isn't,* and that will be that?" Her eyes skipped over the courtyard again, finding my men. Maybe even seeing the thrum of the link between us all.

Her humor faded into a grim certainty. "It isn't. It..." A strange sort of peace came into her voice. "It isn't. But it always was so *small,* anyway."

Wariness prickled through my veins. Behind her, the Voidborn had left off attacking my men. They'd simply *stopped.* As one, they turned to where my stepmother and

I stood. Their glowing eyes locked on Melisandre with a look that chilled me.

Anticipation.

"He told me that, you know," she continued. "He said it, over and over again, even though I couldn't see it. But he was right." Hate and rage twisted her face when she turned back to me, like the words were bitter and terrible but true. "Alaric was *right*."

I fought the urge to retreat from the look in her eyes. It wasn't sane. It didn't even seem like she was actually seeing me.

On the far side of the courtyard, my men were weaving past the Voidborn as fast as they could, trying to reach me but clearly wary as hell at the battle that had just stopped for no reason they could see.

"Stepmother, whatever you're thinking, please don't—"

"There are whole worlds out there." She cocked her head at me with a strangely mechanical curiosity that never reached the cold deadness in her eyes. "Did you know that? Whole *realms* whispering to one another. Telling stories to one another. And I... I really thought I could be satisfied ruling it all from this *one* little world?"

Oh no.

"I am a *goddess*. I am beyond them and will overthrow them all. And you..." She gave a tiny giggle, like it was all so simple. "Why, you will be reduced to ash. The dust of your entire existence will be lost in the void, and if the other realms ever imagine you existed at all, it'll be as barely more than the memory of a dream." Her laughter turned cruel, a hint of the woman I knew coming back into her blue eyes. "Nothing left of Gwyneira and her men except a foolish... little... *fairytale.*"

She snapped her fingers. The ground shook as the tiny fissures of nothingness raced from the courtyard and the castle to converge behind her. The slivers of emptiness swirled together, spiraling in the air at her back until they merged into one inky black portal into oblivion.

"Gwyneira!" Dex ran toward me, the others on his heels and Casimir flying ahead of him.

All around the courtyard, Voidborn surged out of the monsters they'd inhabited. In a flood of black smoke, they dove into the portal.

"What the fuck?" Clay shouted.

"Just *run*, dammit!" Lars snapped back.

A rumble came from the castle, and suddenly, vines and tendrils of rot surged across the courtyard.

"Oh *hell*." Clay waved his arms, frantically urging the others on as they veered around the darkness and strained to reach my side. "Go, go, go!"

But the fungus-like ropes didn't care about them. Climbing over each other, the vines piled higher behind my stepmother's back until they could pass over the edge of the portal to the void.

The moment they touched that darkness, the earth itself groaned. Everywhere the vines rested began to crumble like sand.

Behind my stepmother, the void swelled larger. It wrapped around her like a black cloak and flowed over her like she was sinking into an inky pool.

And just before it embraced her completely, Melisandre's lips curled into a vicious smile. "*This*, my pathetic little stepdaughter, is how your story ends."

She flung her arms wide. Nothingness erupted around her in a wave.

There was no escape.

58
MELISANDRE

Every fragment of my essence sang with power. Every tiny piece that made me who I was finally, finally understood.

I was born to be a goddess.

And my victory was only beginning.

"It was a wretched little realm anyway, pet."

Alaric walked beside me across the nothingness, admiring the ink-black vines growing from beyond the borders of the world I'd once bothered to call mine. At my back, they clawed past the edges of the portal I'd made. The castle still stood beyond it, though that wouldn't last. With every passing moment, my power drained the energy out of that world, fueling the growth of my majesty across the void.

Thousands of tendrils of my power coursed out across the nothingness now. Millions, even. Each one would seek any crack, any weakness or flaw in the veils that surrounded the pathetic *reality* of the realms.

Relentless and unstoppable, they would break open those barriers and pour into the worlds that glowed like a disgusting rainbow of stars against the beautiful, pure black night of oblivion.

And then the true fun would begin.

"It was," I agreed.

Alaric smirked at me. "Did you really think your *hatred* would destroy me down in that tunnel weeks ago?"

"I won, didn't I?"

"By making me more a part of you than I ever would have been otherwise. By *becoming* me to the point you sacrificed your entire realm and set yourself on a path to destroy countless more, on a scale even *we* have never yet achieved." He chuckled. "Rather makes one wonder which of us truly won in the end, don't you think?"

I scoffed with disgust. "*I* did."

He made a thoughtful sound. "We'll see."

Temper flaring, I turned to him. "I grew *beyond* my world, Alaric. That's the truth of it. And your ridiculous nitpicking won't change the fact I crushed you into nothing when I—"

Light flickered at the corner of my eye.

"I think you'll find, pet, that you haven't won *quite* yet. Look."

My gaze followed to where he pointed.

In the distance, an eight-pointed star glimmered. A light as bright and clear as a diamond shone at its heart.

"She's still fighting you," Alaric commented. "The Nine all are."

"*How?*" The word tore from me like a growled curse.

"The void *took* her. She couldn't survive that. *None* of them could."

"And yet." He gestured like the truth was self-explanatory.

Fury stole my words.

Alaric only chuckled. "Vampires are our creation, pet. Brought back to some semblance of life and thus made into vessels for us, same as the orcs or harpies or shifters whose species had once died out only to have us resurrect them. Enough of our power exists within them to let them last a fraction longer in the emptiness than most—a fact I once used to my advantage when *you* were thrown into the void, if you recall. Besides, there are worlds *within* worlds, and the Nine are one unto themselves. Over and over, they acted to create the reality *they* thought should be, until they bent their very world around them. It happens like that sometimes in these petty little realms. Someone rises up so high, they start to embody the energy of the realm itself. But... " He smiled. "That doesn't mean they can't be broken—and through them, break everything."

"But I already *did* that," I snarled.

"Almost. Would you like to see how it truly ends?"

He started forward. Seething, I trailed him.

Gwyneira's little star began to take on definition, revealing the glowing forms of her little band of irritants standing on a ghostly remnant of the world I'd destroyed. At their back, a hint of dull light shone, like a memory of the portal I'd opened. Vines of my power still extended from it, growing out into the darkness.

But all around the pathetic Nine, fragments of light

drifted like she and her men were on the edge of disintegrating into dust and snow.

Alaric smiled to see it. "Remember what I once told you, pet. The Nine aren't this world's salvation." His soulless eyes met mine, and his metallic teeth glinted in the dying light. "They are its downfall."

59
GWYNEIRA

At the heart of oblivion, we were nearly gone. A ghostly scrap of dirt remained beneath our feet, as ephemeral as a dream. A shadow of the portal was at our backs, like a painting so sapped by time, the details had disappeared. Vines choked it, blocking our path and pulsing like they were draining the lifeblood of our realm. Our protection given by the Wall of Erenelle was eroding like glittering sand beneath a brutal wind.

And beyond us was only endless night.

"Stay together," Dex said, scanning the darkness.

Lars nodded. "We'll find a way out of this."

His optimism was welcome—but I had no idea how to do that. Our bonds were holding for the moment, but the darkness before us had a weight, and it was intent upon crushing us like glass.

And we weren't alone.

My breath caught at the realization. My senses

wanted to rebel against this void. Everything in me wanted to run screaming from the dark. But horror riveted me here, watching the emptiness with the sudden knowledge something slithered in the void. Some great and hungry *thing* that knew exactly where we were.

And it was coming closer.

It was watching us as it writhed toward our position like an enormous snake twisting through the night, hissing mad words that chased themselves round and around without end.

Corruption is power is poison is victory is hunger is...

I strained for the distant traces of my connection to the nexus, desperate to pull us back into our world. But the vines had nearly drained it all, and void didn't want to let us go.

"Anyone got a great plan for getting us out of here?" Clay prompted.

"Draw on our power, princess," Dex said. "Use it to reach the nexus and bring us back."

"I'm *trying*. I can't seem to..." I trailed off, my eyes still riveted on darkness, seeking the *thing* coming our way.

"I suspect the issue is a bit more complicated," Casimir said.

Hunching around the wounds on his chest, the demon made a wary sound. "Why is that, vampire?"

"Because," Byron filled in, "with what the queen has done, I'm not sure anything remains to go back to."

A growl left Ozias, displeasure in the sound.

"But—" Niko made a desperate noise.

My head shook. "I can feel it. Just... just a bit. But—"

This isn't the way, a gentle and loving voice whispered so softly, it was as if the speaker was right beside my ear.

The glittering light of our failing protections suddenly swept around us like snowflakes in the night. It washed away the void, taking the slithering beast and any fear too.

Suddenly, we were somewhere else entirely.

Old and familiar stones vibrated gently beneath my feet as if welcoming me. Each of my men still surrounded me. Together, we stood atop a high parapet, a crenelated wall of dark granite lining its edges. Sparks of silver glittered within the rocky surface like it held a million flecks of light. Moss grew in the spaces between each stone—and for a moment, the sight filled me with fear.

But this wasn't my stepmother's rot or decay. The little green curls glinted like they were made of emerald crystal, shimmering with life.

"What happened?" Niko whispered, his dark eyes wide.

I shook my head, speechless.

Clay glanced back and forth like he was checking something. "Are... are we *dead?*"

"This is an unexpected afterlife, if so," Byron replied skeptically.

My mouth moved, searching for words. "It's my home."

The others went silent.

I stepped forward, staring beyond us, overcome with awe. The sky danced with colors and light, like the brilliant glows I'd sometimes see in the northern sky, but without end. Amid it all, a sea of stars shone like diamonds, each of them brushed with shifting colors by the lights and glittering with endless majesty.

Yet the castle wasn't diminished by the infinite beauty above. Age radiated from everything around me, like the moss knew of a time before time began and the stones remembered when they were mountains. What they were now was only a flickering moment in the journey of all they'd been—and all they'd someday be.

The heart of a mountain. The wall protecting us and keeping us from falling.

The dust at the center of a newborn star.

Endless. Infinite. Never beginning or ending. Simply... being.

"Welcome, my precious ones."

I turned. A woman stood beyond us, a dress of stars drifting around her. Misty light rose from her long black hair and drifted in wisps into the brilliant night sky. Her red lips curled when she smiled, and her eyes were so knowing and calm, they instantly eased something inside me that had never known it had been in pain.

I'd only seen her in paintings. None had done her justice.

"Mother?" I whispered.

"Hello, daughter." Eira extended her arms.

I was moving before I finished registering the impulse.

Her arms enfolded me like a warm blanket made of the softest down imaginable. I squeezed my eyes shut, tears prickling.

"You're too close to the edge, my darling child."

I sniffled, pulling back but not letting her go. "Where are we?"

"At the cusp of everything."

I hesitated, confused.

"*Are* we dead, then?" Casimir asked carefully.

My mother shook her head. "Not yet. Perhaps not at all. But you *are* at the farthest reaches of life, the edge before death's fall." Her eyes returned to mine. "The place where things are at their most true."

She brushed my hair back from my cheek. "I am so proud of you, my beautiful girl." She smiled at the others. "Of *all* of you. The brave seven I sent to my daughter. The strong eighth you found and who found you. Each of you are all I could have wished for my daughter and more."

My giants smiled awkwardly, seeming flattered, while Casimir appeared touched and grateful. The demon fidgeted as if he didn't know where to look, and at the sight, my mother's smile became lovingly amused. "Even you, son of Jessora. I sent you too."

The demon blinked, stunned.

A distant rumble carried through the night, making my breath catch with alarm.

My mother only sighed. "Melisandre has played a game so much more dangerous than she knows." Eira gave a small, sad chuckle. "But that is her way. She was broken long before I knew her, and though that breaking wasn't her fault, her choices are still hers alone. Sometimes, people take poison in an effort to cure their pain, but it only destroys whatever good was left inside beyond the breaking. In the end, they burn down everything because, after destroying themselves, destruction has become familiar. Welcome. It is all they know."

"Is..." I faltered, but the question pressed at me. "Is that why she is so determined to kill me?"

Eira shook her head. "She never saw *you*, precious one. And that isn't your fault. A diamond does not cease to be a diamond simply because someone cannot recognize its value." She took my hand. "Others do not exist as people to her, only as playthings and objects on a game board, because that's what she believes the world to be. Yet because you are real and not a toy—and because you survived when she wanted her toy to die—she behaves like a child throwing a tantrum, obsessed with destroying you simply because you didn't do as she wished."

She rested her palm on my cheek. "I know that doesn't make it hurt less, but your pain is *real*. Nothing about Melisandre is, on so many levels now." Eira's mouth tightened. "But that doesn't mean the damage she causes does not exist."

The stars overhead changed. Their radiance spread until they weren't lonely glimmers in the infinite dark, but pinpoints of brightness amid a fabric of light.

"Everything that exists has a reason," my mother said. "Every story has a place where it was true. There are realms upon realms of reality. They always surround us, and all of them whisper to one another. Tell each other their stories. Their dreams. This is what Melisandre threatens, and what she will destroy if you don't stop her now."

Sound carried from the fabric of light, a distant

lullaby of chimes and whispers, like the rushing of a sea deeper and more infinite than I could fathom. Images played out in the glowing radiance as if they had always been there, *right there*. They'd simply been beyond my ability to perceive them.

Worlds of fire. Of deep forests and brilliant sunlight. Of endless oceans, and of impossibly tall steel-and-glass towers that stretched into a brilliant blue sky. In each one, people lived and loved, fought and died, some of them looking like humans and some looking like nothing I'd ever dreamed.

But the tendrils of rot were coming for them all, creeping across the void. Already, they'd found the first little cracks along the barriers that separated one reality from another. With every little breach they found, the rot dug at it relentlessly, widening the gaps, breaking apart the boundaries, forcing their way into those realms.

So they could feed.

"How do we stop her?" I asked.

"You see what is true." My mother's smile turned sad. "And you shatter the sky."

I stared, horrified. "What? That... what does that *mean*? We can't—"

The growling returned, closer now, rumbling out from the darkness. Overhead, the glistening lights of the realms quivered as the rot climbed across them, making the barriers between them start to crumble.

"Go now, my precious ones. The lie Melisandre tells herself is still hunting you." She took my hands. "She is not what she seems, and she never has been. Down at her core, *she* is the flaw in all of their plans. The power she clings to is not hers, and it was taken from the very thing she cannot be." Her gaze swept us all. "Everything you were and everything you are has brought you to this moment. Your bonds reflect those that hold together your world. Trust what you have become."

All around us, the castle and the radiant light of the realms began to fall away like stardust, taking Eira with it.

"Mother!" I cried.

"I love you, my daughter. I always have."

She faded like a dream.

And we stood once more at the edge of a nightmare.

The endless void surrounded the nine of us, with only a shadow of colorless dirt beneath our feet and the sliver of a portal at our backs. The vines still choked it and crawled out in every direction all across the emptiness, just as they had when we saw them from the parapet moments ago. Ghostly traces of the colors that had filled the sky moments before still drifted in the far distance, the glimmer of other realms inside them. But now the vines had reached them.

And already, the distant lights of other realms were starting to falter.

"We have to stop this," Niko said.

Dex scanned it all, shaking his head. "I'm open to suggestions."

A low, contemptuous chuckle came from the darkness. "Your world, your *life* is almost gone, Gwyneira. Why do you still bother to fight?"

I tensed. The hissing, clicking voice seemed made of thousands of smaller voices, all of them so twisted by hate and ravenous hunger that the sound of them made my skin crawl.

The Voidborn.

And my stepmother.

Out of the depths of the void, a monster slithered like a ghostly eel larger than the tallest of buildings and longer than my eyes could see. Scales darker than a moonless night wafted in and out of view like they were not quite fully present, while their edges glinted with silver like blades ready to slice. Smaller shadows with glowing eyes darted around its shifting surface, diving in and out of it like crazed wisps of smoke.

Voidborn. So many, they surpassed any hope of counting them all.

"The Nine," the creature sneered as it wound around us. "*Saviors* of the realm."

The Voidborn flitting around its massive sides cackled.

"That, uh... that fucking thing is the queen, isn't it?" Clay asked softly.

Lars nodded, his eyes on the creature. "Think so."

"Dear *gods*," Niko whispered.

The creature slithered around the fading scrap of land on which we stood. "What fools you are." Twisting sinuously, it veered wide of the dying glow of our world. "You saved nothing."

"Much as I'm loving this encouragement," Clay commented. "Anyone got any ideas?"

I didn't respond, staring at the enormous monster winding around us. It seemed to have no end, and it circled us as if to surround us on every side—left, right, above or below. Yet for every time it coiled closer, it would then veer away.

"We pour our power into the gap to our world," Dex said. "Fuel it enough to return and figure this out when we're not on the edge of oblivion."

"It won't work, my friend," Casimir replied. "Our world is being drained even now by powers from the void. If we pour our power into that, it will only drain us same as the nexuses."

"So we..." Niko made a desperate noise. "We close it. That tear she made. We shut it somehow."

"It's our only connection to our world," Byron countered. "Sever that and..."

"We're trapped here," Lars filled in. "And we die."

The demon growled like he refused to accept that, while Ozias shuddered, grim horror radiating from him.

My heart ached.

"But we've lasted this long," Niko argued, desperate hope in his voice. "These bonds between us... Everything we created in the temple..."

"The bonds we've forged may be a reflection of the nexuses of our world," Casimir said. "But they have not changed reality. Whether it is through the portal closing or our world dying, once the energy of our world is fully gone, we won't last. Even a nexus cannot withstand the absence of all things that is the void."

My eyes tracked the monstrous creature circling us. How *were* we still alive? And why hadn't it attacked yet? It had surrounded us entirely, yet it wasn't constricting down. Was it just toying with us?

The eel drew closer and then pulled back again.

I blinked. The light from our world. That's what it was avoiding. But why had it...

Casimir's words registered. I turned quickly. "What did you say?"

"That even a nexus could not withstand the void."

"No, about the... the reflection." I turned, looking at the creature my stepmother had become, my mind racing. "And reality." My mouth moved, searching for words. "Our bond is a reflection of our world. Our reality. Everything we are... and everything we were... We're a mirror. But she..." I tracked the creature as it circled us again. "She's broken."

"Princess?" Dex prompted.

"Her lie is hunting us. That's what my mother said. That she's not what she seems and she never has been." I stared at the massive eel as it coiled around us again. "And that *she's* the flaw in all their plans."

Giving my men a desperate look. "I... I have an idea. We don't try to hit *this*. We aim for her."

Casimir paused thoughtfully, while Byron's eyes just skimmed back and forth across the ghostly dirt like he was running cross-references at high speed.

"What's the difference, though?" Clay asked. "Her or this, it doesn't—"

"It does matter," Byron said, looking up again. "Mirror, mirror..."

I nodded. "Exactly."

"Then that's good enough." Dex nodded. "We'll follow your lead."

I reached for them. Their magic rushed into me instantly.

"Mm, what's this?" the eel creature murmured. "You've decided to fight *yet* again? You truly do love to suffer, don't you, Gwyneira?"

I turned to face the darkness. "Mirror, mirror," I whispered. "Broken... now it lies."

"The prophecy of the Nine?" My stepmother laughed. "How do you think *that* will stop me, you pathetic little fool?"

"Because you're the broken mirror," I said. "And this is how we reflect the truth." Our magic surged out from me, aimed right at her. "This is how we shatter the skies."

The power struck, and the vast creature she'd become flinched. But even though she faltered, the smaller shadows all around her only hissed and clicked as if cackling with glee.

"Idiotic child," they taunted me. "You think to attack with *this*? We *feed* on the energy of worlds. We feed on *reality* and consume it all."

I smiled. "Except you need hers."

Our power pierced into her shadows. The Voidborn swarmed, intent upon devouring it, fighting frantically to feast and not be scorched by its light.

But they couldn't take it all. Couldn't stop it from lancing through the darkness of her monstrous form like an arrow intent upon one target. One truth.

That she had always been the flaw in their plan, just as my mother said. Because no matter what power she drained from something else, what terror she wreaked on our world, or what kind of annihilating monstrosity she used Voidborn magic to become, at her core the *reality* of Melisandre was that she wasn't strong.

She never had been.

Before she sacrificed her own humanity to take on the powers of a vampire, she was a witch caught in a system every bit as harsh and unjust as the bigotry of Erenelle or Aneira, who thought the only way to triumph over it was through sadism and bloodshed.

Before she stole a crown to call herself a queen, she was a woman so twisted and broken by cruelty, she'd decided the only way to overcome her suffering was through pettiness and hate.

Before she'd become the monster who murdered my mother and who tried to destroy our realm, she'd been a *real* thing, and the only power that had been *hers* was that she hated the world so much, she'd chosen to make a bargain with creatures who despised reality every bit as much as she did.

Her hatred was the only thing about herself she'd ever embraced in all her life. Out of everything she'd stolen or bargained to take, it was the only thing that had ever truly belonged to her from the start.

But nothing else did.

And that made her so very, very weak.

Our power slammed into the deepest, darkest part of the beast, past the layers of magic the Voidborn had given her, past everything she'd become. Down to the center of her essence where that one truth formed the original bedrock of everything she and the Voidborn had built. The central piece that was only, purely, and simply *Melisandre.*

The linchpin of their destruction. The real thing amid their unreality that they'd needed to access our world and make any of this possible.

The true core.

A scream tore from the heart of the beast, and deep within its darkness, something fractured like glass. Cracks spread through the monster, racing through its massive body, radiating out from the inside.

Until it shattered.

Hundreds of Voidborn scattered like leaves. The massive form of the snake began crumbling to dust in their wake, a cascade of disintegrating fragments that disappeared into nothing before they ever came close to the tiny scrap of reality where we stood.

At the edge of where the last remnants of our world touched the void, my stepmother stood. Shudders shook her. Countless hairline cracks covered her skin, her dress, even her hair, as if all she'd been was only a fragile, breaking shell. As the cracks spread, dust wafted from her body like all her power, all her *existence* was disintegrating into the hungry, empty dark. She reached for us only to lurch as her hands and arms began to turn to ash and crumble away.

Tiny wisps of smoke rose from within her as if emanating from every part of her essence. The ghost of glowing yellow eyes wavered before her, watching us above the eerie glint of long metal fangs.

I tensed, bracing for the shifting shadows to coalesce into a Voidborn.

But the yellow eyes grew dull, their glow fading as its

misty form dissipated and blew away like smoke on a breeze.

A faint chuckle escaped my stepmother. "Told you... I won, Alaric." Her gaze slid to me, and her lips curled into a weak sneer as the last of her began drifting off into oblivion. "But he was right about this too. The Nine do destroy the world." Her voice became a whisper on the emptiness. "Such a wretched little realm anyway."

And then she was gone.

Rumbling shook the void.

Clay made a nervous sound. "Anyone else have a bad feeling about..." The last of the dust of the massive creature my stepmother had been drifted away. "Oh, shit."

The cracks that destroyed her hadn't stopped. They'd continued out into the vines, radiating across the emptiness all the way to where the rot chewed at the other realms.

But now, from the inside out, those cracks were changing. In the distance, light suddenly pierced out from them, splintering the darkness like pure energy was breaking through the rotting surface of the vines. In a cascade, the fissures of light spread, all of them gaining speed.

And heading our way.

"We poured our power into the heart of anti-reality to summon reality back again," Casimir said slowly. "And now... it's coming."

"All the energy of our realm." Byron's gaze tracked over the countless cracks of light racing toward us. "All at once."

I stared in horror. "Oh gods. I didn't—"

"No," Dex cut in. "You didn't. We all did. The Nine are one, and"—he shook his head, watching the cascade race closer—"it was the only thing to do."

"But this... this is okay, though, right?" Niko said, the hope in his voice doing nothing for the fear in his eyes. "It'll just go into our realm and bring everything back... and that'll be fine."

Byron shook his head. "That is the power and essence of *everything*. Mountains. Oceans. All the people and anywhere the ley lines she corrupted could touch. And it's going to hit one point of the world. Just *one*."

"You know nature, my friend," Casimir said. "Tell me, how well does a tree fare in the face of an avalanche?"

"Or a volcano," Ozias murmured.

Niko turned, staring out at the light spearing the darkness. "Then what do we do?"

Desperate looks passed between us all. We'd stopped the Voidborn, yes. But the energy of an entire realm?

Light crackled through the dark vines of rot like lightning, racing closer.

"We are like a nexus," Casimir said suddenly.

I turned to him, confused. "What?"

"We are like our world. Our power. Our gifts, each of them like the elements of reality."

"What's your point, man?" Clay demanded.

Dex spoke up before the vampire could, his eyes on the surge of light coming our way. "We let it strike us first. Buffer the hit. Diffuse it so the world might survive."

Clay and Lars stared at him, stunned. Byron turned

away, shaking his head, and horror showed on Niko's face when he turned to me, the loss Dex was proposing so clear in his eyes. The demon shuddered, anguish on his face, while that same feeling radiated through Ozias so strongly I could feel his beast howling inside.

My mouth opened, but I couldn't find words. I knew what that meant, and the incredible likelihood of what would happen then.

We'd die.

I looked over my shoulder at the shadowy portal to our world. The color was gone. Nearly every detail had faded away. Everything my home had ever been was disappearing like a dying dream.

But maybe it didn't have to go.

"Doomed are the Nine," I whispered.

My heart breaking, I turned back to my men. "It's the only hope for the world," I said quietly, a tiny shrug making my shoulders rise and fall. "We have to try."

They stared at me. But one by one, the sorrow faded into acceptance in their eyes.

The crackling light raced closer. It was almost here.

My men came toward me. Our arms wrapped around one another, holding us together.

The friends who'd become family.

The outsiders who'd made each other their home.

The princess who'd found a new life after being left to die in the snow.

"Do you think there was any truth to what Gwyneira's mother said?" Niko asked. "That the realms tell each other their stories? That maybe we'll go on somehow?"

Dex nodded. "I do."

"Beyond any doubt," Byron said, his green gaze unwavering on me.

Niko smiled at the answer. "Good."

Tears burned in my eyes. "But I hope that, even if from now on and forever after we're only a story, they know the truth too."

"What's that, princess?" Byron asked.

I smiled at him as the light swelled so bright, it was blinding. "That once upon a time, we were real."

The blast struck.

60

GWYNEIRA

Birds chirped in the distance. Wings fluttered. Something hard and rough rested against my back.

"Princess?" an elderly voice called from far away. "Princess, can you hear me?"

I opened my eyes only to squint at the light.

A thin and familiar face swam into view. "Harran?"

The steward stared down at me. "Princess! Oh, thank the gods, you're all right."

I blinked in confusion and struggled to move. Dirt and rocks lay beneath me, and a cloudless blue sky hung overhead. Wincing, I started to rub my eyes. "How did I—"

My gaze caught on my arm. A pale shimmer clung to my skin, like the barest sheen of frost.

A groan came from my right. Pressing a hand to his head, Clay sat up and then froze as if registering what he'd just done. "Wait, we're... we're not dead."

His eyes found me, relief splitting his face into a massive grin. Beyond him, Lars stirred.

"Princess?" Niko's voice came from my left.

I turned. Byron and Demon were near his side, the wounds on Demon's chest glowing like banked fire, as if his powers were already working to heal him. A surge of relief and love poured through my link to Ozias behind me, while just ahead, Dex and Casimir sat up groggily.

Confusion crossed my scholar's face. "H-how are we not dead?"

Clay laughed. "Don't question it, man."

Breathless chuckles came from Lars and Dex. A smile tugged at Niko's lips like it wasn't sure it should be there, and I suspected my expression was similar.

Because I wondered the same thing. Moreover, I wasn't the only one with a strange sheen to their skin. We all had it. The shimmer was faint, and it didn't look like my stepmother's silver gleam. More like frost, and unless the light hit it just right I wouldn't even know it was there.

Other details of the courtyard registered. Harran and the nine of us weren't alone.

I froze. While the old steward hovered nearby, looking anxious, all around the courtyard beyond him lay green-skinned men, shifters, and harpies, each of them unmoving.

"Hey, Cas," Clay said. "You all right?"

Casimir didn't answer, looking past me to something at my back.

I turned. My lips parted in shock.

We *also* weren't the only ones who looked different. The royal tree stood behind us.

Every inch of it now glistened, as clear as if it was made out of a diamond.

"What the..." Lars whispered.

Unsteadily, I pushed to my feet and walked toward it. As I drew closer, I could see more detail. How it wasn't simply clear. Inside, the crystal held rings like those found in a tree trunk. Thin veins of glistening liquid pumped through it all.

"It's still alive," I said.

A strange, ethereal feeling brushed over my mind, like distant chimes. On impulse, I reached for the trunk.

"Careful," Dex cautioned.

I nodded, not turning. Gingerly, my fingertips rested on the glass.

My eyes widened. In an instant, my awareness spread out, as if somehow I was here but also... everywhere. In the city. The countryside. In Gentresqua and Cioloren and... my gods, even the Wild Lands.

Everywhere my stepmother's apple trees on the ley lines had been, but those trees had now become like diamonds. And from it all, that same whisper of chiming carried through my mind.

I pulled back with a small gasp. "It... it took the blast too."

"What?" Niko's footsteps came closer.

"We buffered the impact," I said, turning back to them. "But the tree, the ley lines, the nexus..." My gaze rose, and a breath escaped me at the shimmer clinging to the stone walls. "Even the castle... They're part of me. They took it too."

Eyeing the tree, Niko reached out, resting his fingertips on it too.

The chiming in my mind changed. Grew richer, like another layer of sound had joined what I heard.

His wide eyes darted to me. "You feel that?"

I nodded.

Behind us, the others rose, coming closer, reaching out too.

Note by note, the chiming turned to a harmony that stole my breath with its beauty.

"We're connected to it." Wonder filled Lars's voice.

Byron made a noise of agreement. "Not simply a mirror of the world anymore."

"Our energy and it are the same," Casimir said.

"But what does that mean?" Clay asked. "For, you know, *us*?"

Casimir chuckled softly, as if his power had told him something about the diamond trees that the rest of us couldn't yet perceive. "I suspect we will have many, *many* centuries to figure that out."

His gaze met mine.

"Our..." I wetted my lips, fear and hope fluttering in me at the words. "Our bonds will sustain them?" I twitched my head toward the giants.

He nodded. "We and this world are connected. We survive, it survives. And vice versa."

A shaky breath escaped me, so much joy filling my chest it was hard to speak.

But my giants simply grinned. "Guess you'll have to put up with us for a while longer," Clay teased.

I choked on a laugh. "Forever."

His smile broadened.

Groaning came from the courtyard. Alarmed, we turned.

On the flagstones, the monsters were stirring.

"Oh, shit." Clay reached for his sword.

Dex and Lars did the same, while the demon growled.

"Wait." Niko put a hand to Clay's arm, his eyes on the monsters.

For a moment, the creatures only blinked as if they were dazed. But when they spotted one another, cries of relief and pain and joy rose. Green-skinned men and shifters shoved to their feet, grabbing one another in hugs, while harpies wailed and huddled together, winged arms around each other.

A smile tugged at Niko's lips. "I think it's okay."

"What?" Clay gave him an incredulous look.

"Their kind can survive possession," Niko said. "I saw it. And the Voidborn left when the portal opened." His grin broadened. "They're not possessed anymore."

The monsters caught sight of us. The cries of relief and joy subsided as they tensed, pulling back as if bracing for us to attack.

Hands raised, Niko took a step toward them.

"Careful, brother," the demon snarled.

Nodding, Niko didn't take his eyes from the creatures. "Can any of you understand me?"

Wary looks passed between the monsters. One of the green-skinned men stepped forward. "I do." His voice was gruff, and his words had a rough accent that I couldn't hope to identify.

My sweet giant smiled. "My name is Niko. These are my friends." He gestured to us. "We're not your enemies if you're not ours."

The green-skinned man eyed him and then jerked his head in a tight nod.

From among the harpies, one woman rose. Her brown braids were a matted mess on her head, and her wings were missing some of their longer feathers. "Are..." Her beak made her words click. "Are the *dark things* gone?"

Niko nodded.

A shudder that looked driven by pure relief went through the harpy. Behind her, several others closed their eyes like they were thanking their gods.

At the far end of the courtyard, something heavy suddenly banged into the gate. Panicked noises shot through the harpies, while the green-skinned men and shifters tensed like they were preparing to fight.

"Brothers!" More banging followed, along with swearing in Erenlian. A wood beam of the gate splintered under the blows.

A smoky shape flowed through the gap. Gasps rose, but before anyone could attack, the amorphous figure coalesced.

Ruhl huffed a greeting at us and then rose up on his hind legs and knocked the crossbeam on the gate aside.

Brock stormed through, scanning the courtyard fast.

At the sight of Clay and Lars, his furious expression cracked into relief. "Gods of the Stone, are you all right?" He strode toward us quickly.

A strangled noise left Harran. "What? That's a—"

"It's okay," I said quickly. "They're our allies."

The steward stared at me.

Behind Brock, more giants entered the courtyard. Dathan, Ignatius and so many others who'd come with us through the gateway. The robed figures of witches followed proudly on their heels.

"Well," Ignatius said, taking in the tree and us alike. "This is..."

"As it should be," said a familiar voice. The crowd of witches parted.

Rufinia, First Matron of the Jeweled Coven, stood at their center. Her graying cloud of hair was disheveled and she bore a cut on the dark skin of her cheek, but she gave me a smile as she tilted her head in a nod. "Princess Gwyneira."

Harran cleared his throat, cutting me off before I could respond. "If I may, madam," the steward said, his face a picture of rigid propriety. "Not princess." He bowed to me. "*Queen*."

Dex smiled, pride and respect in his eyes. "All hail the queen."

Grins spread across the faces of my men.

I couldn't find words. I'd fought for this for so long, and now...

"So," Clay said like he'd read my mind. "What happens next?"

Byron chuckled. "What would your books say, your highness?"

I stared at him for a moment, thrown. "I-I guess they'd say..." A smile tugged at my lips as the answer came to me. "Now we live happily ever after."

EPILOGUE

GWYNEIRA

Two months later

"Oh, this is a good one." Shifting position against Byron's side on the leather sofa, I angled my book so that he could see.

Glancing up from the novel in his hands, he skimmed where I pointed. Firelight from the massive library fireplace made his green eyes gleam.

As did curiosity.

"That *does* look good." He reached for a thin strip of cloth from the pile at his side. "Red?"

"Mm, pink. That scene in the book yesterday was sexier, but I like the positions in this one."

Nodding, he picked up the cloth. I tucked it between the pages and grinned.

"Your Majesty?" Harran called. "Excuse me, Your Majesty?"

Byron made a regretful noise. "Duty calls, yes?" He kissed the top of my head. "Don't worry, we can keep reading later tonight. Demon will likely enjoy what I found on page two hundred and six. I know *I* will."

I peeked at where he pointed and found myself at a loss for words. "Red for that one. Definitely."

He laughed.

"Your majesty." Harran bustled around the corner of a bookcase, papers clutched in his hands. "My apologies for disturbing your reading time, but we really *must* go over these seating arrangements for the Jeweled Coven's spring equinox dinner. Seating the ruby witches next to the orcs is hardly— Oh." He stopped, blinking at the stacks of books surrounding us. "My, are all these for the, uh... new sections?"

"Mostly." I set my book aside and then nodded to the stack on my left. "That pile is for Valeria when she and Lord Thomas come by for their 'state visit' next week."

I tried to smile past my discomfort, knowing Valeria didn't want me to be upset that the visits weren't merely about rebuilding Aneira but also about making sure she had everything she needed as a new vampire. After we found her and the others my stepmother had turned hiding in the deepest parts of the castle tunnels, it had taken some rather ingenious caging spells cast by Casimir, Byron, and the witches to trap them long enough to give them each a vial of giant blood.

But thank the gods, the treatment had worked, and now contributions from very well compensated Erenlians meant Valeria, Fironia, and so many other victims of my stepmother could start to rebuild to their lives.

"And," I pressed onward, nodding at another stack. "*That* pile includes those historical romances you were curious about a few days ago. Ones you thought the new head cook might like to read with you, right?"

"Ah. Um. Yes." Harran's mouth moved. "T-thank you." He cleared his throat. "I'll see to it that General Valeria's books are packed for safekeeping."

I suppressed a smile at the scarlet flush on his cheeks. "Thank you."

With a shaky breath, he drew himself up again. "Now, about these seating arrangements."

I set my book aside and climbed to my feet, Byron rising behind me. "I'm not sure I see the problem. The—"

Footsteps came our way, moving fast, and then Clay poked his head around a bookcase with a grin. "They're back."

Excitement quivered in my chest. "Harran, the ruby witches will be fine. Just put Leontine next to their leader. They seem quite enamored of each other, and she's fascinated by his people's history. They'll talk for hours and keep everyone else in line at the same time."

Harran floundered. "H-how could you know—"

"A little bird told me." A smile tugged at my lips as the castle quivered ever so slightly beneath my feet. "Now if you'll excuse me."

With Byron on my heels, I hurried after Clay. "Are they okay?"

"Yeah, I think. Cas is Cas, and the pack seems good. Best I can tell for shadow wolves, anyway."

Relief pressed a breath from me.

"What about the Wild Lands?" Byron asked. "Is it like we thought?"

Clay shrugged. "Yeah. Just diamond trees everywhere and not a ghost nor a what-the-fuck to be seen. Probably not going to be too much longer till the orcs and whatnot want to talk trade routes."

Byron gave a low whistle, while I smiled. At first, the orcs, harpies, shifters and all the other creatures who'd been brought back from extinction by the Voidborn had been something of a question for us. Many of them came from lands that didn't exist anymore. Some from entire continents and islands that had long since sunk into the sea. Living among humans and giants was unfamiliar at best, and that was without the fear many humans still felt for them after what the Voidborn had forced those creatures to do.

But to Casimir, the solution was simple. He was the king of an empty country. They were people without a home. Thus, after days of negotiations, the new-old creatures were declared citizens of Zenirya, with each species nominating royal advisors to the throne.

All that had been left was to determine what to do about the Wild Lands—if anything was needed at all. Preliminary scrying spells cast by the witches hinted that, when the energy of our realm returned, the twisted magic of those cursed lands may have been healed somehow, purged of the corruption from the Witch Wars which had made it go feral.

Casimir had taken Ruhl and flown to the west almost immediately, just to see if it was true.

"About time you got here," Lars said from the throne room entrance when we rounded the corner. "I was about to send a search party."

Clay splayed his hands. "Hey, if these two keep expanding the library, we're going to need search parties on constant standby."

I rolled my eyes at them both. "You're just jealous because Brock spent half his last visit exploring the new section on Erenlian history."

"Okay, that's fair." Clay shrugged. "Who knew the guy was such a bookworm?"

"Your Majesty." Dex's voice felt like a warm hug even before he caught me as I came through the doorway.

I hugged him back. "It's about time you got a free moment." I gave Ozias a pointed look. "*Both* of you."

Dex chuckled. "That's what I told the recruits, but did they listen?"

I grinned. His uniform was spotless—his training wouldn't accept anything less—but I could still see the exhaustion in his eyes. After we disbanded all that remained of my stepmother's former group of Huntsmen, Dex had taken charge of rebuilding an elite unit of royal guards to protect us all.

Being leader of the *new* Huntsmen kept him incredibly busy.

"And you?" I asked Ozias. "What's your excuse?"

A low, hungry growl left him as he pulled me into his arms. "Shifters talk too much."

I smothered a giggle. "How horrible for you."

His growl turned into a rumble of warning. "Careful. I haven't gotten to spank you in *days*."

My cheeks flushed with equal parts embarrassment and anticipation. "Well, you two will be home tonight, yes? Because Byron and I had a *very* productive reading time."

Desire lit their eyes, and promise filled Dex's voice when he said, "Oh, we wouldn't miss *that* for the world."

Ruhl turned as we came toward them all. Amorphous shapes of shadow and smoke swirled behind him, separating out into the wolf forms of his pack. His green eyes gleaming, Ruhl tilted his head ever so slightly at the sight of me, almost like a nod of acknowledgement.

I nodded back. One day, I would truly to figure out what he actually was. But until then, Byron and Casimir said they planned to scour the archives for information on nyxvarg.

Maybe they'd find an actual description of the nature of his kind.

Pushing the thoughts aside, I continued on to where Casimir stood conversing with the leader of the harpies. Niko was nearby, talking with several of the orcs who served as healers among their people. Roan stood behind him, his brother's ever-present bodyguard and shadow.

"—easily set up a place for your people in the southern province," Casimir was saying to one of the harpies, "*if* warmer weather is your preference. But the north has—"

At a short sound from the harpy, Casimir cut off and turned. His lips spread into a broad smile at the sight of me. "Ah, my queen."

"I hear it went well."

"Better than well." He enfolded me in a quick hug, seeming near to bursting with excitement. "With the magic of the Wild Lands gone, we found parts of my nation still standing that I haven't seen in over thirty years."

I hesitated, not wanting to dim his enthusiasm, but unable to stop my hope. "Any people?"

He winced. "No. But I made my peace with that possibility years ago. I half-expected never to see *anything* of Zenirya again, so to even have our museums and schools still standing is..." He shook his head, and then a smile crossed his face again. "And I should add, Ruhl also found the *libraries*."

"Oh." I turned to the shadow wolf, who I swore was smirking at me. An answering grin tugged at my lips. "Well, thank you."

One of the wolves behind him huffed, and Ruhl glanced back. Some kind of unspoken communication seemed to pass between them, because his body language changed, becoming almost business-like. Rising from his haunches, he paced to a section of the throne room wall, his pack coming with him.

"What is that about, I wonder?" Byron murmured.

I shook my head. "Are you feeling anything odd about that part of the—"

The stone wavered. Shadows gathered fast, swirling

together quickly to form a dark space taller and wider than any of us.

"Gateway." Byron lifted his hands, defensive magic already swirling around him.

Dex grabbed for his sword. "How the hell did it get past the warding around—"

The sound of someone clearing their throat came from within the darkness.

Something about it was familiar.

"Is that a gateway demon?" Clay asked.

"Doesn't matter." Roan stepped between Niko and the gateway, his muscles tense like he was on the verge of shifting into his demon.

Pfft! came the voice of one of the smaller-sounding gateway demons. *'Doesn't matter' he says. Just for that we shouldn't even—*

A grunt followed, almost like somebody elbowing someone else.

"What the...?" Lars murmured.

Ruhl gave the portal an exasperated look.

Fine! The throat-clearing sound returned, and then the gateway demon made a noise like it was imitating a trumpet. *Introducing his hideousness, his monstrosity-ness, his enormous—*

Get on with it! another demon snapped.

Sounds of a tussle came from within the gateway, like the two demons were wresting, and then a deeper, older voice said tiredly. *Just move. My mate wishes to see her sons.*

I froze. Ahead of me, Niko and Roan did the same.

Something shifted in the darkness, and then a figure swelled into existence.

My eyes widened. It was a demon, larger even than Roan's other form, with jet-black horns curving from his head, broad wings, and long claws on his hands and feet. He wore black leather breeches and a flowing linen shirt the color of smoke. When his eyebrow arched imperiously at the sight of all of us, the expression was so reminiscent of Roan, it stole my breath.

An Erenlian woman stepped from the darkness behind him. Her hair was as black as night, while her skin was light-gray marble. She wore a dress of rich, red velvet that shifted to orange like dancing flames when she moved.

When she saw Niko and Roan, a smile broke out across her face and tears rose in her eyes. "Oh..." She pressed her fingertips to her lips like she was trying to contain herself. "There you both are."

Neither of the brothers moved. I didn't know what to do, whether to speak to break the silence or let them find their way through it first. My eyes darted to one side of the gateway, seeking Ruhl like maybe he had the answer, even if I knew the wolf wouldn't respond.

At the forefront of his pack, the wolf didn't seem perturbed in the slightest. He simply turned to the demon and placed one paw on the creature's massive clawed foot. After a moment passed, the demon nodded, and Ruhl turned back, sinking onto his haunches, utterly calm.

Somehow, the sight helped.

The woman took a step forward, her eyes never

leaving Niko and Roan. "I-I don't know if you... Oh, gods, how to do this?" She drew a steadying breath. "My name is Jessora. I'm your mother."

A shocked breath escaped me, but happiness was on its heels. Their mother?

"Um..." Niko's eyes darted briefly to Roan. "Hi." He cleared his throat. "I mean, hello."

Jessora's smile returned. "Hello. You... you'd be Archerias's son, yes?" An awkward sort of worry flickered over her face. "I'm sorry. I... I don't know what they named you or—"

"Niko," Roan cut in, a tense, protective edge to his voice.

She nodded quickly. "Niko. And you're Roan."

His head moved in brief acknowledgement, cold and cautious. Her smile still flickered back to life at the sight.

Something in my chest twisted at the expression. It was so clear where Niko had gotten his bright and sweet nature.

Her smile unchanged, she nodded to the demon beside her. "This is Xarcist, your father and my... well, his people call it—"

"Your mate," Roan interrupted again.

Xarcist's brow arched. "You're familiar with that, I take it."

Roan's shoulders rolled back and in an instant, he shifted entirely into the demon. "Yes," he said flatly, protectiveness clear in his tone.

Xarcist didn't bristle at the obvious threat. Instead, one corner of his lips curled up in a proud, approving smile.

And that, too, looked so like Roan that it left me speechless.

But at the sight of his demon form, Jessora made a breathless sound of joy. "You... oh. You're..."

With a wary look at Niko, Demon pulled back a bit, seeming thrown. "What?"

Xarcist regarded him, still seeming proud. "There was little chance you and the demonic power within you could both survive intact. Most half-bloods become one or the other—if they don't simply rip themselves apart from within, unable to exist as either side."

My lips parted in shock. That...

Oh gods, so that was why they were the way they were. A demonic force and a man, half and half.

And by some miracle, they'd managed to survive. To coexist.

To become the amazing man and demon who meant the world to me.

"What is your name, son?" Xarcist continued.

The demon was silent.

"We..." Niko glanced at the demon uncomfortably. "We just call him Demon."

Xarcist's brow arched with affront.

"Whatever you're thinking—" Niko took a step forward, "—take care before you speak."

His protectiveness drew Demon back to himself. "I need no other name."

Xarcist watched them both and then tilted his head in a small nod. "So be it. But should you wish to know —" He glanced at Jessora briefly. "—your mother and I would have called you Kaos. That was the name we chose when we..." Pain flickered over his face.

Jessora gave him a loving, sympathetic look. "There was a time when we first met when we thought we would be able to stay together so easily. But soon after I learned I was pregnant, his realm pulled him back again. Crossing between his realm and ours has always been... *perilous*. Almost impossible, really. When Archerias's enemies kidnapped me, Xarcist broke about a hundred laws and combusted an uninhabited pocket realm just to return here to rescue me."

"Small price to stop those who threatened you," Xarcist muttered.

I buried a smile at the sentiment so reminiscent of the demon.

Or rather *Kaos*, if he decided that was he wanted to be called.

"Is that why you never came back for me?" Niko asked. "For *us*?"

Jessora's expression turned sad. "I'm so sorry. With Roan... I was young. Xarcist was gone, my village cast me out for 'consorting with the unnatural,' and when he was born as a—" She winced apologetically at Roan. "—a *dwarf*, I thought..." She shook her head. "I knew nothing of what it meant for my child to be a half-blood. I only wanted you to have a better life than I could give. A life with a family who had the resources to protect you from the cruelty and judgement I knew you'd receive."

A heartbeat passed, and then the demon shifted back into Roan. "They were that... while they lived."

Silence followed his words.

"What happened with me?" Niko asked quietly.

Jessora's pained expression deepened. "I didn't mean to leave you. I swear. After Xarcist rescued me, he and I tried to return to where I'd hidden you in the woods, but the tear he'd opened between realms caught us before we could. I..." Her voice caught. "I never knew if you survived or..."

Xarcist put a massive hand to her shoulder. She reached up, clasping hers over his, accepting the support.

"I'm so sorry," she finished to Niko.

For a moment, my sweet giant seemed at a loss for words. But then he shook his head. "It... it was okay. A healer woman found me. Marnira. She raised me." He smiled. "It was a good childhood. You don't have anything to be sorry for."

Gratitude filled Jessora's eyes. "I prayed to the gods for both of you every day. And when the barriers between the realms weakened and there was the chance to finally come find you again..." She pressed her clasped hands to her lips like she was trying to hold overwhelming emotions inside. "All I—all *we*—want is to be part of your lives, in whatever way you'll let us."

Niko looked over at Roan, hope in his eyes. "I... I would like that."

Roan's wary, distrustful expression didn't change, and his eyes never left his father. "He's a demon. I won't risk that. Not with her."

Xarcist's eyes narrowed, flicking to me. "Your mate,"

he said like he was filling in a blank. His fiery gaze swept Dex, Ozias and the others. "And your..."

"Family." Roan spat the word.

But again, Xarcist didn't seem offended, only proud. "I think you'll find, my son, that while little in all the realms is sacred to a demon, a *mate* is the most sacred of all. And if they are your family, then..." He nodded like he was making a decision that had more weight and solidity than stone. "They are mine as well. Any who harm them or your mate will face my wrath."

Roan was motionless, and my heart went out to him. I crossed to his side, putting a hand to his arm.

A breath entered his lungs. His eyes went to mine.

I smiled, and after a moment, he nodded like he was regaining his footing. "I..." He looked back at Xarcist, only to hesitate with a look I was starting to know well.

His demon was speaking to him.

He cleared his throat. "Kaos and I agree. We would like you to be a part of our lives too." Roan's brow flickered down briefly. "Though he would also like to know if you're going to be ripped out of this realm again and whether we should move our mate away from you for her safety, just in case."

A gruff chuckle burst from Xarcist. "No. Crossing realms *is* dangerous, as your mother said. Or, it *was*. The walls are weaker now. Cracks exist. We won't be pulled away this time."

Apprehension swirled in my gut. My stepmother's destruction had done that. I had no doubt at all.

"Then," Niko started, only to glance at the shadow

wolves like he had a suspicion of the answer to his own question. "How did you know to find us?"

Xarcist sighed. "After we were torn away from this realm before Jessora could return for you, Jessora was heartbroken. And when one's mate suffers..."

Understanding seemed to pass between all my men, as if they knew what he spoke of only too well.

"Thus, I swore to find my mate's sons." Xarcist glanced to one side. "And the nyxvarg took an oath to assist me. They stole across the realms, completing a crossing even my kind would not survive. But as their alpha tells me, when they arrived here, tangled magic delayed them. By the time they could orient themselves enough to conquer it..." His mouth tightened. "Both of my mate's sons were nowhere to be found."

A rolling movement went through Ruhl's body, like he was shrugging off the discomfort of that memory.

I hesitated, but I had to know. "Can you *speak* to him?"

Xarcist's fiery gaze turned to me, respectful and calm. "After a fashion. When they choose to do so, the nyxvarg share images. Emotions and such. In this form, they will truly *speak* only to one another and their mate. But for all others, to receive even the more limited form of their communication is quite rare. It is a sign of their highest respect and esteem."

Ruhl's glowing eyes met mine. He tilted his head in a tiny, acknowledging nod.

Niko looked between Xarcist and the wolves. "So all this time, Ruhl and his pack were here to find... us?"

"Originally, yes. Though I understand they developed a fondness of the strange country in which they found themselves as well. When you stumbled upon them, they acted to protect it *and* you."

Watching Ruhl, Jessora crouched down. "Thank you for protecting my sons." She smiled. "You can go now. Your oath is complete."

I blinked, looking between her and the wolf.

Ruhl caught sight of my reaction. Rising to his feet, he paced over to me.

"What does she mean, go?" I asked him.

The wolf glanced back at Xarcist and Jessora.

"Back before the barriers weakened, the nyxvarg had their own reasons for risking the journey to this realm," Xarcist said. "Their kind have a connection to their destined mate that transcends realms. But the curse of this is that their mate can be in any realm at all. Thus many nyxvarg never find them."

I stared at the wolf. "That longing. The searching."

Ruhl's glowing eyes were solemn.

"But," Xarcist continued, "as we said, the barriers are no longer what they once were. Whatever realms their mates occupy, the nyxvarg may well be able to find them more easily now."

Ruhl sank onto his haunches with an expectant look at me.

I crouched down. His paw came to rest on my knee.

The gratitude that poured from him made tears burn in my eyes. He could feel her now, stronger ever than before. We'd shattered the sky, and with it, the barriers that kept him from the one whose soul was out beyond the darkness, calling to him.

And it was time he and his pack found her.

"But—" my voice broke, "—if you go, we'll miss you. *I'll* miss you."

Gentle affection came from him. He leaned forward, softly bumping his forehead to mine.

Warmth filled me. Friendship.

And the sense that now everything would be all right.

After all, perhaps someday he, his pack, and their mate could come to see us again.

I nodded, sniffling a bit. "I'll hold you to that."

Ruhl's wry smirk returned. He huffed, almost as if chuckling. Rising again, he walked back to his pack. But at the edge of the gateway, he turned, his glowing eyes finding Casimir.

The vampire smiled. "Thank you, my friend."

Ruhl bowed in a solemn, respectful nod. Behind him, smoke rose from the rest of his pack, as if they were on the edge of shifting.

With a huff that radiated excitement, Ruhl threw his head back and gave a wild, exulting howl.

His pack took up the cry. In a surge of swirling darkness, the shadow wolves raced into the gateway.

Their howls faded into the distance.

Ozias put his arm around me. "Are you okay, little mate?"

I smiled, resting my head on his side. "Yeah." I looked over at all my men, my heart swelling at the love in their eyes. "After all, everyone deserves to find their treluria."

———

Thank you for reading Forever After: Crimson Snow. For more stories from Sierra Rowan, please visit sierrarowan.com.

TITLES BY SIERRA ROWAN

Forever After: Crimson Snow

Of Snow So White

Of Blood So Red

Of Fate So Dark

Of Nine So Bold

The Vampire Rebellion Series

Blood Pawn

Blood Captive

Blood Rebel

Blood Queen

Jekylls and Hydes

The Jekyll and Her Hydes

The Misfit and Her Monsters

ABOUT THE AUTHOR

Sierra Rowan is the USA Today bestselling author of action-packed reverse harem paranormal romance and urban fantasy novels. Sierra loves to write stories filled with steam, heart, and adventure where a happily-ever-after is guaranteed, even if it takes a few magical battles and wild escapes to get there.

Get updates about all of Sierra Rowan's books at sierrarowan.com.

amazon.com/author/sierrarowan

bookbub.com/authors/sierra-rowan

goodreads.com/sierrarowan

facebook.com/authorsierrarowan

instagram.com/authorsierrarowan

tiktok.com/@sierrarowanbooks